The Best of
JACK VANCE

THE BEST OF JACK VANCE

With an introduction by
BARRY N. MALZBERG

TAPLINGER PUBLISHING COMPANY

NEW YORK

This edition first published in the United States in 1978 by
TAPLINGER PUBLISHING CO., INC.
New York, New York

Copyright © 1976 by Jack Vance
Published by arrangement with Pocket Books
Division of Simon & Schuster, Inc.
630 Fifth Avenue, New York, New York 10020
All rights reserved. Printed in the U.S.A.

Library of Congress Catalog Number: 78-56984
ISBN 0-8008-0726-X

Contents

Preface to the Collection

QUITE CANDIDLY, I DON'T LIKE TO DISCUSS, LET alone analyze, my own stories. Still, I have been asked to prepare a preface to the following collection, and no subject other than the stories themselves seems appropriate.

These are all stories I like, naturally enough. They date across approximately fifteen years. I have a special affection for "Ullward's Retreat" and "Sail 25." Otherwise there is little I can say that the stories can't say better for themselves.

Instead, I'll make a remark or two about my personal approach to the business of writing. In the first place, I am firmly convinced that the writer who publicizes himself distracts his readers from what should be his single concern: his work. For this reason, after a few early vacillations, I refuse to disseminate photographs, self-analysis, biographical data, critiques and confessions: not from innate reserve, but to focus attention where I think it belongs.

I am aware of using no inflexible or predetermined style. Each story generates its own style, so to speak. In theory, I feel that the only good style is the style which no one notices, but I suppose that in practice this may not be altogether or at all times possible. In actuality the subject of style is much too large to be covered in a sentence or two and no doubt every writer has his own ideas on the subject.

Without further generalities, I commend the reader's attention to the stories themselves.

J. V.

Capturing Vance

I HAVE THIS THEORY THAT THE TITLES OF FIRST published stories are symbolic. They seem to intimate the direction of a career. Certainly it is appropriate that Robert Heinlein, who with John W. Campbell turned this field around in the forties, first appeared in 1939 with "Life-Line" and that Tom Sherred's almost singlehanded attempt to forge new directions in 1948 was called "E for Effort." Then my own first published science-fiction story was called, "We're Coming Through the Windows," amply predicting an eight-year output of some three million words, and Silverberg's in a 1956 *Astounding* was titled, with equal appropriateness, "To Be Continued" (and how!). There may be something profound here. Jack Vance's first piece in a 1947 issue of *Astounding* was "I'll Build Your Dream Castle" * and sandwiched among Simak, Tenn, Asimov, other large figures of that time, it attracted little notice.

But by the early fifties Jack Vance's dream castles were becoming noticeable to a great many. Ten years later he had emerged, notably with "The Last Castle" and *The Dragon Masters* as the logical successor to James Schmitz, the greatest portrayer of total alienness in science-fiction. By this time, 1976, any fool knows that Jack Vance is one of the ten most important writers in the history of the field.

He has accumulated that importance quietly and wholly on the basis of his work. To the best of my knowledge he has never entered the social life of science-fiction, preferring to

---

* Whoops! Reginald's *Contemporary Science-Fiction Authors* says that Vance's first story in 1945 was "The World-Thinker." Same difference, say I.

ix

live iconoclastically and well in the far West where he has let his work and only his work make a contribution. I cannot recall any other writer in science-fiction who has managed to make a similar reputation without self-promotion and social involvement in the field's interstices, which makes even more of a statement as to the value of his fiction.

Vance is remarkable. His landscapes are wholly imagined, his grasp of the fact that future or other worlds will not be merely extensions of our own but entirely alien has never been exceeded in this field. There are two equally legitimate ways of regarding science-fiction. If you look at the genre as necessarily being one kind of thing close-up, then Robert Silverberg is probably the best the field has ever had; but if you look at it in another, equally viable, equally defensible, way, then only James Schmitz can touch Vance. He is simply one of the best there ever has been at grasping that the material of science-fiction will *feel differently* to those who live through it, and has brought that difference alive.

He is also one of only two writers, the other is the brilliant short-story writer Avram Davidson, to have won both science-fiction's Hugo Award and the Edgar Award of the Mystery Writers of America, the latter for best first novel back in the mid-sixties. Most science-fiction readers are unaware of the fact that under his real name John Holbrook, Jack Vance has had an impressive parallel career as mystery novelist. The man is a professional who works to the limits he perceives. As a science-fiction writer, the dimensions of his accomplishment grow in retrospection yearly; Jack Vance is eventually going to be perceived as one of the foundation blocks of the field. He has already influenced two generations of writers: those like Larry Niven and Terry Carr who came up in the sixties doing alien landscapes with rigor and integrity, and younger writers like Gardner Dozois who, thanks to Vance, are now able to take the alienness for granted and work with it comfortably for an audience that has been educated to understand it.

Jack Vance built his dream castle for all of us. Elegantly furnished with loops and spires and rooms yet undiscovered it will not, I suspect (in contradiction to the first line of his novella), be overwhelmed. Ever.

BARRY N. MALZBERG
9 August 1975: New Jersey

The Best of
JACK VANCE

I

SEVERAL YEARS ago Cele Goldsmith edited *Amazing Stories*. One evening at the home of Poul Anderson she produced a set of cover illustrations which she had bought by the dozen for reasons of economy, and asked those present to formulate stories based upon them. Poul rather gingerly accepted a cover whose subject I forget. Frank Herbert was assigned the representation of a human head, with a cutaway revealing an inferno of hellfire, scurrying half-human creatures, and the paraphernalia of a nuclear power plant. I was rather more fortunate and received a picture purporting to display a fleet of spaceships driven by sun-sails. Theoretically the idea is sound, and space scientists have long included this concept among their speculations for future planetary voyages. Astrogation of course becomes immensely complex, but by carefully canting the sail and using planetary and/or solar gravities, any region of the solar system may be visited—not always by the most direct route, but neither did the clipper ships sail great-circle routes.

The disadvantages are the complication of the gear and the tremendous expanse of sail—to be measured in square miles—necessary to accelerate any meaningful mass of ship to any appreciable velocity within a reasonable time-span.

Which brings me back to my cover picture. The artist, no doubt for purposes of artistry, had depicted the ships with sails about the size of spinnakers for a twelve-meter, which at Earth radius from the sun would possibly produce as much as one fly-power of thrust. Additionally the sails were painted in gaudy colors, in defiance of the conventional wisdom which specifies that sun-sails shall be flimsy membranes of plastic, coated with a film of reflective metal a few molecules thick. Still, no matter how illogical the illustration, I felt that I must justify each detail by one means or another. After considerable toil I succeeded, with enormous gratitude that I had not been selected to write about the cutaway head which had been the lot of Frank Herbert.

SAIL 25

1

Henry Belt came limping into the confer-
ence room, mounted the dais, settled himself at the desk. He
looked once around the room: a swift bright glance which,
focusing nowhere, treated the eight young men who faced
him to an almost insulting disinterest. He reached in his
pocket, brought forth a pencil and a flat red book, which he
placed on the desk. The eight young men watched in alsolute
silence. They were much alike: healthy, clean, smart, their
expressions identically alert and wary. Each had heard legends
of Henry Belt, each had formed his private plans and private
determinations.

Henry Belt seemed a man of a different species. His face
was broad, flat, roped with cartilage and muscle, with skin
the color and texture of bacon rind. Coarse white grizzle
covered his scalp, his eyes were crafty slits, his nose a mis-
shapen lump. His shoulders were massive, his legs short and
gnarled.

"First of all," said Henry Belt, with a gap-toothed grin,
"I'll make it clear that I don't expect you to like me. If you
do I'll be surprised and displeased. It will mean that I haven't
pushed you hard enough."

He leaned back in his chair, surveyed the silent group.
"You've heard stories about me. Why haven't they kicked
me out of the service? Incorrigible, arrogant, dangerous
Henry Belt. Drunken Henry Belt. (This last, of course, is
slander. Henry Belt has never been drunk in his life.) Why
do they tolerate me? For one simple reason: out of necessity.
No one wants to take on this kind of job. Only a man like

3

Henry Belt can stand up to it: year after year in space, with nothing to look at but a half-dozen round-faced young scrubs. He takes them out, he brings them back. Not all of them, and not all of those who come back are spacemen today. But they'll all cross the street when they see him coming. Henry Belt? you say. They'll turn pale or go red. None of them will smile. Some of them are high placed now. They could kick me loose if they chose. Ask them why they don't. Henry Belt is a terror, they'll tell you. He's wicked, he's a tyrant. Cruel as an ax, fickle as a woman. But a voyage with Henry Belt blows the foam off the beer. He's ruined many a man, he's killed a few, but those that come out of it are proud to say, I trained with Henry Belt!

"Another thing you may hear: Henry Belt has luck. But don't pay any heed. Luck runs out. You'll be my thirteenth class, and that's unlucky. I've taken out seventy-two young sprats, no different from yourselves; I've come back twelve times: which is partly Henry Belt and partly luck. The voyages average about two years long: how can a man stand it? There's only one who could: Henry Belt. I've got more space-time than any man alive, and now I'll tell you a secret: this is my last time out. I'm starting to wake up at night to strange visions. After this class I'll quit. I hope you lads aren't superstitious. A white-eyed woman told me that I'd die in space. She told me other things and they've all come true. We'll get to know each other well. And you'll be wondering on what basis I make my recommendations. Am I objective and fair? Do I put aside personal animosity? Naturally there won't be any friendship. Well, here's my system. I keep a red book. Here it is. I'll put your names down right now. You, sir?"

"I'm Cadet Lewis Lynch, sir."

"You?"

"Edward Culpepper, sir."

"Marcus Verona, sir."

"Vidal Weske, sir."

"Marvin McGrath, sir."

"Barry Ostrander, sir."

"Clyde von Gluck, sir."

"Joseph Sutton, sir."

Henry Belt wrote the names in the red book. "This is the

system. When you do something to annoy me, I mark you down demerits, At the end of the voyage I total these demerits, add a few here and there for luck, and am so guided. I'm sure nothing could be clearer than this. What annoys me? Ah, that's a question which is hard to answer. If you talk too much: demerits. If you're surly and taciturn: demerits. If you slouch and laze and dog the dirty work: demerits. If you're overzealous and forever scuttling about: demerits. Obsequiousness: demerits. Truculence: demerits. If you sing and whistle: demerits. If you're a stolid bloody bore: demerits. You can see that the line is hard to draw. Here's a hint which can save you many marks. I don't like gossip, especially when it concerns myself. I'm a sensitive man, and I open my red book fast when I think I'm being insulted." Henry Belt once more leaned back in his chair. "Any questions?"

No one spoke.

Henry Belt nodded. "Wise. Best not to flaunt your ignorance so early in the game. In response to the thought passing through each of your skulls, I do not think of myself as God. But you may do so, if you choose. And this"—he held up the red book—"you may regard as the Syncretic Compendium. Very well. Any questions?"

"Yes, sir," said Culpepper.

"Speak, sir."

"Any objection to alcoholic beverages aboard ship, sir?"

"For the cadets, yes indeed. I concede that the water must be carried in any event, that the organic compounds present may be reconstituted, but unluckily the bottles weigh far too much."

"I understand, sir."

Henry Belt rose to his feet. "One last word. Have I mentioned that I run a tight ship? When I say jump, I expect every one of you to jump. This is dangerous work, of course. I don't guarantee your safety. Far from it, especially since we are assigned to old Twenty-Five, which should have been broken up long ago. There are eight of you present. Only six cadets will make the voyage. Before the week is over I will make the appropriate notifications. Any more questions? . . . Very well, then. Cheerio." Limping on his thin legs as if his feet hurt, Henry Belt departed into the back passage.

For a moment or two there was silence. Then von Gluck said in a soft voice, "My gracious."

"He's a tyrannical lunatic," grumbled Weske. "I've never heard anything like it! Megalomania!"

"Easy," said Culpepper. "Remember, no gossiping."

"Bah!" muttered McGrath. "This is a free country. I'll damn well say what I like."

Weske rose to his feet. "A wonder somebody hasn't killed him."

"I wouldn't want to try it," said Culpepper. "He looks tough." He made a gesture, stood up, brow furrowed in thought. Then he went to look along the passageway into which Henry Belt had made his departure. There, pressed to the wall, stood Henry Belt. "Yes, sir," said Culpepper suavely. "I forgot to inquire when you wanted us to convene again."

Henry Belt returned to the rostrum. "Now is as good a time as any." He took his seat, opened his red book. "You, Mr. von Gluck, made the remark 'My gracious' in an offensive tone of voice. One demerit. You, Mr. Weske, employed the terms 'tyrannical lunatic' and 'megalomania,' in reference to myself. Three demerits. Mr. McGrath, you observed that freedom of speech is the official doctrine of this country. It is a theory which presently we have no time to explore, but I believe that the statement in its present context carries an overtone of insubordination. One demerit. Mr. Culpepper, your imperturbable complacence irritates me. I prefer that you display more uncertainty, or even uneasiness."

"Sorry, sir."

"However, you took occasion to remind your colleagues of my rule, and so I will not mark you down."

"Thank you, sir."

Henry Belt leaned back in the chair, stared at the ceiling. "Listen closely, as I do not care to repeat myself. Take notes if you wish. Topic: Solar Sails, Theory and Practice Thereof. Material with which you should already be familiar, but which I will repeat in order to avoid ambiguity.

"First, why bother with the sail when nuclear jet-ships are faster, more dependable, more direct, safer and easier to navigate? The answer is threefold. First, a sail is not a bad way to move heavy cargo slowly but cheaply through space. Secondly, the range of the sail is unlimited, since we employ the mechanical pressure of light for thrust, and therefore need carry neither propulsive machinery, material to be ejected, nor energy source. The solar sail is much lighter than its nuclear-powered counterpart, and may carry a larger complement of men in a larger hull. Thirdly, to train a man for space there is no better instrument than the handling of a sail. The computer naturally calculates sail cant and plots the course; in fact, without the computer we'd be dead ducks. Nevertheless the control of a sail provides working familiarity with the cosmic elementals: light, gravity, mass, space.

"There are two types of sail: pure and composite. The first relies on solar energy exclusively, the second carries a secondary power source. We have been assigned Number Twenty-Five, which is the first sort. It consists of a hull, a large parabolic reflector which serves as radar and radio antenna, as well as reflector for the power generator; and the sail itself. The pressure of radiation, of course, is extremely slight—on the order of an ounce per acre at this distance from the sun. Necessarily the sail must be extremely large and extremely light. We use a fluoro-siliconic film a tenth of a mil in gauge, fogged with lithium to the state of opacity. I believe the layer of lithium is about a thousand two hundred molecules thick. Such a foil weighs about four tons to the square mile. It is fitted to a hoop of thin-walled tubing, from which mono-crystalline iron cords lead to the hull.

"We try to achieve a weight factor of six tons to the square mile, which produces an acceleration of between g/one hundred and g/one thousand, depending on proximity to the sun, angle of cant, circum-solar orbital speed, reflectivity of surface. These accelerations seem minute, but calculation shows them to be cumulatively enormous. G/one hundred yields a velocity increment of eight hundred miles per hour every hour, eighteen thousand miles per hour each day, or five miles per second each day. At this rate interplanetary distances are readily negotiable—with proper manipulation of the sail, I need hardly say.

"The virtues of the sail I've mentioned. It is cheap to build and cheap to operate. It requires neither fuel, nor ejectant. As it travels through space, the great area captures various ions, which may be expelled in the plasma jet powered by the parabolic reflector, which adds another increment to the acceleration.

"The disadvantages of the sail are those of the glider or

sailing ship, in that we must use natural forces with great precision and delicacy.

"There is no particular limit to the size of the sail. On Twenty-Five we use about four square miles of sail. For the present voyage we will install a new sail, as the old is well worn and eroded.

"That will be all for today."

Once more Henry Belt limped down from the dais and out the passage. On this occasion there were no comments.

2

The eight cadets shared a dormitory, attended classes together, ate at the same table in the mess hall. In various shops and laboratories they assembled, disassembled and reassembled computers, pumps, generators, gyro-platforms, star-trackers, communication gear. "It's not enough to be clever with your hands," said Henry Belt. "Dexterity is not enough. Resourcefulness, creativity, the ability to make successful improvisations—these are more important. We'll test you out." And presently each of the cadets was introduced into a room on the floor of which lay a great heap of mingled housings, wires, flexes, gears, components of a dozen varieties of mechanism. "This is a twenty-six-hour test," said Henry Belt. "Each of you has an identical set of components and supplies. There shall be no exchange of parts or information between you. Those whom I suspect of this fault will be dropped from the class, without recommendation. What I want you to build is, first, one standard Aminex Mark Nine Computer. Second, a servo-mechanism to orient a mass ten kilograms toward Mu Hercules. Why Mu Hercules?"

"Because, sir, the solar system moves in the direction of Mu Hercules, and we thereby avoid parallax error. Negligible though it may be, sir."

"The final comment smacks of frivolity, Mr. McGrath, which serves only to distract the attention of those who are trying to take careful note of my instructions. One demerit."

"Sorry, sir. I merely intended to express my awareness that for many practical purposes such a degree of accuracy is unnecessary."

"That idea, cadet, is sufficiently elemental that it need not be labored. I appreciate brevity and precision."

"Yes, sir."

"Thirdly, from these materials, assemble a communication system, operating on one hundred watts, which will permit two-way conversation between Tycho Base and Phobos, at whatever frequency you deem suitable."

The cadets started in identical fashion by sorting the material into various piles, then calibrating and checking the test instruments. Achievement thereafter was disparate. Culpepper and von Gluck, diagnosing the test as partly one of mechanical ingenuity and partly ordeal by frustration, failed to become excited when several indispensable components proved either to be missing or inoperative, and carried each project as far as immediately feasible. McGrath and Weske, beginning with the computer, were reduced to rage and random action. Lynch and Sutton worked doggedly at the computer, Verona at the communication system.

Culpepper alone managed to complete one of the instruments, by the process of sawing, polishing and cementing together sections of two broken crystals into a crude, inefficient, but operative maser unit.

The day after this test McGrath and Weske disappeared from the dormitory, whether by their own volition or notification from Henry Belt, no one ever knew.

The test was followed by weekend leave. Cadet Lynch, attending a cocktail party, found himself in conversation with a Lieutenant-Colonel Trenchard, who shook his head pityingly to hear that Lynch was training with Henry Belt.

"I was up with Old Horrors myself. I tell you, it's a miracle we ever got back. Belt was drunk two-thirds of the voyage."

"How does he escape court-martial?" asked Lynch.

"Very simple. All the top men seem to have trained under Henry Belt. Naturally they hate his guts but they all take a perverse pride in the fact. And maybe they hope that someday a cadet will take him apart."

"Have any ever tried?"

"Oh yes. I took a swing at Henry once. I was lucky to escape with a broken collarbone and two sprained ankles.

If you come back alive, you'll stand a good chance of reaching the top."

The next evening Henry Belt passed the word. "Next Tuesday morning we go up. We'll be gone several months."

On Tuesday morning the cadets took their places in the angel-wagon. Henry Belt presently appeared. The pilot readied for takeoff.

"Hold your hats. On the count . . ." The projectile thrust against the earth, strained, rose, went streaking up into the sky. An hour later the pilot pointed. "There's your boat. Old Twenty-Five. And Thirty-Nine right beside it, just in from space."

Henry Belt stared aghast from the port. "What's been done to the ship? The decoration? The red, the white, the yellow, the checkerboard?"

"Thank some idiot of a landlubber," said the pilot. "The word came to pretty the old boats for a junket of congressmen."

Henry Belt turned to the cadets. "Observe this foolishness. It is the result of vanity and ignorance. We will be occupied several days removing the paint."

They drifted close below the two sails: No. 39 just down from space, spare and polished beside the bedizened structure of No. 25. In 39's exit port a group of men waited, their gear floating at the end of cords.

"Observe those men," said Henry Belt. "They are jaunty. They have been on a pleasant outing around the planet Mars. They are poorly trained. When you gentlemen return you will be haggard and desperate and well trained. Now, gentlemen, clamp your helmets, and we will proceed."

The helmets were secured. Henry Belt's voice came by radio. "Lynch, Ostrander, will remain here to discharge cargo. Verona, Culpepper, von Gluck, Sutton, leap with cords to the ship; ferry across the cargo, stow it in the proper hatches."

Henry Belt took charge of his personal cargo, which consisted of several large cases. He eased them out into space, clipped on lines, thrust them toward 25, leaped after. Pulling himself and the cases to the entrance port he disappeared within.

Discharge of cargo was effected. The crew from 39 trans-ferred to the carrier, which thereupon swung down and away, thrust itself dwindling back toward Earth.

When the cargo had been stowed, the cadets gathered in the wardroom. Henry Belt appeared from the master's cubicle. "Gentlemen, how do you like the surroundings? Eh, Mr. Culpepper?"

"The hull is commodious, sir. The view is superb."

Henry Belt nodded. "Mr. Lynch? Your impressions?"

"I'm afraid I haven't sorted them out yet, sir."

"I see. You, Mr. Sutton?"

"Space is larger than I imagined it, sir."

"True. Space is unimaginable. A good spaceman must either be larger than space, or he must ignore it. Both difficult. Well, gentlemen, I will make a few comments, then I will retire and enjoy the voyage. Since this is my last time out, I intend to do nothing whatever. The operation of the ship will be completely in your hands. I will merely appear from time to time to beam benevolently about, or alas! to make marks in my red book. Nominally I shall be in command, but you six will enjoy complete control over the ship. If you return us safely to Earth I will make an approving entry in my red book. If you wreck us or fling us into the sun, you will be more unhappy than I, since it is my destiny to die in space. Mr. von Gluck, do I perceive a smirk on your face?"

"No, sir, it is a thoughtful half-smile."

"What is humorous in the concept of my demise, may I ask?"

"It will be a great tragedy, sir. I merely was reflecting upon the contemporary persistence of, well, not exactly superstition, but, let us say, the conviction of a subjective cosmos."

Henry Belt made a notation in the red book. "Whatever is meant by this barbaric jargon I'm sure I don't know, Mr. von Gluck. It is clear that you fancy yourself a philosopher and dialectician. I will not fault this, so long as your remarks conceal no overtones of malice and insolence, to which I am extremely sensitive. Now, as to the persistence of superstition, only an impoverished mind considers itself the repository of absolute knowledge. Hamlet spoke on this subject to Horatio, as I recall, in the well-known work by William Shakespeare. I myself have seen strange and terrifying sights. Were they hallucinations? Were they the manipulation of the cosmos by my mind or the mind of someone—or something —other than myself? I do not know. I therefore counsel a flexible attitude toward matters where the truth is still unknown. For this reason: the impact of an inexplicable experience may well destroy a mind which is too brittle. Do I make myself clear?"

"Perfectly, sir."

"Very good. To return, then. We shall set a system of watches whereby each man works in turn with each of the other five. I thereby hope to discourage the formation of special friendships, or cliques.

"You have inspected the ship. The hull is a sandwich of lithium-beryllium, insulating foam, fiber and an interior skin. Very light, held rigid by air pressure rather than by any innate strength of the material. We can therefore afford enough space to stretch our legs and provide all of us with privacy.

"The master's cubicle is to the left; under no circumstances is anyone permitted in my quarters. If you wish to speak to me, knock on my door. If I appear, good. If I do not appear, go away. To the right are six cubicles which you may now distribute among yourselves by lot.

"Your schedule will be two hours study, four hours on watch, six hours off. I will require no specific rate of study progress, but I recommend that you make good use of your time.

"Our destination is Mars. We will presently construct a new sail, then while orbital velocity builds up, you will carefully test and check all equipment aboard. Each of you will compute sail cant and course and work out among yourselves any discrepancies which may appear. I shall take no hand in navigation. I prefer that you involve me in no disaster. If any such occur I shall severely mark down the persons responsible.

"Singing, whistling, humming, are forbidden. I disapprove of fear and hysteria, and mark accordingly. No one dies more than once; we are well aware of the risks of this, our chosen occupation. There will be no practical jokes. You may fight, so long as you do not disturb me or break any instruments; however, I counsel against it, as it leads to resentment, and

I have known cadets to kill each other. I suggest coolness and detachment in your personal relations. Use of the micro-film projector is of course at your own option. You may not use the radio either to dispatch or receive messages. In fact, I have put the radio out of commission, as is my practice. I do this to emphasize the fact that, sink or swim, we must make do with our own resources. Are there any questions? . . . Very good. You will find that if you all behave with scrupulous correctness and accuracy, we shall in due course return safe and sound, with a minimum of demerits and no casualties. I am bound to say, however, that in twelve pre-vious voyages this has failed to occur. Now you select your cubicles, stow your gear. The carrier will bring up the new sail tomorrow, and you will go to work."

3

The carrier discharged a great bundle of three-inch tub-ing: paper-thin lithium hardened with beryllium, reinforced with filaments of mono-crystalline iron—a total length of eight miles. The cadets fitted the tubes end to end, cement-ing the joints. When the tube extended a quarter-mile it was bent bow shaped by a cord stretched between two ends, and further sections added. As the process continued the free end curved far out and around, and presently began to veer back in toward the hull. When the last tube was in place the loose end was hauled down, socketed home, to form a great hoop two and a half miles in diameter.

Henry Belt came out occasionally in his spacesuit to look on, and occasionally spoke a few words of sardonic com-ment, to which the cadets paid little heed. Their mood had changed; this was exhilaration, to be weightlessly afloat above the bright cloud-marked globe, with continent and ocean wheeling massively below. Anything seemed possible, even the training voyage with Henry Belt! When he came out to inspect their work, they grinned at each other with indul-gent amusement. Henry Belt suddenly seemed a rather piti-ful creature, a poor vagabond suited only for drunken bluster. Fortunate indeed that they were less naïve than Henry Belt's previous classes! They had taken Belt seriously; he had cowed them, reduced them to nervous pulp. Not this crew, not by a long shot! They saw through Henry Belt! Just keep your nose clean, do your work, keep cheerful. The training voyage won't last but a few months, and then real life begins. Gut it out, ignore Henry Belt as much as possible. This is the sensible attitude; the best way to keep on top of the situation.

Already the group had made a composite assessment of its members, arriving at a set of convenient labels. Culpepper: smooth, suave, easy-going. Lynch: excitable, argumentative, hot-tempered. Von Gluck: the artistic temperament, delicate with hands and sensibilities. Ostrander: prissy, finicky, over-tidy. Sutton: moody, suspicious, competitive. Verona: the plugger, rough at the edges, but persistent and reliable.

Around the hull swung the gleaming hoop, and now the carrier brought up the sail, a great roll of darkly shining stuff. When unfolded and unrolled, and unfolded many times more, it became a tough gleaming film, flimsy as gold leaf. Unfolded to its fullest extent it was a shimmering disk, already rippling and bulging to the light of the sun. The cadets fitted the film to the hoop, stretched it taut as a drumhead, cemented it in place. Now the sail must carefully be held edge on to the sun, or it would quickly move away, under a thrust of about a hundred pounds.

From the rim, braided-iron threads were led to a ring at the back of the parabolic reflector, dwarfing this as the reflector dwarfed the hull, and now the sail was ready to move.

The carrier brought up a final cargo: water, food, spare parts, a new magazine for the microfilm viewer, mail. Then Henry Belt said, "Make sail."

This was the process of turning the sail to catch the sunlight while the hull moved around Earth away from the sun, canting it parallel to the sun-rays when the ship moved on the sunward leg of its orbit: in short, building up an orbital velocity which in due course would stretch loose the bonds of Terrestrial gravity and send Sail 25 kiting out toward Mars.

During this period the cadets checked every item of equipment aboard the vessel. They grimaced with disgust and dismay at some of the instruments: 25 was an old ship, with antiquated gear. Henry Belt seemed to enjoy their grumbling. "This is a training voyage, not a pleasure cruise. If you wanted your noses wiped, you should have taken a post on the ground. And, I have no sympathy for fault-finders. If you wish a model by which to form your own conduct, observe me."

The moody introspective Sutton, usually the most diffident and laconic of individuals, ventured an ill-advised witticism. "If we modeled ourselves after you, sir, there'd be no room to move for the whiskey."

Out came the red book. "Extraordinary impudence, Mr. Sutton. How can you yield so easily to malice?"

Sutton flushed pink; his eyes glistened, he opened his mouth to speak, then closed it firmly. Henry Belt, waiting politely expectant, turned away. "You gentlemen will perceive that I rigorously obey my own rules of conduct. I am regular as a clock. There is no better, more genial shipmate than Henry Belt. There is not a fairer man alive. Mr. Culpepper, you have a remark to make?"

"Nothing of consequence, sir."

Henry Belt went to the port, glared out at the sail. He swung around instantly. "Who is on watch?"

"Sutton and Ostrander, sir."

"Gentlemen, have you noticed the sail? It has swung about and is canting to show its back to the sun. In another ten minutes we shall be tangled in a hundred miles of guy-wires."

Sutton and Ostrander sprang to repair the situation. Henry Belt shook his head disparagingly. "This is precisely what is meant by the words 'negligence' and 'inattentiveness.' You two have committed a serious error. This is poor spacemanship. The sail must always be in such a position as to hold the wires taut."

"There seems to be something wrong with the sensor, sir," Sutton blurted. "It should notify us when the sail swings behind us."

"I fear I must charge you an additional demerit for making excuses, Mr. Sutton. It is your duty to assure yourself that all the warning devices are functioning properly, at all times. Machinery must never be used as a substitute for vigilance."

Ostrander looked up from the control console. "Someone has turned off the switch, sir. I do not offer this as an excuse, but as an explanation."

"The line of distinction is often hard to define, Mr. Ostrander. Please bear in mind my remarks on the subject of vigilance."

"Yeṣ, sir, but—who turned off the switch?"

"Both you and Mr. Sutton are theoretically hard at work watching for any accident or occurrence. Did you not observe it?"

"No, sir."

"I might almost accuse you of further inattention and neglect, in this case."

Ostrander gave Henry Belt a long, dubious side-glance. "The only person I recall going near the console is yourself, sir. I'm sure you wouldn't do such a thing."

Henry Belt shook his head sadly. "In space you must never rely on anyone for rational conduct. A few moments ago Mr. Sutton unfairly imputed to me an unusual thirst for whiskey. Suppose this were the case? Suppose, as an example of pure irony, that I had indeed been drinking whiskey, that I was in fact drunk?"

"I will agree, sir, that anything is possible."

Henry Belt shook his head again. "That is the type of remark, Mr. Ostrander, that I have come to associate with Mr. Culpepper. A better response would have been, 'In the future, I will try to be ready for any conceivable contingency.' Mr. Sutton, did you make a hissing sound between your teeth?"

"I was breathing, sir."

"Please breathe with less vehemence."

Henry Belt turned away and wandered back and forth about the wardroom, scrutinizing cases, frowning at smudges on polished metal. Ostrander muttered something to Sutton, and both watched Henry Belt closely as he moved here and there. Presently Henry Belt lurched toward them. "You show great interest in my movements, gentlemen."

"We were on the watch for another unlikely contingency, sir."

"Very good, Mr. Ostrander. Stick with it. In space nothing is impossible. I'll vouch for this personally."

4

Henry Belt sent all hands out to remove the paint from the surface of the parabolic reflector. When this had been accomplished, incident sunlight was now focused upon an expanse of photoelectric cells. The power so generated was used to operate plasma jets, expelling ions collected by the vast expanse of sail, further accelerating the ship, thrusting it ever out into an orbit of escape. And finally one day, at an exact instant dictated by the computer, the ship departed from Earth and floated tangentially out into space, off at an angle for the orbit of Mars. At an acceleration of g/100, velocity built up rapidly. Earth dwindled behind; the ship was isolated in space. The cadets' exhilaration vanished, to be replaced by an almost funereal solemnity. The vision of Earth dwindling and retreating is an awesome symbol, equivalent to eternal loss, to the act of dying itself. The more impressionable cadets—Sutton, von Gluck, Ostrander—could not look astern without finding their eyes swimming with tears. Even the suave Culpepper was awed by the magnificence of the spectacle, the sun an aching pit not to be tolerated, Earth a plump pearl rolling on black velvet among a myriad glittering diamonds. And away from Earth, away from the sun, opened an exalted magnificence of another order entirely. For the first time the cadets became dimly aware that Henry Belt had spoken truly of strange visions. Here was death, here was peace, solitude, star-blazing beauty which promised not oblivion in death, but eternity. . . . Streams and spatters of stars. . . . The familiar constellation, the stars with their prideful names presenting themselves like heroes: Achernar, Fomalhaut, Sadal, Suud, Canopus. . . .

Sutton could not bear to look into the sky. "It's not that I feel fear," he told von Gluck, "or yes, perhaps it is fear. It sucks at me, draws me out there. . . . I suppose in due course I'll become accustomed to it."

"I'm not so sure," said von Gluck. "I wouldn't be surprised if space could become a psychological addiction, a need—so that whenever you walked on Earth you felt hot and breathless."

Life settled into a routine. Henry Belt no longer seemed a man, but a capricious aspect of nature, like storm or lightning; and like some natural cataclysm, Henry Belt showed no favoritism, nor forgave one jot or tittle of offense. Apart from the private cubicles no place on the ship escaped his attention. Always he reeked of whiskey, and it became a matter of covert speculation as to exactly how much whiskey he had brought aboard. But no matter how he reeked or how he swayed on his feet, his eyes remained clever and steady, and he spoke without slurring in his paradoxically clear sweet voice.

One day he seemed slightly drunker than usual, and ordered all hands into spacesuits and out to inspect the sail for meteoric puncture. The order seemed sufficiently odd that the cadets stared at him in disbelief. "Gentlemen, you hesitate, you fail to exert yourselves, you luxuriate in sloth. Do you fancy yourselves at the Riviera? Into the spacesuits, on the double, and everybody into space. Check hoop, sail, reflector, struts and sensor. You will be adrift for two hours. When you return I want a comprehensive report. Mr. Lynch, I believe you are in charge of this watch. You will present the report."

"Yes, sir."

"One more matter. You will notice that the sail is slightly bellied by the continual radiation pressure. It therefore acts as a focusing device, the focal point presumably occurring behind the cab. But this is not a matter to be taken for granted. I have seen a man burned to death in such a freak accident. Bear this in mind."

For two hours the cadets drifted through space, propelled by tanks of gas and thrust tubes. All enjoyed the experience except Sutton, who found himself appalled by the immensity of his emotions. Probably least affected was the practical Verona, who inspected the sail with a care exacting enough to satisfy even Henry Belt.

The next day the computer went wrong. Ostrander was in charge of the watch and knocked on Henry Belt's door to make the report.

Henry Belt appeared in the doorway. He apparently had been asleep. "What is the difficulty, Mr. Ostrander?"

"We're in trouble, sir. The computer has gone out."

Henry Belt rubbed his grizzled pate. "This is not an unusual circumstance. We prepare for this contingency by schooling all cadets thoroughly in computer design and repair. Have you identified the difficulty?"

"The bearings which suspend the data-separation disks have broken. The shaft has several millimeters play and as a result there is total confusion in the data presented to the analyzer."

"An interesting problem. Why do you present it to me?"

"I thought you should be notified, sir. I don't believe we carry spares for this particular bearing."

Henry Belt shook his head sadly. "Mr. Ostrander, do you recall my statement at the beginning of this voyage, that you six gentlemen are totally responsible for the navigation of the ship?"

"Yes, sir. But—"

"This is an applicable situation. You must either repair the computer, or perform the calculations yourself."

"Very well, sir. I will do my best."

5

Lynch, Verona, Ostrander and Sutton disassembled the mechanism, removed the worn bearing. "Confounded antique!" said Lynch. "Why can't they give us decent equipment? Or if they want to kill us, why not shoot us and save us all trouble."

"We're not dead yet," said Verona. "You've looked for a spare?"

"Naturally. There's nothing remotely like this."

Verona looked at the bearing dubiously. "I suppose we could cast a babbitt sleeve and machine it to fit. That's what we'll have to do—unless you fellows are awfully fast with your math."

Sutton glanced out the port, quickly turned his eyes away. "I wonder if we should cut sail."

"Why?" asked Ostrander.

"We don't want to build up too much velocity. We're already going thirty miles a second."

"Mars is a long way off."

"And if we miss, we go shooting past. Then where are we?"

"Sutton, you're a pessimist. A shame to find morbid tendencies in one so young." This from von Gluck.

"I'd rather be a live pessimist than a dead comedian."

The new sleeve was duly cast, machined and fitted. Anxiously the alignment of the data disks was checked. "Well," said Verona doubtfully, "there's wobble. How much that affects the functioning remains to be seen. We can take some of it out by shimming the mount. . . ."

Chims of tissue paper were inserted and the wobble seemed to be reduced. "Now—feed in the data," said Sutton. "Let's see how we stand."

Coordinates were fed into the system; the indicator swung. "Enlarge sail cant four degrees," said von Gluck; "we're making too much left concentric. Projected course. . . ." He tapped buttons, watched the bright line extend across the screen, swing around a dot representing the center of gravity of Mars. "I make it an elliptical pass, about twenty thousand miles out. That's at present acceleration, and it should toss us right back at Earth."

"Great. Simply great. Let's go, Twenty-Five!" This was Lynch. "I've heard of guys dropping flat on their faces and kissing Earth when they put down. Me, I'm going to live in a cave the rest of my life."

Sutton went to look at the data disks. The wobble was slight but perceptible. "Good Lord," he said huskily. "The other end of the shaft is loose too."

Lynch started to spit curses; Verona's shoulders slumped. "Let's get to work and fix it."

Another bearing was cast, machined, polished, mounted. The disks wobbled, scraped. Mars, an ocher disk, shouldered ever closer in from the side. With the computer unreliable the cadets calculated and plotted the course manually. The results were at slight but significant variance with those of the computer. The cadets looked dourly at each other. "Well," growled Ostrander, "there's error. Is it the instruments? The calculation? The plotting? Or the computer?"

Culpepper said in a subdued voice, "Well, we're not about to crash head-on at any rate."

Verona went back to study the computer. "I can't imagine why the bearings don't work better. . . . The mounting brackets—could they have shifted?" He removed the side housing, studied the frame, then went to the case for tools.

"What are you going to do?" demanded Sutton.

"Try to ease the mounting brackets around. I think that's our trouble."

"Leave me alone! You'll bugger the machine so it'll never work."

Verona paused, looked questioningly around the group. "Well? What's the verdict?"

"Maybe we'd better check with the old man," said Ostrander nervously.

"All well and good—but you know what he'll say."

"Let's deal cards. Ace of spades goes to ask him."

Culpepper received the ace. He knocked on Henry Belt's door. There was no response. He started to knock again, but restrained himself.

He returned to the group. "Wait till he shows himself. I'd rather crash into Mars than bring forth Henry Belt and his red book."

The ship crossed the orbit of Mars well ahead of the looming red planet. It came toppling at them with a peculiar clumsy grandeur, a mass obviously bulky and globular, but so fine and clear was the detail, so absent the perspective, that the distance and size might have been anything. Instead of swinging in a sharp elliptical curve back toward Earth, the ship swerved aside in a blunt hyperbola and proceeded outward, now at a velocity of close to fifty miles a second. Mars receded astern and to the side. A new part of space lay ahead. The sun was noticeably smaller. Earth could no longer be differentiated from the stars. Mars departed quickly and politely, and space seemed lonely and forlorn.

Henry Belt had not appeared for two days. At last Culpepper went to knock on the door—once, twice, three times: a strange face looked out. It was Henry Belt, face haggard, skin like pulled taffy. His eyes glared red, his hair seemed matted and more unkempt than hair a quarter-inch should be. But he spoke in his quiet clear voice. "Mr. Culpepper, your merciless din has disturbed me. I am quite put out with you."

"Sorry, sir. We feared that you were ill."

Henry Belt made no response. He looked past Culpepper, around the circle of faces. "You gentlemen are unwontedly serious. Has this presumptive illness of mine caused you all distress?"

Sutton spoke in a rush. "The computer is out of order."

"Why then, you must repair it."

"It's a matter of altering the housing. If we do it incorrectly—"

"Mr. Sutton, please do not harass me with the hour-by-hour minutiae of running the ship."

"But, sir, the matter has become serious; we need your advice. We missed the Mars turn-around—"

"Well, I suppose there's always Jupiter. Must I explain the basic elements of astrogation to you?"

"But the computer's out of order—definitely."

"Then, if you wish to return to Earth, you must perform the calculations with pencil and paper. Why is it necessary to explain the obvious?"

"Jupiter is a long way out," said Sutton in a shrill voice. "Why can't we just turn around and go home?" This last was almost a whisper.

"I see I've been too easy on you cads," said Henry Belt. "You stand around idly; you chatter nonsense while the machinery goes to pieces and the ship flies at random. Everybody into spacesuits for sail inspection. Come now. Let's have some snap. What are you all? Walking corpses? You, Mr. Culpepper, why the delay?"

"It occurred to me, sir, that we are approaching the asteroid belt. As I am chief of the watch, I consider it my duty to cant sail to swing us around the area."

"You may do this; then join the rest in hull-and-sail inspection."

"Yes, sir."

The cadets donned spacesuits, Sutton with the utmost reluctance. Out into the dark void they went, and now here was loneliness indeed.

When they returned, Henry Belt had returned to his compartment.

"As Mr. Belt points out, we have no great choice," said Ostrander. "We missed Mars, so let's hit Jupiter. Luckily it's in good position—otherwise we'd have to swing out to Saturn or Uranus—"

"They're off behind the sun," said Lynch. "Jupiter's our last chance."

"Let's do it right then. I say, let's make one last attempt to set those confounded bearings. . . ."

But now it seemed as if the wobble and twist had been eliminated. The disks tracked perfectly, the accuracy monitor glowed green.

"Great!" yelled Lynch. "Feed it the dope. Let's get going!

All sail for Jupiter. Good Lord, but we're having a trip!"
"Wait till it's over," said Sutton. Since his return from sail inspection he had stood to one side, cheeks pinched, eyes staring. "It's not over yet. And maybe it's not meant to be."
The other five pretended not to have heard him. The computer spat out figures and angles. There was a billion miles to travel. Acceleration was less, due to the diminution in the intensity of sunlight. At least a month must pass befóre Jupiter came close.

6

The ship, great sail spread to the fading sunlight, fled like a ghost—out, always out. Each of the cadets had quietly performed the same calculation, and arrived at the same result. If the swing around Jupiter were not performed with exactitude, if the ship were not slung back like a stone on a string, there was nothing beyond. Saturn, Uranus, Neptune, Pluto were far around the sun; the ship, speeding at a hundred miles a second, could not be halted by the waning gravity of the sun, nor yet sufficiently accelerated in a concentric direction by sail and jet into a true orbit. The very nature of the sail made it useless as a brake; always the thrust was outward. Within the hull seven men lived and thought, and the psychic relationship worked and stirred like yeast in a vat of decaying fruit. The fundamental similarity, the human identity of the seven men, was utterly canceled; apparent only were the disparities. Each cadet appeared to others only as a walking characteristic, and Henry Belt was an incomprehensible Thing, who appeared from his compartment at unpredictable times, to move quietly here and there with the blind blank grin of an archaic Attic hero.
Jupiter loomed and bulked. The ship, at last within reach of the Jovian gravity, sidled over to meet it. The cadets gave ever more careful attention to the computer, checking and counter-checking the instructions. Verona was the most assiduous at this, Sutton the most harassed and ineffectual. Lynch growled and cursed and sweat; Ostrander complained in a thin peevish voice. Von Gluck worked with the calm of pessimistic fatalism; Culpepper seemed unconcerned, almost debonair, a blandness which bewildered Ostrander, infuriated Lynch, awoke a malignant hate in Sutton. Verona

and von Gluck on the other hand seemed to derive strength and refreshment from Culpepper's placid acceptance of the situation. Henry Belt said nothing. Occasionally he emerged from his compartment, to survey the wardroom and the cadets with the detached interest of a visitor to an asylum.

It was Lynch who made the discovery. He signaled it with an odd growl of sheer dismay, which brought a resonant questioning sound from Sutton. "My God, my God," muttered Lynch.

Verona was at his side. "What's the trouble?"

"Look. This gear. When we replaced the disks we dephased the whole apparatus one notch. This white dot and this other white dot should synchronize. They're one sprocket apart. All the results would check and be consistent because they'd all be off by the same factor."

Verona sprang into action. Off came the housing, off came various components. Gently he lifted the gear, set it back into correct alignment. The other cadets leaned over him as he worked, except Culpepper, who was chief of the watch.

Henry Belt appeared. "You gentlemen are certainly diligent in your navigation," he said presently. "Perfectionists almost."

"We do our best," grated Lynch between set teeth. "It's a damn shame sending us out with a machine like this."

The red book appeared. "Mr. Lynch, I mark you down not for your private sentiments, which are of course yours to entertain, but for voicing them and thereby contributing to an unhealthy atmosphere of despairing and hysterical pessimism."

A tide of red crept from Lynch's neck. He bent over the computer, made no comment. But Sutton suddenly cried out, "What else do you expect from us? We came out here to learn, not to suffer, or to fly on forever!" He gave a ghastly laugh. Henry Belt listened patiently. "Think of it!" cried Sutton. "The seven of us. In this capsule, forever!"

"I am afraid that I must charge you two demerits for your outburst, Mr. Sutton. A good spaceman maintains his dignity at all costs."

Lynch looked up from the computer. "Well, now we've got a corrected reading. Do you know what it says?"

Henry Belt turned him a look of polite inquiry.

"We're going to miss," said Lynch. "We're going to pass

by just as we passed Mars. Jupiter is pulling us around and sending us out toward Gemini."

The silence was thick in the room. Henry Belt turned to look at Culpepper, who was standing by the porthole, photographing Jupiter with his personal camera.

"Mr. Culpepper?"

"Yes, sir."

"You seem unconcerned by the prospect which Mr. Sutton has set forth."

"I hope it's not imminent."

"How do you propose to avoid it?"

"I imagine that we will radio for help, sir."

"You forget that I have destroyed the radio."

"I remember noting a crate marked 'Radio Parts' stored in the starboard jet-pod."

"I am sorry to disillusion you, Mr. Culpepper. That case is mislabeled."

Ostrander jumped to his feet, left the wardroom. There was the sound of moving crates. A moment of silence. Then he returned. He glared at Henry Belt. "Whiskey, bottles of whiskey."

Henry Belt nodded. "I told you as much."

"But now we have no radio," said Lynch in an ugly voice.

"We never have had a radio, Mr. Lynch. You were warned that you would have to depend on your own resources to bring us home. You have failed, and in the process doomed me as well as yourself. Incidentally, I must mark you all down ten demerits for a faulty cargo check."

"Demerits," said Ostrander in a bleak voice.

"Now, Mr. Culpepper," said Henry Belt. "What is your next proposal?"

"I don't know, sir."

Verona spoke in a placatory voice. "What would you do, sir, if you were in our position?"

Henry Belt shook his head. "I am an imaginative man, Mr. Verona, but there are certain leaps of the mind which are beyond my powers." He returned to his compartment.

Von Gluck looked curiously at Culpepper. "It is a fact. You're not at all concerned."

"Oh, I'm concerned. But I believe that Mr. Belt wants to get home too. He's too good a spaceman not to know exactly what he's doing."

The door from Henry Belt's compartment slid back. Henry Belt stood in the opening. "Mr. Culpepper, I chanced to overhear your remark, and I now note down ten demerits against you. This attitude expresses a complacence as dangerous as Mr. Sutton's utter funk." He looked about the room. "Pay no heed to Mr. Culpepper. He is wrong. Even if I could repair this disaster, I would not raise a hand. For I expect to die in space."

7

The sail was canted vectorless, edgewise to the sun. Jupiter was a smudge astern. There were five cadets in the wardroom. Culpepper, Verona, and von Gluck sat talking in low voices. Ostrander and Lynch lay crouched, arms to knees, faces to the wall. Sutton had gone two days before. Quietly donning his spacesuit he had stepped into the exit chamber and thrust himself headlong into space. A propulsion unit gave him added speed, and before any of the cadets could intervene he was gone.

Shortly thereafter Lynch and Ostrander succumbed to inanition, a kind of despondent helplessness: manic-depression in its most stupefying phase. Culpepper the suave, Verona the pragmatic and von Gluck the sensitive remained.

They spoke quietly to themselves, out of earshot of Henry Belt's room. "I still believe," said Culpepper, "that somehow there is a means to get ourselves out of this mess, and that Henry Belt knows it."

Verona said, "I wish I could think so. . . . We've been over it a hundred times. If we set sail for Saturn or Neptune or Uranus, the outward vector of thrust plus the outward vector of our momentum will take us far beyond Pluto before we're anywhere near a trajectory of control. The plasma jets could stop us if we had enough energy, but the shield can't supply it and we don't have another power source. . . ."

Von Gluck hit his fist into his hand. "Gentlemen," he said in a soft, delighted voice. "I believe we have sufficient energy at hand. We will use the sail. Remember? It is bellied. It can function as a mirror. It spreads five square miles of surface. Sunlight out here is thin—but so long as we collect enough of it—"

"I understand!" said Culpepper. "We back off the hull till the reactor is at the focus of the sail and turn on the jets!"

Verona said dubiously, "We'll still be receiving radiation pressure. And what's worse, the jets will impinge back on the sail. Effect—cancellation. We'll be nowhere."

"If we cut the center out of the sail—just enough to allow the plasma through—we'd beat that objection. As for the radiation pressure—we'll surely do better with the plasma drive."

"What do we use to make plasma? We don't have the stock."

"Anything that can be ionized. The radio, the computer, your shoes, my shirt, Culpepper's camera, Henry Belt's whiskey. . . ."

8

The angel-wagon came up to meet Sail 25, in orbit beside Sail 40, which was just making ready to take out a new crew.

The cargo carrier drifted near, eased into position. Three men sprang across space to Sail 40, a few hundred yards behind 25, tossed lines back to the carrier, pulled bales of cargo and equipment across the gap.

The five cadets and Henry Belt, clad in spacesuits, stepped out into the sunlight. Earth spread below, green and blue, white and brown, the contours so precious and dear to bring tears to the eyes. The cadets transferring cargo to Sail 40 gazed at them curiously as they worked. At last they were finished, and the six men of Sail 25 boarded the carrier.

"Back safe and sound, eh Henry?" said the pilot. "Well, I'm always surprised."

Henry Belt made no answer. The cadets stowed their cargo, and standing by the port, took a final look at Sail 25. The carrier retro-jetted; the two sails seemed to rise above them.

The lighter nosed in and out of the atmosphere, braked, extended its wings, glided to an easy landing on the Mojave Desert.

The cadets, their legs suddenly loose and weak to the unaccustomed gravity, limped after Henry Belt to the carry-all, seated themselves and were conveyed to the administration complex. They alighted from the carry-all, and now Henry Belt motioned the five to the side.

"Here, gentlemen, is where I leave you. Tonight I will check my red book and prepare my official report. But I believe I can present you an unofficial résumé of my impressions. Mr. Lynch and Mr. Ostrander, I feel that you are ill suited either for command or for any situation which might inflict prolonged emotional pressure upon you. I cannot recommend you for space-duty.

"Mr. von Gluck, Mr. Culpepper and Mr. Verona, all of you meet my minimum requirements for a recommendation, although I shall write the words 'Especially Recommended' only beside the names Clyde von Gluck and Marcus Verona. You brought the sail back to Earth by essentially faultless navigation.

"So now our association ends. I trust you have profited by it." Henry Belt nodded briefly to each of the five and limped off around the building.

The cadets looked after him. Culpepper reached in his pocket and brought forth a pair of small metal objects which he displayed in his palm. "Recognize these?"

"Hmf," said Lynch in a flat voice. "Bearings for the computer disks. The original ones."

"I found them in the little spare parts tray. They weren't there before."

Von Gluck nodded. "The machinery always seemed to fail immediately after sail check, as I recall."

Lynch drew in his breath with a sharp hiss. He turned, strode away. Ostrander followed him. Culpepper shrugged. To Verona he gave one of the bearings, to von Gluck the other. "For souvenirs—or medals. You fellows deserve them."

"Thanks, Ed," said von Gluck.

"Thanks," muttered Verona. "I'll make a stickpin of this thing."

The three, not able to look at each other, glanced up into the sky where the first stars of twilight were appearing, then continued on into the building where family and friends and sweethearts awaited them.

THIS STORY is one of my favorites. Having said so much, I suppose that I am obliged to respond to the question: why?

To extol one's own work is sheer recklessness; on the other hand unabashed candor is refreshing and perhaps a virtue; therefore I will venture one or two comments in regard to "Ullward's Retreat."

I consider the story well constructed from a technical standpoint, and I feel that in spite of its overt frivolity, the story makes a number of profound statements upon the human condition. There are no villains in this piece, and no heroes; we are confronted only with human captiousness and human vanity.

II

ULLWARD'S RETREAT

BRUHAM ULLWARD HAD INVITED THREE FRIENDS to lunch at his ranch: Ted and Ravelin Seehoe, and their adolescent daughter Iugenae. After an eye-bulging feast, Ullward offered around a tray of the digestive pastilles which had won him his wealth.

"A wonderful meal," said Ted Seehoe reverently. "Too much, really. I'll need one of these. The algae was absolutely marvelous."

Ullward made a smiling easy gesture. "It's the genuine stuff."

Ravelin Seehoe, a fresh-faced, rather positive young woman of eighty or ninety, reached for a pastille. "A shame there's not more of it. The synthetic we get is hardly recognizable as algae."

"It's a problem," Ullward admitted. "I clubbed up with some friends; we bought a little mat in the Ross Sea and grow all our own."

"Think of that!" exclaimed Ravelin. "Isn't it frightfully expensive?"

Ullward pursed his lips whimsically. "The good things in life come high. Luckily, I'm able to afford a bit extra."

"What I keep telling Ted—" began Ravelin, then stopped as Ted turned her a keen warning glance.

Ullward bridged the rift. "Money isn't everything. I have a flat of algae, my ranch; you have your daughter—and I'm sure you wouldn't trade."

Ravelin regarded Iugenae critically. "I'm not so sure."

Ted patted Iugenae's hand. "When do you have your own

30

child, Lamster Ullward?" (*Lamster: contraction of Land-master—the polite form of address in current use.*)

"Still some time yet. I'm thirty-seven billion down the list."

"A pity," said Ravelin Seehoe brightly, "when you could give a child so many advantages."

"Someday, someday, before I'm too old."

"A shame," said Ravelin, "but it has to be. Another fifty billion people and we'd have no privacy whatever!" She looked admiringly around the room, which was used for the sole purpose of preparing food and dining.

Ullward put his hands on the arms of his chair, hitched forward a little. "Perhaps you'd like to look around the ranch?" He spoke in a casual voice, glancing from one to the other.

Iugenae clapped her hands; Ravelin beamed. "If it wouldn't be too much trouble!" "Oh, we'd love to, Lamster Ullward!" cried Iugenae. "I've always wanted to see your ranch," said Ted. "I've heard so much about it."

"It's an opportunity for Iugenae I wouldn't want her to miss," said Ravelin. She shook her finger at Iugenae. "Remember, Miss Puss, notice everything very carefully—and don't *touch*!"

"May I take pictures, Mother?"

"You'll have to ask Lamster Ullward."

"Of course, of course," said Ullward. "Why in the world not?" He rose to his feet—a man of more than middle stature, more than middle pudginess, with straight sandy hair, round blue eyes, a prominent beak of a nose. Almost three hundred years old, he guarded his health with great zeal, and looked little more than two hundred.

He stepped to the door, checked the time, touched a dial on the wall. "Are you ready?"

"Yes, we're quite ready," said Ravelin.

Ullward snapped back the wall, to reveal a view over a sylvan glade. A fine oak tree shaded a pond growing with rushes. A path led through a field toward a wooded valley a mile in the distance.

"Magnificent," said Ted. "Simply magnificent!"

They stepped outdoors into the sunlight. Iugenae flung her arms out, twirled, danced in a circle. "Look! I'm all alone! I'm out here all by myself!"

"Iugenae!" called Ravelin sharply. "Be careful! Stay on the path! That's real grass and you mustn't damage it."

Iugenae ran ahead to the pond. "Mother!" she called back. "Look at these funny little jumpy things! And look at the flowers!"

"The animals are frogs," said Ullward. "They have a very interesting life-history. You see the little fishlike things in the water?"

"Aren't they funny! Mother, do come here!"

"Those are called tadpoles and they will presently become frogs, indistinguishable from the ones you see."

Ravelin and Ted advanced with more dignity, but were as interested as Iugenae in the frogs.

"Smell the fresh air," Ted told Ravelin. "You'd think you were back in the early times."

"It's absolutely exquisite," said Ravelin. She looked around her. "One has the feeling of being able to wander on and on and on."

"Come around over here," called Ullward from beyond the pool. "This is the rock garden."

In awe, the guests stared at the ledge of rock, stained with red and yellow lichen, tufted with green moss. Ferns grew from a crevice; there were several fragile clusters of white flowers.

"Smell the flowers, if you wish," Ullward told Iugenae. "But please don't touch them; they stain rather easily."

Iugenae sniffed. "Mmmm!"

"Are they real?" asked Ted.

"The moss, yes. That clump of ferns and these little succulents are real. The flowers were designed for me by a horticulturist and are exact replicas of certain ancient species. We've actually improved on the odor."

"Wonderful, wonderful," said Ted.

"Now come this way—no, don't look back; I want you to get the total effect. . . ." An expression of vexation crossed his face.

"What's the trouble?" asked Ted.

"It's a damned nuisance," said Ullward. "Hear that sound?"

Ted became aware of a faint rolling rumble, deep and almost unheard. "Yes. Sounds like some sort of factory."

"It is. On the floor below. A rug-works. One of the looms creates this terrible row. I've complained, but they pay no attention. . . . Oh, well, ignore it. Now stand over here—look around!"

His friends gasped in rapture. The view from this angle was a rustic bungalow in an Alpine valley, the door being the opening into Ullward's dining room.

"What an illusion of distance!" exclaimed Ravelin. "A person would almost think he was alone."

"A beautiful piece of work," said Ted. "I'd swear I was looking into ten miles—at least five miles—of distance."

"I've got a lot of space here," said Ullward proudly. "Almost three-quarters of an acre. Would you like to see it by moonlight?"

"Oh, could we?"

Ullward went to a concealed switch-panel; the sun seemed to race across the sky. A fervent glow of sunset lighted the valley; the sky burned peacock blue, gold, green, then came twilight—and the rising full moon came up behind the hill.

"This is absolutely marvelous," said Ravelin softly. "How can you bring yourself to leave it?"

"It's hard," admitted Ullward. "But I've got to look after business too. More money, more space."

He turned a knob; the moon floated across the sky, sank. Stars appeared, forming the age-old patterns. Ullward pointed out the constellations and the first-magnitude stars by name, using a pencil-torch for a pointer. Then the sky flushed with lavender and lemon-yellow and the sun appeared once more. Unseen ducts sent a current of cool air through the glade.

"Right now I'm negotiating for an area behind this wall here." He tapped at the depicted mountainside, an illusion given reality and three-dimensionality by laminations inside the pane. "It's quite a large area—over a hundred square feet. The owner wants a fortune, naturally."

"I'm surprised he wants to sell," said Ted. "A hundred square feet means real privacy."

"There's been a death in the family," explained Ullward. "The owner's four-great-grandfather passed on and the space is temporarily surplus."

Ted nodded. "I hope you're able to get it."

"I hope so too. I've got rather flamboyant ambitions—eventually I hope to own the entire quarterblock—but it

takes time. People don't like to sell their space and everyone is anxious to buy."

"Not we," said Ravelin cheerfully. "We have our little
home. We're snug and cozy and we're putting money aside
for investment."

"Wise," agreed Ullward. "A great many people are space-
poor. Then when a chance to make real money comes up,
they're under-capitalized. Until I scored with the digestive
pastilles, I lived in a single rented locker. I was cramped—
but I don't regret it today."

They returned through the glade toward Ullward's house,
stopping at the oak tree. "This is my special pride," said
Ullward. "A genuine oak tree!"

"Genuine?" asked Ted in astonishment. "I assumed it was
simulated."

"So many people do," said Ullward. "No, it's genuine."

"Take a picture of the tree, Iugenae, please. But don't
touch it. You might damage the bark."

"Perfectly all right to touch the bark," assured Ullward.
He looked up into the branches, then scanned the ground.
He stooped, picked up a fallen leaf. "This grew on the tree,"
he said. "Now, Iugenae, I want you to come with me." He
went to the rock garden, pulled a simulated rock aside, to
reveal a cabinet with washbasin. "Watch carefully." He
showed her the leaf. "Notice? It's dry and brittle and brown."

"Yes, Lamster Ullward." Iugenae craned her neck.

"First I dip it in this solution." He took a beaker full of
dark liquid from a shelf. "So. That restores the green color.
We wash off the excess, then dry it. Now we rub this next
fluid carefully into the surface. Notice, it's flexible and strong
now. One more solution—a plastic coating—and there we
are, a true oak leaf, perfectly genuine. It's yours."

"Oh, Lamster Ullward! Thank you ever so much!" She
ran off to show her father and mother, who were standing
by the pool, luxuriating in the feeling of space, watching the
frogs. "See what Lamster Ullward gave me!"

"You be very careful with it," said Ravelin. "When we
get home, we'll find a nice little frame and you can hang it
in your locker."

The simulated sun hung in the western sky. Ullward led
the group to a sundial. "An antique, countless years old.
Pure marble, carved by hand. It works too—entirely func-

tional. Notice. Three-fifteen by the shadow on the dial. . . ."
He peered at his beltwatch, squinted at the sun. "Excuse me
one moment." He ran to the control board, made an adjustment. The sun lurched ten degrees across the sky. Ullward
returned, checked the sundial. "That's better. Notice. Three-
fifty by the sundial, three-fifty by my watch. Isn't that something now?"

"It's wonderful," said Ravelin earnestly.

"It's the loveliest thing I've ever seen," chirped Iugenae.

Ravelin looked around the ranch, sighed wistfully. "We
hate to leave, but I think we must be returning home."

"It's been a wonderful day, Lamster Ullward," said Ted.
"A wonderful lunch, and we enjoyed seeing your ranch."

"You'll have to come out again," invited Ullward. "I always enjoy company."

He led them into the dining room, through the living
room-bedroom to the door. The Seehoe family took a last
look across the spacious interior, pulled on their mantles,
stepped into their runshoes, made their farewells. Ullward
slid back the door. The Seehoes looked out, waited till a
gap appeared in the traffic. They waved good-bye, pulled the
hoods over their heads, stepped out into the corridor.

The runshoes spun them toward their home, selecting the
appropriate turnings, sliding automatically into the correct
lift- and drop-pits. Deflection fields twisted them through the
throngs. Like the Seehoes, everyone wore mantle and hood
of filmy reflective stuff to safeguard privacy. The illusion-
pane along the ceiling of the corridor presented a view of
towers dwindling up into a cheerful blue sky, as if the
pedestrian were moving along one of the windy upper passages.

The Seehoes approached their home. Two hundred yards
away, they angled over to the wall. If the flow of traffic
carried them past, they would be forced to circle the block
and make another attempt to enter. Their door slid open as
they spun near; they ducked into the opening, swinging
around on a metal grab-bar.

They removed their mantles and runshoes, sliding skillfully past each other. Iugenae pivoted into the bathroom and
there was room for both Ted and Ravelin to sit down. The
house was rather small for the three of them; they could
well have used another twelve square feet, but rather than

pay exorbitant rent, they preferred to save the money with an eye toward Iugenae's future.

Ted sighed in satisfaction, stretching his legs luxuriously under Ravelin's chair. "Ullward's ranch notwithstanding, it's nice to be home."

Iugenae backed out of the bathroom.

Ravelin looked up. "It's time for your pill, dear."

Iugenae screwed up her face. "Oh, Mama! Why do I have to take pills? I feel perfectly well."

"They're good for you, dear."

Iugenae sullenly took a pill from the dispenser. "Runy says you make us take pills to keep us from growing up."

Ted and Ravelin exchanged glances.

"Just take your pill," said Ravelin, "and never mind what Runy says."

"But how is it that I'm thirty eight and Ermara Burk's only thirty two; and she's got a figure and I'm like a slat?"

"No arguments, dear. Take your pill."

Ted jumped to his feet. "Here, Babykin, sit down."

Iugenae protested, but Ted held up his hand. "I'll sit in the niche. I've got a few calls that I have to make."

He sidled past Ravelin, seated himself in the niche in front of the communication screen. The illusion-pane behind him was custom-built—Ravelin, in fact, had designed it herself. It simulated a merry little bandit's den, the walls draped in red and yellow silk, a bowl of fruit on the rustic table, a guitar on the bench, a copper teakettle simmering on the countertop stove. The pane had been rather expensive, but when anyone communicated with the Seehoes, it was the first thing they saw, and here the house-proud Ravelin had refused to stint.

Before Ted could make his call, the signal light flashed. He answered; the screen opened to display his friend Loren Aigle, apparently sitting in an airy arched rotunda, against a background of fleecy clouds—an illusion which Ravelin had instantly recognized as an inexpensive stock effect.

Loren and Elme, his wife, were anxious to hear of the Seehoe's visit to the Ullward ranch. Ted described the afternoon in detail.

"Space, space and more space! Isolation pure and simple! Absolute privacy! You can hardly imagine it! A fortune in illusion-panes."

"Nice," said Loren Aigle. "I'll tell you one you'll find hard to believe. Today I registered a whole planet to a man." Loren worked in the Certification Bureau of the Extraterrestrial Properties Agency.

Ted was puzzled and uncomprehending. "A whole planet? How so?"

Loren explained. "He's a free-lance spaceman. Still a few left."

"But what's he planning to do with an entire planet?"

"Live there, he claims."

"Alone?"

Loren nodded. "I had quite a chat with him. Earth is all very well, he says, but he prefers the privacy of his own planet. Can you imagine that?"

"Frankly, no! I can't imagine the fourth dimension either. What a marvel, though!"

The conversation ended and the screen faded. Ted swung around to his wife. "Did you hear that?"

Ravelin nodded; she had heard but not heeded. She was reading the menu supplied by the catering firm to which they subscribed. "We won't want anything heavy after that lunch. They've got simulated synthetic algae again."

Ted grunted. "It's never as good as the genuine synthetic."

"But it's cheaper and we've all had an enormous lunch."

"Don't worry about me, Mom!" sang Iugenae. "I'm going out with Runy."

"Oh, you are, are you? And where are you going, may I ask?"

"A ride around the world. We're catching the seven o'clock shuttle, so I've got to hurry."

"Come right home afterward," said Ravelin severely. "Don't go anywhere else."

"For heaven's sake, Mother, you'd think I was going to elope or something."

"Mind what I say, Miss Puss. I was a girl once myself. Have you taken your medicine?"

"Yes, I've taken my medicine."

Iugenae departed; Ted slipped back into the niche. "Who are you calling now?" asked Ravelin.

"Lamster Ullward. I want to thank him for going to so much trouble for us."

Ravelin agreed that an algae-and-margarine call was no more than polite.

Ted called, expressed his thanks, then—almost as an afterthought—chanced to mention the man who owned a planet.

"An entire planet?" inquired Ullward. "It must be inhabited."

"No, I understand not, Lamster Ullward. Think of it! Think of the privacy!"

"Privacy!" exclaimed Ullward bluffly. "My dear fellow, what do you call this?"

"Oh, naturally, Lamster Ullward—you have a real showplace."

"The planet must be very primitive," Ullward reflected. "An engaging idea, of course—if you like that kind of thing. Who is this man?"

"I don't know, Lamster Ullward. I could find out, if you like."

"No, no, don't bother. I'm not particularly interested. Just an idle thought." Ullward laughed his hearty laugh. "Poor man. Probably lives in a dome."

"That's possible, of course, Lamster Ullward. Well, thanks again, and good night."

The spaceman's name was Kennes Mail. He was short and thin, tough as synthetic herring, brown as toasted yeast. He had a close-cropped pad of gray hair, a keen, if ingenuous, blue gaze. He showed a courteous interest in Ullward's ranch, but Ullward thought his recurrent use of the word "clever" rather tactless.

As they returned to the house, Ullward paused to admire his oak tree.

"It's absolutely genuine, Lamster Mail! A living tree, survival of past ages! Do you have trees as fine as that on your planet?"

Kennes Mail smiled. "Lamster Ullward, that's just a shrub. Let's sit somewhere and I'll show you photographs."

Ullward had already mentioned his interest in acquiring extraterrestrial property; Mail, admitting that he needed money, had given him to understand that some sort of deal might be arranged. They sat at a table; Mail opened his case. Ullward switched on the wallscreen.

"First I'll show you a map," said Mail. He selected a rod,

dropped it into the table socket. On the wall appeared a world projection: oceans, an enormous equatorial landmass named Gaea; the smaller subcontinents Atalanta, Persephone, Alcyone. A box of descriptive information read:

MAIL'S PLANET

Claim registered and endorsed at Extraterrestrial Properties Agency

Surface area:	.87 Earth normal
Gravity:	.93 Earth normal
Diurnal rotation:	22.15 Earth hours
Annual revolution:	2.97 Earth years
Atmosphere:	Invigorating
Climate:	Salubrious
Noxious conditions and infiuences:	None
Population:	1

Mail pointed to a spot on the eastern shore of Gaea. "I live here. Just got a rough camp at present. I need money to do a bit better for myself. I'm willing to lease off one of the smaller continents, or, if you prefer, a section of Gaea, say from Murky Mountains west to the ocean."

Ullward, with a cheerful smile, shook his head. "No sections for me, Lamster Mail. I want to buy the world outright. You set your price; if it's within reason, I'll write a check."

Mail glanced at him sidewise. "You haven't even seen the photographs."

"True." In a businesslike voice, Ullward said, "By all means, the photographs."

Mail touched the projection button. Landscapes of an unfamiliar wild beauty appeared on the screen. There were mountain crags and roaring rivers, snow-powdered forests, ocean dawns and prairie sunsets, green hillsides, meadows spattered with blossoms, beaches white as milk.

"Very pleasant," said Ullward. "Quite nice." He pulled out his checkbook. "What's your price?"

Mail chuckled and shook his head. "I won't sell. I'm willing to lease off a section—providing my price is met and my rules are agreed to."

Ullward sat with compressed lips. He gave his head a quick little jerk. Mail started to rise to his feet.

"No, no," said Ullward hastily. "I was merely thinking. . . . Let's look at the map again."

Mail returned the map to the screen. Ullward made careful inspection of the various continents, inquired as to physiography, climate, flora and fauna.

Finally he made his decision. "I'll lease Gaea."

"No, Lamster Ullward!" declared Mail. "I'm reserving this entire area—from Murky Mountains and the Calliope River east. This western section is open. It's maybe a little smaller than Atalanta or Persephone, but the climate is warmer."

"There aren't any mountains on the western section," Ullward protested. "Only these insignificant Rock Castle Crags."

"They're not so insignificant," said Mail. "You've also got the Purple Bird Hills, and down here in the south is Mount Cairasco—a live volcano. What more do you need?"

Ullward glanced across his ranch. "I'm in the habit of thinking big."

"West Gaea is a pretty big chunk of property."

"Very well," said Ullward. "What are your terms?"

"So far as money goes, I'm not greedy," Mail said. "For a twenty-year lease: two hundred thousand a year, the first five years in advance."

Ullward made a startled protest. "Great guns, Lamster Mail! That's almost half my income!"

Mail shrugged. "I'm not trying to get rich. I want to build a lodge for myself. It costs money. If you can't afford it, I'll have to speak to someone who can."

Ullward said in a nettled voice, "I can afford it, certainly —but my entire ranch here cost less than a million."

"Well, either you want it or you don't," said Mail. "I'll tell you my rules, then you can make up your mind."

"What rules?" demanded Ullward, his face growing red.

"They're simple and their only purpose is to maintain privacy for both of us. First, you have to stay on your own property. No excursions hither and yon on my property. Second, no subleasing. Third, no residents except yourself, your family and your servants. I don't want any artists' colony springing up, nor any wild, noisy resort atmosphere.

Naturally you're entitled to bring out your guests, but they've got to keep your property just like yourself."

He looked sidewise at Ullward's glum face. "I'm not trying to be tough, Lamster Ullward. Good fences make good neighbors, and it's better that we have the understanding now than hard words and beam-gun evictions later."

"Let me see the photographs again," said Ullward. "Show me West Gaea."

He looked, heaved a deep sigh. "Very well, I agree."

The construction crew had departed. Ullward was alone on West Gaea. He walked around the new lodge, taking deep breaths of pure quiet air, thrilling to the absolute solitude and privacy. The lodge had cost a fortune, but how many other people of Earth owned—leased, rather—anything to compare with this?

He walked out on the front terrace, gazed proudly across miles—genuine unsimulated miles—of landscape. For his home site, he had selected a shelf in the foothills of the Ullward Range (as he had renamed the Purple Bird Hills). In front spread a great golden savannah dotted with blue-green trees; behind rose a tall gray cliff.

A stream rushed down a cleft in the rock, leaping, splashing, cooling the air, finally flowing into a beautiful clear pool, beside which Ullward had erected a cabana of red, green and brown plastic. At the base of the cliff and in crevices grew clumps of spiky blue cactus, lush green bushes covered with red trumpet-flowers, a thick-leafed white plant holding up a stalk clustered with white bubbles.

Solitude! The real thing! No thumping of factories, no roar of traffic two feet from one's bed. One arm outstretched, the other pressed to his chest, Ullward performed a stately little jig of triumph on the terrace. Had he been able, he might have turned a cartwheel. When a person has complete privacy, absolutely nothing is forbidden!

Ullward took a final turn up and down the terrace, made a last appreciative survey of the horizon. The sun was sinking through banks of fire-fringed clouds. Marvelous depth of color, a tonal brilliance to be matched only in the very best illusion-panes!

He entered the lodge, made a selection from the nutrition locker. After a leisurely meal, he returned to the lounge. He stood thinking for a moment, then went out upon the terrace, strolled up and down. Wonderful! The night was full of stars, hanging like blurred white lamps, almost as he had always imagined them.

After ten minutes of admiring the stars, he returned into the lodge. Now what? The wallscreen, with its assortment of recorded programs. Snug and comfortable, Ullward watched the performance of a recent musical comedy.

Real luxury, he told himself. Pity he couldn't invite his friends out to spend the evening. Unfortunately impossible, considering the inconvenient duration of the trip between Mail's Planet and Earth. However—only three days until the arrival of his first guest. She was Elf Intry, a young woman who had been more than friendly with Ullward on Earth. When Elf arrived, Ullward would broach a subject which he had been mulling over for several months—indeed, ever since he had first learned of Mail's Planet.

Elf Intry arrived early in the afternoon, coming down to Mail's Planet in a capsule discharged from the weekly Outer Ring Express packet. A woman of normally good disposition, she greeted Ullward in a seethe of indignation. "Just who is that brute around the other side of the planet? I thought you had absolute privacy here!"

"That's just old Mail," said Ullward evasively. "What's wrong?"

"The fool on the packet set me the wrong coordinates and the capsule came down on a beach. I noticed a house and then I saw a naked man jumping rope behind some bushes. I thought it was you, of course. I went over and said 'Boo!' You should have heard the language he used!" She shook her head. "I don't see why you allow such a boor on your planet."

The buzzer on the communication screen sounded. "That's Mail now," said Ullward. "You wait here. I'll tell him how to speak to my guests!"

He presently returned to the terrace. Elf came over to him, kissed his nose. "Ully, you're pale with rage! I hope you didn't lose your temper."

"No," said Ullward. "We merely—well, we had an understanding. Come along, look over the property."

He took Elf around to the back, pointing out the swimming pool, the waterfall, the mass of rock above. "You won't see that effect on any illusion-pane! That's genuine rock!"

"Lovely, Ully. Very nice. The color might be just a trifle darker, though. Rock doesn't look like that."

"No?" Ullward inspected the cliff more critically. "Well, I can't do anything about it. How about the privacy?"

"Wonderful! It's so quiet, it's almost eerie!"

"Eerie?" Ullward looked around the landscape. "It hadn't occurred to me."

"You're not sensitive to these things, Ully. Still, it's very nice, if you can tolerate that unpleasant creature Mail so close."

"Close?" protested Ullward. "He's on the other side of the continent!"

"True," said Elf. "It's all relative, I suppose. How long do you expect to stay out here?"

"That depends. Come along inside. I want to talk with you."

He seated her in a comfortable chair, brought her a globe of Gluco-Fructoid Nectar. For himself, he mixed ethyl alcohol, water, a few drops of Haig's Oldtime Esters.

"Elf, where do you stand in the reproduction list?"

She raised her fine eyebrows, shook her head. "So far down, I've lost count. Fifty or sixty billion."

"I'm down thirty-seven billion. It's one reason I bought this place. Waiting list, piffle! Nobody stops Bruham Ullward's breeding on his own planet!"

Elf pursed her lips, shook her head sadly. "It won't work, Ully."

"And why not?"

"You can't take the children back to Earth. The list would keep them out."

"True, but think of living here, surrounded by children. All the children you wanted! And utter privacy to boot! What more could you ask for?"

Elf sighed. "You fabricate a beautiful illusion-pane, Ully. But I think not. I love the privacy and solitude—but I thought there'd be more people to be private from."

The Outer Ring Express packet came past four days later. Elf kissed Ullward good-bye. "It's simply exquisite here,

Ully. The solitude is so magnificent, it gives me gooseflesh.
I've had a wonderful visit." She climbed into the capsule.
"See you on Earth."

"Just a minute," said Ullward suddenly. "I want you to
post a letter or two for me."

"Hurry. I've only got twenty minutes."

Ullward was back in ten minutes. "Invitations," he told
her breathlessly. "Friends."

"Right." She kissed his nose. "Good-bye, Ully." She
slammed the port; the capsule rushed away, whirling up to
meet the packet.

The new guests arrived three weeks later; Frobisher Wor-
beck, Liornetta Stobart, Harris and Hyla Cabe, Ted and
Ravelin and Iugenae Seehoe, Juvenal Aquister and his son
Runy.

Ullward, brown from long days of lazing in the sun,
greeted them with great enthusiasm. "Welcome to my little
retreat! Wonderful to see you all! Frobisher, you pink-
cheeked rascal! And Iugenae! Prettier than ever! Be careful, Ravelin—I've got my eye on your daughter! But Runy's
here, guess I'm out of the picture! Liornetta, damned glad
you could make it! And Ted! Great to see you, old chap!
This is all your doing, you know! Harris, Hyla, Juvenal—
come on up! We'll have a drink, a drink, a drink!"

Running from one to the other, patting arms, herding the
slow-moving Frobisher Worbeck, he conducted his guests up
the slope to the terrace. Here they turned to survey the pan-
orama. Ullward listened to their remarks, mouth pursed
against a grin of gratification.

"Magnificent!"

"Grand!"

"Absolutely genuine!"

"The sky is so far away, it frightens me!"

"The sunlight's so pure!"

"The genuine thing's always best, isn't it?"

Runy said a trifle wistfully, "I thought you were on a
beach, Lamster Ullward."

"Beach? This is mountain country, Runy. Land of the
wide open spaces! Look out over that plain!"

Liornetta Stobart patted Runy's shoulder. "Not every
planet has beaches, Runy. The secret of happiness is to be
content with what one has."

Ullward laughed gaily. "Oh, I've got beaches, never fear for that! There's a fine beach—ha, ha—five hundred miles due west. Every step Ullward domain!"

"Can we go?" said Iugenae excitedly. "Can we go, Lamster Ullward?"

"We certainly can! That shed down the slope is headquarters for the Ullward Airlines. We'll fly to the beach, swim in Ullward Ocean! But now refreshment! After that crowded capsule, your throats must be like paper!"

"It wasn't too crowded," said Ravelin Seehoe. "There were only nine of us." She looked critically up at the cliff. "If that were an illusion-pane, I'd consider it grotesque."

"My dear Ravelin!" cried Ullward. "It's impressive! Magnificent!"

"All of that," agreed Frobisher Worbeck, a tall sturdy man, white haired, red jowled, with a blue benevolent gaze. "And now, Bruham, what about those drinks?"

"Of course. Ted, I know you of old. Will you tend bar? Here's the alcohol, here's the water, here are the esters. Now, you two," Ullward called to Runy and Iugenae. "How about some nice cold soda pop?"

"What kind is there?" asked Runy.

"All kinds, all flavors. This is Ullward's Retreat! We've got methylamyl glutamine, cycloprodacterol phosphate, metathiobromine-four-glycocitrose. . . ."

Runy and Iugenae expressed their preferences; Ullward brought the globes, then hurried to arrange tables and chairs for the adults. Presently everyone was comfortable and relaxed.

Iugenae whispered to Ravelin, who smiled and nodded indulgently. "Lamster Ullward, you remember the beautiful oak leaf you gave Iugenae?"

"Of course I do."

"It's still as fresh a green as ever. I wonder if Iugenae might have a leaf or two from some of these other trees?"

"My dear Ravelin!" Ullward roared with laughter. "She can have an entire tree!"

"Oh, Mother! Can—"

"Iugenae, don't be ridiculous!" snapped Ted. "How could we get it home? Where would we plant the thing? In the bathroom?"

Ravelin said, "You and Runy find some nice leaves, but don't wander too far."

"No, Mother." She beckoned to Runy. "Come along, dope. Bring a basket."

The others of the party gazed out over the plain. "A beautiful view, Ullward," said Frobisher Worbeck. "How far does your property extend?"

"Five hundred miles west to the ocean, six hundred miles east to the mountains, eleven hundred miles north and two hundred miles south."

Worbeck shook his head solemnly. "Nice. A pity you couldn't get the whole planet. Then you'd have real privacy!"

"I tried, of course," said Ullward. "The owner refused to consider the idea."

"A pity."

Ullward brought out a map. "However, as you see, I have a fine volcano, a number of excellent rivers, a mountain range, and down here on the delta of Cinnamon River an absolutely miasmic swamp."

Ravelin pointed to the ocean. "Why, it's Lonesome Ocean! I thought the name was Ullward Ocean."

Ullward laughed uncomfortably. "Just a figure of speech —so to speak. My rights extend ten miles. More than enough for swimming purposes."

"No freedom of the seas here, eh, Lamster Ullward?" laughed Harris Cabe.

"Not exactly," confessed Ullward.

"A pity," said Frobisher Worbeck.

Hyla Cabe pointed to the map. "Look at these wonderful mountain ranges! The Magnificent Mountains! And over here—the Elysian Gardens! I'd love to see them, Lamster Ullward."

Ullward shook his head in embarrassment. "Impossible, I'm afraid. They're not on my property. I haven't seen them myself."

His guests stared at him in astonishment. "But surely—"

"It's an atom-welded contract with Lamster Mail," Ullward explained. "He stays on his property, I stay on mine. In this way, our privacy is secure."

"Look," Hyla Cabe said aside to Ravelin. "The Unimaginable Caverns! Doesn't it make you simply wild not to be able to see them?"

Aquister said hurriedly, "It's a pleasure to sit here and just breathe this wonderful fresh air. No noise, no crowds, no bustle or hurry."

The party drank and chatted and basked in the sunshine until late afternoon. Enlisting the aid of Ravelin Seehoe and Hyla Cabe, Ullward set out a simple meal of yeast pellets, processed protein, thick pieces of algae crunch.

"No animal flesh, cooked vegetation?" questioned Worbeck curiously.

"Tried them the first day," said Ullward. "Revolting. Sick for a week."

After dinner, the guests watched a comic melodrama on the wallscreen. Then Ullward showed them to their various cubicles, and after a few minutes of badinage and calling back and forth, the lodge became quiet.

Next day, Ullward ordered his guests into their bathing suits. "We're off to the beach, we'll gambol on the sand, we'll frolic in the surf of Lonesome Ullward Ocean!"

The guests piled happily into the air-car. Ullward counted heads. "All aboard! We're off!"

They rose and flew west, first low over the plain, then high into the air, to obtain a panoramic view of the Rock Castle Crags.

"The tallest peak—there to the north—is almost ten thousand feet high. Notice how it juts up, just imagine the mass! Solid rock! How'd you like that dropped on your toe, Runy? Not so good, eh? In a moment, we'll see a precipice over a thousand feet straight up and down. There—now! Isn't that remarkable?"

"Certainly impressive," agreed Ted.

"What those Magnificent Mountains must be like!" said Harris Cabe with a wry laugh.

"How tall are they, Lamster Ullward?" inquired Liornetta Stobart.

"What? Which?"

"The Magnificent Mountains."

"I don't know for sure. Thirty or forty thousand feet, I suppose."

"What a marvelous sight they must be!" said Frobisher Worbeck. "Probably make these look like foothills."

"These are beautiful too," Hyla Cabe put in hastily.

"Oh, naturally," said Frobisher Worbeck. "A damned fine sight! You're a lucky man, Bruham!"

Ullward laughed shortly, turned the air-car west. They flew across a rolling forested plain and presently Lonesome Ocean gleamed in the distance. Ullward slanted down, landed the air-car on the beach, and the party alighted.

The day was warm, the sun hot. A fresh wind blew in from the ocean. The surf broke upon the sand in massive roaring billows.

The party stood appraising the scene. Ullward swung his arms. "Well, who's for it? Don't wait to be invited! We've got the whole ocean to ourselves!"

Ravelin said, "It's so rough! Look how that water crashes down!"

Liornetta Stobart turned away with a shake of her head. "Illusion-pane surf is always so gentle. This could lift you right up and give you a good shaking!"

"I expected nothing quite so vehement," Harris Cabe admitted.

Ravelin beckoned to Iugenae. "You keep well away, Miss Puss. I don't want you swept out to sea. You'd find it Lonesome Ocean indeed!"

Runy approached the water, waded gingerly into a sheet of retreating foam. A comber thrashed down at him and he danced quickly back up the shore.

"The water's cold," he reported.

Ullward poised himself. "Well, here goes! I'll show you how it's done!" He trotted forward, stopped short, then flung himself into the face of a great white comber.

The party on the beach watched.

"Where is he?" asked Hyla Cabe.

Iugenae pointed. "I saw part of him out there. A leg, or an arm."

"There he is!" cried Ted. "Woof! Another one's caught him. I suppose some people might consider it sport. . . ."

Ullward staggered to his feet, lurched through the retreating wash to shore. "Hah! Great! Invigorating! Ted! Harris! Juvenal! Take a go at it!"

Harris shook his head. "I don't think I'll try it today, Bruham."

"The next time for me too," said Juvenal Aquister. "Perhaps it won't be so rough."

"But don't let us stop you!" urged Ted. "You swim as long as you like. We'll wait here for you."

"Oh, I've had enough for now," said Ullward. "Excuse me while I change."

When Ullward returned, he found his guests seated in the air-car. "Hello! Everyone ready to go?"

"It's hot in the sun," explained Liornetta, "and we thought we'd enjoy the view better from inside."

"When you look through the glass, it's almost like an illusion-pane," said Iugenae.

"Oh, I see. Well, perhaps you're ready to visit other parts of the Ullward domain?"

The proposal met with approval; Ullward took the air-car into the air. "We can fly north over the pine woods, south over Mount Cairasco, which unfortunately isn't erupting just now."

"Anywhere you like, Lamster Ullward," said Frobisher Worbeck. "No doubt it's all beautiful."

Ullward considered the varied attractions of his leasehold. "Well, first to the Cinnamon Swamp."

For two hours they flew, over the swamp, across the smoking crater of Mount Cairasco, east to the edge of Murky Mountains, along Calliope River to its source in Goldenleaf Lake. Ullward pointed out noteworthy views, interesting aspects. Behind him, the murmurs of admiration dwindled and finally died.

"Had enough?" Ullward called back gaily. "Can't see half a continent in one day! Shall we save some for tomorrow?"

There was a moment's stillness. Then Liornetta Stobart said, "Lamster Ullward, we're simply dying for a peek at the Magnificent Mountains. I wonder—do you think we could slip over for a quick look? I'm sure Lamster Mail wouldn't really mind."

Ullward shook his head with a rather stiff smile. "He's made me agree to a very definite set of rules. I've already had one brush with him."

"How could he possibly find out?" asked Juvenal Aquister.

"He probably wouldn't find out," said Ullward, "but—"

"It's a damned shame for him to lock you off into this drab little peninsula!" Frobisher Worbeck said indignantly.

"Please, Lamster Ullward," Iugenae wheedled.

"Oh, very well," Ullward said recklessly.

He turned the air-car east. The Murky Mountains passed below. The party peered from the windows, exclaiming at the marvels of the forbidden landscape.

"How far are the Magnificent Mountains?" asked Ted.

"Not far. Another thousand miles."

"Why are you hugging the ground?" asked Frobisher Worbeck. "Up in the air, man! Let's see the countryside!"

Ullward hesitated. Mail was probably asleep. And, in the last analysis, he really had no right to forbid an innocent little—

"Lamster Ullward," called Runy, "there's an air-car right behind us."

The air-car drew up level. Kennes Mail's blue eyes met Ullward's across the gap. He motioned Ullward down.

Ullward compressed his mouth, swung the air-car down. From behind him came murmurs of sympathy and outrage.

Below was a dark pine forest; Ullward set down in a pretty little glade. Mail landed nearby, jumped to the ground, signaled to Ullward. The two men walked to the side. The guests murmured together and shook their heads.

Ullward presently returned to the air-car. "Everybody please get in," he said crisply.

They rose into the air and flew west. "What did the chap have to say for himself?" queried Worbeck.

Ullward chewed at his lips. "Not too much. Wanted to know if I'd lost the way. I told him one or two things. Reached an understanding. . . ." His voice dwindled, then rose in a burst of cheerfulness. "We'll have a party back at the lodge. What do we care for Mail and his confounded mountains?"

"That's the spirit, Bruham!" cried Frobisher Worbeck.

Both Ted and Ullward tended bar during the evening. Either one or the other mingled rather more alcohol to rather less esters into the drinks than standard practice recommended. As a result, the party became quite loud and gay. Ullward damned Mail's interfering habits; Worbeck explored six thousand years of common law in an effort to prove Mail a domineering tyrant; the women giggled; Iugenae and Runy watched cynically, then presently went off to attend to their own affairs.

In the morning, the group slept late. Ullward finally tottered out on the terrace, to be joined one at a time by the others. Runy and Iugenae were missing.

"Young rascals," groaned Worbeck. "If they're lost, they'll have to find their own way back. No search parties for me."

At noon, Runy and Iugenae returned in Ullward's air-car.

"Good heavens," shrieked Ravelin. "Iugenae, come here this instant! Where have you been?"

Juvenal Aquister surveyed Runy sternly. "Have you lost your mind, taking Lamster Ullward's air-car without his permission?"

"I asked him last night," Runy declared indignantly. "He said yes, take anything except the volcano because that's where he slept when his feet got cold, and the swamp because that's where he dropped his empty containers."

"Regardless," said Juvenal in disgust, "you should have had better sense. Where have you been?"

Runy fidgeted. Iugenae said, "Well, we went south for a while, then turned and went east—I think it was east. We thought if we flew low, Lamster Mail wouldn't see us. So we flew low, through the mountains, and pretty soon we came to an ocean. We went along the beach and came to a house. We landed to see who lived there, but nobody was home."

Ullward stifled a groan.

"What would anyone want with a pen of birds?" asked Runy.

"Birds? What birds? Where?"

"At the house. There was a pen with a lot of big birds, but they kind of got loose while we were looking at them and all flew away."

"Anyway," Iugenae continued briskly, "we decided it was Lamster Mail's house, so we wrote a note, telling what everybody thinks of him and pinned it to his door."

Ullward rubbed his forehead. "Is that all?"

"Well, practically all." Iugenae became diffident. She looked at Runy and the two of them giggled nervously.

"There's more?" yelled Ullward. "What, in heaven's name?"

"Nothing very much," said Iugenae, following a crack in the terrace with her toe. "We put a booby-trap over the door —just a bucket of water. Then we came home."

The screen buzzer sounded from inside the lodge. Everybody looked at Ullward. Ullward heaved a deep sigh, rose to his feet, went inside.

That very afternoon, the Outer Ring Express packet was due to pass the junction point. Frobisher Worbeck felt sudden and acute qualms of conscience for the neglect his business suffered while he dawdled away hours in idle enjoyment.

"But my dear old chap!" exclaimed Ullward. "Relaxation is good for you!"

True, agreed Frobisher Worbeck, if one could make himself oblivious to the possibility of fiasco through the carelessness of underlings. Much as he deplored the necessity, in spite of his inclination to loiter for weeks, he felt impelled to leave—and not a minute later than that very afternoon.

Others of the group likewise remembered important business which they had to see to, and those remaining felt it would be a shame and an imposition to send up the capsule half empty and likewise decided to return.

Ullward's arguments met unyielding walls of obstinacy. Rather glumly, he went down to the capsule to bid his guests farewell. As they climbed through the port, they expressed their parting thanks:

"Bruham, it's been absolutely marvelous!"

"You'll never know how we've enjoyed this outing, Lamster Ullward!"

"The air, the space, the privacy—I'll never forget!"

"It was the most, to say the least."

The port thumped into its socket. Ullward stood back, waving rather uncertainly.

Ted Seehoe reached to press the *Active* button. Ullward sprang forward, pounded on the port.

"Wait!" he bellowed. "A few things I've got to attend to! I'm coming with you!"

"Come in, come in," said Ullward heartily, opening the door to three of his friends; Coble and his wife Heulia Sansom, and Coble's young, pretty cousin Landine. "Glad to see you!"

"And we're glad to come! We've heard so much of your wonderful ranch, we've been on pins and needles all day!"

"Oh, come now! It's not so marvelous as all that!"

"Not to you, perhaps—you live here!"

Ullward smiled. "Well, I must say I live here and still like it. Would you like to have lunch, or perhaps you'd prefer to walk around for a few minutes? I've just finished making a few changes, but I'm happy to say everything is in order."

"Can we just take a look?"

"Of course. Come over here. Stand just so. Now—are you ready?"

"Ready."

Ullward snapped the wall back.

"Ooh!" breathed Landine. "Isn't it beautiful!"

"The space, the open feeling!"

"Look, a tree! What a wonderful simulation!"

"That's no simulation," said Ullward. "That's a genuine tree!"

"Lamster Ullward, are you telling the truth?"

"I certainly am. I never tell lies to a lovely young lady. Come along, over this way."

"Lamster Ullward, that cliff is so convincing, it frightens me."

Ullward grinned. "It's a good job." He signaled a halt. "Now—turn around."

The group turned. They looked out across a great golden savannah, dotted with groves of blue-green trees. A rustic lodge commanded the view, the door being the opening into Ullward's living room.

The group stood in silent admiration. Then Heulia sighed. "Space. Pure space."

"I'd swear I was looking miles," said Coble.

Ullward smiled, a trifle wistfully. "Glad you like my little retreat. Now what about lunch? Genuine algae!"

SOMETIMES THE source of a story is a mystery even to the writer himself: a seepage from his subconscious. Other times the derivation is clear and direct. In the case of "The Last Castle," both situations are equally true.

The germ of the story was contained in an article dealing with Japanese social interactions. As is well known, Japanese society is highly formalized—much more thoroughly so in the past than during the relatively egalitarian times since the last war.

During the nineteenth century, when a samurai deigned to converse with a person of lower rank, each used markedly different vocabularies, with honorifics precisely calculated to the difference in status. When the person of lower degree discussed the samurai's activities or intentions, he used a special convention. Never would he pose a simple question such as: "Will your lordship go boar-hunting tomorrow?" This would impute to his lordship a coarse and undignified fervor, a sweating, earnest lip-licking zeal, which his lordship would have found offensively below his dignity. Instead the underling might ask: "Will your lordship tomorrow amuse himself by trifling at the hunting of a boar?"

III

54

In short, the aristocrat was conceded sensibilities of such exquisite nicety, competences of such awful grandeur, that he need only toy with all ordinary activities, in a mood of whimsy or caprice, in order to achieve dazzling successes.

So, "The Last Castle" concerns a society of somewhat similar folk, and examines their behavior when the society is subjected to great stress.

THE LAST CASTLE

‹‹‹‹‹‹‹‹‹‹‹‹‹‹‹‹‹‹‹‹‹‹‹‹‹‹‹‹‹‹‹‹‹

1

1.

TOWARD THE END OF A STORMY SUMMER AFTER-
noon, with the sun finally breaking out under ragged black
rain-clouds, Castle Janeil was overwhelmed and its population destroyed. Until almost the last moment factions among
the castle clans contended as to how Destiny properly should
be met. The gentlemen of most prestige and account elected
to ignore the entire undignified circumstance and went about
their normal pursuits, with neither more nor less punctilio
than usual. A few cadets,. desperate to the point of hysteria,
took up weapons and prepared to resist the final assault. Still
others, perhaps a quarter of the total population, waited
passively, ready—almost happy—to expiate the sins of the
human race. In the end, death came uniformly to all, and all
extracted as much satisfaction from their dying as this
essentially graceless process could afford. The proud sat
turning the pages of their beautiful books, discussing the
qualities of a century-old essence, or fondling a favorite
Phane, and died without deigning to heed the fact. The
hotheads raced up the muddy slope which, outraging all normal rationality, loomed above the parapets of Janeil. Most
were buried under sliding rubble, but a few gained the ridge
to gun, hack and stab, until they themselves were shot,
crushed by the half-alive power-wagons, hacked or stabbed.
The contrite waited in the classic posture of expiation—on

their knees, heads bowed—and perished, so they believed, by a process in which the Meks were symbols and human sin the reality. In the end all were dead: gentlemen, ladies, Phanes in the pavilions; Peasants in the stables. Of all those who had inhabited Janeil, only the Birds survived, creatures awkward, gauche and raucous, oblivious to pride and faith, more concerned with the wholeness of their hides than the dignity of their castle. As the Meks swarmed down over the parapets, the Birds departed their cotes and, screaming strident insults, flapped east toward Hagedorn, now the last castle of Earth.

2.

Four months before, the Meks had appeared in the park before Janeil, fresh from the Sea Island massacre. Climbing to the turrets and balconies, sauntering the Sunset Promenade, from ramparts and parapets, the gentlemen and ladies of Janeil, some two thousand in all, looked down at the brown-gold warriors. Their mood was complex—amused indifference, flippant disdain, and a substratum of doubt and foreboding; all the product of three basic circumstances—their own exquisitely subtle civilization, the security provided by Janeil's walls, and the fact that they could conceive no recourse, no means for altering circumstances.

The Janeil Meks had long since departed to join the revolt; there remained only Phanes, Peasants and Birds from which to fashion what would have been the travesty of a punitive force. At the moment there seemed no need for such a force. Janeil was deemed impregnable. The walls, two hundred feet tall, were black rock-melt contained in the meshes of a silver-blue steel alloy. Solar cells provided energy for all the needs of the castle, and in the event of emergency, food could be synthesized from carbon dioxide and water vapor, as well as syrup for Phanes, Peasants and Birds. Such a need was not envisaged. Janeil was self-sufficient and secure, though inconveniences might arise when machinery broke down and there were no Meks to repair it. The situation then was disturbing but hardly desperate. During the day the gentlemen so inclined brought forth energy-guns and sport-rifles and killed as many Meks as the extreme range allowed.

After dark the Meks brought forward power-wagons and

earth-movers, and began to raise a dike around Janeil. The folk of the castle watched without comprehension until the dike reached a height of fifty feet and dirt began to spill down against the walls. Then the dire purpose of the Meks became apparent, and insouciance gave way to dismal foreboding. All the gentlemen of Janeil were erudite in at least one realm of knowledge; certain were mathematical theoreticians, while others had made a profound study of the physical sciences. Some of these, with a detail of Peasants to perform the sheerly physical exertion, attempted to restore the energy-cannon to functioning condition. Unluckily, the cannon had not been maintained in good order. Various components were obviously corroded or damaged. Conceivably these components might have been replaced from the Mek shops on the second sublevel, but none of the group had any knowledge of the Mek nomenclature or warehousing system. Warrick Madency Arban (Arban of the Madency family in the Warrick clan) suggested that a work-force of Peasants search the warehouse, but in view of the limited mental capacity of the Peasants, nothing was done and the whole plan to restore the energy-cannon came to naught.

The gentlefolk of Janeil watched in fascination as the dirt piled higher and higher around them, in a circular mound like a crater. Summer neared its end, and on one stormy day dirt and rubble rose above the parapets, and began to spill over into the courts and piazzas: Janeil must soon be buried and all within suffocated. It was then that a group of impulsive young cadets, with more élan than dignity, took up weapons and charged up the slope. The Meks dumped dirt and stone upon them, but a handful gained the ridge where they fought in a kind of dreadful exaltation.

Fifteen minutes the fight raged and the earth became sodden with rain and blood. For one glorious moment the cadets swept the ridge clear, and had not most of their fellows been lost under the rubble, anything might have occurred. But the Meks regrouped and thrust forward. Ten men were left, then six, then four, then one, then none. The Meks marched down the slope, swarmed over the battlements, and with somber intensity killed all within. Janeil, for seven hundred years the abode of gallant gentlemen, and gracious ladies, had become a lifeless hulk.

3.

The Mek, standing as if a specimen in a museum case, was a manlike creature, native, in his original version, to a planet of Etamin. His tough rusty-bronze hide glistened metallically as if oiled or waxed; the spines thrusting back from scalp and neck shone like gold, and indeed were coated with a conductive copper-chrome film. His sense organs were gathered in clusters at the site of a man's ears; his visage—it was often a shock, walking the lower corridors, to come suddenly upon a Mek—was corrugated muscle, not dissimilar to the look of an uncovered human brain. His maw, a vertical irregular cleft at the base of this "face," was an obsolete organ by reason of the syrup sac which had been introduced under the skin of the shoulders; the digestive organs, originally used to extract nutrition from decayed swamp vegetation and coelenterates, had atrophied. The Mek typically wore no garment except possibly a work-apron or a tool-belt, and in the sunlight his rust-bronze skin made a handsome display. This was the Mek solitary, a creature intrinsically as effective as man—perhaps more by virtue of his superb brain which also functioned as a radio transceiver. Working in the mass, by the teeming thousands, he seemed less admirable, less competent: a hybrid of subman and cockroach.

Certain savants, notably Morninglight's D. R. Jardine and Salonson of Tuang, considered the Mek bland and phlegmatic, but the profound Claghorn of Castle Hagedorn asserted otherwise. The emotions of the Mek, said Claghorn, were different from human emotions, and only vaguely comprehensible to man. After diligent research Claghorn isolated over a dozen Mek emotions.

In spite of such research, the Mek revolt came as an utter surprise, no less to Claghorn, D. R. Jardine and Salonson than to anyone else. Why? asked everyone. How could a group so long submissive have contrived so murderous a plot?

The most reasonable conjecture was also the simplest: the Mek resented servitude and hated the Earthmen who had removed him from his natural environment. Those who argued against this theory claimed that is projected human emotions and attitudes into a nonhuman organism, that the

Mek had every reason to feel gratitude toward the gentlemen who had liberated him from the conditions of Etamin Nine. To this, the first group would inquire, "Who projects human attitudes now?" And the retort of their opponents was often, "Since no one knows for certain, one projection is no more absurd than another."

2

1.

Castle Hagedorn occupied the crest of a black diorite crag overlooking a wide valley to the south. Larger, more majestic than Janeil, Hagedorn was protected by walls a mile in circumference, and three hundred feet tall. The parapets stood a full nine hundred feet above the valley, with towers, turrets and observation aeries rising even higher. Two sides of the crag, at east and west, dropped sheer to the valley. The north and south slopes, a trifle less steep, were terraced and planted with vines, artichokes, pears and pomegranates. An avenue rising from the valley circled the crag and passed through a portal into the central plaza. Opposite stood the great Rotunda, with at either side the tall Houses of the twenty-eight families.

The original castle, constructed immediately after the return of men to Earth, stood on the site now occupied by the plaza. The tenth Hagedorn, assembling an enormous force of Peasants and Meks, had built the new walls, after which he demolished the old castle. The twenty-eight Houses dated from this time, five hundred years before.

Below the plaza were three service levels: the stables and garages at the bottom, next the Mek shops and Mek living quarters, then the various storerooms, warehouses and special shops—bakery, brewery, lapidary, arsenal, repository and the like.

The current Hagedorn, twenty-sixth of the line, was a Claghorn of the Overwheles. His selection had occasioned general surprise, because O.C. Charle, as he had been before his elevation, was a gentleman of no remarkable presence. His elegance, flair and erudition were only ordinary; he had never been notable for any significant originality of thought. His physical proportions were good; his face was square and

The clans of Hagedorn, their colors and associated families:

CLANS	COLORS	FAMILIES
Xanten	yellow; black piping	Haude, Quay, Idelsea, Esledune, Salonson, Roseth.
Beaudry	dark blue; white piping	Onwane, Zadig, Prine, Fer, Sesune.
Overwhele	gray, green; red rosettes	Claghorn, Abreu, Woss, Hinken, Zumbeld.
Aure	brown, black	Zadhause, Fotergil, Marune, Baudune, Godalming, Lesmanic.
Isseth	purple, dark red	Mazeth, Floy, Luder-Hepman, Uegus, Kerrithew, Bethune.

The first gentleman of the castle, elected for life, is known as "Hagedorn."

The clan chief, selected by the family elders, bears the name of his clan, thus: "Xanten," "Beaudry," "Overwhele," "Aure," "Isseth"—both clans and clan chiefs.

The family elder, selected by household heads, bears the name of his family. Thus "Idelsea," "Zadhause," "Bethune," and "Claghorn," are both families and family elders.

The remaining gentlemen and ladies bear first the clan, then the family, then the personal name. Thus: Aure Zadhause Ludwick, abbreviated to A.Z. Ludwick, and Beaudry Fer Dariane, abbreviated to B.F. Dariane.

bony, with a short straight nose, a benign brow and narrow gray eyes. His expression, normally a trifle abstracted—his detractors used the word "vacant"—by a simple lowering of the eyelids, a downward twitch of the coarse blond eyebrows, at once became stubborn and surly, a fact of which O.C. Charle, or Hagedorn, was unaware.

The office, while exerting little or no formal authority, exerted a pervasive influence, and the style of the gentleman who was Hagedorn affected everyone. For this reason the selection of Hagedorn was a matter of no small importance, subject to hundreds of considerations, and it was the rare candidate who failed to have some old solecism or gaucherie discussed with embarrassing candor. While the candidate might never take overt umbrage, friendships were inevitably sundered, rancors augmented, reputations blasted. O.C. Charle's elevation represented a compromise between two factions among the Overwheles, to which clan the privilege of selection had fallen.

The gentlemen between whom O.C. Charle represented a compromise were both highly respected, but distinguished by basically different attitudes toward existence. The first was the talented Garr of the Zumbeld family. He exemplified the traditional virtues of Castle Hagedorn: he was a notable connoisseur of essences, and he dressed with absolute savoir, with never so much as a pleat nor a twist of the characteristic Overwhele rosette awry. He combined insouciance and flair with dignity; his repartee coruscated with brilliant allusions and turns of phrase; when aroused his wit was utterly mordant. He could quote every literary work of consequence; he performed expertly upon the nine-stringed lute, and was thus in constant demand at the Viewing of Antique Tabards. He was an antiquarian of unchallenged erudition and knew the locale of every major city of Old Earth, and could discourse for hours upon the history of the ancient times. His military expertise was unparelleled at Hagedorn, and challenged only by D.K. Magdah of Castle Delora and perhaps Brusham of Tuang. Faults? Flaws? Few could be cited: over-punctilio which might be construed as waspishness; an intrepid pertinacity which could be considered ruthlessness. O.Z. Garr could never be dismissed as insipid or indecisive, and his personal courage was beyond dispute. Two years before, a stray band of Nomads had ventured into Lucerne Valley, slaughtering Peasants, stealing cattle and going so far as to fire an arrow into the chest of an Isseth cadet. O.Z. Garr instantly assembled a punitive company of Meks, loaded them aboard a dozen power-wagons, and set forth in pursuit of the Nomads, finally overtaking them near Drene River, by the ruins of Worster Cathedral. The Nomads were unexpectedly strong, unexpectedly crafty, and were not content to turn tail and flee. During the fighting, O.Z. Garr displayed the most exemplary demeanor, directing the attack from the seat of his power-wagon, a pair of Meks standing by with shields to ward away arrows. The conflict ended in a rout of the Nomads; they left twenty-seven lean, black-cloaked corpses strewn on the field, while only twenty Meks lost their lives.

O.Z. Garr's opponent in the election was Claghorn, elder of the Claghorn family. As with O.Z. Garr, the exquisite discriminations of Hagedorn society came to Claghorn as easily as swimming to a fish. He was no less erudite than O.Z. Garr, though hardly so versatile, his principal field of study being the Meks, their physiology, linguistic modes, and social patterns. Claghorn's conversation was more profound, but less entertaining and not so trenchant as that of O.Z. Garr; he seldom employed the extravagant tropes and allusions which characterized Garr's discussions, preferring a style of speech which was unadorned. Claghorn kept no Phanes; O.Z. Garr's four matched Gossamer Dainties were marvels of delight, and at the Viewing of Antique Tabards Garr's presentations were seldom outshone. The important contrast between the two men lay in their philosophic outlook. O.Z. Garr, a traditionalist, a fervent exemplar of his society, subscribed to its tenets without reservation. He was beset by neither doubt nor guilt; he felt no desire to alter the conditions which afforded more than two thousand gentlemen and ladies lives of great richness. Claghorn, while by no means an Expiationist, was known to feel dissatisfaction with the general tenor of life at Castle Hagedorn, and argued so plausibly that many folk refused to listen to him, on the grounds that they became uncomfortable. But an indefinable malaise ran deep, and Claghorn had many influential supporters.

When the time came for ballots to be cast, neither O.Z. Garr nor Claghorn could muster sufficient support. The office finally was conferred upon a gentleman who never in his most optimistic reckonings had expected it—a gentleman of decorum and dignity but no great depth; without flippancy, but likewise without vivacity; affable but disinclined to force an issue to a disagreeable conclusion: O.C. Charle, the new Hagedorn.

Six months later, during the dark hours before dawn, the Hagedorn Meks evacuated their quarters and departed, taking with them power-wagons, tools, weapons and electrical equipment. The act had clearly been long in the planning, for simultaneously the Meks at each of the eight other castles made a similar departure.

The initial reaction at Castle Hagedorn, as elsewhere, was incredulity, then shocked anger, then—when the implications of the act were pondered—a sense of foreboding and calamity.

The new Hagedorn, the clan chiefs and certain other notables appointed by Hagedorn met in the formal council chamber to consider the matter. They sat around a great table covered with red velvet: Hagedorn at the head; Xanten and Isseth at his left; Overwhele, Aure and Beaudry at his right; then the others, including O.Z. Garr, I.K. Linus, A.G. Bernal, a mathematical theoretician of great ability, and B.F. Wyas, an equally sagacious antiquarian who had identified the sites of many ancient cities—Palmyra, Lübeck, Eridu, Zanesville, Burton-on-Trent and Massilia, among others. Certain family elders filled out the council: Marune and Baudune of Aure; Quay, Roseth and Idelsea of Xanten; Uegus of Isseth, Claghorn of Overwhele.

All sat silent for a period of ten minutes, arranging their minds and performing the silent act of psychic accommodation known as "intression."

At last Hagedorn spoke. "The castle is suddenly bereft of its Meks. Needless to say, this is an inconvenient condition, to be adjusted as swiftly as possible. Here, I am sure, we find ourselves of one mind."

He looked around the table. All thrust forward carved ivory tablets to signify assent—all save Claghorn, who however did not stand it on end to signify dissent.

Isseth, a stern white-haired gentleman magnificently handsome in spite of his seventy years, spoke in a grim voice. "I see no point in cogitation or delay. What we must do is clear. Admittedly the Peasants are poor material from which to recruit an armed force. Nonetheless, we must assemble them, equip them with sandals, smocks and weapons so that they do not discredit us, and put them under good leadership: O.Z. Garr or Xanten. Birds can locate the vagrants, whereupon we will track them down, order the Peasants to give them a good drubbing, and herd them home on the double."

Xanten, thirty-five years old—extraordinarily young to be a clan chief—and a notorious firebrand, shook his head. "The idea is appealing but impractical. Peasants simply could not stand up to the Meks, no matter how we trained them."

The statement was manifestly accurate. The Peasants, small andromorphs originally of Spica Ten, were not so much timid as incapable of performing a vicious act.

A dour silence held the table. O.Z. Garr finally spoke. "The dogs have stolen our power-wagons, otherwise I'd be tempted to ride out and chivy the rascals home with a whip." *

"A matter of perplexity," said Hagedorn, "is syrup. Naturally they carried away what they could. When this is exhausted—what then? Will they starve? Impossible for them to return to their original diet. What was it? Swamp mud? Eh, Claghorn, you're the expert in these matters. Can the Meks return to a diet of mud?"

"No," said Claghorn. "The organs of the adult are atrophied. If a cub were started on the diet, he'd probably survive."

"Just as I assumed." Hagedorn scowled portentously down at his clasped hands to conceal his total lack of any constructive proposal.

A gentleman in the dark blue of the Beaudrys appeared in the doorway; he poised himself, held high his right arm and bowed so that the fingers swept the floor.

---

* This, only an approximate translation, fails to capture the pungency of the language. Several words have no contemporary equivalents. "Skirkling," as in "to send skirkling," denotes a frantic pell-mell flight in all directions, accompanied by a vibration or twinkling or jerking motion. To "volith" is to toy idly with a matter, the implication being that the person involved is of such Jovian potency that all difficulties dwindle to contemptible triviality. "Raudlebogs" are the semi-intelligent beings of Etamin Four, who were brought to Earth, trained first as gardeners, then construction laborers, then sent home in disgrace because of certain repulsive habits they refused to forgo.

The statement of O.Z. Garr, therefore, becomes something like this: "Were power-wagons at hand, I'd volith riding forth with a whip to send the raudlebogs skirkling home."

Hagedorn rose to his feet. "Come forward, B.F. Robarth; what is your news?" For this was the significance of the newcomer's genuflection.

"The news is a message broadcast from Halcyon. The Meks have attacked; they have fired the structure and are slaughtering all. The radio went dead one minute ago."

All swung around, some jumped to their feet. "Slaughter?" croaked Claghorn.

"I am certain that by now Halcyon is no more."

Claghorn sat staring with eyes unfocused. The others discussed the dire news in voices heavy with horror.

Hagedorn once more brought the council back to order. "This is clearly an extreme situation—the gravest, perhaps, of our entire history. I am frank to state that I can suggest no decisive counteract."

Overwhele inquired, "What of the other castles? Are they secure?"

Hagedorn turned to B.F. Robarth. "Will you be good enough to make general radio contact with all other castles, and inquire as to their condition?"

Xanten said, "Others are as vulnerable as Halcyon: Sea Island and Delora, in particular, and Maraval as well."

Claghorn emerged from his reverie. "The gentlemen and ladies of these places, in my opinion, should consider taking refuge at Janeil or here, until the uprising is quelled."

Others around the table looked at him in surprise and puzzlement. O.Z. Garr inquired in the silkiest of voices: "You envision the gentlefolk of these castles scampering to refuge at the cock-a-hoop swaggering of the lower orders?"

"Indeed, should they wish to survive," responded Claghorn politely. A gentleman of late middle age, Claghorn was stocky and strong, with black-gray hair, magnificent green eyes, and a manner which suggested great internal force under stern control. "Flight by definition entails a certain diminution of dignity," he went on to say. "If O.Z. Garr can propound an elegant manner of taking to one's heels, I will be glad to learn it, and everyone else should likewise heed, because in the days to come the capability may be of comfort to all."

Hagedorn interposed before O.Z. Garr could reply. "Let us keep to the issues. I confess I cannot see to the end of all this. The Meks have demonstrated themselves to be murderers; how can we take them back into our service? But if we don't—well, to say the least, conditions will be austere until we can locate and train a new force of technicians. We must consider along these lines."

"The spaceships!" exclaimed Xanten. "We must see to them at once!"

"What's this?" inquired Beaudry, a gentleman of rock-hard face. "How do you mean, 'see to them'?"

"They must be protected from damage! What else? They are our link to the Home Worlds. The maintenance Meks probably have not deserted the hangars, since, if they propose to exterminate us, they will want to deny us the spaceships."

"Perhaps you care to march with a levy of Peasants to take the hangars under firm control?" suggested O.Z. Garr in a somewhat supercilious voice. A long history of rivalry and mutual detestation existed between himself and Xanten.

"It may be our only hope," said Xanten. "Still—how does one fight with a levy of Peasants? Better that I fly to the hangars and reconnoiter. Meanwhile, perhaps you, and others with military expertise, will take in hand the recruitment and training of a Peasant militia."

"In this regard," stated O.Z. Garr, "I await the outcome of our current deliberations. If it develops that there lies the optimum course, I naturally will apply my competences to the fullest degree. If your own capabilities are best fulfilled by spying out the activities of the Meks, I hope that you will be largehearted enough to do the same."

The two gentlemen glared at each other. A year previously their enmity had almost culminated in a duel. Xanten, a gentleman tall, clean-limbed and nervously active, was gifted with great natural flair, but likewise evinced a disposition too easy for absolute elegance. The traditionalists considered him "sthross," indicating a manner flawed by an almost imperceptible slackness and lack of punctilio: not the best possible choice for clan chief.

Xanten's response to O.Z. Garr was blandly polite. "I shall be glad to take this task upon myself. Since haste is of the essence I will risk the accusation of precipitousness and leave at once. Hopefully I return to report tomorrow." He rose, performed a ceremonious bow to Hagedorn, another all-inclusive salute to the council and departed.

He crossed to Esledune House, where he maintained an apartment on the thirteenth level: four rooms furnished in the style known as Fifth Dynasty, after an epoch in the history of the Altair Home Planets, from which the human race had returned to Earth. His current consort, Araminta, a lady of the Onwane family, was absent on affairs of her own, which suited Xanten well enough. After plying him with questions she would have discredited his simple explanation, preferring to suspect an assignation at his country place. Truth to tell, he had become bored with Araminta and had reason to believe that she felt similarly—or perhaps his exalted rank had provided her less opportunity to preside at glittering social functions than she had expected. They had bred no children. Araminta's daughter by a previous connection had been tallied to her. Her second child must then be tallied to Xanten, preventing him from siring another child.*

Xanten doffed his yellow council vestments, and, assisted by a young Peasant buck, donned dark yellow hunting-breeches with black trim, a black jacket, black boots. He drew a cap of soft black leather over his head, and slung a pouch over his shoulder, into which he loaded weapons: a coiled blade, an energy-gun.

Leaving the apartment, he summoned the lift and descended to the first-level armory, where normally a Mek clerk would have served him. Now Xanten, to his vast disgust, was forced to take himself behind the counter, and rummage here and there. The Meks had removed most of the sport-rifles, all the pellet ejectors and heavy energy-guns; an ominous circumstance, thought Xanten. At last he found a steel sling-whip, spare power slugs for his gun, a brace of fire grenades and a high-powered monocular.

He returned to the lift and rode to the top level, ruefully considering the long climb when eventually the mechanism broke down, with no Meks at hand to make repairs. He thought of the apoplectic furies of rigid traditionalists such as Beaudry and chuckled: eventful days lay ahead!

---

* The population of Castle Hagedorn was fixed; each gentleman and each lady was permitted a single child. If by chance another were born the parent must either find someone who had not yet sired to sponsor it, or dispose of it another way. The usual procedure was to give the child into the care of the Expiationists.

Stopping at the top level, he crossed to the parapets and proceeded around to the radio room. Customarily three Mek specialists connected into the apparatus by wires clipped to their quills sat typing messages as they arrived; now B.F. Robarth stood before the mechanism, uncertainly twisting the dials, his mouth wry with deprecation and distaste for the job.

"Any further news?" Xanten asked.

B.F. Robarth gave him a sour grin. "The folk at the other end seem no more familiar with this cursed tangle than I. I hear occasional voices. I believe that the Meks are attacking Castle Delora."

Claghorn had entered the room behind Xanten. "Did I hear you correctly? Delora Castle is gone?"

"Not gone yet, Claghorn. But as good as gone. The Delora walls are little better than a picturesque crumble."

"Sickening situation!" muttered Xanten. "How can sentient creatures perform such evil? After all these centuries, how little we actually know of them!" As he spoke he recognized the tactlessness of his remark; Claghorn had devoted much time to a study of the Meks.

"The act itself is not astounding," said Claghorn shortly. "It has occurred a thousand times in human history."

Mildly surprised that Claghorn should use human history in reference to a case involving the suborders, Xanten asked, "You were never aware of this vicious aspect to the Mek nature?"

"No. Never. Never indeed."

Claghorn seemed unduly sensitive, thought Xanten. Understandable, all in all. Claghorn's basic doctrine as set forth during the Hagedorn selection was by no means simple, and Xanten neither understood it nor completely endorsed what he conceived to be its goals; but it was plain that the revolt of the Meks had cut the ground out from under Claghorn's feet. Probably to the somewhat bitter satisfaction of O.Z. Garr, who must feel vindicated in his traditionalist doctrines.

Claghorn said tersely, "The life we've been leading couldn't last forever. It's a wonder it lasted as long as it did."

"Perhaps so," said Xanten in a soothing voice. "Well, no matter. All things change. Who knows? The Peasants may be planning to poison our food. . . . I must go." He bowed to Claghorn, who returned him a crisp nod, and to B.F. Robarth, then departed the room.

He climbed the spiral staircase—almost a ladder—to the cotes, where the Birds lived in an invincible disorder, occupying themselves with gambling, quarrels and a version of chess, with rules incomprehensible to every gentleman who had tried to understand it.

Castle Hagedorn maintained a hundred Birds, tended by a gang of long-suffering Peasants, whom the Birds held in vast disesteem. The Birds were garish, garrulous creatures, pigmented red, yellow or blue, with long necks, jerking inquisitive heads and an inherent irreverence which no amount of discipline or tutelage could overcome. Spying Xanten, they emitted a chorus of rude jeers: "Somebody wants a ride! Heavy thing!" "Why don't the self-anointed two-footers grow wings for themselves?" "My friend, never trust a Bird! We'll sky you, then fling you down on your fundament!"

"Quiet!" called Xanten. "I need six fast silent Birds for an important mission. Are any capable of such a task?"

"Are any capable, he asks!" "*A ros ros ros*! When none of us have flown for a week!" "Silence? We'll give you silence, yellow and black!"

"Come then. You. You. You of the wise eye. You there. You with the cocked shoulder. You with the green pompon. To the basket."

The Birds designated, jeering, grumbling, reviling the Peasants, allowed their syrup sacs to be filled, then flapped to the wicker seat where Xanten waited. "To the space depot at Vincenne," he told them. "Fly high and silently. Enemies are abroad. We must learn what harm if any has been done to the spaceships."

"To the depot, then!" Each Bird seized a length of rope tied to an overhead framework; the chair was yanked up with a jerk calculated to rattle Xanten's teeth, and off they flew, laughing, cursing each other for not supporting more of the load, but eventually all accommodating themselves to the task and flying with a coordinated flapping of the thirty-six sets of wings. To Xanten's relief, their garrulity lessened; silently they flew south, at a speed of fifty or sixty miles per hour.

The afternoon was already waning. The ancient countryside, scene to so many comings and goings, so much triumph and so much disaster, was laced with long black shadows. Looking down, Xanten reflected that though the human stock was native to this soil, and though his immediate ancestors had maintained their holdings for seven hundred years, Earth still seemed an alien world. The reason of course was by no means mysterious or rooted in paradox. After the Six-Star War, Earth had lain fallow for three thousand years, unpopulated save for a handful of anguished wretches who somehow had survived the cataclysm and who had become semibarbaric Nomads. Then seven hundred years ago certain rich lords of Altair, motivated to some extent by political disaffection, but no less by caprice, had decided to return to Earth. Such was the origin of the nine great strongholds, the resident gentlefolk and the staffs of specialized andromorphs. . . . Xanten flew over an area where an antiquarian had directed excavations, revealing a plaza flagged with white stone, a broken obelisk, a tumbled statue. . . . The sight, by some trick of association, stimulated Xanten's mind to an astonishing vision, so simple and yet so grand that he looked around, in all directions, with new eyes. The vision was Earth repopulated with men, the land cultivated, Nomads driven back into the wilderness.

At the moment the image was farfetched. And Xanten, watching the soft contours of Old Earth slide below, pondered the Mek revolt which had altered his life with such startling abruptness.

Claghorn had long insisted that no human condition endured forever, with the corollary that the more complicated such a condition, the greater its susceptibility to change. In which case the seven-hundred-year continuity at Castle Hagedorn—as artificial, extravagant and intricate as life could be—became an astonishing circumstance in itself. Claghorn had pushed his thesis further. Since change was inevitable, he argued that the gentlefolk should soften the impact by anticipating and controlling the changes—a doctrine which had been attacked with great fervor. The traditionalists labeled all of Claghorn's ideas demonstrable fallacy, and cited the very stability of castle life as proof of its viability. Xanten had inclined first one way, then the other, emotionally involved with neither cause. If anything, the fact of O.Z. Garr's traditionalism had nudged him toward Claghorn's views, and now it seemed as if events had vindicated Claghorn. Change had come, with an impact of the maximum harshness and violence.

There were still questions to be answered, of course. Why had the Meks chosen this particular time to revolt? Conditions had not altered appreciably for five hundred years, and the Meks had never previously hinted dissatisfaction. In fact they had revealed nothing of their feelings, though no one had ever troubled to ask them—save Claghorn.

The Birds were veering east to avoid the Ballarat Mountains, to the west of which were the ruins of a great city, never satisfactorily identified. Below lay the Lucerne Valley, at one time a fertile farmland. If one looked with great concentration, the outline of the various holdings could sometimes be distinguished. Ahead, the spaceship hangars were visible, where Mek technicians maintained four spaceships, jointly the property of Hagedorn, Janeil, Tuang, Morninglight and Maraval, though, for a variety of reasons, the ships were never used.

The sun was setting. Orange light twinkled and flickered on the metal walls. Xanten. called instructions up to the Birds: "Circle down. Alight behind that line of trees, but fly low so that none will see."

Down on stiff wings curved the Birds, six ungainly necks stretched toward the ground. Xanten was ready for the impact; the Birds never seemed able to alight easily when they carried a gentleman. When the cargo was something in which they felt a personal concern, dandelion fluff would never have been disturbed by the jar.

Xanten expertly kept his balance, instead of tumbling and rolling in the manner preferred by the Birds. "You all have syrup," he told them. "Rest; make no noise; do not quarrel. By tomorrow's sunset, if I am not here, return to Castle Hagedorn and say that Xanten was killed."

"Never fear!" cried the Birds. "We will wait forever!" "At any rate till tomorrow's sunset!" "If danger threatens, if you are pressed—*a ros ros ros!* Call for the Birds." "*A ros!* We are ferocious when aroused!"

"I wish it were true," said Xanten. "The Birds are arrant cowards; this is well-known. Still, I value the sentiment. Remember my instructions, and quiet above all! I do not wish to be set upon and stabbed because of your clamor."

The Birds made indignant sounds. "Injustice, injustice! We are quiet as the dew!"

"Good." Xanten hurriedly moved away lest they should bellow new advice or reassurances after him.

Passing through the forest, he came to an open meadow at the far edge of which, perhaps a hundred yards distant, was the rear of the first hangar. He stopped to consider. Several factors were involved. First: the maintenance Meks, with the metal structure shielding them from radio contact, might still be unaware of the revolt. Hardly likely, he decided, in view of the otherwise careful planning. Second: the Meks, in continuous communication with their fellows, acted as a collective organism. The aggregate functions more competently than its parts, and the individual was not prone to initiative. Hence, vigilance was likely to be extreme. Third: if they expected anyone to attempt a discreet approach, they would necessarily scrutinize most closely the route which he proposed to take.

Xanten decided to wait in the shadows another ten minutes, until the setting sun shining over his shoulder should most effectively blind any who might watch.

Ten minutes passed. The hangars, burnished by the dying sunlight, bulked long, tall, completely quiet. In the intervening meadow long golden grass waved and rippled in a cool breeze. . . . Xanten took a deep breath, hefted his pouch, arranged his weapons and strode forth. It did not occur to him to crawl through the grass.

He reached the back of the nearest hangar without challenge. Pressing his ear to the metal he heard nothing. He walked to the corner, looked down the side: no sign of life. Xanten shrugged. Very well, then—to the door.

He walked beside the hangar, the setting sun casting a long black shadow ahead of him. He came to a door opening into the hangar administrative office. Since there was nothing to be gained by trepidation, Xanten thrust the door aside and entered.

The offices were empty. The desks, where centuries before underlings had sat, calculating invoices and bills of lading, were bare, polished free of dust. The computers and information banks, black enamel, glass, white and red switches, looked as if they had been installed only the day before.

Xanten crossed to a glass pane overlooking the hangar floor, shadowed under the bulk of the ship.

He saw no Meks. But on the floor of the hangar, arranged in neat rows and heaps, were elements and assemblies of the ship's control mechanism. Service panels gaped wide into the hull to show where the devices had been detached.

Xanten stepped from the office out into the hangar. The spaceship had been disabled, put out of commission. Xanten looked along the neat rows of parts. Certain savants of various castles were expert in the theory of space-time transfer; S.X. Rosenbox of Maraval had even derived a set of equations which, if translated into machinery, eliminated the troublesome Hamus effect. But not one gentleman, even were he so oblivious to personal honor as to touch a hand to a tool, would know how to replace, connect and tune the mechanisms heaped upon the hangar floor.

The malicious work had been done—when? Impossible to say.

Xanten returned to the office, stepped back out into the twilight, and walked to the next hangar. Again no Meks; again the spaceship had been gutted of its control mechanism. Xanten proceeded to the third hangar, where conditions were the same.

At the fourth hangar he discerned the faint sounds of activity. Stepping into the office, looking through the glass wall into the hangar, he found Meks working with their usual economy of motion, in a near-silence which was uncanny.

Xanten, already uncomfortable from skulking through the forest, became enraged by the cool destruction of his property. He strode forth into the hangar. Slapping his thigh to attract attention, he called in a harsh voice, "Return the components to place! How dare you vermin act in such a manner!"

The Meks turned about their black countenances to study him through black-beaded lens-clusters at each side of their heads.

"What!" bellowed Xanten. "You hesitate?" He brought forth his steel whip, usually more of a symbolic adjunct than a punitive instrument, and slashed it against the ground. "Obey! This ridiculous revolt is at its end!"

The Meks still hesitated, and events wavered in the balance. None made a sound, though messages were passing among them, appraising the circumstances, establishing a consensus. Xanten could allow them no such leisure. He marched forward, wielding the whip, striking at the only area where the Meks felt pain: the ropy face. "To your duties," he roared. "A fine maintenance crew are you! A destruction crew is more like it!"

The Meks made the soft blowing sound which might mean anything. They fell back, and now Xanten noted one standing at the head of the companionway leading into the ship: a Mek larger than any he had seen before, and one in some fashion different. This Mek was aiming a pellet gun at his head. With an unhurried flourish, Xanten whipped away a Mek who had leaped forward with a knife, and without deigning to aim, fired at and destroyed the Mek who stood on the companionway, even as the slug sang past his head.

The other Meks were nevertheless committed to an attack. All surged forward. Lounging disdainfully against the hull, Xanten shot them as they came, moving his head once to avoid a chunk of metal, again reaching to catch a throw-knife and hurl it into the face of him who had thrown it.

The Meks drew back, and Xanten guessed that they had agreed on a new tactic: either to withdraw for weapons, or perhaps to confine him within the hangar. In any event no more could be accomplished here. He made play with the whip and cleared an avenue to the office. With tools, metal bars and forgings striking the glass behind him, he sauntered through the office and out into the night.

The full moon was rising: a great yellow globe casting a smoky saffron glow, like an antique lamp. Mek eyes were not well adapted for night-seeing, and Xanten waited by the door. Presently Meks began to pour forth, and Xanten hacked at their necks as they came.

The Meks drew back inside the hangar. Wiping his blade, Xanten strode off the way he had come, looking neither right nor left. He stopped short. The night was young. Something tickled his mind: the recollection of the Mek who had fired the pellet gun. He had been larger, possibly a darker bronze, but, more significantly, he had displayed an indefinable poise, almost authority—though such a word, when used in connection with the Meks, was anomalous. On the other hand, someone must have planned the revolt, or at least originated the concept. It might be worthwhile to extend the reconnaissance, though his primary information had been secured.

Xanten turned back and crossed the landing area to the barracks and garages. Once more, frowning in discomfort, he felt the need for discretion. What times these were! when a gentleman must skulk to avoid such as the Meks! He stole up behind the garages where a half dozen power-wagons * lay dozing.

Xanten looked them over. All were of the same sort, a metal frame with four wheels, an earth-moving blade at the front. Nearby must be the syrup stock. Xanten presently found a bin containing a number of canisters. He loaded a dozen on a nearby wagon, slashed the rest with his knife, so that the syrup gushed across the ground. The Meks used a somewhat different formulation; their syrup would be stocked at a different locale, presumably inside the barracks.

Xanten mounted a power-wagon, twisted the *awake* key, tapped the *go* button and pulled a lever which set the wheels into reverse motion. The power-wagon lurched back. Xanten halted it, turned it so that it faced the barracks. He did likewise with three others, then set them all into motion, one after the other. They trundled forward; the blades cut open the metal wall of the barracks, the roof sagged. The power-wagons continued, pushing the length of the interior, crushing all in their way.

Xanten nodded in profound satisfaction and returned to the power-wagon he had reserved for his own use. Mounting to the seat, he waited. No Meks issued from the barracks. Apparently they were deserted, with the entire crew busy at the hangars. Still, hopefully, the syrup stocks had been destroyed, and many might perish by starvation.

From the direction of the hangars came a single Mek, evidently attracted by the sounds of destruction. Xanten crouched on the seat, and as it passed, coiled his whip

---

* Power-wagons, like the Meks, originally swamp-creatures from Etamin Nine, were great rectangular slabs of muscle, slung into a rectangular frame and protected from sunlight, insects and rodents by a synthetic pelt. Syrup sacs communicated with their digestive apparatus, wires led to motor nodes in the rudimentary brain. The muscles were clamped to rocker arms which actuated rotors and drive-wheels. The power-wagons, economical, long-lived and docile, were principally used for heavy cartage, earth-moving, heavy tillage and other arduous jobs.

around the stocky neck. He heaved; the Mek spun to the ground.

Xanten leaped down, seized its pellet gun. Here was another of the larger Meks, and now Xanten saw it to be without a syrup sac, a Mek in the original state. Astounding! How did the creature survive? Suddenly there were many new questions to be asked—hopefully a few to be answered. Standing on the creature's head, Xanten hacked away the long antenna quills which protruded from the back of the Mek's scalp. It was now insulated, alone, on its own resources—a situation to reduce the most stalward Mek to apathy.

"Up!" ordered Xanten. "Into the back of the wagon!" He cracked the whip for emphasis.

The Mek at first seemed disposed to defy him, but after a blow or two obeyed. Xanten climbed into the seat and started the power-wagon, directed it to the north. The Birds would be unable to carry both himself and the Mek—or in any event they would cry and complain so raucously that they might as well be believed at first. They might or might not wait until the specified hour of tomorrow's sunset; as likely as not they would sleep the night in a tree, awake in a surly mood and return at once to Castle Hagedorn.

All through the night the power-wagon trundled, with Xanten on the seat and his captive huddled in the rear.

3

1.

The gentlefolk of the castles, for all their assurance, disliked to wander the countryside by night, by reason of what some derided as superstitious fear. Others cited travelers benighted beside moldering ruins and their subsequent visions: the eldritch music they had heard, or the whimper of moon-mirkins, or the far horns of spectral huntsmen. Others had seen pale lavender and green lights, and wraiths which ran with long strides through the forest; and Hode Abbey, now a dank tumble, was notorious for the White Hag and the alarming toll she exacted.

A hundred such cases were known, and while the hard-headed scoffed, none needlessly traveled the countryside by night. Indeed, if ghosts truly haunt the scenes of tragedy and heartbreak, then the landscape of Old Earth must be home to ghosts and specters beyond all numbering—especially that region across which Xanten rolled in the power-wagon, where every rock, every meadow, every vale and swale was crusted thick with human experience.

The moon rose high; the wagon trundled north along an ancient road, the cracked concrete slabs shining pale in the moonlight. Twice Xanten saw flickering orange lights off to the side, and once, standing in the shade of a cypress tree, he thought he saw a tall quiet shape, silently watching him pass. The captive Mek sat plotting mischief, Xanten well knew. Without its quills it must feel depersonified, bewildered, but Xanten told himself that it would not do to doze.

The road led through a town, certain structures of which still stood. Not even the Nomads took refuge in these old towns, fearing either miasma or perhaps the redolence of grief.

The moon reached the zenith. The landscape spread away in a hundred tones of silver, black and gray. Looking about, Xanten thought that for all the notable pleasures of civilized life, there was yet something to be said for the spaciousness and simplicity of Nomadland. The Mek made a stealthy movement. Xanten did not so much as turn his head. He cracked his whip in the air. The Mek became quiet.

All through the night the power-wagon rolled along the old road, with the moon sinking into the west. The eastern horizon glowed green and lemon-yellow, and presently, as the pallid moon disappeared, the sun rose over the distant line of mountains. At this moment, off to the right, Xanten spied a drift of smoke.

He halted the wagon. Standing up on the seat, he craned his neck to spy a Nomad encampment about a quarter-mile distant. He could distinguish three or four dozen tents of various sizes and a dozen dilapidated power-wagons. On the hetman's tall tent he thought he saw a black ideogram that he recognized. If so, this would be the tribe which not long before had trespassed on the Hagedorn domain, and which O.Z. Garr had repulsed.

Xanten settled himself upon the seat, composed his garments, set the power-wagon in motion and guided it toward the camp.

A hundred black-cloaked men, tall and lean as ferrets,

watched his approach. A dozen sprang forward, and whipping arrows to bows, aimed them at his heart. Xanten turned them a glance of supercilious inquiry, drove the wagon up to the hetman's tent, halted. He rose to his feet. "Hetman," he called. "Are you awake?"

The hetman parted the canvas which closed off his tent, peered out and after a moment came forth. Like the others he wore a garment of limp black cloth, swathing head and body alike. His face thrust through a square opening: narrow blue eyes, a grotesquely long nose, a chin long, skewed and sharp.

Xanten gave him a curt nod. "Observe this." He jerked his thumb toward the Mek in the back of the wagon. The hetman flicked aside his eyes, studied the Mek a tenth-second and returned to a scrutiny of Xanten. "His kind have revolted against the gentlemen," said Xanten. "In fact they massacre all the men of Earth. Hence, we of Castle Hagedorn make this offer to the Nomads. Come to Castle Hagedorn. We will feed, clothe and arm you. We will train you to discipline and the arts of formal warfare. We will provide the most expert leadership within our power. We will then annihilate the Meks, expunge them from Earth. After the campaign, we will train you to technical skills, and you may pursue profitable and interesting careers in the service of the castles."

The hetman made no reply for a moment. Then his weathered face split into a ferocious grin. He spoke in a voice which Xanten found surprisingly well modulated. "So your beasts have finally risen up to rend you! A pity they forbore so long! Well, it is all one to us. You are both alien folk and sooner or later your bones must bleach together."

Xanten pretended incomprehension. "If I understand you aright, you assert that in the face of alien assault, all men must fight a common battle; and then, after the victory, cooperate still to their mutual advantage. Am I correct?"

The hetman's grin never wavered. "You are not men. Only we of Earth soil and Earth water are men. You and your weird slaves are strangers together. We wish you success in your mutual slaughter."

"Well, then," declared Xanten, "I heard you aright after all. Appeals to your loyalty are ineffectual, so much is clear. What of self-interest, then? The Meks, failing to expunge the gentlefolk of the castles, will turn upon the Nomads and kill them as if they were so many ants."

"If they attack us, we will war on them," said the hetman. "Otherwise let them do as they will."

Xanten glanced thoughtfully at the sky. "We might be willing, even now, to accept a contingent of Nomads into the service of Castle Hagedorn, this to form a cadre from which a larger, more versatile group may be formed."

From the side, another Nomad called in an offensively jeering voice, "You will sew a sac on our backs where you can pour your syrup, hey?"

Xanten replied in an even voice, "The syrup is highly nutritious and supplies all bodily needs."

"Why, then, do you not consume it yourself?"

Xanten disdained reply.

The hetman spoke. "If you wish to supply us weapons, we will take them, and use them against whomever threatens us. But do not expect us to defend you. If you fear for your lives, desert your castles and become Nomads."

"Fear for our lives?" exclaimed Xanten. "What nonsense! Never! Castle Hagedorn is impregnable, as is Janeil, and most of the other castles as well."

The hetman shook his head. "Any time we choose we could take Hagedorn, and kill all you popinjays in your sleep."

"What!" cried Xanten in outrage. "Are you serious?"

"Certainly. On a black night we would send a man aloft on a great kite and drop him down on the parapets. He would lower a line, haul up ladders and in fifteen minutes the castle is taken."

Xanten pulled at his chin. "Ingenious, but impractical. The Birds would detect such a kite. Or the wind would fail at a critical moment. . . . All this is beside the point. The Meks fly no kites. They plan to make a display against Janeil and Hagedorn, then, in their frustration, go forth and hunt Nomads."

The hetman moved back a step. "What then? We have survived similar attempts by the men of Hagedorn. Cowards all. Hand to hand, with equal weapons, we would make you eat the dirt like the dogs you are."

Xanten raised his eyebrows in elegant disdain. "I fear that you forget yourself. You address a clan chief of Castle

Hagedorn. Only fatigue and boredom restrain me from punishing you with this whip."

"Bah!" said the hetman. He crooked a finger to one of his archers. "Spit this insolent lordling."

The archer discharged his arrow, but Xanten, who had been expecting some such act, fired his energy-gun, destroying arrow, bow and the archer's hands. He said, "I see I must teach you common respect for your betters; so it means the whip after all." Seizing the hetman by the scalp, he coiled the whip smartly once, twice, thrice around the narrow shoulders. "Let this suffice. I cannot compel you to fight, but at least I can demand decent respect." He leaped to the ground, and seizing the hetman, pitched him into the back of the wagon alongside the Mek. Then, backing the power-wagon around, he departed the camp without so much as a glance over his shoulder, the thwart of the seat protecting his back from arrows.

The hetman scrambled erect, drew his dagger. Xanten turned his head slightly. "Take care! Or I will tie you to the wagon and you shall run behind in the dust."

The hetman hesitated, made a spitting sound between his teeth, drew back. He looked down at his blade, turned it over and sheathed it with a grunt. "Where do you take me?"

Xanten halted the wagon. "No farther. I merely wished to leave your camp with dignity, without dodging and ducking a hail of arrows. You may alight. I take it you still refuse to bring your men into the service of Castle Hagedorn?"

The hetman once more made the spitting sound between his teeth. "When the Meks have destroyed the castles, we shall destroy the Meks, and Earth will be cleared of starthings."

"You are a gang of intractable savages. Very well, alight, return to your encampment. Reflect well before you again show disrespect to a Castle Hagedorn clan chief."

"Bah," muttered the hetman. Leaping down from the wagon, he stalked back down the track toward his camp.

2.

About noon Xanten came to Far Valley, at the edge of the Hagedorn lands. Nearby was a village of Expiationists:

malcontents and neurasthenics in the opinion of castle gentlefolk, and a curious group by any standards. A few had held enviable rank; certain others were savants of recognized erudition; but others yet were persons of neither dignity nor reputation, subscribing to the most bizarre and extreme of philosophies. All now performed toil no different from that relegated to the Peasants, and all seemed to take a perverse satisfaction in what—by castle standards—was filth, poverty and degradation.

As might be expected, their creed was by no means homogeneous. Some might better have been described as "nonconformists" or "disassociationists"; another group were "passive expiationists"; and others still, a minority, argued for a dynamic program.

Between castle and village was little intercourse. Occasionally the Expiationists bartered fruit or polished wood for tools, nails, medicaments; or the gentlefolk might make up a party to watch the Expiationists at their dancing and singing. Xanten had visited the village on many such occasions and had been attracted by the artless charm and informality of the folk at their play. Now, passing near the village, Xanten turned aside to follow a lane which wound between tall blackberry hedges and out upon a little common where goats and cattle grazed. Xanten halted the wagon in the shade and saw that the syrup sac was full. He looked back at his captive. "What of you? If you need syrup, pour yourself full. But no, you have no sac. What, then, do you feed upon? Mud? Unsavory fare. I fear none here is rank enough for your taste. Ingest syrup or munch grass, as you will; only do not stray overfar from the wagon, for I watch with an intent eye."

The Mek, sitting hunched in a corner, gave no signal that it comprehended, nor did it move to take advantage of Xanten's offer.

Xanten went to a watering trough and, holding his hands under the trickle which issued from a lead pipe, rinsed his face, then drank a swallow or two from his cupped hand.

Turning, he found that a dozen folk of the village had approached. One he knew well, a man who might have become Godalming, or even Aure, had he not become infected with expiationism.

Xanten performed a polite salute. "A.G. Philidor: it is I, Xanten."

"Xanten, of course. But here I am A.G. Philidor no longer, merely Philidor."

Xanten bowed. "My apologies; I have neglected the full rigor of your informality."

"Spare me your wit," said Philidor. "Why do you bring us a shorn Mek? For adoption, perhaps?" This last alluded to the gentlefolk practice of bringing over-tally babies to the village.

"Now who flaunts his wit? But you have not heard the news?"

"News arrives here last of all. The Nomads are better informed."

"Prepare yourself for surprise. The Meks have revolted against the castles. Halcyon and Delora are demolished, and all killed; perhaps others by this time."

Philidor shook his head. "I am not surprised."

"Well, then, are you not concerned?"

Philidor considered. "To this extent. Our own plans, never very feasible, become more farfetched than ever."

"It appears to me," said Xanten, "that you face grave and immediate danger. The Meks surely intend to wipe out every vestige of humanity. You will not escape."

Philidor shrugged. "Conceivably the danger exists. . . . We will take counsel and decide what to do."

"I can put forward a proposal which you may find attractive," said Xanten. "Our first concern, of course, is to suppress the revolt. There are at least a dozen Expiationist communities, with an aggregate population of two or three thousand—perhaps more. I propose that we recruit and train a corps of highly disciplined troops, supplied from the Castle Hagedorn armory, led by Hagedorn's most expert military theoreticians."

Philidor stared at him incredulously. "You expect us, the Expiationists, to become your soldiers?"

"Why not?" asked Xanten ingenuously. "Your life is at stake no less than ours."

"No one dies more than once."

Xanten in his turn evinced shock. "What? Can this be a former gentleman of Hagedorn speaking? Is this the face a man of pride and courage turns to danger? Is this the lesson of history? Of course not! I need not instruct you in this; you are as knowledgeable as I."

Philidor nodded. "I know that the history of man is not his technical triumphs, his kills, his victories. It is a composite, a mosaic of a trillion pieces, the account of each man's accommodation with his conscience. This is the true history of the race."

Xanten made an airy gesture. "A.G. Philidor, you oversimplify grievously. Do you consider me obtuse? There are many kinds of history. They interact. You emphasize morality. But the ultimate basis of morality is survival. What promotes survival is good; what induces mortifaction is bad."

"Well spoken!" declared Philidor. "But let me propound a parable. May a nation of a million beings destroy a creature who otherwise will infect all with a fatal disease? Yes, you will say. Once more: ten starving beasts hunt you, that they may eat. Will you kill them to save your life? Yes, you will say again, though here you destroy more than you save. Once more: a man inhabits a hut in a lonely valley. A hundred spaceships descend from the sky, and attempt to destroy him. May he destroy these ships in self-defense, even though he is one and they are a hundred thousand? Perhaps you say yes. What, then, if a whole world, a whole race of beings, pits itself against this single man? May he kill all? What if the attackers are as human as himself? What if he were the creature of the first instance, who otherwise will infect a world with disease? You see, there is no area where a simple touchstone avails. We have searched and found none. Hence, at the risk of sinning against Survival, we—I, at least; I can only speak for myself—have chosen a morality which at least allows me calm. I kill—nothing. I destroy—nothing."

"Bah," said Xanten contemptuously. "If a Mek platoon entered this valley and began to kill your children, you would not defend them?"

Philidor compressed his lips, turned away. Another man spoke. "Philidor has defined morality. But who is absolutely moral? Philidor, or I, or you, might desert his morality in such a case."

Philidor said, "Look about you. Is there anyone here you recognize?"

Xanten scanned the group. Nearby stood a girl of extra-ordinary beauty. She wore a white smock and in the dark hair curling to her shoulders she wore a red flower. Xanten nodded. "I see the maiden O.Z. Garr wished to introduce into his ménage at the castle."

"Exactly," said Philidor. "Do you recall the circumstances?"

"Very well indeed," said Xanten. "There was vigorous objection from the Council of Notables—if for no other reason than the threat to our laws of population control. O.Z. Garr attempted to sidestep the law in this fashion. 'I keep Phanes,' he said. 'At times I maintain as many as six, or even eight, and no one utters a word of protest. I will call this girl Phane and keep her among the rest.' I and others protested. There was almost a duel over this matter. O.Z. Garr was forced to relinquish the girl. She was given into my custody and I conveyed her to Far Valley."

Philidor nodded. "All this is correct. Well—we attempted to dissuade Garr. He refused to be dissuaded, and threatened us with his hunting force of perhaps thirty Meks. We stood aside. Are we moral? Are we strong or weak?"

"Sometimes it is better," said Xanten, "to ignore morality. Even though O.Z. Garr is a gentleman and you are but Ex-piationists. . . . Likewise in the case of the Meks. They are destroying the castles, and all the men of Earth. If morality means supine acceptance, then morality must be abandoned!"

Philidor gave a sour chuckle. "What a remarkable situ-ation. The Meks are here, likewise Peasants and Birds and Phanes, all altered, transported and enslaved for human pleasure. Indeed, it is this fact that occasions our guilt, for which we must expiate, and now you want us to compound this guilt!"

"It is a mistake to brood overmuch about the past," said Xanten. "Still, if you wish to preserve your option to brood, I suggest that you fight Meks now, or at the very least take refuge in the castle."

"Not I," said Philidor. "Perhaps others may choose to do so."

"You will wait to be killed?"

"No. I and no doubt others will take refuge in the remote mountains."

Xanten clambered back aboard the power-wagon. "If you change your mind, come to Castle Hagedorn."

He departed.

The road continued along the valley, wound up a hillside, crossed a ridge. Far ahead, silhouetted against the sky, stood Castle Hagedorn.

4

1.

Xanten reported to the council.

"The spaceships cannot be used. The Meks have rendered them inoperative. Any plan to solicit assistance from the Home Worlds is pointless."

"This is sorry news," said Hagedorn with a grimace. "Well, then, so much for that."

Xanten continued. "Returning by power-wagon I encountered a tribe of Nomads. I summoned the hetman and explained to him the advantages of serving Castle Hagedorn. The Nomads, I fear, lack both grace and docility. The hetman gave so surly a response that I departed in disgust.

"At Far Valley I visited the Expiationist village, and made a similar proposal, but with no great success. They are as idealistic as the Nomads are churlish. Both are of a fugitive tendency. The Expiationists spoke of taking refuge in the mountains. The Nomads presumably will retreat into the steppes."

Beaudry snorted. "How will flight help them? Perhaps they gain a few years—but eventually the Meks will find every last one of them; such is their methodicity."

"In the meantime," O.Z. Garr declared peevishly, "we might have organized them into an efficient combat corps, to the benefit of all. Well, then, let them perish; we are secure."

"Secure, yes," said Hagedorn gloomily. "But what when the power fails? When the lifts break down? When air circulation cuts off so that we either stifle or freeze? What then?"

O.Z. Garr gave his head a grim shake. "We must steel ourselves to undignified expedients, with as good grace as possible. But the machinery of the castle is sound, and I expect small deterioration or failure for conceivably five or ten years. By that time anything may occur."

Claghorn, who had been leaning indolently back in his seat, spoke at last. "This essentially is a passive program. Like the defection of the Nomads and Expiationists, it looks very little beyond the immediate moment."

O.Z. Garr spoke in a voice carefully polite. "Claghorn is well aware that I yield to none in courteous candor, as well as optimism and directness: in short, the reverse of passivity. But I refuse to dignify a stupid little inconvenience by extending it serious attention. How can he label this procedure passivity? Does the worthy and honorable head of the Claghorns have a proposal which more effectively maintains our status, our standards, our self-respect?"

Claghorn nodded slowly, with a faint half-smile which O.Z. Garr found odiously complacent. "There is a simple and effective method by which the Meks might be defeated."

"Well, then!" cried Hagedorn. "Why hesitate? Let us hear it!"

Claghorn looked around the red velvet-covered table, considering the faces of all: the dispassionate Xanten; Beaudry, burly, rigid, face muscles clenched in an habitual expression unpleasantly like a sneer; old Isseth, as handsome, erect and vital as the most dashing cadet; Hagedorn, troubled, glum, his inward perplexity all too evident; the elegant Garr; Overwhele, thinking savagely of the inconveniences of the future; Aure, toying with his ivory tablet, either bored, morose or defeated; the others displaying various aspects of doubt, foreboding, hauteur, dark resentment, impatience; and in the case of Floy, a quiet smile—or as Isseth later characterized it, an imbecilic smirk—intended to convey his total disassociation from the entire irksome matter.

Claghorn took stock of the faces, and shook his head. "I will not at the moment broach this plan, as I fear it is unworkable. But I must point out that under no circumstances can Castle Hagedorn be as before, even should we survive the Mek attack."

"Bah!" exclaimed Beaudry. "We lose dignity, we become ridiculous, by even so much as discussing the beasts."

Xanten stirred himself. "A distasteful subject, but remember! Halcyon is destroyed, and Delora, and who knows what others? Let us not thrust our heads in the sand! The Meks will not waft away merely because we ignore them."

"In any event," said O. Z. Garr. "Janeil is secure and we

are secure. The other folk, unless they are already slaughtered, might do well to visit us during the inconvenience, if they can justify the humiliation of flight to themselves. I myself believe that the Meks will soon come to heel, anxious to return to their posts."

Hagedorn shook his head gloomily. "I find this hard to believe. But very well, then, we shall adjourn."

2.

The radio communication system was the first of the castle's vast array of electrical and mechanical devices to break down. The failure occurred so soon and so decisively that certain of the theoreticians, notably I. K. Harde and Uegus, postulated sabotage by the departing Meks. Others remarked that the system had never been absolutely dependable, that the Meks themselves had been forced to tinker continuously with the circuits, that the failure was simply a result of faulty engineering. I. K. Harde and Uegus inspected the unwieldy apparatus, but the cause of failure was not obvious. After a half hour of consultation they agreed that any attempt to restore the system would necessitate complete redesign and reengineering, with consequent construction of testing and calibration devices, and the fabrication of a complete new family of components. "This is manifestly impossible," stated Uegus in his report to the council. "Even the simplest useful system would require several technician-years. There is not even one single technician to hand. We must therefore await the availability of trained and willing labor."

"In retrospect," stated Isseth, the oldest of the clan chiefs, "it is clear that in many ways we have been less than provident. No matter that the men of the Home Worlds are vulgarians! Men of shrewder calculation than our own would have maintained interworld connection."

"Lack of shrewdness and providence were not the deterring factors," stated Claghorn. "Communication was discouraged simply because the early lords were unwilling that Earth should be overrun with Home-World parvenus. It is as simple as that."

Isseth grunted, and started to make a rejoinder, but Hagedorn said hastily, "Unluckily, as Xanten tells us, the spaceships have been rendered useless, and while certain of our number have a profound knowledge of the theoretical considerations, again who is there to perform the toil? Even were the hangars and spaceships themselves under our control."

O. Z. Garr declared, "Give me six platoons of Peasants and six power-wagons equipped with high-energy cannon, and I'll regain the hangars; no difficulties there!"

Beaudry said, "Well, here's a start, at least. I'll assist in the training of the Peasants, and though I know nothing of cannon operation, rely on me for any advice I can give."

Hagedorn looked around the group, frowned, pulled at his chin. "There are difficulties to this program. First, we have at hand only the single power-wagon in which Xanten returned from his reconnaissance. Then, what of our energy-cannons? Has anyone inspected them? The Meks were entrusted with maintenance, but it is possible, even likely, that they wrought mischief here as well. O.Z. Garr, you are reckoned an expert military theoretician; what can you tell us in this regard?"

"I have made no inspection to date," stated O. Z. Garr. "Today the Display of Antique Tabards will occupy us all until the Hour of Sundown Appraisal*." He looked at his watch. "Perhaps now is as good a time as any to adjourn, until I am able to provide detailed information in regard to the cannons."

Hagedorn nodded his heavy head. "The time indeed grows late. Your Phanes appear today?"

"Only two," replied O. Z. Garr. "The Lazule and the Eleventh Mystery. I can find nothing suitable for the Gossamer Delights nor my little Blue Fay, and the Gloriana still requires tutelage. Today B. Z. Maxelwane's Variflors should repay the most attention."

"Yes," said Hagedorn. "I have heard other remarks to this effect. Very well, then, until tomorrow. Eh, Claghorn, you have something to say?"

"Yes, indeed," Claghorn said mildly. "We have all too

---

* Display of Antique Tabards; Hour of Sundown Appraisal: the literal sense of the first term was yet relevant; that of the second had become lost and the phrase was a mere formalism, connoting that hour of late afternoon when visits were exchanged, and wines, liqueurs and essences tasted: in short, a time of relaxation and small talk before the more formal convivialities of dining.

little time at our disposal. Best that we make the most of it. I seriously doubt the efficacy of Peasant troops; to pit Peasants against Meks is like sending rabbits against wolves. What we need, rather than rabbits, are panthers."

"Ah, yes," Hagedorn said vaguely. "Yes, indeed."

"Where, then, are panthers to be found?" Claghorn looked inquiringly around the table. "Can no one suggest a source? A pity. Well, then, if panthers fail to appear, I suppose rabbits must do. Let us go about the business of converting rabbits into panthers, and instantly. I suggest that we postpone all fetes and spectacles until the shape of our future is more certain."

Hagedorn raised his eyebrows, opened his mouth to speak, closed it again. He looked intently at Claghorn to ascertain whether or not he joked. Then he looked dubiously around the table.

Beaudry gave a rather brassy laugh. "It seems that erudite Claghorn cries panic."

O. Z. Garr stated: "Surely, in all dignity, we cannot allow the impertinence of our servants to cause us such eye-rolling alarm. I am embarrassed even to bring the matter forward."

"I am not embarrassed," said Claghorn, with the full-faced complacence which so exasperated O. Z. Garr. "I see no reason why you should be. Our lives are threatened, in which case a trifle of embarrassment, or anything else, becomes of secondary importance."

O. Z. Garr rose to his feet, performed a brusque salute in Claghorn's direction, of such a nature as to constitute a calculated affront. Claghorn, rising, performed a similar salute, so grave and overly complicated as to invest Garr's insult with burlesque overtones. Xanten, who detested O. Z. Garr, laughed aloud.

O. Z. Garr hesitated, then, sensing that under the circumstances taking the matter further would be regarded as poor form, strode from the chamber.

3.

The Viewing of Antique Tabards, an annual pageant of Phanes wearing sumptuous garments, took place in the Great Rotunda to the north of the central plaza. Possibly half of the gentlemen, but less than a quarter of the ladies, kept Phanes. These were creatures native to the caverns of Albireo Seven's moon: a docile race, both playful and affectionate, which after several thousand years of selective breeding had become sylphs of piquant beauty. Clad in a delicate gauze which issued from pores behind their ears, along their upper arms and down their backs, they were the most inoffensive of creatures, anxious always to please, innocently vain. Most gentlemen regarded them with affection, but rumors sometimes told of ladies drenching an especially hated Phane in tincture of ammonia, which matted her pelt and destroyed her gauze forever.

A gentleman besotted by a Phane was considered a figure of fun. The Phane though so carefully bred as to seem a delicate girl, if used sexually became crumpled and haggard, with gauzes drooping and discolored, and everyone would know that such and such a gentleman had misused his Phane. In this regard, at least, the women of the castles might exert their superiority, and did so by conducting themselves with such extravagant provocation that the Phanes in contrast seemed the most ingenuous and fragile of nature sprites. Their life-span was perhaps thirty years, during the last ten of which, after they had lost their beauty, they encased themselves in mantles of gray gauze and performed menial tasks in boudoirs, kitchens, pantries, nurseries and dressing rooms.

The Viewing of Antique Tabards was an occasion more for the viewing of Phanes than the tabards, though these, woven of Phane-gauze, were of great intrinsic beauty in themselves.

The Phane owners sat in a lower tier, tense with hope and pride, exulting when one made an especially splendid display, plunging into black depths when the ritual postures were performed with other than grace and elegance. During each display, highly formal music was plucked from a lute by a gentleman from a clan different to that of the Phane owner, the owner never playing the lute to the performance of his own Phane. The display was never overtly a competition and no formal acclamation was allowed, but all watching made up their minds as to which was the most entrancing and graceful of the Phanes, and the repute of the owner was thereby exalted.

The current Viewing was delayed almost half an hour by

reason of the defection of the Meks, and certain hasty improvisations had been necessary. But the gentlefolk of Castle Hagedorn were in no mood to be critical and took no heed of the occasional lapses as a dozen young Peasant bucks struggled to perform unfamiliar tasks. The Phanes were as entrancing as ever, bending, twisting, swaying to plangent chords of the lute, fluttering their fingers as if feeling for raindrops, crouching suddenly and gliding, then springing upright as straight as wands, finally bowing and skipping from the platform.

Halfway through the program a Peasant sidled awkwardly into the Rotunda, and mumbled in an urgent manner to the cadet who came to inquire his business. The cadet at once made his way to Hagedorn's polished jet booth. Hagedorn listened, nodded, spoke a few terse words and settled calmly back in his seat as if the message had been of no consequence, and the gentlefolk of the audience were reassured.

The entertainment proceeded. O.Z. Garr's delectable pair made a fine show, but it was generally felt that Lirlin, a young Phane belonging to Isseth Floy Gazuneth, for the first time at a formal showing, made the most captivating display.

The Phanes appeared for a last time, moving all together through a half-improvised minuet, then performing a final half gay, half regretful salute, departed the Rotunda. For a few moments more the gentlemen and ladies would remain in their booths, sipping essences, discussing the display, arranging affairs and assignations. Hagedorn sat frowning, twisting his hands. Suddenly he rose to his feet. The Rotunda instantly became silent.

"I dislike intruding an unhappy note at so pleasant an occasion," said Hagedorn. "But the news has just been given to me, and it is fitting that all should know. Janeil Castle is under attack. The Meks are there in great force, with hundreds of power-wagons. They have circled the castle with a dike which prevents any effective use of the Janeil energy-cannon.

"There is no immediate danger to Janeil, and it is difficult to comprehend what the Meks hope to achieve, the Janeil walls being all of two hundred feet high.

"The news, nevertheless, is somber, and it means that eventually we must expect a similar investment—though it is even more difficult to comprehend how Meks could hope to inconvenience us. Our water derives from four wells sunk deep into the earth. We have great stocks of food. Our energy is derived from the sun. If necessary, we could condense water and synthesize food from the air—at least I have been so assured by our great biochemical theoretician, X. B. Ladisname. Still—this is the news. Make of it what you will. Tomorrow the Council of Notables will meet."

5

1.

"Well, then," said Hagedorn to the council, "for once let us dispense with formality. O. Z. Garr: what of our cannon?"

O. Z. Garr, wearing the magnificent gray and green uniform of the Overwhele Dragoons, carefully placed his morion on the table, so that the panache stood erect. "Of twelve cannon, four appear to be functioning correctly. Four have been sabotaged by excision of the power-leads. Four have been sabotaged by some means undetectable to careful investigation. I have commandeered a half dozen Peasants who demonstrate a modicum of mechanical ability, and have instructed them in detail. They are currently engaged in splicing the leads. This is the extent of my current information in regard to the cannon."

"Moderately good news," said Hagedorn. "What of the proposed corps of armed Peasants?"

"The project is under way. A. F. Mull and I. A. Berzelius are now inspecting Peasants with a view to recruitment and training. I can make no sanguine projection as to the military effectiveness of such a corps, even if trained and led by such as A. F. Mull, I. A. Berzelius and myself. The Peasants are a mild, ineffectual race, admirably suited to the grubbing of weeds, but with no stomach whatever for fighting."

Hagedorn glanced around the council. "Are there any other suggestions?"

Beaudry spoke in a harsh, angry voice. "Had the villains but left us our power-wagons, we might have mounted the cannon aboard—the Peasants are equal to this, at least. Then we could roll to Janeil and blast the dogs from the rear."

"These Meks seem utter fiends!" declared Aure. "What conceivably do they have in mind? Why, after all these centuries, must they suddenly go mad?"

"We all ask ourselves the same questions," said Hagedorn. "Xanten, you returned from reconnaissance with a captive. Have you attempted to question him?"

"No," said Xanten. "Truth to tell, I haven't thought of him since."

"Why not attempt to question him? Perhaps he can provide a clue or two."

Xanten nodded assent. "I can try. Candidly, I expect to learn nothing."

"Claghorn, you are the Mek expert," said Beaudry. "Would you have thought the creatures capable of so intricate a plot? What do they hope to gain? Our castles?"

"They are certainly capable of precise and meticulous planning," said Claghorn. "Their ruthlessness surprises me —more, possibly, than it should. I have never known them to covet our material possessions, and they show no tendency toward what we consider the concomitants of civilization: fine discriminations of sensation and the like. I have often speculated—I won't dignify the conceit with the status of a theory—that the structural logic of a brain is of rather more consequence than we reckon with. Our own brains are remarkable for their utter lack of rational structure. Considering the haphazard manner in which our thoughts are formed, registered, indexed and recalled, any single rational act becomes a miracle. Perhaps we are incapable of rationality; perhaps all thought is a set of impulses generated by one emotion, monitored by another, ratified by a third. In contrast, the Mek brain is a marvel of what seems to be careful engineering. It is roughly cubical and consists of microscopic cells interconnected by organic fibrils, each a monofilament molecule of negligible electrical resistance. Within each cell is a film of silica, a fluid of variable conductivity and dielectric properties, a cusp of a complex mixture of metallic oxides. The brain is capable of storing great quantities of information in an orderly pattern. No fact is lost, unless it is purposely forgotten, a capacity which the Meks possess. The brain also functions as a radio transceiver, possibly as a radar transmitter and detector, though this again is speculation.

"Where the Mek brain falls short is in its lack of emotional color. One Mek is precisely like another, without any personality differentiation perceptible to us. This, clearly, is a function of their communicative system: unthinkable for a unique personality to develop under these conditions. They served us efficiently and—so we thought—loyally, because they felt nothing about their condition, neither pride in achievement, nor resentment, nor shame. Nothing whatever. They neither loved us nor hated us, nor do they now. It is hard for us to conceive this emotional vacuum, when each of us feels something about everything. We live in a welter of emotions. They are as devoid of emotion as an ice cube. They were fed, housed and maintained in a manner they found satisfactory. Why did they revolt? I have speculated at length, but the single reason which I can formulate seems so grotesque and unreasonable that I refuse to take it seriously. If this after all is the correct explanation. . . ." His voice drifted away.

"Well?" demanded O. Z. Garr peremptorily. "What, then?"

"Then—it is all the same. They are committed to the destruction of the human race. My speculation alters nothing."

Hagedorn turned to Xanten. "All this should assist you in your inquiries."

"I was about to suggest that Claghorn assist me, if he is so inclined," said Xanten.

"As you like," said Claghorn, "though in my opinion the information, no matter what, is irrelevant. Our single concern should be a means to repel them and to save our lives."

"And—except the force of 'panthers' you mentioned at our previous session—you can conceive of no subtle weapon?" asked Hagedorn wistfully. "A device to set up electrical resonances in their brains, or something similar?"

"Not feasible," said Claghorn. "Certain organs in the creatures' brains function as overload switches. Though it is true that during this time they might not be able to communicate." After a moment's reflection he added thoughtfully, "Who knows? A. G. Bernal and Uegus are theoreticians with a profound knowledge of such projections. Perhaps they might construct such a device, or several, against a possible need."

Hagedorn nodded dubiously, and looked toward Uegus. "Is this possible?"

Uegus frowned. " 'Construct'? I can certainly design such an instrument. But the components—where? Scattered through the storerooms helter-skelter, some functioning, others not. To achieve anything meaningful I must become no better than an apprentice, a Mek." He became incensed, and his voice hardened. "I find it hard to believe that I should be forced to point out this fact. Do you hold me and my talents, then, of such small worth?"

Hagedorn hastened to reassure him. "Of course not! I for one would never think of impugning your dignity."

"Never!" agreed Claghorn. "Nevertheless, during this present emergency, we will find indignities imposed upon us by events, unless now we impose them upon ourselves."

"Very well," said Uegus, a humorless smile trembling at his lips. "You shall come with me to the storeroom. I will point out the components to be brought forth and assembled; you shall perform the toil. What do you say to that?"

"I say yes, gladly, if it will be of real utility. However, I can hardly perform the labor for a dozen different theoreticians. Will any others serve besides myself?"

No one responded. Silence was absolute, as if every gentleman present held his breath.

Hagedorn started to speak, but Claghorn interrupted. "Pardon, Hagedorn, but here, finally, we are stuck upon a basic principle, and it must be settled now."

Hagedorn looked desperately around the council. "Has anyone relevant comment?"

"Claghorn must do as his innate nature compels," declared O. Z. Garr in the silkiest of voices. "I cannot dictate to him. As for myself, I can never demean my status as a gentleman of Hagedorn. This creed is as natural to me as drawing breath; if ever it is compromised I become a travesty of a gentleman, a grotesque mask of myself. This is Castle Hagedorn, and we represent the culmination of human civilization. Any compromise therefore becomes degradation; any expedient diminution of our standards becomes dishonor. I have heard the word 'emergency' used. What a deplorable sentiment! To dignify the ratlike snappings and gnashings of such as the Meks with the word 'emergency' is to my mind unworthy of a gentleman of Hagedorn!"

A murmur of approval went around the council table.

Claghorn leaned far back in his seat, chin on his chest, as if in relaxation. His clear blue eyes went from face to face, then returned to O. Z. Garr whom he studied with dispassionate interest. "Obviously you direct your words to me," he said, "and I appreciate their malice. But this is a small matter." He looked away from O. Z. Garr, to stare up at the massive diamond and emerald chandelier. "More important is the fact that the council as a whole, in spite of my earnest persuasion, seems to endorse your viewpoint. I can urge, expostulate, insinuate no longer, and I will now leave Castle Hagedorn. I find the atmosphere stifling. I trust that you survive the attack of the Meks, though I doubt that you will. They are a clever, resourceful race, untroubled by qualms or preconceptions, and we have long underestimated their quality."

Claghorn rose from his seat, inserted the ivory tablet into its socket. "I bid you all farewell."

Hagedorn hastily jumped to his feet and held forth his arms imploringly. "Do not depart in anger, Claghorn! Reconsider! We need your wisdom, your expertise!"

"Assuredly you do," said Claghorn. "But even more, you need to act upon the advice I have already extended. Until then, we have no common ground, and any further interchange is futile and tiresome." He made a brief, all-inclusive salute and departed the chamber.

Hagedorn slowly resumed his seat. The others made uneasy motions, coughed, looked up at the chandelier, studied their ivory tablets. O. Z. Garr muttered something to B. F. Wyas who sat beside him, who nodded solemnly. Hagedorn spoke in a subdued voice. "We will miss the presence of Claghorn, his penetrating if unorthodox insights. . . . We have accomplished little. Uegus, perhaps you will give thought to the projector under discussion. Xanten, you were to question the captive Mek. O. Z. Garr, you undoubtedly will see to the repair of the energy-cannon. . . . Aside from these small matters, it appears that we have evolved no general plan of action, to help either ourselves or Janeil."

Marune spoke. "What of the other castles? Are they

still extant? We have had no news. I suggest that we send Birds to each castle, to learn their condition."

Hagedorn nodded. "Yes, this is a wise motion. Perhaps you will see to this, Marune?"

"I will do so."

"Good. We will now adjourn."

2.

The Birds dispatched by Marune of Aure, one by one returned. Their reports were similar:

"Sea Island is deserted. Marble columns are tumbling along the beach. Pearl Dome is collapsed. Corpses float in the Water Garden."

"Maraval reeks of death. Gentlemen, Peasants, Phanes— all dead. Alas! Even the Birds have departed!"

"Delora: *a ros ros ros!* A dismal scene! No sign of life!"

"Alume is desolate. The great wooden door is smashed. The Green Flame is extinguished."

"There is nothing at Halcyon. The Peasants were driven into a pit."

"Tuang: silence."

"Morninglight: death."

6

1.

Three days later, Xanten constrained six Birds to a lift-chair, directed them first on a wide sweep around the castle, then south to Far Valley.

The Birds aired their usual complaints, then bounded down the deck in great ungainly hops which threatened to throw Xanten immediately to the pavement. At last gaining the air, they flew up in a spiral; Castle Hagedorn became an intricate miniature far below, each House marked by its unique cluster of turrets and aeries, its own eccentric roof line, its long streaming pennon.

The Birds performed the prescribed circle, skimming the crags and spires of North Ridge; then, setting wings aslant the upstream, they coasted away toward Far Valley.

Over the pleasant Hagedorn domain flew the Birds and

Xanten: over orchards, fields, vineyards, Peasant villages. They crossed Lake Maude with its pavilions and docks, the meadows beyond where the Hagedorn cattle and sheep grazed, and presently came to Far Valley, at the limit of Hagedorn lands.

Xanten indicated where he wished to alight; the Birds, who would have preferred a site closer to the village where they could have watched all that transpired, grumbled and cried out in wrath and set Xanten down so roughly that had he not been alert the shock would have pitched him head over heels.

Xanten alighted without elegance but at least remained on his feet. "Await me here!" he ordered. "Do not stray; attempt no flamboyant tricks among the lift-straps. When I return I wish to see six quiet Birds, in neat formation, lift-straps untwisted and untangled. No bickering, mind you! No loud caterwauling, to attract unfavorable comment! Let all be as I have ordered!"

The Birds sulked, stamped their feet, ducked aside their necks, made insulting comments just under the level of Xanten's hearing. Xanten, turning them a final glare of admonition, walked down the lane which led to the village.

The vines were heavy with ripe blackberries and a number of the girls of the village filled baskets. Among them was the girl O. Z. Garr had thought to preempt for his personal use. As Xanten passed, he halted and performed a courteous salute. "We have met before, if my recollection is correct."

The girl smiled, a half rueful, half whimsical smile. "Your recollection serves you well. We met at Hagedorn, where I was taken a captive. And later, when you conveyed me here, after dark, though I could not see your face." She extended her basket. "Are you hungry. Will you eat?"

Xanten took several berries. In the course of the conversation he learned that the girl's name was Glys Meadowsweet, that her parents were not known to her, but were presumably gentlefolk of Castle Hagedorn who had exceeded their birth tally. Xanten examined her even more carefully than before, but could see resemblance to none of the Hagedorn families. "You might derive from Castle Delora. If there is any family resemblance I can detect, it is to the Cosanzas of Delora— a family noted for the beauty of its ladies."

"You are not married?" she asked artlessly.

"No," said Xanten, and indeed he had dissolved his relationship with Araminta only the day before. "What of you?"

She shook her head. "I would never be gathering blackberries otherwise; it is work reserved for maidens. . . . Why do you come to Far Valley?"

"For two reasons. The first to see you." Xanten heard himself say this with surprise. But it was true, he realized with another small shock of surprise. "I have never spoken with you properly and I have always wondered if you were as charming and gay as you are beautiful."

The girl shrugged and Xanten could not be sure whether she was pleased or not, compliments from gentlemen sometimes setting the stage for a sorry aftermath. "Well, no matter. I came also to speak to Claghorn."

"He is yonder," she said in a voice toneless, even cool, and pointed. "He occupies that cottage." She returned to her blackberry picking. Xanten bowed and proceeded to the cottage the girl had indicated.

Claghorn, wearing loose knee-length breeches of gray homespun, worked with an ax chopping faggots into stove-lengths. At the sight of Xanten he halted his toil, leaned on the ax and mopped his forehead. "Ah, Xanten, I am pleased to see you. How are the folk of Castle Hagedorn?"

"As before. There is little to report, even had I come to bring you news."

"Indeed, indeed?" Claghorn leaned on the ax handle surveying Xanten with a bright blue gaze.

"At our last meeting," went on Xanten, "I agreed to question the captive Mek. After doing so I am distressed that you were not at hand to assist, so that you might have resolved certain ambiguities in the responses."

"Speak on," said Claghorn. "Perhaps I shall be able to do so now."

"After the council meeting I descended immediately to the storeroom where the Mek was confined. It lacked nutriment; I gave it syrup and a pail of water, which it sipped sparingly, then evinced a desire for minced clams. I summoned kitchen help and sent them for this commodity and the Mek ingested several pints. As I have indicated, it was an unusual Mek, standing as tall as myself and lacking a syrup sac. I conveyed it to a different chamber, a storeroom for brown plush furniture, and ordered it to a seat.

"I looked at the Mek and it looked at me. The quills which I removed were growing back; probably it could at least receive from Meks elsewhere. It seemed a superior beast, showing neither obsequiousness nor respect, and answered my questions without hesitation.

"First I remarked: 'The gentlefolk of the castles are astounded by the revolt of the Meks. We had assumed that your life was satisfactory. Were we wrong?'

" 'Evidently.' I am sure that this was the word signaled, though never had I suspected the Meks of dryness or wit of any sort.

" 'Very well, then,' I said. 'In what manner?'

" 'Surely it is obvious,' he said. 'We no longer wished to toil at your behest. We wished to conduct our lives by our own traditional standards.'

"The response surprised me. I was unaware that the Meks possessed standards of any kind, much less traditional standards."

Claghorn nodded. "I have been similarly surprised by the scope of the Mek mentality."

"I reproached the Mek: 'Why kill? Why destroy our lives in order to augment your own?' As soon as I had put the question I realized that it had been unhappily phrased. The Mek, I believe, realized the same; however, in reply he signaled something very rapidly which I believe was: 'We knew we must act with decisiveness. Your own protocol made this necessary. We might have returned to Etamin Nine, but we prefer this world Earth, and will make it our own, with our own great slipways, tubs and basking ramps.'

"This seemed clear enough, but I sensed an adumbration extending yet beyond. I said, 'Comprehensible. But why kill, why destroy? You might have taken yourself to a different region. We could not have molested you.'

" 'Infeasible, by your own thinking. A world is too small for two competing races. You intended to send us back to dismal Etamin Nine.'

" 'Ridiculous!' I said. 'Fantasy, absurdity. Do you take me for a mooncalf?'

" 'No,' the creature insisted. 'Two of Castle Hagedorn's notables were seeking the highest post. One assured us that, if elected, this would become his life's aim.'

" 'A grotesque misunderstanding,' I told him. 'One man, a lunatic, cannot speak for all men!'

" 'No? One Mek speaks for all Meks. We think with one mind. Are not men of a like sort?'

" 'Each thinks for himself. The lunatic who assured you this tomfoolery is an evil man. But at least matters are clear. We do not propose to send you to Etamin Nine. Will you withdraw from Janeil, take yourselves to a far land and leave us in peace?'

" 'No,' he said. 'Affairs have proceeded too far. We will now destroy all men. The truth of the statement is clear: one world is too small for two races.'

" 'Unluckily, then, I must kill you,' I told him. 'Such acts are not to my liking, but, with opportunity, you would kill as many gentlemen as possible.' At this the creature sprang upon me and I killed it with an easier mind than had it sat staring.

"Now you know all. It seems that either you or O. Z. Garr stimulated the cataclysm. O. Z. Garr? Unlikely. Impossible. Hence, you, Claghorn, you! have this weight upon your soul!"

Claghorn frowned down at the ax. "Weight, yes. Guilt, no. Ingenuousness, yes; wickedness, no."

Xanten stood back. "Claghorn, your coolness astounds me! Before, when rancorous folk like O. Z. Garr conceived you a lunatic—"

"Peace, Xanten!" exclaimed Claghorn. "This extravagant breast-beating becomes maladroit. What have I done wrong? My fault is that I tried too much. Failure is tragic, but a phthisic face hanging over the cup of the future is worse. I meant to become Hagedorn, I would have sent the slaves home. I failed, the slaves revolted. So do not speak another word. I am bored with the subject. You cannot imagine how your bulging eyes and your concave spine oppress me."

"Bored you may be," cried Xanten. "You decry my eyes, my spine—but what of the thousands dead?"

"How long would they live in any event? Lives as cheap as fish in the sea. I suggest that you put by your reproaches and devote a similar energy to saving yourself. Do you realize that a means exists? You stare at me blankly. I assure you that what I say is true, but you will never learn the means from me."

"Claghorn," said Xanten, "I flew to this spot intending to blow your arrogant head from your body—" Claghorn, no longer heeding, had returned to his wood-chopping.

"Claghorn!" cried Xanten. "Attend me!"

"Xanten, take your outcries elsewhere, if you please. Remonstrate with your Birds."

Xanten swung on his heel and marched back down the lane. The girls picking berries looked at him questioningly and moved aside. Xanten halted to look up and down the lane. Glys Meadowsweet was nowhere to be seen. In a new fury he continued. He stopped short. On a fallen tree a hundred feet from the Birds sat Glys Meadowsweet, examining a blade of grass as if it had been an astonishing artifact of the past. The Birds, for a marvel, had actually obeyed him and waited in a fair semblance of order.

Xanten looked up toward the heavens, kicked at the turf. He drew a deep breath and approached Glys Meadowsweet. He noted that she had tucked a flower into her long loose hair.

After a second or two she looked up and searched his face. "Why are you so angry?"

Xanten slapped his thigh, then seated himself beside her. " 'Angry'? No. I am out of my mind with frustration. Claghorn is as obstreperous as a sharp rock. He knows how Castle Hagedorn can be saved but he will not divulge his secret."

Glys Meadowsweet laughed—an easy, merry sound, like nothing Xanten had ever heard at Castle Hagedorn. " 'Secret'? When even I know it?"

"It must be a secret," said Xanten. "He will not tell me."

"Listen. If you fear the Birds will hear, I will whisper." She spoke a few words into his ear.

Perhaps the sweet breath befuddled Xanten's mind. But the explicit essence of the revelation failed to strike home into his consciousness. He made a sound of sour amusement. "No secret there. Only what the prehistoric Scythians termed *bathos*. Dishonor to the gentlemen! Do we dance with the Peasants? Do we serve the Birds essences and discuss with them the sheen of our Phanes?"

" 'Dishonor,' then?" She jumped to her feet. "Then it is also dishonor for you to talk to me, to sit here with me, to make ridiculous suggestions—"

"I made no suggestions!" protested Xanten. "I sit here in all decorum—"

"Too much decorum, too much honor!" With a display of passion which astounded Xanten, Glys Meadowsweet tore the flower from her hair and hurled it to the ground. "There! Hence!"

"No," said Xanten in sudden humility. He bent, picked up the flower, kissed it, replaced it in her hair. "I am not over-honorable. I will try my best." He put his arms on her shoulders, but she held him away.

"Tell me," she inquired with a very mature severity, "do you own any of those peculiar insect-women?"

"I? Phanes? I own no Phanes."

With this, Glys Meadowsweet relaxed and allowed Xanten to embrace her, while the Birds clucked, guffawed and made vulgar scratching sounds with their wings.

7

1.

The summer waxed warm. On June 30 Janeil and Hagedorn celebrated the Fete of Flowers, even though the dike was rising high around Janeil. Shortly after, Xanten flew six select Birds into Castle Janeil by night, and proposed to the council that the population be evacuated by Bird-lift—as many as possible, as many who wished to leave. The council listened with stony faces and without comment passed on to a consideration of other affairs.

Xanten returned to Castle Hagedorn. Using the most careful methods, speaking only to trusted comrades, Xanten enlisted thirty or forty cadets and gentlemen to his persuasion, though inevitably he could not keep the doctrinal thesis of his program secret.

The first reaction of the traditionalists was mockery and charges of poltroonery. At Xanten's insistence, challenges were neither issued nor accepted by his hot-blooded associates.

On the evening of September 9 Castle Janeil fell. The news was brought to Castle Hagedorn by excited Birds who told the grim tale again and again in voices ever more hysterical.

Hagedorn, now gaunt and weary, automatically called a council meeting; it took note of the gloomy circumstances. "We, then, are the last castle! The Meks cannot conceivably do us harm; they can build dikes around our castle walls for twenty years and only work themselves to distraction. We are secure; but yet it is a strange and portentous thought to realize that at last, here at Castle Hagedorn, live the last gentlemen of the race!"

Xanten spoke in a voice strained with earnest conviction. "Twenty years—fifty years—what difference to the Meks? Once they surround us, once they deploy, we are trapped. Do you comprehend that now is our last opportunity to escape the great cage that Castle Hagedorn is to become?"

" 'Escape,' Xanten? What a word! For shame!" hooted O. Z. Garr. "Take your wretched band, escape! To steppe or swamp or tundra! Go as you like, with your poltroons, but be good enough to give over these incessant alarms!"

"Garr, I have found conviction since I became a 'poltroon.' Survival is good morality. I have this from the mouth of a noted savant."

"Bah! Such as whom?"

"A.G. Philidor, if you must be informed of every detail."

O.Z. Garr clapped his hand to his forehead. "Do you refer to Philidor, the Expiationist? He is of the most extreme stripe, an Expiationist to out-expiate all the rest! Xanten, be sensible, if you please!"

"There are years ahead for all of us," said Xanten in a wooden voice, "if we free ourselves from the castle."

"But the castle is our life!" declared Hagedorn. "In essence, Xanten, what would we be without the castle? Wild animals? Nomads?"

"We would be alive."

O.Z. Garr gave a snort of disgust and turned away to inspect a wall hanging.

Hagedorn shook his head in doubt and perplexity. Beaudry threw his hands up into the air. "Xanten, you have the effect of unnerving us all. You come in here and inflict this dreadful sense of urgency—but why? In Castle Hagedorn we are as safe as in our mothers' arms. What do we gain by throwing aside all—honor, dignity, comfort, civilized niceties —for no other reason than to slink through the wilderness?"

"Janeil was safe," said Xanten. "Today where is Janeil?

Death, mildewed cloth, sour wine. What we gain by *slinking* is the assurance of survival. And I plan much more than simple *slinking*."

"I can conceive of a hundred occasions when death is better than life!" snapped Isseth. "Must I die in dishonor and disgrace? Why may my last years not be passed in dignity?"

Into the room came B.F. Robarth. "Councilmen, the Meks approach Castle Hagedorn."

Hagedorn cast a wild look around the chamber. "Is there a consensus? What must we do?"

Xanten threw up his hands. "Everyone must do as he thinks best! I argue no more: I am done, Hagedorn. Will you adjourn the council so that we may be about our affairs? I to my *slinking*?"

"Council is adjourned," said Hagedorn, and all went to stand on the ramparts.

Up the avenue into the castle trooped Peasants from the surrounding countryside, packets slung over their shoulders. Across the valley, at the edge of Bartholomew Forest, was a clot of power-wagons and an amorphous brown-gold mass: Meks.

Aure pointed west. "Look—there they come, up the Long Swale." He turned, peered east. "And look, there at Bambridge: Meks!"

By common consent, all swung about to scan North Ridge. O.Z. Garr pointed to a quiet line of brown-gold shapes. "There they wait, the vermin! They have penned us in! Well, then, let them wait!" He swung away, rode the lift down to the plaza, and crossed swiftly to Zumbeld House, where he worked the rest of the afternoon with his Gloriana, of whom he expected great things.

2.

The following day the Meks formalized the investment. Around Castle Hagedorn a great circle of Mek activity made itself apparent: sheds, warehouses, barracks. Within this periphery, just beyond the range of the energy-cannon, power-wagons thrust up mounds of dirt.

During the night these mounds lengthened toward the castle, similarly the night after. At last the purpose of the mounds became clear: they were a protective cover above passages or tunnels leading toward the crag on which Castle Hagedorn rested.

The following day several of the mounds reached the base of the crag. Presently a succession of power-wagons loaded with rubble began to flow from the far end. They issued, dumped their loads and once again entered the tunnels.

Eight of these aboveground tunnels had been established. From each trundled endless loads of dirt and rock, gnawed from the crag on which Castle Hagedorn sat. To the gentlefolk who crowded the parapets the meaning of the work at last became clear.

"They make no attempt to bury us," said Hagedorn. "They merely mine out the crag from below us!"

On the sixth day of the siege, a great segment of the hillside shuddered, slumped and a tall pinnacle of rock reaching almost up to the base of the walls collapsed.

"If this continues," muttered Beaudry, "our time will be less than that of Janeil."

"Come, then," called O.Z. Garr, suddenly active. "Let us try our energy-cannon. We'll blast open their wretched tunnels, and then what will the rascals do?" He went to the nearest emplacement and shouted down for Peasants to remove the tarpaulin.

Xanten, who happened to be standing nearby, said, "Allow me to assist you." He jerked away the tarpaulin. "Shoot now, if you will."

O.Z. Garr stared at him uncomprehendingly, then leaped forward and swiveled the great projector about so that it aimed at a mound. He pulled the switch; the air crackled in front of the ringed snout, rippled, flickered with purple sparks. The target area steamed, became black, then dark red, then slumped into an incandescent crater. But the underlying earth, twenty feet in thickness, afforded too much insulation; the molten puddle became white-hot but failed to spread or deepen. The energy-cannon gave a sudden chatter, as electricity short-circuited through corroded insulation. The cannon went dead. O.Z. Garr inspected the mechanism in anger and disappointment; then, with a gesture of repugnance, he turned away. The cannons were clearly of limited effectiveness.

Two hours later, on the east side of the crag, another great sheet of rock collapsed, and just before sunset a similar mass sheered from the western face, where the wall of the castle rose almost in an uninterrupted line from the cliff below.

At midnight Xanten and those of his persuasion, with their children and consorts, departed Castle Hagedorn. Six teams of Birds shuttled from the flight deck to a meadow near Far Valley, and long before dawn had transported the entire group. There were none to bid them farewell.

3.

A week later another section of the east cliff fell away, taking a length of rock-melt buttress with it. At the tunnel mouths the piles of excavated rubble had become alarmingly large.

The terraced south face of the crag was the least disturbed, the most spectacular damage having occurred to east and west. Suddenly, a month after the initial assault, a great section of the terrace slumped forward, leaving an irregular crevasse which interrupted the avenue and hurled down the statues of former notables emplaced at intervals along the avenue's balustrade.

Hagedorn called a council meeting. "Circumstances," he said in a wan attempt at facetiousness, "have not bettered themselves. Our most pessimistic expectations have been exceeded: a dismal situation. I confess that I do not relish the prospect of toppling to my death among all my smashed belongings."

Aure made a desperate gesture. "A similar thought haunts me! Death—what of that? All must die! But when I think of my precious belongings, I become sick. My books trampled! my fragile vases smashed! my tabards ripped! my rugs buried! my Phanes strangled! my heirloom chandeliers flung aside! These are my nightmares."

"Your possessions are no less precious than any others," said Beaudry shortly. "Still, they have no life of their own, when we are gone, who cares what happens to them?"

Marune winced. "A year ago I put down eighteen dozen flasks of prime essence; twelve dozen Green Rain; three each of Balthazar and Faidor. Think of these, if you would contemplate tragedy!"

"Had we only known!" groaned Aure. "I would have—I would have. . . . " His voice trailed away.

O. Z. Garr stamped his foot in impatience. "Let us avoid lamentation at all costs! We had a choice, remember? Xanten beseeched us to flee; now he and his like go skulking and foraging through the north mountains with the Expiationists. We chose to remain, for better or worse, and unluckily the worse is occurring. We must accept the fact like gentlemen."

To this the council gave melancholy assent. Hagedorn brought forth a flask of priceless Rhadamanth, and poured with a prodigality which previously would have been unthinkable. "Since we have no future—to our glorious past!"

That night disturbances were noted here and there around the ring of Mek investment: flames at four separate points, a faint sound of hoarse shouting. On the following day it seemed that the tempo of activity had lessened a trifle.

During the afternoon, however, a vast segment of the east cliff fell away. A moment later, as if after majestic deliberation, the tall east wall split off and toppled, leaving the backs of six great Houses exposed to the open sky.

An hour after sunset a team of Birds settled to the flight-deck. Xanten jumped from the seat. He ran down the circular staircase to the ramparts and came down to the plaza by Hagedorn's palace.

Hagedorn, summoned by a kinsman, came forth to stare at Xanten in surprise. "What do you do here? We expected you to be safely north with the Expiationists!"

"The Expiationists are not safely north," said Xanten. "They have joined the rest of us. We are fighting."

Hagedorn's jaw dropped. "Fighting? The gentlemen are fighting Meks?"

"As vigorously as possible."

Hagedorn shook his head in wonder. "The Expiationists too? I understood that they had planned to flee north."

"Some have done so, including A.G. Philidor. There are factions among the Expiationists just as here. Most are not ten miles distant. The same with the Nomads. Some have taken their power-wagons and fled. The rest kill Meks with fanatic fervor. Last night you saw our work. We fired four storage warehouses, destroyed syrup tanks, killed a hundred or more Meks, as well as a dozen power-wagons. We suffered losses, which hurt us because there are few of us and many Meks. This is why I am here. We need more men. Come fight beside us!"

Hagedorn turned, motioning to the great central plaza. "I will call forth the folk from their Houses. Talk to everyone."

4.

The Birds, complaining bitterly at the unprecedented toil, worked all night, transporting the gentlemen who, sobered by the imminent destruction of Castle Hagedorn, were now willing to abandon all scruples and fight for their lives. The staunch traditionalists still refused to compromise their honor, but Xanten gave them cheerful assurance: "Remain here, then, prowling the castle like so many furtive rats. Take what comfort you can in the fact that you are being protected; the future holds little else for you."

And many who heard him stalked away in disgust.

Xanten turned to Hagedorn. "What of you? Do you come or do you stay?"

Hagedorn heaved a deep sigh, almost a groan. "Castle Hagedorn is at an end. No matter what the eventuality. I come with you."

5.

The situation had suddenly altered. The Meks, established in a loose ring around Castle Hagedorn, had calculated upon no resistance from the countryside and little from the castle. They had established their barracks and syrup depots with thought only for convenience and none for defense; raiding parties, consequently, were able to approach, inflict damage and withdraw before sustaining serious losses of their own. Those Meks posted along North Ridge were harassed almost continuously, and finally were driven down with many losses. The circle around Castle Hagedorn became a cusp; then two days later, after the destruction of five more syrup depots, the Meks drew back even farther. Throwing up earthworks before the two tunnels leading under the south face of the crag, they established a more or less tenable defensive position, but now instead of beleaguering, they became the beleaguered, even though power-wagons of broken rock still issued from the crag. Within the area thus defended, the Meks concentrated their remaining syrup stocks, tools, weapons, ammunition. The area outside the earthworks was floodlit after dark and guarded by Meks armed with pellet guns, making any frontal assault impractical. For a day the raiders kept to the shelter of the surrounding orchards, appraising the new situation. Then a new tactic was attempted. Six light carriages were improvised and loaded with bladders of a light inflammable oil, with a fire grenade attached. To each of these carriages ten Birds were harnessed, and at midnight sent aloft, with a man for each carriage. Flying high, the Birds then glided down through the darkness over the Mek position, where the fire bombs were dropped. The area instantly seethed with flame. The syrup depot burned; the power-wagons, awakened by the flames, rolled frantically back and forth, crushing Meks and stores, colliding with each other, adding vastly to the terror of the fire. The Meks who survived took shelter in the tunnels. Certain of the floodlights were extinguished, and taking advantage of the confusion, the men attacked the earthworks. After a short, bitter battle, the men killed all the sentinels and took up positions commanding the mouths of the tunnels, which now contained all that remained of the Mek army. It seemed as if the Mek uprising had been put down.

8

1.

The flames died. The human warriors—three hundred men from the castle, two hundred Expiationists and about three hundred Nomads—gathered about the tunnel mouth and, during the balance of the night, considered methods to deal with the immured Meks. At sunrise, those men of Castle Hagedorn, whose children and consorts were yet inside, went to bring them forth. With them, upon their return, came a group of castle gentlemen: among them Beaudry, O.Z. Garr, Isseth and Aure. They greeted their onetime peers, Hagedorn, Xanten, Claghorn and others, crisply, but with a certain austere detachment which recognized that loss of prestige incurred by those who fought Meks as if they were equals.

"Now what is to happen?" Beaudry inquired of Hagedorn. "The Meks are trapped but you can't bring them forth. Not impossibly they have syrup stored within for the power-wagons; they may well survive for months."

O.Z. Garr, assessing the situation from the standpoint of a military theoretician, came forward with a plan of action. "Fetch down the cannon—or have your underlings do so—and mount them on power-wagons. When the vermin are sufficiently weak, roll the cannon in and wipe out all but a labor force for the castle: we formerly worked four hundred, and this should suffice."

"Ha!" exclaimed Xanten. "It gives me great pleasure to inform you that this will never be. If any Meks survive they will repair the spaceships and instruct us in their mainte-nance and we will then transport them and Peasants back to their native worlds."

"How, then, do you expect us to maintain our lives?" de-manded Garr coldly.

"You have the syrup generator. Fit yourselves with sacs and drink syrup."

Garr tilted back his head, stared coldly down his nose. "This is your voice, yours alone, and your insolent opinion. Others are to be heard from. Hagedorn—you were once a gentleman. Is this also your philosophy, that civilization should wither?"

"It need not wither," said Hagedorn, "provided that all of us—you as well as we—toil for it. There can be no more slaves. I have become convinced of this."

O.Z. Garr turned on his heel, swept back up the avenue into the castle, followed by the most traditional-minded of his comrades. A few moved aside and talked among them-selves in low tones, with one or two black looks for Xanten and Hagedorn.

From the ramparts of the castle came a sudden outcry: "The Meks! They are taking the castle! They swarm up the lower passages! Attack, save us!"

The men below stared up in consternation. Even as they looked, the castle portals swung shut.

"How is this possible?" demanded Hagedorn. "I swear all entered the tunnels!"

"It is only too clear," said Xanten bitterly. "While they undermined, they drove a tunnel up to the lower levels!"

Hagedorn started forward as if he would charge up the crag alone, then halted. "We must drive them out. Unthinkable that they pillage our castle!"

"Unfortunately," said Claghorn, "the walls bar us as effectively as they did the Meks."

"We can send up a force by Bird-car! Once we consolidate, we can hunt them down, exterminate them."

Claghorn shook his head. "They can wait on the ramparts and flight deck and shoot down the Birds as they approach. Even if we secured a foothold there would be great bloodshed: one of us killed for every one of them. And they still outnumber us three or four to one."

Hagedorn groaned. "The thought of them reveling among my possessions, strutting about in my clothes, swilling my essences—it sickens me!"

"Listen!" said Claghorn. From on high they heard the hoarse yells of men, the crackle of energy-cannon. "Some of them, at least, hold out on the ramparts!"

Xanten went to a nearby group of Birds who were for once awed and subdued by events. "Lift me up above the castle, out of range of the pellets, but where I can see what the Meks do!"

"Care, take care!" croaked one of the Birds. "Ill things occur at the castle."

"Never mind; convey me up, above the ramparts!"

The Birds lifted him, swung in a great circle around the crag and above the castle, sufficiently distant to be safe from the Mek pellet guns. Beside those cannon which yet operated stood thirty men and women. Between the great Houses, the Rotunda and the palace, everywhere the cannon could not be brought to bear, swarmed Meks. The plaza was littered with corpses: gentlemen, ladies and their children—all those who had elected to remain at Castle Hagedorn.

At one of the cannon stood O.Z. Garr. Spying Xanten he gave a shout of hysterical rage, swung up the cannon, fired a bolt. The Birds, screaming, tried to swerve aside, but the bolt smashed two. Birds, car, Xanten fell in a great tangle. By some miracle, the four yet alive caught their balance and a hundred feet from the ground, with a frenzied groaning effort, they slowed their fall, steadied, hovered an instant, sank to the ground. Xanten staggered free of the tangle. Men came running. "Are you safe?" called Claghorn.

"Safe, yes. Frightened as well." Xanten took a deep breath and went to sit on an outcrop of rock.

"What's happening up there?" asked Claghorn.

"All dead," said Xanten, "all but a score. Garr has gone mad. He fired on me."

"Look! Meks on the ramparts!" cried A.L. Morgan.

"There!" cried someone else. "Men! They jump! . . . No, they are flung!"

Some were men, some were Meks whom they had dragged with them; with awful slowness they toppled to their deaths. No more fell. Castle Hagedorn was in the hands of the Meks.

Xanten considered the complex silhouette, at once so familiar and so strange. "They can't hope to hold out. We need only destroy the sun-cells, and they can synthesize no syrup."

"Let us do it now," said Claghorn, "before they think of this and man the cannon! Birds!"

He went off to give the orders, and forty Birds, each clutching two rocks the size of a man's head, flapped up, circled the castle and presently returned to report the sun-cells destroyed.

Xanten said, "All that remains is to seal the tunnel entrances against a sudden eruption, which might catch us off guard—then patience."

"What of the Peasants in the stables—and the Phanes?" asked Hagedorn in a forlorn voice.

Xanten gave his head a slow shake. "He who was not an Expiationist before must become one now."

Claghorn muttered, "They can survive two months—no more."

But two months passed, and three months, and four months: then one morning the great portals opened and a haggard Mek stumbled forth. He signaled: "Men: we starve. We have maintained your treasures. Give us our lives or we destroy all before we die."

Claghorn responded: "These are our terms. We give you your lives. You must clean the castle, remove and bury the corpses. You must repair the spaceships and teach us all you know regarding them. We will then transport you to Etamin Nine."

2.

Five years later Xanten and Glys Meadowsweet, with their two children, had reason to travel north from their home near Sande River. They took occasion to visit Castle Hagedorn, where now lived only two or three dozen folk, among them Hagedorn.

He had aged, so it seemed to Xanten. His hair was white; his face, once bluff and hearty, had become thin, almost waxen. Xanten could not determine his mood.

They stood in the shade of a walnut tree, with castle and crag looming above them. "This is now a great museum," said Hagedorn. "I am curator, and this will be the function of all the Hagedorns who come after me, for there is incalculable treasure to guard and maintain. Already the feeling of antiquity has come to the castle. The Houses are alive with ghosts. I see them often, especially on the nights of the fetes. . . . Ah, those were the times, were they not, Xanten?"

"Yes, indeed," said Xanten. He touched the heads of his two children. "Still, I have no wish to return to them. We are men now, on our own world, as we never were before."

Hagedorn gave a somewhat regretful assent. He looked up at the vast structure, as if now were the first occasion he had laid eyes on it. "The folk of the future—what will they think of Castle Hagedorn? Its treasures, its books, its tabards?"

"They will come, they will marvel," said Xanten. "Almost as I do today."

"There is much at which to marvel. Will you come within, Xanten? There are still flasks of noble essence laid by."

"Thank you, no," said Xanten. "There is too much to stir old memories. We will go our way, and I think immediately."

Hagedorn nodded sadly. "I understand very well. I myself am often given to reverie these days. Well then, goodbye, and journey home with pleasure."

"We will do so, Hagedorn. Thank you and good-bye."

THE IDEA behind this story is highly ingenious and novel; in fact I'll go so far as to say "inspired." I wish only that I had formulated it myself. In point of fact the concept was generated somewhere within the hyperdimensional recesses of Damon Knight's intellect.

This is how I happened to write the story. During the time that Damon edited the magazine *World's Beyond,* I sold him two stories: "The New Prime" and "The Secret." One day in casual conversation he outlined the idea upon which "Abercrombie Station" is built, and in effect commissioned the story.

I produced the required verbiage, but just as I imprinted the final period, *World's Beyond* folded and I sold the story elsewhere. A year or two later I saw Damon, who by this time had forgotten the entire transaction. He paid me a generous if rather wistful compliment upon the theme of the story. "Oddly enough," said Damon, "at one time I had a very similar notion, but never got around to writing the story."

I finally inquired, "Damon, don't you remember when you tossed me this idea and ordered it written up for *World's Beyond?*"

Damon was and is much too polite to con-

IV

116

tradict me, and I take this occasion to acknowledge his contribution to the story which follows.

An interesting footnote to my connection with *World's Beyond* concerns "The Secret," the second story I sold Damon. When *World's Beyond* folded it carried with it into limbo the still unpublished story which thereupon mysteriously vanished and was seen no more. About five years later I rewrote the story, using the same title. Again "The Secret" disappeared, somewhere after leaving Scott Meredith's office, but before finding a market. I have searched high and low for carbons to these stories without success; both versions have vanished without a trace. I can surmise only that I brushed upon an elemental verity, most truly secret indeed, and that one or another of the Upper Forces saw fit to expunge the dangerous knowledge before it gained currency. I will not attempt a third version; I value my life and sanity, and can take a hint.

ABERCROMBIE STATION

‹‹‹‹‹‹‹‹‹‹‹‹‹‹‹‹‹‹‹‹‹‹‹‹‹‹‹‹‹‹‹‹‹

1

THE DOORKEEPER WAS A BIG HARD-LOOKING MAN with an unwholesome horse-face, a skin like corroded zinc. Two girls spoke to him, asking arch questions.

Jean saw him grunt noncommittally. "Just stick around; I can't give out no dope."

He motioned to the girl sitting beside Jean, a blond girl, very smartly turned out. She rose to her feet; the doorkeeper slid back the door. The blond girl walked swiftly through into the inner room; the door closed behind her.

She moved tentatively forward, stopped short.

A man sat quietly on an old-fashioned leather couch, watching through half-closed eyes.

Nothing frightening here, was her initial impression. He was young—twenty-four or twenty-five. Mediocre, she thought, neither tall nor short, stocky nor lean. His hair was nondescript, his features without distinction, his clothes unobtrusive and neutral.

He shifted his position, opened his eyes a flicker. The blond girl felt a quick pang. Perhaps she had been mistaken.

"How old are you?"

"I'm—twenty."

"Take off your clothes."

She stared, hands tight and white knuckled on her purse. Intuition came suddenly; she drew a quick shallow breath. *Obey him once, give in once, he'll be your master as long as you live.*

"No . . . no, I won't."

118

She turned quickly, reached for the door-slide. He said unemotionally, "You're too old anyway."

The door jerked aside; she walked quickly through the outer room, looking neither right nor left.

A hand touched her arm. She stopped, looked down into a face that was jet, pale rose, ivory. A young face with an expression of vitality and intelligence: black eyes, short black hair, a beautiful clear skin, mouth without makeup.

Jean asked, "What goes on? What kind of job is it?"

The blond girl said in a tight voice, "I don't know. I didn't stay to find out. It's nothing nice." She turned, went through the outer door.

Jean sank back into the chair, pursed her lips speculatively. A minute passed. Another girl, nostrils flared wide, came from the inner room, crossed to the door, looking neither right nor left.

Jean smiled faintly. She had a wide mouth, expansive and flexible. Her teeth were small, white, very sharp.

The doorkeeper motioned to her. She jumped to her feet, entered the inner room.

The quiet man was smoking. A silvery plume rose past his face, melted into the air over his head. Jean thought, *There's something strange in his complete immobility. He's too tight, too compressed.*

She put her hands behind her back and waited, watching carefully.

"How old are you?"

This was a question she usually found wise to evade. She tilted her head sidewise, smiling, a mannerism which gave her a wild and reckless look. "How old do you think I am?"

"Sixteen or seventeen."

"That's close enough."

He nodded. "Close enough. What's your name?"

"Jean Parlier."

"Whom do you live with?"

"No one. I live alone."

"Father? Mother?"

"Dead."

"Grandparents? Guardian?"

"I'm alone."

He nodded. "Any trouble with the law on that account?"

She considered him warily. "No."

He moved his head enough to send a kink running up the feather of smoke. "Take off your clothes."

"Why?"

"It's a quick way to check your qualifications."

"Well—yes. In a way I guess it is. . . . Physical or moral?"

He made no reply, sat looking at her impassively, the gray skein of smoke rising past his face.

She shrugged, put her hands to her sides, to her neck, to her waist, to her back, to her legs, and stood without clothes.

He put the cigarette to his mouth, puffed, sat up, stubbed it out, rose to his feet, walked slowly forward.

He's trying to scare me, she thought, and smiled quietly to herself. He could try.

He stopped two feet away, stood looking down into her eyes. "You really want a million dollars?"

"That's why I'm here."

"You took the advertisement in the literal sense of the words?"

"Is there any other way?"

"You might have construed the language as—metaphor, hyperbole."

She grinned, showing her sharp white teeth. "I don't know what those words mean. Anyway, I'm here. If the advertisement was only intended for you to look at me naked, I'll leave."

His expression did not change. Peculiar, thought Jean, how his body moved, his head turned, but his eyes always seemed fixed. He said as if he had not heard her, "Not too many girls have applied."

"That doesn't concern me. I want a million dollars. What is it? Blackmail? Impersonation?"

He passed over her question. "What would you do with a million if you had it?"

"I don't know. . . . I'll worry about that when I get it. Have you checked my qualifications? I'm cold."

He turned quickly, strode to the couch, seated himself. She slipped into her clothes, came over to the couch, took a tentative seat facing him.

He said dryly, "You fill the qualifications almost too well!"

"How so?"

"It's unimportant."

Jean tilted her head, laughed. She looked like a healthy, very pretty high-school girl who might be the better for more sunshine. "Tell me what I'm to do to earn a million dollars."

"You're to marry a wealthy young man, who suffers from —let us call it, an incurable disease. When he dies, his property will be yours. You will sell his property to me for a million dollars."

"Evidently he's worth more than a million dollars."

He was conscious of the questions she did not ask. "There's somewhere near a billion involved."

"What kind of disease does he have? I might catch it myself."

"I'll take care of the disease end. You won't catch it if you keep your nose clean."

"Oh—oh, I see—tell me more about him. Is he handsome? Big? Strong? I might feel sorry if he died."

"He's eighteen years old. His main interest is collecting." Sardonically: "He likes zoology too. He's an eminent zoologist. His name is Earl Abercrombie. He owns"—he gestured up—"Abercrombie Station."

Jean stared, then laughed feebly. "That's a hard way to make a million dollars . . . Earl Abercrombie. . . ."

"Squeamish?"

"Not when I'm awake. But I do have nightmares."

"Make up your mind."

She looked modestly to where she had folded her hands in her lap. "A million isn't a very large cut out of a billion."

He surveyed her with something like approval. "No, it isn't."

She rose to her feet, slim as a dancer. "All you do is sign a check. I have to marry him, get in bed with him."

"They don't use beds on Abercrombie Station."

"Since he lives on Abercrombie, he might not be interested in me."

"Earl is different," said the quiet man. "Earl likes gravity girls."

"You must realize that once he dies, you'd be forced to accept whatever I chose to give you. Or the property might be put in charge of a trustee."

"Not necessarily. The Abercrombie Civil Regulation allows property to be controlled by anyone sixteen or over. Earl is eighteen. He exercises complete control over the Station, subject to a few unimportant restrictions. I'll take care of that end." He went to the door, slid it open. "Hammond."

The man with the long face came wordlessly to the door. "I've got her. Send the others home."

He closed the door, turned to Jean. "I want you to have dinner with me."

"I'm not dressed for dinner."

"I'll send up the couturier. Try to be ready in an hour."

He left the room. The door closed. Jean stretched, threw back her head, opened her mouth in a soundless exultant laugh. She raised her arms over her head, took a step forward, turned a supple cartwheel across the rug, bounced to her feet beside the window.

She knelt, rested her head on her hands, looked across Metropolis. Dusk had come. The great gray-golden sky filled three-quarters of her vision. A thousand feet below was the wan gray, lavender and black crumble of surface buildings, the pallid roadways streaming with golden motes. To the right, aircraft slid silently along force-guides to the mountain suburbs—tired normal people bound to pleasant normal homes. What would they think if they knew that she, Jean Parlier, was watching? For instance, the man who drove that shiny Skyfarer with the pale green chevrets. . . . She built a picture of him: pudgy, forehead creased with lines of worry. He'd be hurrying home to his wife, who would listen tolerantly while he boasted or grumbled. Cattle-women, cow-women, thought Jean without rancor. What man could subdue her? Where was the man who was wild and hard and bright enough? . . . Remembering her new job, she grimaced. Mrs. Earl Abercrombie. She looked up into the sky. The stars were not yet out and the lights of Abercrombie Station could not be seen.

A million dollars, think of it! "What will you do with a million dollars?" her new employer had asked her, and now that she returned to it, the idea was uncomfortable, like a lump in her throat.

What would she feel? How would she. . . . Her mind moved away from the subject, recoiled with the faintest trace of anger, as if it were a subject not to be touched upon. "Rats," said Jean. "Time to worry about it after I get it. . . . A million dollars. Not too large a cut out of a billion, actually. Two million would be better." Her eyes followed a slim red airboat diving along a sharp curve into the parking area: a sparkling new Marshall Moon-Chaser. Now there was something she wanted. It would be one of her first purchases.

The door slid open. Hammond the doorkeeper looked in briefly. Then the couturier entered, pushing his wheeled kit before him, a slender little blond man with rich topaz eyes. The door closed.

Jean turned away from the window. The couturier—André was the name stenciled on the enamel of the box—spoke for more light, walked around her, darting glances up and down her body.

"Yes," he muttered, pressing his lips in and out. "Ah, yes. . . . Now what does the lady have in mind?"

"A dinner gown, I suppose."

He nodded. "Mr. Fotheringay mentioned formal evening wear."

So that was his name—Fotheringay.

André snapped up a screen. "Observe, if you will, a few of my effects; perhaps there is something to please you."

Models appeared on the screen, stepping forward, smiling, turning away.

Jean said, "Something like that."

André made a gesture of approval, snapped his fingers. "Mademoiselle has good taste. And now we shall see . . . if mademoiselle will let me help her. . . ."

He deftly unzipped her garments, laid them on the couch.

"First—we refresh ourselves." He selected a tool from his kit, and, holding her wrist between delicate thumb and forefinger, sprayed her arms with cool mist, then warm, perfumed air. Her skin tingled, fresh, invigorated.

André tapped his chin. "Now, the foundation."

She stood, eyes half closed, while he bustled around her, striding off, making whispered comments, quick gestures with significance only to himself.

He sprayed her with gray-green web, touched and pulled as the strands set. He adjusted knurled knobs at the ends of a flexible tube, pressed it around her waist, swept it away and it trailed shining black-green silk. He artfully twisted and wound his tube. He put the frame back in the kit, pulled, twisted, pinched, while the silk set.

He sprayed her with wan white, quickly jumped forward,

folded, shaped, pinched, pulled, bunched and the stuff fell in twisted bands from her shoulders and into a full rustling skirt.

"Now—gauntlets." He covered her arms and hands with warm black-green pulp which set into spangled velvet, adroitly cut with scissors to bare the back of her hand.

"Slippers." Black satin, webbed with emerald-green phosphorescence.

"Now—the ornaments." He hung a red bauble from her right ear, slipped a cabochon ruby on her right hand.

"Scent—a trace. The Levailleur, indeed." He flicked her with an odor suggestive of a Central Asia flower patch. "And mademoiselle is dressed. And may I say"—he bowed with a flourish—"most exquisitely beautiful."

He manipulated his cart, one side fell away. A mirror uncoiled upward.

Jean inspected herself. Vivid naiad. When she acquired that million dollars—two million would be better—she'd put André on her permanent payroll.

André was still muttering compliments. "—Elan supreme. She is magic. Most striking. Eyes will turn. . . ."

The door slid back. Fotheringay came into the room. André bowed low, clasped his hands.

Fotheringay glanced at her. "You're ready. Good. Come along."

Jean thought, *We might as well get this straight right now.* "Where?"

He frowned slightly, stood aside while André pushed his cart out.

Jean said, "I came here of my own free will. I walked into this room under my own power. Both times I knew where I was going. Now you say 'Come along.' First I want to know where. Then I'll decide whether or not I'll come."

"You don't want a million dollars very badly."

"Two million. I want it badly enough to waste an afternoon investigating. . . . But—if I don't get it today, I'll get it tomorrow. Or next week. Somehow I'll get it; a long time ago I made my mind up. So?" She performed an airy curtsy.

His pupils contracted. He said in an even voice, "Very well. Two million. I am now taking you to dinner on the roof, where I will give you your instructions."

2

They drifted under the dome, in a greenish plastic bubble. Below them spread the commercial fantasy of an outworld landscape: gray sward; gnarled red and green trees casting dramatic black shadows; a pond of fluorescent green liquid; panels of exotic blossoms; beds of fungus.

The bubble drifted easily, apparently at random, now high under the near-invisible dome, now low under the foliage. Successive courses appeared from the center of the table, along with chilled wine and frosted punch.

It was wonderful and lavish, thought Jean. But why should Fotheringay spend his money on her? Perhaps he entertained romantic notions. . . . She dallied with the idea, inspected him covertly. . . . The idea lacked conviction. He seemed to be engaging in none of the usual gambits. He neither tried to fascinate her with his charm, nor swamp her with synthetic masculinity. Much as it irritated Jean to admit it, he appeared—indifferent.

Jean compressed her lips. The idea was disconcerting. She essayed a slight smile, a side glance up under lowered lashes.

"Save it," said Fotheringay. "You'll need it all when you get up to Abercrombie."

Jean returned to her dinner. After a minute she said calmly, "I was—curious."

"Now you know."

Jean thought to tease him, draw him out. "Know what?"

"Whatever it was you were curious about."

"Pooh. Men are mostly alike. They all have the same button. Push it, they all jump in the same direction."

Fotheringay frowned, glanced at her under narrowed eyes. "Maybe you aren't so precocious after all."

Jean became tense. In a curious indefinable way, the subject was very important, as if survival were linked with confidence in her own sophistication and flexibility. "What do you mean?"

"You make the assumption most pretty girls make," he said with a trace of scorn. "I thought you were smarter than that."

Jean frowned. There had been little abstract thinking in her background. "Well, I've never had it work out differently. Although I'm willing to admit there are exceptions. . . . It's a kind of game. I've never lost. If I'm kidding myself, it hasn't made much difference so far."

Fotheringay relaxed. "You've been lucky."

Jean stretched out her arms, arched her body, smiled as if at a secret. "Call it luck."

"Luck won't work with Earl Abercrombie."

"You're the one who used the word luck. I think it's, well—ability."

"You'll have to use your brains too." He hesitated, then said, "Actually, Earl likes—odd things."

Jean sat looking at him, frowning.

He said coolly, "You're making up your mind how best to ask the question, 'What's odd about me?' "

Jean snapped, "I don't need you to tell me what's odd about me. I know what it is myself."

Fotheringay made no comment.

"I'm completely on my own," said Jean. "There's not a soul in all the human universe that I care two pins for. I do just exactly as I please." She watched him carefully. He nodded indifferently. Jean quelled her exasperation, leaned back in her chair, studied him as if he were in a glass case. . . . A strange young man. Did he ever smile? She thought of the Capellan Fibrates who by popular superstition were able to fix themselves along a man's spinal column and control his intelligence. Fotheringay displayed a coldness strange enough to suggest such a possession. . . . A Capellan could manipulate but one hand at a time. Fotheringay held a knife in one hand, a fork in the other and moved both hands together. So much for that.

He said quietly, "I watched your hands too."

Jean threw back her head and laughed—a healthy adolescent laugh. Fotheringay watched her without discernible expression.

She said, "Actually, you'd like to know about me, but you're too stiff-necked to ask."

"You were born at Angel City on Codiron," said Fotheringay. "Your mother abandoned you in a tavern, a gambler named Joe Parlier took care of you until you were ten, when you killed him and three other men and stowed away on the Gray Line Packet *Bucyrus*. You were taken to the Waif's Home at Paie on Bella's Pride. You ran away and the superintendent was found dead. . . . Shall I go on? There's five more years of it."

Jean sipped her wine, nowise abashed. "You've worked fast. . . . But you've misrepresented. You said, 'There's five years more of it, shall I go on?' as if you were able to go on. You don't know anything about the next five years."

Fotheringay's face changed by not a flicker. He said as if she had not spoken, "Now listen carefully. This is what you'll have to look out for."

"Go ahead. I'm all ears." She leaned back in her chair. A clever technique, ignoring an unwelcome situation as if it never existed. Of course, to carry it off successfully, a certain temperament was required. A cold fish like Fotheringay managed very well.

"Tonight a man named Webbard meets us here. He is chief steward at Abercrombie Station. I happen to be able to influence certain of his actions. He will take you up with him to Abercrombie and install you as a servant in the Abercrombie private chambers."

Jean wrinkled her nose. "Servant? Why can't I go to Abercrombie as a paying guest?"

"It wouldn't be natural. A girl like you would go up to Capricorn or *Verge*. Earl Abercrombie is extremely suspicious. He'd be certain to fight shy of you. His mother, old Mrs. Clara, watches him pretty closely, and keeps drilling into his head the idea that all the Abercrombie girls are after his money. As a servant you will have opportunity to meet him in intimate circumstances. He rarely leaves his study; he's absorbed in his collecting."

"My word," murmured Jean. "What does he collect?"

"Everything you can think of," said Fotheringay, moving his lips upward in a quick grimace, almost a smile. "I understand from Webbard, however, that he is rather romantic, and has carried on a number of flirtations among the girls of the Station."

Jean screwed up her mouth in fastidious scorn. Fotheringay watched her impassively.

"When do I—commence?"

"Webbard goes up on the supply barge tomorrow. You'll go with him."

A whisper of sound from the buzzer. Fotheringay touched the button. "Yes?"

"Mr. Webbard for you, sir."

Fotheringay directed the bubble down to the landing stage. Webbard was waiting; the fattest man Jean had ever seen.

The plaque on the door read, *Richard Mycroft, Attorney-at-Law.* Somewhere far back down the years, someone had said in Jean's hearing that Richard Mycroft was a good attorney.

The receptionist was a dark woman of about thirty-five, with a direct penetrating eye. "Do you have an appointment?"

"No," said Jean. "I'm in rather a hurry."

The receptionist hesitated a moment, then bent over the communicator. "A young lady—Miss Jean Parlier—to see you. New business."

"Very well."

The receptionist nodded to the door. "You can go in," she said shortly.

She doesn't like me, thought Jean. *Because I'm what she was and what she wants to be again.*

Mycroft was a square man with a pleasant face. Jean constructed a wary defense against him. If you liked someone and he knew it, he felt obligated to advise and interfere. She wanted no advice, no interference. She wanted two million dollars.

"Well, young lady," said Mycroft. "What can I do for you?"

He's treating me like a child, thought Jean. *Maybe I look like a child to him.* She said, "It's a matter of advice. I don't know much about fees. I can afford to pay you a hundred dollars. When you advise me a hundred dollars' worth, let me know and I'll go away."

"A hundred dollars buys a lot of advice," said Mycroft. "Advice is cheap."

"Not from a lawyer."

Mycroft became practical. "What are your troubles?"

"It's understood that this is all confidential?"

"Certainly." Mycroft's smile froze into a polite grimace.

"It's nothing illegal—so far as I'm concerned—but I don't want you passing out any quiet hints to—people that might be interested."

Mycroft straightened himself behind his desk. "A lawyer is expected to respect the confidence of his client."

"Okay. . . . Well, it's like this." She told him of Fotheringay, of Abercrombie Station and Earl Abercrombie. She said that Earl Abercrombie was sick with an incurable disease. She made no mention of Fotheringay's convictions on that subject. It was a matter she herself kept carefully brushing out of her mind. Fotheringay had hired her. He told her what to do, told her that Earl Abercrombie was sick. That was good enough for her. If she had asked too many questions, found that things were too nasty even for her stomach, Fotheringay would have found another girl less inquisitive. . . . She skirted the exact nature of Earl's disease. She didn't actually know herself. She didn't want to know.

Mycroft listened attentively, saying nothing.

"What I want to know is," said Jean, "is the wife sure to inherit on Abercrombie? I don't want to go to a lot of trouble for nothing. And after all Earl is under twenty-one; I thought that in the event of his death it was best to—well, make sure of everything first."

For a moment Mycroft made no move, but sat regarding her quietly. Then he tamped tobacco into a pipe.

"Jean," he said, "I'll give you some advice. It's free. No strings on it."

"Don't bother," said Jean. "I don't want the kind of advice that's free. I want the kind I have to pay for."

Mycroft grimaced. "You're a remarkably wise child."

"I've had to be. . . . Call me a child, if you wish."

"Just what will you do with a million dollars? Or two million, I understand it to be?"

Jean stared. Surely the answer was obvious . . . or was it? When she tried to find an answer, nothing surfaced.

"Well," she said vaguely, "I'd like an airboat, some nice clothes, and maybe. . . ." In her mind's eye she suddenly saw herself surrounded by friends. Nice people, like Mr. Mycroft.

"If I were a psychologist and not a lawyer," said Mycroft, "I'd say you wanted your mother and father more than you wanted two million dollars."

Jean became very heated. "No, no! I don't want them at all. They're dead." As far as she was concerned they were dead. They had died for her when they left her on Joe Parlier's pool table in the old Aztec Tavern.

Jean said indignantly, "Mr. Mycroft, I know you mean well, but tell me what I want to know."

"I'll tell you," said Mycroft, "because if I didn't, someone else would. Abercrombie property, if I'm not mistaken, is regulated by its own civil code. . . . Let's see—" He twisted in his chair, pushed buttons on his desk.

On the screen appeared the index to the Central Law Library. Mycroft made further selections, narrowing down selectively. A few seconds later he had the information. "Property control begins at sixteen. Widow inherits at minimum fifty, percent; the entire estate unless specifically stated otherwise in the will."

"Good," said Jean. She jumped to her feet. "That's what I wanted to make sure of."

Mycroft asked, "When do you leave?"

"This afternoon."

"I don't need to tell you that the idea behind the scheme is—not moral."

"Mr. Mycroft, you're a dear. But I don't have any morals."

He tilted his head, shrugged, puffed on his pipe. "Are you sure?"

"Well—yes." Jean considered a moment. "I suppose so. Do you want me to go into details?"

"No. I think what I meant to say was, are you sure you know what you want out of life?"

"Certainly. Lots of money."

Mycroft grinned. "That's really not a good answer. What will you buy with your money?"

Jean felt irrational anger rising in her throat. "Oh—lots of things." She rose to her feet. "Just what do I owe you, Mr. Mycroft?"

"Oh—ten dollars. Give it to Ruth."

"Thank you, Mr. Mycroft." She stalked out of his office.

As she marched down the corridor she was surprised to find that she was angry with herself as well as irritated with Mr. Mycroft. He had no right making people wonder about themselves. It wouldn't be so bad if she weren't wondering a little already.

But this was all nonsense. Two million dollars was two million dollars. When she was rich, she'd call on Mr. Mycroft and ask him if honestly he didn't think it was worth a few little lapses.

And today—up to Abercrombie Station. She suddenly became excited.

3

The pilot of the Abercrombie supply barge was emphatic. "No, sir, I think you're making a mistake, nice little girl like you."

He was a chunky man in his thirties, hard-bitten and positive. Sparse blond hair crusted his scalp, deep lines gave his mouth a cynical slant. Webbard, the Abercrombie chief steward, was billeted astern, in the special handling locker. The usual webbings were inadequate to protect his corpulence; he floated chin-deep in a tankful of emulsion the same specific gravity as his body.

There was no passenger cabin and Jean had slipped into the seat beside the pilot. She wore a modest white frock, a white toque, a gray-and-black-striped jacket.

The pilot had few good words for Abercrombie Station. "Now it's what I call a shame, taking a kid like you to serve the likes of them. . . . Why don't they get one of their own kind? Surely both sides would be the happier."

Jean said innocently, "I'm going up for only just a little bit."

"So you think. It's catching. In a year you'll be like the rest of them. The air alone is enough to sicken a person, rich and sweet like olive oil. Me, I never set foot outside the barge unless I can't help it."

"Do you think I'll be—safe?" She raised her lashes, turned him her reckless sidelong look.

He licked his lips, moved in his seat. "Oh, you'll be safe enough," he muttered. "At least from them that's been there a while. You might have to duck a few just fresh from Earth. . . . After they've lived on the Station a bit their ideas change, and they wouldn't spit on the best part of an Earth girl."

"Hmmph." Jean compressed her lips. Earl Abercrombie had been born on the Station.

"But I wasn't thinking so much of that," said the pilot. It was hard, he thought, talking straight sense to a kid so

young and inexperienced. "I meant in that atmosphere you'll
be apt to let yourself go. Pretty soon you'll look like the
rest of 'em—never want to leave. Some aren't *able* to leave
—couldn't stand it back on Earth if they wanted to."

"Oh—I don't think so. Not in my case."

"It's catching," said the pilot vehemently. "Look, kid—
I know. I've ferried out to all the stations, I've seen 'em
come and go. Each station has its own kind of weirdness,
and you can't keep away from it." He chuckled self-consciously. "Maybe that's why I'm so batty myself. . . . Now
take Madeira Station. Gay. Frou-frou." He made a mincing
motion with his fingers. "That's Madeira. You wouldn't know
much about that. . . . But take Balchester Aerie, take Merlin
Dell, take the Starhome—"

"Surely, some are just pleasure resorts?"

The pilot grudgingly admitted that of the twenty-two resort
satellites, fully half were as ordinary as Miami Beach. "But
the others—oh, Moses!" He rolled his eyes back. "And
Abercrombie is the worst."

There was silence in the cabin. Earth was a monstrous
green, blue, white and black ball over Jean's shoulder. The
sun made a furious hole in the sky below. Ahead were the
stars—and a set of blinking blue and red lights.

"Is that Abercrombie?"

"No, that's the Masonic Temple. Abercrombie is on out a
ways. . . ." He looked diffidently at her from the corner of
his eyes. "Now—look! I don't want you to think I'm fresh.
Or maybe I do. But if you're hard up for a job—why don't
you come back to Earth with me? I got a pretty nice shack
in Long Beach—nothing fancy—but it's on the beach, and
it'll be better than working for a bunch of sideshow freaks."

Jean said absently, "No thanks." The pilot pulled in his
chin, pulled his elbows close against his body, glowered.

An hour passed. From behind came a rattle, and a small
panel slid back. Webbard's pursy face showed through. The
barge was coasting on free momentum, gravity was negated.
"How much longer to the Station?"

"It's just ahead. Half an hour, more or less, and we'll be
fished up tight and right."

Webbard grunted, withdrew.

Yellow and green lights winked ahead. "That's Abercrombie," said the pilot. He reached out to a handle. "Brace

yourself." He pulled. Pale blue check-jets streamed out ahead.

From behind came a thump and an angry cursing. The pilot grinned. "Got him good." The jets roared a minute, died. "Every trip it's the same way. Now in a minute he'll stick his head through the panel and bawl me out."

The portal slid back. Webbard showed his furious face. "Why in thunder don't you warn me before you check? I just now took a blow that might have hurt me! You're not much of a pilot, risking injuries of that sort!"

The pilot said in a droll voice, "Sorry, sir, sorry indeed. Won't happen again."

"It had better not! If it does, I'll make it my business to see that you're discharged."

The portal snapped shut. "Sometimes I get him better than others," said the pilot. "This was a good one, I could tell by the thump."

He shifted in his seat, put his arm around Jean's shoulders, pulled her against him. "Let's have a little kiss, before we fish home."

Jean leaned forward, reached out her arm. He saw her face coming toward him—bright wonderful face, onyx, pale rose, ivory, smiling, hot with life. . . . She reached past him, thrust the check-valve. Four jets thrashed forward. The barge jerked. The pilot fell into the instrument panel, comical surprise written on his face.

From behind came a heavy resonant thump.

The pilot pulled himself back into his seat, knocked back the check-valve. Blood oozed from his chin, forming a little red wen. Behind them the portal snapped open. Webbard's face, black with rage, looked through.

When he had finally finished, and the portal had closed, the pilot looked at Jean, who was sitting quietly in her seat, the corners of her mouth drawn up dreamily.

He said from deep in his throat, "If I had you alone, I'd beat you half to death."

Jean drew her knees up under her chin, clasped her arms around and looked silently ahead.

Abercrombie Station had been built to the Fitch cylinder design: a power and service core, a series of circular decks, a transparent sheath. To the original construction a number of modifications and annexes had been added. An outside deck circled the cylinder, sheet steel to hold the magnetic grapples of small boats, cargo binds, magnetic shoes, anything which was to be fixed in place for a greater or lesser time. At each end of the cylinder, tubes connected to dependent constructions. The first, a sphere, was the private residence of the Abercrombies. The second, a cylinder, rotated at sufficient speed to press the water it contained evenly over its inner surface to a depth of ten feet; this was the Station swimming pool, a feature found on only three of the resort satellites.

The supply barge inched close to the dock, bumped. Four men attached constrictor tackle to rings in the hull, heaved the barge along to the supply port. The barge settled into its socket, grapples shot home, the ports sucked open.

Chief Steward Webbard was still smoldering, but now a display of anger was beneath his dignity. Disdaining magnetic shoes, he pulled himself to the entrance, motioned to Jean. "Bring your baggage."

Jean went to her neat little trunk, jerked it into the air, found herself floundering helpless in the middle of the cargo space. Webbard impatiently returned with magnetic clips for her shoes, and helped her float the trunk into the Station.

She was breathing different, rich air. The barge had smelled of ozone, grease, hemp sacking, but the Station. . . . Without consciously trying to identify the odor, Jean thought of waffles with butter and syrup mixed with talcum powder.

Webbard floated in front of her, an imposing spectacle. His fat no longer hung on him in folds; it ballooned out in an even perimeter. His face was smooth as a watermelon, and it seemed as if his features were incised, carved, rather than molded. He focused his eyes at a point above her dark head. "We had better come to an understanding, young lady."

"Certainly, Mr. Webbard."

"As a favor to my friend, Mr. Fotheringay, I have brought you here to work. Beyond this original and singular act, I am no longer responsible. I am not your sponsor. Mr. Fotheringay recommended you highly, so see that you give satisfaction. Your immediate superior will be Mrs. Blaiskell, and you must obey her implicitly. We have very strict rules here at Abercrombie—fair treatment and good pay—but you must earn it. Your work must speak for itself, and you can expect no special favors." He coughed. "Indeed, if I may say so, you are fortunate in finding employment here; usually we hire people more of our own sort, it makes for harmonious conditions."

Jean waited with demurely bowed head. Webbard spoke on further, detailing specific warnings, admonitions, injunctions.

Jean nodded dutifully. There was no point antagonizing pompous old Webbard. And Webbard thought that here was a respectful young lady, thin and very young and with a peculiar frenetic gleam in her eye, but sufficiently impressed by his importance. . . . Good coloring too. Pleasant features. If she only could manage two hundred more pounds of flesh on her bones, she might have appealed to his grosser nature.

"This way, then," said Webbard.

He floated ahead, and by some magnificent innate power continued to radiate the impression of inexorable dignity even while plunging headfirst along the corridor.

Jean came more sedately, walking on her magnetic clips, pushing the trunk ahead as easily as if it had been a paper bag.

They reached the central core, and Webbard, after looking back over his bulging shoulders, launched himself up the shaft.

Panes in the wall of the core permitted a view of the various halls, lounges, refectories, salons. Jean stopped by a room decorated with red plush drapes and marble statuary. She stared, first in wonder, then in amusement.

Webbard called impatiently, "Come along now, miss, come along."

Jean pulled herself away from the pane. "I was watching the guests. They looked like—" She broke into a sudden giggle.

Webbard frowned, pursed his lips. Jean thought he was about to demand the grounds for her merriment, but evidently he felt it beneath his dignity. He called, "Come along now, I can spare you only a moment."

She turned one last glance into the hall, and now she laughed aloud.

Fat women, like bladder-fish in an aquarium tank. Fat women, round and tender as yellow peaches. Fat women, miraculously easy and agile in the absence of gravity. The occasion seemed to be an afternoon musicale. The hall was crowded and heavy with balls of pink flesh draped in blouses and pantaloons of white, pale blue and yellow.

The current Abercrombie fashion seemed designed to accent the round bodies. Flat bands like Sam Browne belts molded the breasts down and out, under the arms. The hair was parted down the middle, skinned smoothly back to a small roll at the nape of the neck. Flesh, bulbs of tender flesh, smooth shiny balloons. Tiny twitching features, dancing fingers and toes, eyes and lips roguishly painted. On Earth any one of these women would have sat immobile, a pile of sagging sweating tissue. At Abercrombie Station— the so-called "Adipose Alley"—they moved with the ease of dandelion puffs, and their faces and bodies were smooth as butterballs.

"Come, come, come!" barked Webbard. "There's no loitering at Abercrombie!"

Jean restrained the impulse to slide her trunk up the core against Webbard's rotund buttocks, a tempting target.

He waited for her at the far end of the corridor.

"Mr. Webbard," she asked thoughtfully, "how much does Earl Abercrombie weigh?"

Webbard tilted his head back, glared reprovingly down his nose. "Such intimacies, miss, are not considered polite conversation here."

Jean said, "I merely wondered if he were as—well, imposing as you are."

Webbard sniffed. "I couldn't answer you. Mr. Abercrombie is a person of great competence. His—presence is a matter you must learn not to discuss. It's not proper, not done."

"Thank you, Mr. Webbard," said Jean meekly.

Webbard said, "You'll catch on. You'll make a good girl yet. Now, through the tube, and I'll take you to Mrs. Blaiskell."

Mrs. Blaiskell was short and squat as a kumquat. Her head was steel-gray, and skinned back modishly to the roll behind her neck. She wore tight black rompers, the uniform of the Abercrombie servants, so Jean was to learn.

Jean suspected that she made a poor impression on Mrs.

Blaiskell. She felt the snapping gray eyes search her from head to foot, and kept her own modestly downcast.

Webbard explained that Jean was to be trained as a maid, and suggested that Mrs. Blaiskell use her in the Pleasaunce and the bedrooms.

Mrs. Blaiskell nodded. "Good idea. The young master is peculiar, as everyone knows, but he's been pestering the girls lately and interrupting their duties; wise to have one in there such as her—no offense, miss, I just mean it's the gravity that does it—who won't be so apt to catch his eye."

Webbard signed to her, and they floated off a little distance, conversing in low whispers.

Jean's mouth quivered at the corners. Old fools!

Five minutes passed. Jean began to fidget. Why didn't they do something? Take her somewhere. She suppressed her restlessness. Life! How good, how zestful! She wondered, *Will I feel this same joy when I'm twenty? When I'm thirty, forty?* She drew back the corners of her mouth. *Of course I will! I'll never let myself change. . . . But life must be used to its best. Every flicker of ardor and excitement must be wrung free and tasted.* She grinned. Here she floated, breathing the overripe air of Abercrombie Station. In a way it was adventure. It paid well—two million dollars, and only for seducing an eighteen-year-old boy. Seducing him, marrying him—what difference? Of course he was Earl Abercrombie, and if he were as imposing as Mr. Webbard. . . . She considered Webbard's great body in wry speculation. Oh well, two million was two million. If things got too bad, the price might go up. Ten million, perhaps. Not too large a cut out of a billion.

Webbard departed without a word, twitching himself easily back down the core.

"Come," said Mrs. Blaiskell. "I'll show you your room. You can rest and tomorrow I'll take you around."

4

Mrs. Blaiskell stood by, frankly critical, while Jean fitted herself into black rompers. "Lord have mercy, but you mustn't pinch in the waist so! You're rachity and thin to starvation now, poor child; you mustn't point it up so! Perhaps we can find a few airfloats to fill you out; not that it's essential, Lord knows, since you're but a dust-maid. Still, it always improves a household to have a staff of pretty women, and young Earl, I will say this for him and all his oddness, he does appreciate a handsome woman. . . . Now then, your bosom, we must do something there; why, you're nearly flat! You see, there's no scope to allow a fine drape down under the arms, see?" She pointed to her own voluminous rolls of adipose. "Suppose we just roll up a bit of cushion and—"

"No," said Jean tremulously. Was it possible that they thought her so ugly? "I won't wear padding."

Mrs. Blaiskell sniffed. "It's your own self that's to benefit, my dear. I'm sure it's not me that's the wizened one."

Jean bent over her black slippers. "No, you're very sleek."

Mrs. Blaiskell nodded proudly. "I keep myself well shaped out, and all the better for it. It wasn't so when I was your age, miss, I'll tell you; I was on Earth then—"

"Oh, you weren't born here?"

"No, miss, I was one of the poor souls pressed and ridden by gravity, and I burned up my body with the effort of mere conveyance. No, I was born in Sydney, Australia, of decent kind folk, but they were too poor to buy me a place on Abercrombie. I was lucky enough to secure just such a position as you have, and that was while Mr. Justus and old Mrs. Eva, his mother—that's Earl's grandmother—was still with us. I've never been down to Earth since. I'll never set foot on the surface again."

"Don't you miss the festivals and great buildings and all the lovely countryside?"

"Pah!" Mrs. Blaiskell spat the word. "And be pressed into hideous folds and wrinkles? And ride in a cart, and be stared at and snickered at by the home people? Thin as sticks they are with their constant worry and fight against the pull of the soil! No, miss, we have our own sceneries and fetes; there's a pavanne for tomorrow night, a Grand Masque Pantomime, a Pageant of Beautiful Women, all in the month ahead. And best, I'm among my own people, the round ones, and I've never a wrinkle on my face. I'm fine and full-blown, and I wouldn't trade with any of them below."

Jean shrugged. "If you're happy, that's all that matters." She looked at herself in the mirror with satisfaction. Even if fat Mrs. Blaiskell thought otherwise, the black rompers looked well on her, now that she'd fitted them snug to her hips and waist. Her legs—slender, round and shining ivory —were good, this she knew. Even if weird Mr. Webbard and odd Mrs. Blaiskell thought otherwise. Wait till she tried them on young Earl. He preferred gravity girls; Fotheringay had told her so. And yet—Webbard and Mrs. Blaiskell had hinted otherwise. Maybe he liked both kinds . . .? Jean smiled, a little tremulously. If Earl liked both kinds, then he would like almost anything that was warm, moved and breathed. And that certainly included herself.

If she asked Mrs. Blaiskell outright, she'd be startled and shocked. Good proper Mrs. Blaiskell. A motherly soul, not like the matrons in the various asylums and waifs' homes of her experience. Strapping big women those had been—practical and quick with their hands. . . . But Mrs. Blaiskell was nice; she would never have deserted her child on a pool table. Mrs. Blaiskell would have struggled and starved herself to keep her child and raise her nicely. . . . Jean idly speculated how it would seem with Mrs. Blaiskell for a mother. And Mr. Mycroft for a father. It gave her a queer prickly feeling, and also somehow called up from deep inside a dark dull resentment tinged with anger.

Jean moved uneasily, fretfully. *Never mind the nonsense! You're playing a lone hand. What would you want with relatives? What an ungodly nuisance!* She would never have been allowed this adventure up to Abercrombie Station. . . . On the other hand, with relatives there would be many fewer problems on how to spend two million dollars.

Jean sighed. Her own mother wasn't kind and comfortable like Mrs. Blaiskell. She couldn't have been, and the whole matter became an academic question. *Forget it, put it clean out of your mind.*

Mrs. Blaiskell brought forward service shoes, worn to some extent by everyone at the Station: slippers with magnetic coils in the soles. Wires led to a power bank at the belt. By adjusting a rheostat, any degree of magnetism could be achieved.

"When a person works, she needs a footing," Mrs. Blaiskell explained. "Of course there's not much to do, once you get on to it. Cleaning is easy, with our good filters; still, there's sometimes a stir of dust and always a little film of oil that settles from the air."

Jean straightened up. "Okay, Mrs. B., I'm ready. Where do we start?"

Mrs. Blaiskell raised her eyebrows at the familiarity, but was not seriously displeased. In the main, the girl seemed to be respectful, willing and intelligent. And—significantly— not the sort to create a disturbance with Mr. Earl.

Twitching a toe against a wall, she propelled herself down the corridor, halted by a white door, slid back the panel.

They entered the room as if from the ceiling. Jean felt an instant of vertigo, pushing herself headfirst at what appeared to be a floor.

Mrs. Blaiskell deftly seized a chair, swung her body around, put her feet to the nominal floor. Jean joined her. They stood in a large round room, apparently a section across the building. Windows opened on space, stars shone in from all sides; the entire zodiac was visible with a sweep of the eyes.

Sunlight came up from below, shining on the ceiling, and off to one quarter hung the half-moon, hard and sharp as a new coin. The room was rather too opulent for Jean's taste. She was conscious of an overwhelming surfeit of mustard-saffron carpet, white paneling with gold arabesques, a round table clamped to the floor, surrounded by chairs footed with magnetic casters. A crystal chandelier thrust rigidly down; rotund cherubs peered at intervals from the angle between wall and ceiling.

"The Pleasaunce," said Mrs. Blaiskell. "You'll clean in here every morning first thing." She described Jean's duties in detail.

"Next we go to—" She nudged Jean. "Here's old Mrs. Clara, Earl's mother. Bow your head, just as I do."

A woman dressed in rose-purple floated into the room. She wore an expression of absentminded arrogance, as if in all the universe there were no doubt, uncertainty or equivocation. She was almost perfectly globular, as wide as she was tall. Her hair was silver-white, her face a bubble of smooth flesh, daubed apparently at random with rouge. She wore stones spread six inches down over her bulging bosom and shoulders.

Mrs. Blaiskell bowed her head unctuously. "Mrs. Clara,

dear, allow me to introduce the new parlor maid; she's new up from Earth and very handy."

Mrs. Clara Abercrombie darted Jean a quick look. "Emaciated creature."

"Oh, she'll healthen up," cooed Mrs. Blaiskell. "Plenty of good food and hard work will do wonders for her; after all, she's only a child."

"Mmmph. Hardly. It's blood, Blaiskell, and well you know it."

"Well, yes of course, Mrs. Clara."

Mrs. Clara continued in a brassy voice, darting glances around the room. "Either it's good blood you have or vinegar. This girl here, she'll never be really comfortable, I can see it. It's not in her blood."

"No, ma'am, you're correct in what you say."

"It's not in Earl's blood either. He's the one I'm worried for. Hugo was the rich one, but his brother Lionel after him, poor dear Lionel, and——"

"What about Lionel?" said a husky voice. Jean twisted. This was Earl. "Who's heard from Lionel?"

"No one, my dear. He's gone, he'll never be back. I was but commenting that neither one of you ever reached your growth, showing all bone as you do."

Earl scowled past his mother, past Mrs. Blaiskell, and his gaze fell on Jean. "What's this? Another servant? We don't need her. Send her away. Always ideas for more expense."

"She's for your rooms, Earl, my dear," said his mother.

"Where's Jessy? What was wrong with Jessy?"

Mrs. Clara and Mrs. Blaiskell exchanged indulgent glances. Jean turned Earl a slow arch look. He blinked, then frowned. Jean dropped her eyes, traced a pattern on the rug with her toe, an operation which she knew sent interesting movements along her leg. Earning the two million dollars wouldn't be as irksome as she had feared. Because Earl was not at all fat. He was stocky, solid, with bull shoulders and a bull neck. He had a close crop of tight blond curls, a florid complexion, a big waxy nose, a ponderous jaw. His mouth was good, drooping sullenly at the moment.

He was something less than attractive, thought Jean. On Earth she would have ignored him, or if he persisted, stung him to fury with a series of insults. But she had been expecting far worse: a bulbous creature like Webbard, a human balloon. . . . Of course there was no real reason for Earl to be fat; the children of fat people were as likely as not to be of normal size.

Mrs. Clara was instructing Mrs. Blaiskell for the day, Mrs. Blaiskell nodding precisely on each sixth word and ticking off points on her stubby little fingers.

Mrs. Clara finished, Mrs. Blaiskell nodded to Jean. "Come, miss, there's work to be done."

Earl called after them, "Mind now, no one in my study!"

Jean asked curiously, "Why doesn't he want anyone in his study?"

"That's where he keeps all his collections. He won't have a thing disturbed. Very strange sometimes, Mr. Earl. You'll just have to make allowances, and be on your good behavior. In some ways he's harder to serve than Mrs. Clara."

"Earl was born here?"

Mrs. Blaiskell nodded. "He's never been down to Earth. Says it's a place of crazy people, and the Lord knows, he's more than half right."

"Who are Hugo and Lionel?"

"They're the two oldest. Hugo is dead, Lord rest him, and Lionel is off on his travels. Then under Earl there's Harper and Dauphin and Millicent and Clarice. That's all Mrs. Clara's children, all very proud and portly. Earl is the skinny lad of the lot, and very lucky too, because when Hugo died, Lionel was off gadding and so Earl inherited. . . . Now here's his suite, and what a mess."

As they worked Mrs. Blaiskell commented on various aspects of the room. "That bed now! Earl wasn't satisfied with sleeping under a saddleband like the rest of us, no! He wears pajamas of magnetized cloth, and that weights him against the cushion almost as if he lived on Earth. . . . And this reading and studying, my word, there's nothing the lad won't think of! And his telescope! He'll sit in the cupola and focus on Earth by the hour."

"Maybe he'd like to visit Earth?"

Mrs. Blaiskell nodded. "I wouldn't be surprised if you were close on it there. The place has a horrid fascination for him. But he can't leave Abercrombie, you know."

"That's strange. Why not?"

Mrs. Blaiskell darted her wise look. "Because then he forfeits his inheritance; that's in the original charter, that the owner must remain on the premises." She pointed to a gray door. "That there's his study. And now I'm going to give you a peep in, so you won't be tormented by curiosity and perhaps make trouble for yourself when I'm not around to keep an eye open. . . . Now don't be excited by what you see; there's nothing to hurt you."

With the air of a priestess unveiling mystery, Mrs. Blaiskell fumbled a moment with the door-slive, manipulating it in a manner which Jean was not able to observe.

The door swung aside. Mrs. Blaiskell smirked as Jean jumped back in alarm.

"Now, now, now, don't be alarmed; I told you there was nothing to harm you. That's one of Master Earl's zoological specimens, and rare trouble and expense he's gone to—"

Jean sighed deeply, and gave closer inspection to the horned black creature which stood on two legs just inside the door, poised and leaning as if ready to embrace the intruder in leathery black arms.

"That's the most scary part," said Mrs. Blaiskell in quiet satisfaction. "He's got his insects and bugs there"—she pointed—"his gems there, his old music disks there, his stamps there, his books along that cabinet. Nasty things, I'm ashamed of him. Don't let me know of your peeking in them nasty books that Mr. Earl gloats over."

"No, Mrs. Blaiskell," said Jean meekly. "I'm not interested in that kind of thing. If it's what I think it is."

Mrs. Blaiskell nodded emphatically. "It's what you think it is and worse." She did not expand on the background of her familiarity with the library, and Jean thought it inappropriate to inquire.

Earl stood behind them. "Well?" he asked in a heavy sarcastic voice. "Getting an eyeful?" He kicked himself across the room, slammed shut the door.

Mrs. Blaiskell said in a conciliatory voice, "Now, Mr. Earl, I was just showing the new girl what to avoid, what not to look at, and I didn't want her swounding of heart stoppage if innocent-like she happened to peek inside."

Earl grunted. "If she peeps inside while I'm there, she'll be 'swounding' from something more than heart stoppage."

"I'm a good cook too," said Jean. She turned away. "Come, Mrs. Blaiskell, let's leave until Mr. Earl has recovered his temper. I won't have him hurting your feelings."

Mrs. Blaiskell stammered, "Now, then! Surely there's no harm. . . ." She stopped. Earl had gone into his study and slammed the door.

Mrs. Blaiskell's eyes glistened with thick tears. "Ah, my dear, I do so dislike harsh words. . . ."

They worked in silence and finished the bedroom. At the door Mrs. Blaiskell said confidentially into Jean's ears, "Why do you think Earl is so gruff and grumpy?"

"I've no idea," breathed Jean. "None whatever."

"Well," said Mrs. Blaiskell warily, "it all boils down to this: his appearance. He's so self-conscious of his thinness that he's all eaten up inside. He can't bear to have anyone see him; he thinks they're sneering. I've heard him tell Mrs. Clara so. Of course they're not; they're just sorry. He eats like a horse, he takes gland-pellets, but still he's that spindly and all hard tense muscle." She inspected Jean thoroughly. "I think we'll put you on the same kind of regimen, and see if we can't make a prettier woman out of you." Then she shook her head doubtfully, clicked her tongue. "It might not be in your blood, as Mrs. Clara says. I hardly can see that it's in your blood. . . ."

5

There were tiny red ribbons on Jean's slippers, a red ribbon in her hair, a coquettish black beauty spot on her cheek. She had altered her rompers so that they clung unobtrusively to her waist and hips.

Before she left the room she examined herself in the mirror. *Maybe it's me that's out of step! How would I look with a couple hundred more pounds of grade? No. I suppose not. I'm the gamin type. I'll look like a wolverine when I'm sixty, but for the next forty years—watch out.*

She took herself along the corridor, past the Pleasaunce, the music rooms, the formal parlor, the refectory, up into the bedrooms. She stopped by Earl's door, flung it open, entered, pushing the electrostatic duster ahead of her.

The room was dark; the transpar walls were opaque under the action of the scrambling field.

Jean found the dial, turned up the light.

Earl was awake. He lay on his side, his yellow magnetic pajamas pressing him into the mattress. A pale blue quilt was pulled up to his shoulders, his arm lay across his face. Under the shadow of his arm his eye smoldered out at Jean.

He lay motionless, too outraged to move.

Jean put her hands on her hips, said in her clear young voice, "Get up, you sluggard! You'll get as fat as the rest of them lounging around till all hours. . . ."

The silence was choked and ominous. Jean bent to peer under Earl's arm. "Are you alive?"

Without moving Earl said in a harsh low voice, "Exactly what do you thing you're doing?"

"I'm about my regular duties. I've finished the Pleasaunce. Next comes your room."

His eyes went to a clock. "At seven o'clock in the morning?"

"Why not? The sooner I get done, the sooner I can get to my own business."

"Your own business be damned. Get out of here, before you get hurt."

"No, sir. I'm a self-determined individual. Once my work is done, there's nothing more important than self-expression."

"Get out!"

"I'm an artist, a painter. Or maybe I'll be a poet this year. Or a dancer. I'd make a wonderful ballerina. Watch." She essayed a pirouette, but the impulse took her up to the ceiling—not ungracefully, this she made sure.

She pushed herself back. "If I had magnetic slippers I could twirl an hour and a half. Grand jetés are easy. . . ."

He raised himself on his elbow, blinking and glaring, as if on the verge of launching himself at her.

"You're either crazy—or so utterly impertinent as to amount to the same thing."

"Not at all," said Jean. "I'm very courteous. There might be a difference of opinion, but still it doesn't make you automatically right."

He slumped back on the bed. "Argue with old Webbard," he said thickly. "Now—for the last time—get out!"

"I'll go," said Jean, "but you'll be sorry."

"Sorry?" His voice had risen nearly an octave. "Why should I be sorry?"

"Suppose I took offense at your rudeness and told Mr. Webbard I wanted to quit?"

Earl said through tight lips, "I'm going to talk to Mr. Webbard today and maybe you'll be asked to quit. . . . Miraculous!" he told himself bitterly. "Scarecrow maids breaking in at sunup. . . ."

Jean stared in surprise. "Scarecrow! Me? On Earth I'm considered a very pretty girl. I can get away with things like this, disturbing people, because I'm pretty."

"This is Abercrombie Station," said Earl in a dry voice. "Thank God!"

"You're rather handsome yourself," said Jean tentatively.

Earl sat up, his face tinged with angry blood. "Get out of here!" he shouted. "You're discharged!"

"Pish," said Jean. "You wouldn't dare fire me."

"I wouldn't dare?" asked Earl in a dangerous voice. "Why wouldn't I dare?"

"Because I'm smarter than you are."

Earl made a husky sound in his throat. "And just what makes you think so?"

Jean laughed. "You'd be very nice, Earl, if you weren't so touchy."

"All right, we'll take that up first. Why am I so touchy?"

Jean shrugged. "I said you were nice-looking and you blew a skull-fuse." She waved away an imaginary fluff from the back of her hand. "I call that touchiness."

Earl wore a grim smile that made Jean think of Fotheringay. Earl might be tough if pushed far enough. But not as tough as—well, say Ansel Clellan. Or Fiorenzo. Or Party MacClure. Or Fotheringay. Or herself, for that matter.

He was staring at her, as if he were seeing her for the first time. This is what she wanted. "Why do you think you're smarter, then?"

"Oh, I don't know. . . . Are you smart?"

His glance darted off to the doors leading to his study; a momentary quiver of satisfaction crossed his face. "Yes, I'm smart."

"Can you play chess?"

"Of course I play chess," he said belligerently. "I'm one of the best chess players alive."

"I could beat you with one hand." Jean had played chess four times in her life.

"I wish you had something I wanted," he said slowly. "I'd take it away from you."

Jean gave him an arch look. "Let's play for forfeits."

"No!"

"Ha!" She laughed, eyes sparkling.

He flushed. "Very well."

Jean picked up her duster. "Not now, though." She had accomplished more than she had hoped for. She looked ostentatiously over her shoulder. "I've got to work. If Mrs. Blaiskell finds me here she'll accuse you of seducing me."

He snorted with twisted lips. He looked like an angry blond boar, thought Jean. But two million dollars was two million dollars. And it wasn't as bad as if he'd been fat. The idea had been planted in his mind. "You be thinking of the forfeit," said Jean. "I've got to work."

She left the room, turning him a final glance over her shoulder which she hoped was cryptic.

The servants' quarters were in the main cylinder, the Abercrombie Station proper. Jean sat quietly in a corner of the mess hall, watching and listening while the other servants had their elevenses: cocoa gobbed heavy with whipped cream, pastries, ice cream. The talk was high pitched, edgy. Jean wondered at the myth that fat people were languid and easygoing.

From the corner of her eye she saw Mr. Webbard float into the room, his face tight and gray with anger.

She lowered her head over her cocoa, watching him from under her lashes.

Webbard looked directly at her, his lips sucked in and his bulbous cheeks quivered. For a moment it seemed that he would drift at her, attracted by the force of his anger alone; somehow he restrained himself. He looked around the room until he spied Mrs. Blaiskell. A flick of his fingers sent him to where she sat at the end table, held by magnets appropriately fastened to her rompers.

He bent over her, muttered in her ear. Jean could not hear his words, but she saw Mrs. Blaiskell's face change and her eyes go seeking around the room.

Mr. Webbard completed his dramatization and felt better. He wiped the palms of his hands along the ample area of his dark blue corduroy trousers, twisted with a quick wriggle of his shoulders and sent himself to the door with a flick of his toe.

Marvelous, thought Jean, the majesty, the orbital massiveness of Webbard's passage through the air. The full moonface, heavy lidded, placid; the rosy cheeks, the chins and jowls puffed round and tumescent, glazed and oily, without blemish, mar or wrinkle; the hemisphere of the chest, then the bifurcate lower half, in the rich dark blue corduroy: the whole marvel coasting along with the inexorable momentum of an ore barge. . . .

Jean became aware that Mrs. Blaiskell was motioning to her from the doorway, making cryptic little signals with her fat fingers.

Mrs. Blaiskell was waiting in the little vestibule she called her office, her face scene to shifting emotions. "Mr. Webbard has given me some serious information," she said in a voice intended to be stern.

Jean displayed alarm. "About me?"

Mrs. Blaiskell nodded decisively. "Mr. Earl complained of some very strange behavior this morning. At seven o'clock or earlier. . . ."

Jean gasped. "Is it possible, that Earl has had the audacity to—"

"*Mr.* Earl," Mrs. Blaiskell corrected primly.

"Why, Mrs. Blaiskell, it was as much as my life was worth to get away from him!"

Mrs. Blaiskell blinked uneasily. "That's not precisely the way Mr. Webbard put it. He said you—"

"Does that sound reasonable? Is that likely, Mrs. B.?"

"Well—no," Mrs. Blaiskell admitted, putting her hand to her chin, and tapping her teeth with a fingernail. "Certainly it seems odd, come to consider a little more closely." She looked at Jean. "But how is it that—"

"He called me into his room, and then—" Jean had never been able to cry, but she hid her face in her hands.

"There, now," said Mrs. Blaiskell. "I never believed Mr. Webbard anyway. Did he—did he—" She found herself unable to phrase the question.

Jean shook her head. "It wasn't for want of trying."

"Just goes to show," muttered Mrs. Blaiskell. "And I thought he'd grown out of that nonsense."

" 'Nonsense'?" The word had been invested with a certain overtone that set it out of context.

Mrs. Blaiskell was embarrassed. She shifted her eyes.

"Earl has passed through several stages, and I'm not sure
which has been the most troublesome. . . . A year or two
ago—two years, because this was while Hugo was still alive
and the family was together—he saw so many Earth films
that he began to admire Earth women, and it had us all
worried. Thank heaven, he's completely thrown off that un-
wholesomeness, but it's gone to make him all the more shy
and self-conscious." She sighed. "If only one of the pretty
girls of the Station would love him for himself, for his
brilliant mind . . . but no, they're all romantic and they're
more taken by a rich round body and fine flesh, and poor
gnarled Earl is sure that when one of them does smile his
way she's after his money, and very likely true, so I say!"
She looked at Jean speculatively. "It just occurred to me that
Earl might be veering back to his old—well, strangeness.
Not that you're not a nice well-meaning creature, because
you are."

Well, well, thought Jean dispiritedly. Evidently she had
achieved not so much this morning as she had hoped. But
then, every campaign had its setbacks.

"In any event, Mr. Webbard has asked that I give you
different duties, to keep you from Mr. Earl's sight, because
he's evidently taken an antipathy to you. . . . And after this
morning I'm sure you'll not object."

"Of course not," said Jean absently. Earl, that bigoted,
warped, wretch of a boy!

"For today, you'll just watch the Pleasaunce and service
the periodicals and water the atrium plants. Tomorrow—well,
we'll see."

Jean nodded and turned to leave. "One more thing," said
Mrs. Blaiskell in a hesitant voice. Jean paused. Mrs. Blaiskell could not seem to find the right words.

They came in a sudden surge, all strung together. "Be a
little careful of yourself, especially when you're alone near
Mr. Earl. This is Abercrombie Station, you know, and he's
Earl Abercrombie, and the High Justice, and some very
strange things happen. . . ."

Jean said in a shocked whisper, "Physical violence, Mrs.
Blaiskell?"

Mrs. Blaiskell stammered and blushed. "Yes, I suppose
you'd call it that. . . . Some very disgraceful things have
come to light. Not nice, though I shouldn't be saying it to

you, who's only been with us a day. But, be careful. I wouldn't want your soul on my conscience."

"I'll be careful," said Jean in a properly hushed voice.

Mrs. Blaiskell nodded her head, an indication that the interview was at an end.

Jean returned to the refectory. It was really very nice for Mrs. Blaiskell to worry about her. It was almost as if Mrs. Blaiskell were fond of her. Jean sneered automatically. That was too much to expect. Women always disliked her because their men were never safe when Jean was near. Not that Jean consciously flirted—at least, not always—but there was something about her that interested men, even the old ones. They paid lip-service to the idea that Jean was a child, but their eyes wandered up and down, the way a young man's eyes wandered.

But out here on Abercrombie Station it was different. Ruefully Jean admitted that no one was jealous of her, no one on the entire Station. It was the other way around; she was regarded as an object for pity. But it was still nice of Mrs. Blaiskell to take her under her wing; it gave Jean a pleasant warm feeling. Maybe if and when she got hold of that two million dollars—and her thoughts went to Earl. The warm feeling drained from her mind.

Earl, hoity-toity Earl, was ruffled because she had disturbed his rest. So bristle-necked Earl thought she was gnarled and stunted! Jean pulled herself to the chair. Seating herself with a thump, she seized up her bulb of cocoa and sucked at the spout.

Earl! She pictured him: the sullen face, the kinky blond hair, the overripe mouth, the stocky body he so desperately yearned to fatten. This was the man she must inveigle into matrimony. On Earth, on almost any other planet in the human universe, it would be child's play—

This was Abercrombie Station!

She sipped her cocoa, considering the problem. The odds that Earl would fall in love with her and come through with a legitimate proposal seemed slim. Could he be tricked into a position where in order to save face or reputation he would be forced to marry her? Probably not. At Abercrombie Station, she told herself, marriage with her represented almost the ultimate loss of face. Still, there were avenues to be explored. Suppose she beat Earl at chess, could she make marriage the forfeit? Hardly. Earl would be too sly and dishonorable to pay up. It was necessary to make him *want* to marry her, and that would entail making herself desirable in his eyes, which in turn made necessary a revision of Earl's whole outlook. To begin with, he'd have to feel that his own person was not entirely loathsome (although it was). Earl's morale must be built up to a point where he felt himself superior to the rest of Abercrombie Station, and where he would be proud to marry one of his own kind.

A possibility at the other pole: if Earl's self-respect were so utterly blasted and reduced, if he could be made to feel so despicable and impotent that he would be ashamed to show his face outside his room, he might marry her as the best bet in sight. . . . And still another possibility: revenge. If Earl realized that the fat girls who flattered him were actually ridiculing him behind his back, he might marry her from sheer spite.

One last possibility. Duress. Marriage or death. She considered poisons and antidotes, diseases and cures, a straightforward gun in the ribs. . . .

Jean angrily tossed the empty cocoa bulb into the waste hopper. Trickery, sex lure, flattery, browbeating, revenge, fear—which was the most farfetched? All were ridiculous.

She decided she needed more time, more information. Perhaps Earl had a weak spot she could work on. If they had a community of interests, she'd be much further advanced. Examination of his study might give her a few hints.

A bell chimed, a number dropped on a call-board and a voice said, "Pleasaunce."

Mrs. Blaiskell appeared. "That's you, miss. Now go in, nice as you please, and ask Mrs. Clara what it is that's wanted, and then you can go off duty till three."

6

Mrs. Clara Abercrombie, however, was not present. The Pleasaunce was occupied by twenty or thirty young folk, talking and arguing with rather giddy enthusiasm. The girls wore pastel satins, velvets, gauzes, tight around their rotund pink bodies, with frothy little ruffles and anklets, while the young men affected elegant dark grays and blues and tawny beiges, with military trim of white and scarlet.

Ranged along a wall were a dozen stage settings in miniature. Above, a ribbon of paper bore the words: *Pandora in Elis. Libretto by A. Percy Stevanic, music by Colleen O'Casey.*

Jean looked around the room to see who had summoned her. Earl raised his finger peremptorily. Jean walked on her magnetic shoes to where he floated near one of the miniature stage sets. He turned to a mess of cocoa and whipped cream, clinging like a tumor to the side of the set—evidently a broken bulb.

"Clean up that spill," Earl said in a flinty voice.

Jean thought, *He half wants to rub it in, half wants to act as if he doesn't recognize me.* She nodded dutifully. "I'll get a container and a sponge."

When she returned, Earl was across the room talking earnestly to a girl whose globular body was encased in a gown of brilliant rose velvet. She wore rosebuds over each ear and played with a ridiculous little white dog, while she listened to Earl with a halfhearted affection of interest.

Jean worked as slowly as possible, watching from the corners of her eyes. Snatches of conversation reached her: "Lapwill's done simply a marvelous job on the editing, but I don't see that he's given Myras the same scope—" "If the pageant grosses ten thousand dollars, Mrs. Clara says she'll put another ten thousand toward the construction fund. Think of it! a Little Theater all our own!" Excited and conspiratorial whispers ran through the Pleasaunce, "—and for the water scene why not have the chorus float across the sky as moons?"

Jean watched Earl. He hung on the fat girl's words, and spoke with a pathetic attempt at intimate comradeship and jocularity. The girl nodded politely, twisted up her features into a smile. Jean noticed her eyes followed a hearty youth whose physique bulged out his plum-colored breeches like wind bellying a spinnaker. Earl perceived the girl's inattention. Jean saw him falter momentarily, then work even harder at his badinage. The fat girl licked her lips, swung her ridiculous little dog on its leash, and glanced over to where the purple-trousered youth bellowed with laughter.

A sudden idea caused Jean to hasten her work. Earl no

doubt would be occupied here until lunchtime—two hours away. And Mrs. Blaiskell had relieved her from duty till three.

She took herself from the hall, disposed of the cleaning equipment, dived up the corridor to Earl's private chambers. At Mrs. Clara's suite she paused, listening at the door. Snores!

Another fifty feet to Earl's chambers. She looked quickly up and down the corridor, slid back the door and slipped cautiously inside.

The room was silent as Jean made a quick survey. Closet, dressing room to one side, sun-flooded bathroom to the other. Across the room was the tall gray door into the study. A sign hung upon the door, apparently freshly made:

PRIVATE.   DANGER.   DO NOT ENTER.

Jean paused to consider. What kind of danger? Earl might have set devious safeguards over his private chamber.

She examined the door-slide button. It was overhung by an apparently innocent guard—which might or might not control an alarm circuit. She pressed her belt-buckle against the shutter in such a way as to maintain an electrical circuit, then moved the guard aside, pressed the button with her fingernail—gingerly. She knew of buttons which darted out hypodermics when pressed.

There was no whisper of machinery. The door remained in place.

Jean blew fretfully between her teeth. No keyhole, no buttons to play a combination on. . . . Mrs. Blaiskell had found no trouble. Jean tried to reconstruct her motions. She moved to the slide, set her head to where she could see the reflection of the light from the wall. . . . There was a smudge on the gloss. She looked closely and a telltale glint indicated a photoelectric eye.

She put her finger on the eye, pressed the slide-button. The door slipped open. In spite of having been forewarned, Jean recoiled from the horrid black shape which hung forward as if to grapple her.

She waited. After a moment the door fell gently back into place.

Jean returned to the outer corridor, stationed herself

where she could duck into Mrs. Clara's apartments if a suspicious shape came looming up the corridor. Earl might not have contented himself with the protection of a secret electric lock.

Five minutes passed. Mrs. Clara's personal maid passed by, a globular little Chinese, eyes like two shiny black beetles, but no one else.

Jean pushed herself back to Earl's room, crossed to the study door. Once more she read the sign:

PRIVATE.   DANGER.   DO NOT ENTER.

She hesitated. "I'm sixteen years old. Going on seventeen. Too young to die. It's just like that odd creature to furnish his study with evil tricks." She shrugged off the notion. "What a person won't do for money."

She opened the door, slipped through.

The door closed behind her. Quickly she moved out from under the poised demon-shape and turned to examine Earl's sanctum. She looked right, left, up, down.

"There's a lot to see here," she muttered. "I hope Earl doesn't run out of sheep's-eyes for his fat girl, or decide he wants a particular newspaper clipping. . . ."

She turned power into her slipper magnets, and wondered where to begin. The room was more like a warehouse or museum than a study, and gave the impression of wild confusion arranged, sorted, and filed by an extraordinary finicky mind.

After a fashion, it was a beautiful room, imbued with an atmosphere of erudition in its dark wood-tones. The far wall glowed molten with rich color—a rose window from the old Chartres cathedral, in full effulgence under the glare of free-space sunlight.

"Too bad Earl ran out of outside wall," said Jean. "A collection of stained glass windows runs into a lot of wall-space, and one is hardly a collection. . . . Perhaps there's another room. . . ." For the study, large as it was, apparently occupied only half the space permitted by the dimensions of Earl's suite. "But—for the moment—I've got enough here to look at."

Racks, cases, files, walnut-and-leaded-glass cabinets surfaced the walls; glass-topped displays occupied the floor. To her left was a battery of tanks. In the first series swam eels, hundreds of eels: Earth eels, eels from the outer worlds. She opened a cabinet. Chinese coins hung on pegs, each documented with crabbed boyish handwriting.

She circled the room, marveling at the profusion.

There were rock crystals from forty-two separate planets, all of which appeared identical to Jean's unpracticed eye.

There were papyrus scrolls, Mayan codices, medieval parchments illuminated with gold and Tyrian purple, Ogham runes on moldering sheepskin, clay cylinders incised with cuneiform.

Intricate wood carvings—fancy chains, cages within cages, amazing interlocking spheres, seven vested Brahmin temples.

Centimeter cubes containing samples of every known element. Thousands of postage stamps, mounted on leaves, swung out of a circular cabinet.

There were volumes of autographs of famous criminals, together with their photographs and Bertillon and Pevetsky measurements. From one corner came the rich aromas of perfumes—a thousand little flagons minutely described and coded, together with the index and code explanation, and these again had their origin on a multitude of worlds. There were specimens of fungus growths from all over the universe, and there were racks of miniature phonograph records, an inch across, microformed from the original pressings.

She found photographs of Earl's everyday life, together with his weight, height and girth measurement in crabbed handwriting, and each picture bore a colored star, a colored square and either a red or blue disk. By this time Jean knew the flavor of Earl's personality. Near at hand there would be an index and explanation. She found it, near the camera which took the pictures. The disks referred to bodily functions; the stars, by a complicated system she could not quite comprehend, described Earl's morale, his frame of mind. The colored squares recorded his love life. Jean's mouth twisted in a wry grin. She wandered aimlessly on, fingering the physiographic globes of a hundred planets and examining maps and charts.

The cruder aspects of Earl's personality were represented in a collection of pornographic photographs, and near at hand an easel and canvas where Earl was composing a lewd study of his own. Jean pursed her mouth primly. The prospect of marrying Earl was becoming infinitely less enchanting.

She found an alcove filled with little chessboards, each set up in a game. A numbered card and record of moves was attached to each board. Jean picked up the inevitable index book and glanced through. Earl played postcard chess with opponents all over the universe. She found his record of wins and losses. He was slightly but not markedly a winner. One man, William Angelo of Toronto, beat him consistently. Jean memorized the address, reflecting that if Earl ever took up her challenge to play chess, now she knew how to beat him. She would embroil Angelo in a game, and send Earl's moves to Angelo as her own and play Angelo's return moves against Earl. It would be somewhat circuitous and tedious, but foolproof—almost.

She continued her tour of the study. Seashells, moths, dragonflies, fossil trilobites, opals, torture implements, shrunken human heads. If the collection represented bona fide learning, thought Jean, it would have taxed the time and ability of any four Earth geniuses. But the hoard was essentially mindless and mechanical, nothing more than a boy's collection of college pennants or signs or match-box covers on a vaster scale.

One of the walls opened out into an ell, and here was communication via a freight hatch to outside space. Unopened boxes, crates, cases, bundles—apparently material as yet to be filed in Earl's rookery—filled the room. At the corner another grotesque and monumental creature hung poised, as if to clutch at her, and Jean felt strangely hesitant to wander within its reach. This one stood about eight feet tall. It wore the shaggy coat of a bear and vaguely resembled a gorilla, although the face was long and pointed, peering out from under the fur, like that of a French poodle.

Jean thought of Fotheringay's reference to Earl as an "eminent zoologist." She looked around the room. The stuffed animals, the tanks of eels, Earth tropical fish and Maniacan polywriggles were the only zoological specimens in sight. Hardly enough to qualify Earl as a zoologist. Of course, there was an annex to the room. . . . She heard a sound. A click at the outer door.

Jean dived behind the stuffed animal, heart thudding in

her throat. With exasperation she told herself, *He's an eigh-teen-year-old boy. . . . If I can't face him down, out-argue, out-think, out-fight him, and come out on top generally, then it's time for me to start crocheting table mats for a living.* Nevertheless, she remained hidden.

Earl stood quietly in the doorway. The door swung shut behind him. His face was flushed and damp, as if he had just recovered from anger or embarrassment. His delft-blue eyes gazed unseeingly down the roof, gradually came into focus.

He frowned, glanced suspiciously right and left, sniffed. Jean made herself small behind the shaggy fur. Could he smell her?

He coiled up his legs, kicked against the wall, dived directly toward her. Under the creature's arm she saw him approaching, bigger, bigger, bigger, arms at his sides, head turned up like a diver. He thumped against the hairy chest, put his feet to the ground, stood not six feet distant.

He was muttering under his breath. She heard him plainly. "Damnable insult. . . . If she only *knew! Hah!*" He laughed a loud scornful bark. "*Hah!*"

Jean relaxed with a near-audible sigh. Earl had not seen her, and did not suspect her presence.

He whistled aimlessly between his teeth, indecisively. At last he walked to the wall, reached behind a bit of ornate fretwork. A panel swung aside, a flood of bright sunlight poured through the opening into the study.

Earl was whistling a tuneless cadence. He entered the room but did not shut the door. Jean darted from behind her hiding place, looked in, swept the room with her eyes. Possibly she gasped.

Earl was standing six feet away, reading from a list. He looked up suddenly, and Jean felt the brush of his eyes.

He did not move. . . . Had he seen her?

For a moment he made no sound, no stir. Then he came to the door, stood staring up the study and held this position for ten or fifteen seconds. From behind the stuffed gorilla-thing Jean saw his lips move, as if he were silently calculating.

She licked her lips, thinking of the inner room.

He went out into the alcove, among the unopened boxes and bales. He pulled up several, floated them toward the open door, and they drifted into the flood of sunshine. He pushed other bundles aside, found what he was seeking, and sent another bundle after the rest.

He pushed himself back to the door, where he stood suddenly tense, nose dilated, eyes keen, sharp. He sniffed the air. His eyes swung to the stuffed monster. He approached it slowly, arms hanging loose from his shoulders.

He looked behind, expelled his breath in a long drawn hiss, grunted. From within the annex Jean thought, *He can either smell me, or it's telepathy!* She had darted into the room while Earl was fumbling among the crates, and ducked under a wide divan. Flat on her stomach she watched Earl's inspection of the stuffed animal, and her skin tingled. *He smells me, he feels me, he senses me.*

Earl stood in the doorway, looking up and down the study. Then he carefully, slowly, closed the door, threw a bolt home, turned to face into the inner room.

For five minutes he busied himself with his crates, unbundling, arranging the contents, which seemed to be bottles of white powder, on shelves.

Jean pushed herself clear of the floor, up against the underside of the divan and moved to a position where she could see without being seen. Now she understood why Fotheringay had spoken of Earl as an "eminent zoologist."

There was another word which would fit him better, an unfamiliar word which Jean could not immediately dredge out of her memory. Her vocabulary was no more extensive than any girl of her own age, but the word had made an impression.

Teratology. That was the word. Earl was a teratologist.

Like the objects in his other collections, the monsters were only such creatures as lent themselves to ready, almost haphazard collecting. They were displayed in glass cabinets. Panels at the back screened off the sunlight, and at absolute zero, the things would remain preserved indefinitely without taxidermy or embalming.

They were a motley, though monstrous group. There were true human monsters, macro- and micro-cephalics, hermaphrodites, creatures with multiple limbs and with none, creatures sprouting tissues like buds on a yeast cell, twisted hoop-men, faceless things, things green, blue and gray.

And then there were other specimens equally hideous, but

possibly normal in their own environment: the miscellany of a hundred life-bearing planets.

To Jean's eyes, the ultimate travesty was a fat man, displayed in a place of prominence! Possibly he had gained the conspicuous position on his own merits. He was corpulent to a degree Jean had not considered possible. Beside him Webbard might show active and athletic. Take this creature to Earth, he would slump like a jellyfish. Out here on Abercrombie he floated free, bloated and puffed like the throat of a singing frog! Jean looked at his face—looked again! Tight blond curls on his head. . . .

Earl yawned, stretched. He proceeded to remove his clothes. Stark naked he stood in the middle of the room. He looked slowly, sleepily along the ranks of his collection.

He made a decision, moved languidly to one of the cubicles. He pulled a switch.

Jean heard a faint musical hum, a hissing, smelled heady ozone. A moment passed. She heard a sigh of air. The inner door of a glass cubicle opened. The creature within, moving feebly, drifted out into the room. . . .

Jean pressed her lips tight together; after a moment looked away.

Marry Earl? She winced. *No, Mr. Fotheringay. You marry him yourself, you're as able as I am. . . . Two million dollars?* She shuddered. Five million sounded better. For five million she might marry him. But that's as far as it would go. She'd put on her own ring, there'd be no kissing of the bride. She was Jean Parlier, no plaster saint. But enough was enough, and this was too much.

7

Presently Earl left the room. Jean lay still, listened. No sound came from outside. She must be careful. Earl would surely kill her if he found her here. She waited five minutes. No sound, no motion reached her. Cautiously she edged herself out from under the divan.

The sunlight burned her skin with a pleasant warmth, but she hardly felt it. Her skin seemed stained; the air seemed tainted and soiled her throat, her lungs. She wanted a bath. . . . Five million dollars would buy lots of baths. Where was the index? Somewhere would be an index. There had to be an index. . . . Yes. She found it, and quickly consulted the proper entry. It gave her much meat for thought.

There was also an entry describing the revitalizing mechanism. She glanced at it hurriedly, understanding little. Such things existed, she knew. Tremendous magnetic fields streamed through the protoplasm, gripping and binding tight each individual atom, and when the object was kept at absolute zero, energy expenditure dwindled to near-nothing. Switch off the clamping field, kick the particles back into motion with a penetrating vibration, and the creature returned to life.

She returned the index to its place, pushed herself to the door.

No sound came from outside. Earl might be writing or coding the events of the day on his phonogram. . . . Well, so then? She was not helpless. She opened the door, pushed boldly through.

The study was empty!

She dived to the outer door, listened. A faint sound of running water reached her ears. Earl was in the shower. This would be a good time to leave.

She pressed the door-slide. The door snapped open. She stepped out into Earl's bedroom, pushed herself across to the outer door.

Earl came out of the bathroom, his stocky fresh-skinned torso damp with water.

He stood stock-still, then hastily draped a towel around his middle. His face suddenly went mottled red and pink. "What are you doing in here?"

Jean said sweetly, "I came to check on your linen, to see if you needed towels."

He made no answer, but stood watching her. He said harshly, "Where have you been this last hour?"

Jean made a flippant gesture. "Here, there. Were you looking for me?"

He took a stealthy step forward. "I've a good mind to—"

"To what?" Behind her she fumbled for the door-slide.

"To—"

The door opened.

"Wait," said Earl. He pushed himself forward.

Jean slipped out into the corridor, a foot ahead of Earl's hands.

"Come back in," said Earl, making a clutch for her.

From behind them Mrs. Blaiskell said in a horrified voice, "Well, I never! Mr. Earl!" She had appeared from Mrs. Clara's room.

Earl backed into his room hissing unvoiced curses. Jean looked in after him. "The next time you see me, you'll wish you'd played chess with me."

"Jean!" barked Mrs. Blaiskell.

Earl asked in a hard voice, "What do you mean?"

Jean had no idea what she meant. Her mind raced. Better keep her ideas to herself. "I'll tell you tomorrow morning." She laughed mischievously. "About six or six-thirty."

"Miss Jean!" cried Mrs. Blaiskell angrily. "Come away from that door this instant!"

Jean calmed herself in the servants' refectory with a pot of tea.

Webbard came in, fat, pompous and fussy as a hedgehog. He spied Jean and his voice rose to a reedy oboe tone. "Miss, miss!"

Jean had a trick she knew to be effective, thrusting out her firm young chin, squinting, charging her voice with metal. "Are you looking for me?"

Webbard said, "Yes, I certainly am. Where on earth—"

"Well, I've been looking for you. Do you want to hear what I'm going to tell you in private or not?"

Webbard blinked. "Your tone of voice is impudent, miss. If you please—"

"Okay," said Jean. "Right here, then. First of all, I'm quitting. I'm going back to Earth. I'm going to see—"

Webbard held up his hand in alarm, looked around the refectory. Conversation along the tables had come to a halt. A dozen curious eyes were watching.

"I'll interview you in my office," said Webbard.

The door slid shut behind her. Webbard pressed his rotundity into a chair; magnetic strands in his trousers held him in place. "Now, what is all this? I'll have you know there've been serious complaints."

Jean said disgustedly, "Tie a can to it, Webbard. Talk sense."

Webbard was thunderstruck. "You're an impudent minx!"

"Look. Do you want me to tell Earl how I landed the job?"

Webbard's face quivered. His mouth fell open; he blinked four or five times rapidly. "You wouldn't dare to—"

Jean said patiently, "Forget the master-slave routine for five minutes, Webbard. This is man-to-man talk."

"What do you want?"

"I've a few questions I want to ask you."

"Well?"

"Tell me about old Mr. Abercrombie, Mrs. Clara's husband."

"There's nothing to tell. Mr. Justus was a very distinguished gentleman."

"He and Mrs. Clara had how many children?"

"Seven."

"And the oldest inherits the Station?"

"The oldest, always the oldest. Mr. Justus believed in firm organization. Of course the other children were guaranteed a home here at the Station, those who wished to stay."

"And Hugo was the oldest. How long after Mr. Justus did he die?"

Webbard found the conversation distasteful. "This is all footling nonsense," he growled in a deep voice.

"How long?"

"Two years."

"And what happened to him?"

Webbard said briskly, "He had a stroke. Cardiac complaint. Now, what's all this I hear about your quitting?"

"How long ago?"

"Ah—two years."

"And then Earl inherited?"

Webbard pursed his lips. "Mr. Lionel unfortunately was off the Station, and Mr. Earl became legal master."

"Rather nice timing, from Earl's viewpoint."

Webbard puffed out his cheeks. "Now then, young lady, we've had enough of that! If—"

"Mr. Webbard, let's have an understanding once and for all. Either you answer my questions and stop this blustering or I'll ask someone else. And when I'm done, that someone else will be asking you questions too."

"You insolent little trash!" snarled Webbard.

Jean turned toward the door. Webbard grunted, thrashed

himself forward. Jean gave her arm a shake; out of nowhere a blade of quivering glass appeared in her hand.

Webbard floundered in alarm, trying to halt his motion through the air. Jean put up her foot, pushed him in the belly, back toward his chair.

She said, "I want to see a picture of the entire family."

"I don't have any such pictures."

Jean shrugged. "I can go to any public library and dial the Who's-Who." She looked him over coolly, as she coiled her knife. Webbard shrank back in his chair. Perhaps he thought her a homicidal maniac. Well, she wasn't a maniac and she wasn't homicidal either, unless she was driven to it. She asked easily, "Is it a fact that Earl is worth a billion dollars?"

Webbard snorted. "A billion dollars? Ridiculous! The family owns nothing but the Station and lives off the income. A hundred million dollars would build another twice as big and luxurious."

"Where did Fotheringay get that figure?" she asked wonderingly.

"I couldn't say," Webbard replied shortly.

"Where is Lionel now?"

Webbard pulled his lips in and out desperately. "He's— resting somewhere along the Riviera."

"Hm. . . . You say you don't have any photographs?"

Webbard scratched his chin. "I believe that there's a shot of Lionel. . . . Let me see. . . . Yes, just a moment." He fumbled in his desk, pawed and peered, and at last came up with a snapshot. "Mr. Lionel."

Jean examined the photograph with interest. "Well, well." The face in the photograph and the face of the fat man in Earl's zoological collection were the same. "Well, well." She looked up sharply. "And what's his address?"

"I'm sure I don't know," Webbard responded with some return of his mincing dignity.

"Quit dragging your feet, Webbard."

"Oh, well—the Villa Passe-temps, Juan-les-pins."

"I'll believe it when I see your address file. Where is it?"

Webbard began breathing hard. "Now see here, young lady, there's serious matters at stake!"

"Such as what?"

"Well—" Webbard lowered his voice, glanced conspiratorially at the walls of the room. "It's common knowledge at the Station that Mr. Earl and Mr. Lionel are—well, not friendly. And there's a rumor—a rumor, mind you—that Mr. Earl has hired a well-known criminal to kill Mr. Lionel."

That would be Fotheringay, Jean surmised.

Webbard continued. "So you see, it's necessary that I exercise the utmost caution. . . ."

Jean laughed. "Let's see that file."

Webbard finally indicated a card file. Jean said, "You know, where it is; pull it out."

Webbard glumly sorted through the cards. "Here."

The address was: Hotel Atlantide, Apartment 3001, French Colony, Metropolis, Earth.

Jean memorized the address, then stood irresolutely, trying to think of further questions. Webbard smiled slowly. Jean ignored him, stood nibbling her fingertips. Times like this she felt the inadequacy of her youth. When it came to action—fighting, laughing, spying, playing games, making love—she felt complete assurance. But the sorting out of possibilities and deciding which were probable and which irrational was when she felt less than sure. Such as now. . . . Old Webbard, the fat blob, had calmed himself and was gloating. Well, let him enjoy himself. . . . She had to get to Earth. She had to see Lionel Abercrombie. Possibly Fotheringay had been hired to kill him, possibly not. Possibly Fotheringay knew where to find him, possibly not. Webbard knew Fotheringay; probably he had served as Earl's intermediary. Or possibly Webbard was performing some intricate evolutions of his own. It was plain that, now, her interests were joined with Lionel's, rather than Fotheringay's, because marrying Earl was clearly out of the question. Lionel must stay alive. If this meant double-crossing Fotheringay, too bad for Fotheringay. He could have told her more about Earl's "zoological collection" before he sent her up to marry Earl. . . . Of course, she told herself, Fotheringay would have no means of knowing the peculiar use Earl made of his specimens.

"Well?" asked Webbard with an unpleasant grin.

"When does the next ship leave for Earth?"

"The supply barge is heading back tonight."

"That's fine. If I can fight off the pilot. You can pay me now."

"Pay you? You've only done a day's work. You owe the Station for transportation, your uniform, your meals—"

"Oh, never mind." Jean turned, pulled herself into the corridor, went to her room, packed her belongings.

Mrs. Blaiskell pushed her head through the door. "Oh, there you are. . . ." She sniffed. "Mr. Earl has been inquiring for you. He wants to see you at once." It was plain that she disapproved.

"Sure," said Jean. "Right away."

Mrs. Blaiskell departed.

Jean pushed herself along the corridor to the loading deck. The barge pilot was assisting in the loading of some empty metal drums. He saw Jean and his face changed. "You again?"

"I'm going back to Earth with you. You were right. I don't like it here."

The pilot nodded sourly. "This time you ride in the storage. That way neither of us gets hurt. . . . I couldn't promise a thing if you're up forward."

"Suits me," said Jean. "I'm going aboard."

When Jean reached the Hotel Atlantide in Metropolis she wore a black dress and black pumps which she felt made her look older and more sophisticated. Crossing the lobby she kept a wary lookout for the house detective. Sometimes they nursed unkind suspicions toward unaccompanied young girls. It was best to avoid the police, keep them at a distance. When they found that she had no father, no mother, no guardian, their minds were apt to turn to some dreary government institution. On several occasions rather extreme measures to ensure her independence had been necessary.

But the Hotel Atlantide detective took no heed of the black-haired girl quietly crossing the lobby, if he saw her at all. The lift attendant observed that she seemed restless, as with either a great deal of pent enthusiasm or nervous. A porter on the thirtieth floor noticed her searching for an apartment number and mentally labeled her a person unfamiliar with the hotel. A chambermaid watched her press the bell at Apartment 3001, saw the door open, saw the girl jerk back in surprise, then slowly enter the apartment.

Strange, thought the chambermaid, and speculated mildly for a few moments. Then she went to recharge the foam dispensers in the public bathrooms, and the incident passed from her mind.

The apartment was spacious, elegant, expensive. Windows overlooked Central Gardens and the Morison Hall of Equity behind. The furnishings were the work of a professional decorator, harmonious and sterile; a few incidental objects around the room, however, hinted of a woman's presence. But Jean saw no woman. There was only herself and Fotheringay.

Fotheringay wore subdued gray flannels and dark necktie. In a crowd of twenty people he would vanish.

After an instant of surprise he stood back. "Come in."

Jean darted glances around the room, half expecting a fat crumpled body. But possibly Lionel had not been at home, and Fotheringay was waiting.

"Well," he asked, "what brings you here?" He was watching her covertly. "Take a seat."

Jean sank into a chair, chewed at her lip. Fotheringay watched her catlike. Walk carefully. She prodded her mind. What legitimate excuse did she have for visiting Lionel? Perhaps Fotheringay had expected her to double-cross him. . . . Where was Hammond? Her neck tingled. Eyes were on her neck. She looked around quickly.

Someone in the hall tried to dodge out of sight. Not quickly enough. Inside Jean's brain a film of ignorance broke to release a warm soothing flood of knowledge.

She smiled, her sharp white little teeth showing between her lips. It had been a fat woman whom she had seen in the hall, a very fat woman, rosy, flushed, quivering.

"What are you smiling at?" inquired Fotheringay.

She used his own technique. "Are you wondering who gave me your address?"

"Obviously Webbard."

Jean nodded. "Is the lady your wife?"

Fotheringay's chin raised a hairbreadth. "Get to the point."

"Very well." She hitched herself forward. There was still a possibility that she was making a terrible mistake, but the risk must be taken. Questions would reveal her uncertainty, diminish her bargaining position. "How much money can you raise—right now? Cash."

"Ten or twenty thousand."

Her face must have showed disappointment.

"Not enough?"

"No. You sent me on a bum steer."

Fotheringay sat silently.

"Earl would no more make a pass at me than bite off his tongue. His taste in women is—like yours."

Fotheringay displayed no irritation. "But two years ago—"

"There's a reason for that." She raised her eyebrows ruefully. "Not a nice reason."

"Well, get on with it."

"He liked Earth girls because they were freaks. In his opinion, naturally. Earl likes freaks."

Fotheringay rubbed his chin, watching her with blank wide eyes. "I never thought of that."

"Your scheme might have worked out if Earl were halfway right-side up. But I just don't have what it takes."

Fotheringay smiled frostily. "You didn't come here to tell me that."

"No. I know how Lionel Abercrombie can get the Station for himself. . . . Of course your name is Fotheringay."

"If my name is Fotheringay, why did you come here looking for me?"

Jean laughed, a gay ringing laugh. "Why do you think I'm looking for you? I'm looking for Lionel Abercrombie. Fotheringay is no use to me unless I can marry Earl. I can't. I haven't got enough of that stuff. Now I'm looking for Lionel Abercrombie."

8

Fotheringay tapped a well-manicured finger on a well-flanneled knee, and said quietly, "I'm Lionel Abercrombie."

"How do I know you are?"

He tossed her a passport. She glanced at it, tossed it back.

"Okay. Now—you have twenty thousand. That's not enough. I want two million. . . . If you haven't got it, you haven't got it. I'm not unreasonable. But I want to make sure I get it when you do have it. . . . So—you'll write me a deed, a bill of sale, something legal that gives me your interest in Abercrombie Station. I'll agree to sell it back to you for two million dollars."

Fotheringay shook his head. "That kind of agreement is binding on me but not on you. You're a minor."

Jean said, "The sooner I get clear of Abercrombie the better. I'm not greedy. You can have your billion dollars. I merely want two million. . . . Incidentally, how do you figure a billion? Webbard says the whole setup is only worth a hundred million."

Lionel's mouth twisted in a wintry smile. "Webbard didn't include the holdings of the Abercrombie guests. Some very rich people are fat. The fatter they get, the less they like life on Earth."

"They could always move to another resort station."

Lionel shook his head. "It's not the same atmosphere. Abercrombie is Fatman's World. The one small spot in all the universe where a fat man is proud of his weight." There was a wistful overtone in his voice.

Jean said softly, "And you're lonesome for Abercrombie yourself."

Lionel smiled grimly. "Is that so strange?"

Jean shifted in her chair. "Now we'll go to a lawyer. I know a good one. Richard Mycroft. I want this deed drawn up without loopholes. Maybe I'll have to find myself a guardian, a trustee."

"You don't need a guardian."

Jean smiled complacently. "For a fact, I don't."

"You still haven't told me what this project consists of."

"I'll tell you when I have the deed. You don't lose a thing giving away property you don't own. And after you give it away, it's to my interest to help you get it."

Lionel rose to his feet. "It had better be good."

"It will be."

The fat woman came into the room. She was obviously an Earth girl, bewildered and delighted by Lionel's attentions. Looking at Jean her face became clouded with jealousy.

Out in the corridor Jean said wisely, "You get her up to Abercrombie, she'll be throwing you over for one of those fat rascals."

"Shut up!" said Lionel, in a voice like the whetting of a scythe.

The pilot of the supply barge said sullenly, "I don't know about this."

Lionel asked quietly, "You like your job?"

The pilot muttered churlishly, but made no further protest. Lionel buckled himself into the seat beside him. Jean, the horse-faced man named Hammond, two elderly men of professional aspect and uneasy manner settled themselves in the cargo hold.

The ship lifted free of the dock, pushed up above the atmosphere, lined out into Abercrombie's orbit.

The Station floated ahead, glinting in the sunlight.

The barge landed on the cargo deck, the handlers tugged it into its socket, the port sighed open.

"Come on," said Lionel. "Make it fast. Let's get it over with." He tapped Jean's shoulder. "You're first."

She led the way up the main core. Fat guests floated down past them, light and round as soapbubbles, their faces masks of surprise at the sight of so many bone-people.

Up the core, along the vinculum into the Abercrombie private sphere. They passed the Pleasaunce, where Jean caught a glimpse of Mrs. Clara, fat as a blutworst, with the obsequious Webbard.

They passed Mrs. Blaiskell. "Why, Mr. Lionel!" she gasped. "Well, I never, I never!"

Lionel brushed past. Jean, looking over her shoulder into his face, felt a qualm. Something dark smoldered in his eyes. Triumph, malice, vindication, cruelty. Something not quite human. If nothing else, Jean was extremely human, and was wont to feel uneasy in the presence of out-world life. . . . She felt uneasy now.

"Hurry," came Lionel's voice. "Hurry."

Past Mrs. Clara's chambers, to the door of Earl's bedroom. Jean pressed the button; the door slid open.

Earl stood before a mirror, tying a red and blue silk cravat around his bull-neck. He wore a suit of pearl-gray gabardine, cut very full and padded to make his body look round and soft. He saw Jean in the mirror, behind her the hard face of his brother Lionel. He whirled, lost his footing, drifted ineffectually into the air.

Lionel laughed. "Get him, Hammond. Bring him along."

Earl stormed and raved. He was the master here, everybody get out. He'd have them all jailed, killed. He'd kill them himself. . . .

Hammond searched him for weapons, and the two professional-looking men stood uncomfortably in the background muttering to each other.

"Look here, Mr. Abercrombie," one of them said at last. "We can't be a party to violence. . . ."

"Shut up," said Lionel. "You're here as witnesses, as medical men. You're being paid to look, that's all. If you don't like what you see, that's too bad." He motioned to Jean. "Get going."

Jean pushed herself to the study door. Earl called out sharply: "Get away from there, get away! That's private, that's my private study!"

Jean pressed her lips together. It was impossible to avoid feeling pity for poor gnarled Earl. But—she thought of his "zoological collection." Firmly she covered the electric eye, pressed the button. The door swung open, revealing the glory of the stained glass glowing with the fire of heaven.

Jean pushed herself to the furry two-legged creature. Here she waited.

Earl made some difficulty about coming through the door. Hammond manipulated his elbows; Earl belched up a hoarse screech, flung himself forward, panting like a winded chicken.

Lionel said, "Don't fool with Hammond, Earl. He likes hurting people."

The two witnesses muttered wrathfully. Lionel quelled them with a look.

Hammond seized Earl by the seat of the pants, raised him over his head, walked with magnetic shoes gripping the deck across the cluttered floor of the study, with Earl flailing and groping helplessly.

Jean fumbled in the fretwork over the panel into the annex. Earl screamed, "Keep your hands out of there! Oh, how you'll pay, how you'll pay for this, how you'll pay!" His voice hoarsened, he broke into sobs.

Hammond shook him, like a terrier shaking a rat.

Earl sobbed louder.

The sound grated on Jean's ears. She frowned, found the button, pushed. The panel flew open.

They all moved into the bright annex, Earl completely broken, sobbing and pleading.

"There it is," said Jean.

Lionel swung his gaze along the collection of monstrosities. The out-world things, the dragons, basilisks, griffins, the armored insects, the great-eyed serpents, the tangles of muscle, the coiled creatures of fang, brain, cartilage. And then there were the human creatures, no less grotesque. Lionel's eyes stopped at the fat man.

He looked at Earl, who had fallen numbly silent.

"Poor old Hugo," said Lionel. "You ought to be ashamed of yourself, Earl."

Earl made a sighing sound.

Lionel said, "But Hugo is dead. . . . He's as dead as any of the other things. Right, Earl?" He looked at Jean. "Right?"

"I guess that's right," said Jean uneasily. She found no pleasure baiting Earl.

"Of course he's dead," panted Earl.

Jean went to the little key controlling the magnetic field.

Earl screamed, "You witch! You witch!"

Jean depressed the key. There was a musical hum, a hissing, a smell of ozone. A moment passed. There came a sigh of air. The cubicle opened with a sucking sound. Hugo drifted into the room.

He twitched his arms, gagged and retched, made a thin crying sound in his throat.

Lionel turned to his two witnesses. "Is this man alive?"

They muttered excitedly, "Yes, yes!"

Lionel turned to Hugo. "Tell them your name."

Hugo whispered feebly, pressed his elbows to his body, pulled up his atrophied little legs, tried to assume a fetal position.

Lionel asked the two men, "Is this man sane?"

They fidgeted. "That of course is hardly a matter we can determine offhand." There was further mumbling about tests, cephalographs, reflexes.

Lionel waited a moment. Hugo was gurgling, crying like a baby. "Well—is he sane?"

The doctors said, "He's suffering from severe shock. The deep-freeze classically has the effect of disturbing the synapses—"

Lionel asked sardonically, "Is he in his right mind?"

"Well—no."

Lionel nodded. "In that case—you're looking at the new master of Abercrombie Station."

Earl protested, "You can't get away with that, Lionel! He's been insane a long time, and you've been off the Station!"

Lionel grinned wolfishly. "Do you want to take the matter into Admiralty Court at Metropolis?"

Earl fell silent. Lionel looked at the doctors, who were whispering heatedly together.

"Talk to him," said Lionel. "Satisfy yourself whether he's in his right mind or not."

The doctors dutifully addressed Hugo, who made mewing sounds. They came to an uncomfortable but definite decision. "Clearly this man is not able to conduct his own affairs."

Earl pettishly wrenched himself from Hammond's grasp. "Let go of me."

"Better be careful," said Lionel. "I don't think Hammond likes you."

"I don't like Hammond," said Earl viciously. "I don't like anyone." His voice dropped in pitch. "I don't even like myself." He stood staring into the cubicle which Hugo had vacated.

Jean sensed a tide of recklessness rising in him. She opened her mouth to speak.

But Earl had already started.

Time stood still. Earl seemed to move with bewildering slowness, but the others stood as if frozen in jelly.

Time turned on for Jean. "I'm getting out of here!" she gasped, knowing what the half-crazed Earl was about to do.

Earl ran down the line of his monsters, magnetic shoes slapping on the deck. As he ran, he flipped switches. When he finished he stood at the far end of the room. Behind him things came to life.

Hammond gathered himself, plunged after Jean. A black arm apparently groping at random caught hold of his leg. There was a dull cracking sound. Hammond bawled out in terror.

Jean started through the door. She jerked back, shrieking. Facing her was the eight-foot gorilla-thing with the French poodle face. Somewhere along the line Earl had thrown a switch relieving it from magnetic catalepsy. The black eyes shone, the mouth dripped, the hands clenched and unclenched. Jean shrank back.

There were horrible noises from behind. She heard Earl gasping in sudden fear. But she could not turn her eyes from the gorilla-thing. It drifted into the room. The black dog-eyes looked deep into Jean's. She could not move! A great black arm, groping mindlessly, fell past Jean's shoulder, touched the gorilla-thing.

There was screaming bedlam. Jean pressed herself against the wall. A green flapping creature, coiling and uncoiling, twisted out into the study, smashing racks, screens, displays, sending books, minerals, papers, mechanisms, cases and cabinets floating and crashing. The gorilla-thing came after, one of its arms twisted and loose. A rolling flurry of webbed feet, scales, muscular tail and a human body followed— Hammond and a griffin from a world aptly named Pest-Hole.

Jean darted through the door, thought to hide in the alcove. Outside, on the deck, was Earl's spaceboat. She shoved herself across to the port.

Behind, frantically scrambling, came one of the doctors whom Lionel had brought along for a witness.

Jean called, "Over here, over here!"

The doctor threw himself into the spaceboat.

Jean crouched by the port, ready to slam it at any approach of danger. . . . She sighed. All her hopes, plans, future had exploded. Death, debacle, catastrophe were hers instead.

She turned to the doctor. "Where's your partner?"

"Dead! Oh Lord, oh Lord, what can we do?"

Jean turned her head to look at him, lips curling in disgust. Then she saw him in a new, flattering light. A disinterested witness. He looked like money. He could testify that for at least thirty seconds Lionel had been master of Abercrombie Station. Thirty seconds was enough to transfer title to her. Whether Hugo were sane or not didn't matter because Hugo had died thirty seconds before the metal frog with the knife-edged scissor-bill had fixed on Lionel's throat.

Best to make sure. "Listen," said Jean. "This may be important. Suppose you were to testify in court. Who died first, Hugo or Lionel?"

The doctor sat quiet a moment. "Why, Hugo! I saw his neck broken while Lionel was still alive."

"Are you sure?"

"Oh, yes." He tried to pull himself together. "We must do something."

"Okay," said Jean. "What shall we do?"

"I don't know."

From the study came a gurgling sound, and an instant later, a woman's scream. "God!" said Jean. "The things have got out into the inner bedroom. . . . What they won't do to Abercrombie Station. . . ." She lost control and retched against the hull of the boat.

A brown face like a poodle dog's, spotted red with blood, peered around the corner at them. Stealthily it pulled itself closer.

Mesmerized, Jean saw that now its arm had been twisted entirely off. It darted forward. Jean fell back, slammed the port. A heavy body thudded against the metal.

They were closed in Earl's spaceboat. The man had fainted. Jean said, "Don't die on me, fellow. You're worth money. . . ."

Faintly through the metal came crashing and thumping. Then came the muffled *spatttt* of proton guns.

The guns sounded with monotonous regularity. *Spatttt . . . spattt . . . spattt . . . spattt . . . spattt. . . .*

Then there was utter silence.

Jean inched open the port. The alcove was empty. Across her vision drifted the broken body of the gorilla-thing.

Jean ventured into the alcove, looked out into the study. Thirty feet distant stood Webbard, planted like a pirate captain on the bridge of his ship. His face was white and wadded; pinched lines ran from his nose around his nearly invisible mouth. He carried two big proton guns; the orifices of both were white-hot.

He saw Jean; his eyes took on a glitter. "You! It's you that's caused all this, your sneaking and spying!"

He jerked up his proton guns.

"No!" cried Jean. "It's not my fault!"

Lionel's voice came weakly. "Put down those guns, Webbard." Clutching his throat he pushed himself into the study. "That's the new owner," he croaked sardonically. "You wouldn't want to murder your boss, would you?"

Webbard blinked in astonishment. "Mr. Lionel!"

"Yes," said Lionel. "Home again. . . . And there's quite a mess to clean up, Webbard. . . ."

Jean looked at the bankbook. The figures burned into the plastic, spread almost all the way across the tape.

"Two million dollars."

Mycroft puffed on his pipe, looked out the window. "There's a matter you should be considering," he said. "That's the investment of your money. You won't be able to do it by yourself; other parties will insist on dealing with a responsible entity—that is to say, a trustee or a guardian."

"I don't know much about these things," said Jean. "I—rather assumed that you'd take care of them."

Mycroft reached over, tapped the dottle out of his pipe.

"Don't you want to?" asked Jean.

Mycroft said with a compressed distant smile, "Yes, I want to. . . . I'll be glad to administer a two-million-dollar estate. In effect, I'll become your legal guardian, until you're of age. We'll have to get a court order of appointment. The effect of the order will be to take control of the money out of your hands; we can include in the articles, however, a clause guaranteeing you the full income—which I assume is what you want. It should come to—oh, say fifty thousand a year after taxes."

"That suits me," said Jean listlessly. "I'm not too interested in anything right now. . . . There seems to be something of a letdown."

Mycroft nodded. "I can see how that's possible."

Jean said, "I have the money. I've always wanted it, now I have it. And now—" She held out her hands, raised her eyebrows. "It's just a number in a bankbook. . . . Tomorrow morning I'll get up and say to myself, 'What shall I do today? Shall I buy a house? Shall I order a thousand dollars worth of clothes? Shall I start out on a two-year tour of Argo Navis?' And the answer will come out, 'No, the hell with it all.' "

"What you need," said Mycroft, "are some friends, nice girls your own age."

Jean's mouth moved in rather a sickly smile. "I'm afraid we wouldn't have much in common. . . . It's probably a good idea, but—it wouldn't work out." She sat passively in the chair, her wide mouth drooping.

Mycroft noticed that in repose it was a sweet generous mouth.

She said in a low voice, "I can't get out of my head the idea that somewhere in the universe I must have a mother and a father. . . ."

Mycroft rubbed his chin. "People who'd abandon a baby in a saloon aren't worth thinking about, Jean."

"I know," she said in a dismal voice. "Oh, Mr. Mycroft, I'm so damn lonely. . . ." Jean was crying, her head buried in her arms.

Mycroft irresolutely put his hand on her shoulder, patted awkwardly.

After a moment she said, "You'll think I'm an awful fool."

"No," said Mycroft gruffly. "I think nothing of the kind. I wish that I . . ." He could not put it into words.

She pulled herself together, rose to her feet. "Enough of this. . . ." She turned his head up, kissed his chin. "You're really very nice, Mr. Mycroft. . . . But I don't want sympathy. I hate it. I'm used to looking out for myself."

Mycroft returned to his seat, loaded his pipe to keep his fingers busy. Jean picked up her little handbag. "Right now I've got a date with a couturier named André. He's going to dress me to an inch of my life. And then I'm going to—" She broke off. "I'd better not tell you. You'd be alarmed and shocked."

He cleared his throat. "I expect I would."

She nodded brightly. "So long." Then she left his office.

Mycroft cleared his throat again, hitched up his trousers, settled his jacket, returned to his work. . . . Somehow it appeared dull, drab, gray. His head ached.

He said, "I feel like going out and getting drunk. . . ."

Ten minutes passed. His door opened. Jean looked in.

"Hello, Mr. Mycroft."

"Hello, Jean."

"I changed my mind. I thought it would be nicer if I took you out to dinner, and then maybe we could go to a show. . . . Would you like that?"

"Very much," said Mycroft.

T HE SYMBOLIC adjuncts used to enlarge the human personality are of course numerous. Clothes comprise a most important category of these symbols and sometimes when people are gathered together it is amusing to examine garments, unobtrusively of course, and to reflect that each article has been selected wih solicitous care with the intention of creating some particular effect.

Despite the symbolic power of clothes, men and women are judged, by and large, by circumstances more difficult to control: posture, accent, voice timbre, the shape and color of their bodies, and most significant of all, their faces. Voices can be modulated, diets and exercise, theoretically at least, force the body into socially acceptable contours. What can be done to the face? Enormous effort has been expended in this direction. Jowls are hoisted, eyebrows attached or eliminated, noses cropped, de-hooked, de-humped. The hair is tormented into a thousand styles: puffed, teased, wet, dried, hung this way or that: all to formulate a fashionable image. Nonetheless, all pretenses are transparent; nature-fakery yields to the critical eye. No matter what our inclinations, whether or not we like our faces, we are forced to

V

177

live with them, and to accept whatever favor, censure or derision we willy-nilly incur.

Except those intricate and intelligent folk of the world Sirene, whose unorthodox social habits are considered in the following pages.

THE MOON MOTH

THE HOUSEBOAT HAD BEEN BUILT TO THE MOST exacting standards of Sirenese craftmanship, which is to say, as close to the absolute as human eye could detect. The planking of waxy dark wood showed no joints, the fastenings were platinum rivets countersunk and polished flat. In style, the boat was massive, broad beamed, steady as the shore itself, without ponderosity or slackness of line. The bow bulged like a swan's breast, the stem rising high, then crooking forward to support an iron lantern. The doors were carved from slabs of a mottled black-green wood; the windows were many sectioned, paned with squares of mica, stained rose, blue, pale green and violet. The bow was given to service facilities and quarters for the slaves; amidships were a pair of sleeping cabins, a dining saloon and a parlor saloon, opening upon an observation deck at the stern.

Such was Edwer Thissell's houseboat, but ownership brought him neither pleasure nor pride. The houseboat had become shabby. The carpeting had lost its pile; the carved screens were chipped; the iron lantern at the bow sagged with rust. Seventy years ago the first owner, on accepting the boat, had honored the builder and had been likewise honored; the transaction (for the process represented a great deal more than simple giving and taking) had augmented the prestige of both. That time was far gone; the houseboat now commanded no prestige whatever. Edwer Thissell, resident on Sirene only three months, recognized the lack but could do nothing about it: this particular houseboat was the best he could get.

He sat on the rear deck practicing the *ganga,* a zitherlike instrument not much larger than his hand. A hundred yards inshore, surf defined a strip of white beach; beyond rose jungle, with the silhouette of craggy black hills against the sky. Mireille shone hazy and white overhead, as if through a tangle of spider web; the face of the ocean pooled and puddled with mother-of-pearl luster. The scene had become as familiar, though not as boring, as the *ganga,* at which he had worked two hours, twanging out the Sirenese scales, forming chords, traversing simple progressions. Now he put down the *ganga* for the *zachinko,* this a small sound-box studded with keys, played with the right hand. Pressure on the keys forced air through reeds in the keys themselves, producing a concertinalike tone. Thissel ran off a dozen quick scales, making very few mistakes. Of the six instruments he had set himself to learn, the *zachinko* had proved the least refractory (with the exception, of course, of the *hymerkin,* that clacking, slapping, clattering device of wood and stone used exclusively with the slaves).

Thissell practiced another ten minutes, then put aside the *zachinko.* He flexed his arms, wrung his aching fingers. Every waking moment since his arrival had been given to the instruments: the *hymerkin,* the *ganga,* the *zachinko,* the *kiv,* the *strapan,* the *gomapard.* He had practiced scales in nineteen keys and four modes, chords without number, intervals never imagined on the Home Planets. Trills, arpeggios, slurs, click-stops and nasalization; damping and augmentation of overtones; vibratos and wolf-tones; concavities and convexities. He practiced with a dogged, deadly diligence, in which his original concept of music as a source of pleasure had long become lost. Looking over the instruments Thissell resisted an urge to fling all six into the Titanic.

He rose to his feet, went forward through the parlor saloon, the dining saloon, along a corridor past the galley and came out on the foredeck. He bent over the rail, peered down into the underwater pens where Toby and Rex, the slaves, were harnessing the dray-fish for the weekly trip to Fan, eight miles north. The youngest fish, either playful or captious, ducked and plunged. Its streaming black muzzle broke water, and Thissell, looking into its face, felt a peculiar qualm: the fish wore no mask!

Thissell laughed uneasily, fingering his own mask, the Moon Moth. No question about it, he was becoming acclimated to Sirene! A significant stage had been reached when the naked face of a fish caused him shock!

The fish were finally harnessed; Toby and Rex climbed aboard, red bodies glistening, black cloth masks clinging to their faces. Ignoring Thissell they stowed the pen, hoisted anchor. The dray-fish strained, the harness tautened, the houseboat moved north.

Returning to the afterdeck, Thissell took up the *strapan*—this a circular sound-box eight inches in diameter. Forty-six wires radiated from a central hub to the circumference where they connected to either a bell or a tinkle-bar. When plucked, the bells rang, the bars chimed; when strummed, the instrument gave off a twanging, jingling sound. When played with competence, the pleasantly acid dissonances produced an expressive effect; in an unskilled hand, the results were less felicitous, and might even approach random noise. The *strapan* was Thissell's weakest instrument and he practiced with concentration during the entire trip north.

In due course the houseboat approached the floating city. The dray-fish were curbed, the houseboat warped to a mooring. Along the dock a line of idlers weighed and gauged every aspect of the houseboat, the slaves and Thissell himself, according to Sirenese habit. Thissell, not yet accustomed to such penetrating inspection, found the scrutiny unsettling, all the more so for the immobility of the masks. Self-consciously adjusting his own Moon Moth, he climbed the ladder to the dock.

A slave rose from where he had been squatting, touched knuckles to the black cloth at his forehead, and sang on a three-tone phrase of interrogation: "The Moon Moth before me possibly expresses the identity of Ser Edwer Thissell?"

Thissell tapped the *hymerkin* which hung at his belt and sang: "I am Ser Thissell."

"I have been honored by a trust," sang the slave. "Three days from dawn to dusk I have waited on the dock; three nights from dusk to dawn I have crouched on a raft below this same dock listening to the feet of the Night-men. At last I behold the mask of Ser Thissell."

Thissell evoked an impatient clatter from the *hymerkin*. "What is the nature of this trust?"

"I carry a message, Ser Thissell. It is intended for you."

Thissell held out his left hand, playing the *hymerkin* with his right. "Give me the message."

"Instantly, Ser Thissell."

The message bore a heavy superscription:

EMERGENCY COMMUNICATION! RUSH!

Thissell ripped open the envelope. The message was signed by Castel Cromartin, Chief Executive of the Interworld Policies Board, and after the formal saluation read:

ABSOLUTELY URGENT the following orders be executed! Aboard *Carina Cruzeiro,* destination Fan, date of arrival January 10 U.T., is notorious assassin, Haxo Angmark. Meet landing with adequate authority, effect detention and incarceration of this man. These instructions must be successfully implemented. Failure is unacceptable.

ATTENTION! Haxo Angmark is superlatively dangerous. Kill him without hesitation at any show of resistance.

Thissell considered the message with dismay. In coming to Fan as Consular Representative he had expected nothing like this; he felt neither inclination nor competence in the matter of dealing with dangerous assassins. Thoughtfully he rubbed the fuzzy gray cheek of his mask. The situation was not completely dark; Esteban Rolver, Director of the Spaceport, would doubtless cooperate, and perhaps furnish a platoon of slaves.

More hopefully, Thissell reread the message, January 10, Universal Time. He consulted a conversion calendar. Today, 40th in the Season of Bitter Nectar—Thissell ran his finger down the column, stopped. January 10. Today.

A distant rumble caught his attention. Dropping from the mist came a dull shape: the lighter returning from contact with the *Carina Cruzeiro.*

Thissell once more reread the note, raised his head, studied the descending lighter. Aboard would be Haxo Angmark. In five minutes he would emerge upon the soil of

Sirene. Landing formalities would detain him possibly twenty minutes. The landing field lay a mile and a half distant, joined to Fan by a winding path through the hills.

Thissell turned to the slave. "When did this message arrive?"

The slave leaned forward uncomprehendingly. Thissell reiterated his question, singing to the clack of the *hymerkin:* "This message: you have enjoyed the honor of its custody how long?"

The slave sang: "Long days have I waited on the wharf, retreating only to the raft at the onset of dusk. Now my vigil is rewarded; I behold Ser Thissell."

Thissell turned away, walked furiously up the dock. Ineffective, inefficient Sirenese! Why had they not delivered the message to his houseboat? Twenty-five minutes—twenty-two now. . . .

At the esplanade Thissell stopped, looked right, then left, hoping for a miracle: some sort of air-transport to wisk him to the spaceport, where, with Rolver's aid, Haxo Angmark might still be detained. Or better yet, a second message canceling the first. Something, anything. . . . But air-cars were not to be found on Sirene, and no second message appeared.

Across the esplanade rose a meager row of permanent structures, built of stone and iron and so proof against the efforts of the Night-men. A hostler occupied one of these structures, and as Thissell watched a man in a splendid pearl and silver mask emerged riding one of the lizardlike mounts of Sirene.

Thissell sprang forward. There was still time; with luck he might yet intercept Haxo Angmark. He hurried across the esplanade.

Before the line of stalls stood the hostler, inspecting his stock with solicitude, occasionally burnishing a scale or whisking away an insect. There were five of the beasts in prime condition, each as tall as a man's shoulder, with massive legs, thick bodies, heavy wedge-shaped heads. From their fore-fangs, which had been artificially lengthened and curved into near circles, gold rings depended; the scales of each had been stained in diaper-pattern; purple and green, orange and black, red and blue, brown and pink, yellow and silver.

Thissell came to a breathless halt in front of the hoslter.

He reached for his *kiv**, then hesitated. Could this be considered a casual personal encounter? The *zachinko* perhaps? But the statement of his needs hardly seemed to demand the formal approach. Better the *kiv* after all. He struck a chord, but by error found himself stroking the *ganga*. Beneath his mask Thissell grinned apologetically; his relationship with this hostler was by no means on an intimate basis. He hoped that the hostler was of sanguine disposition, and in any event the urgency of the occasion allowed no time to select an exactly appropriate instrument. He struck a second chord, and, playing as well as agitation, breathlessness and lack of skill allowed, sang out a request: "Ser Hostler, I have immediate need of a swift mount. Allow me to select from your herd."

The hostler wore a mask of considerable complexity which Thissell could not identify: a construction of varnished brown cloth, pleated gray leather and, high on the forehead, two large green and scarlet globes, minutely segmented like insect-eyes. He inspected Thissell a long moment, then, rather ostentatiously selecting his *stimic,*** executed a brilliant progression of trills and rounds, of an import Thissell failed to grasp. The hostler sang, "Ser Moon Moth, I fear that my steeds are unsuitable to a person of your distinction."

Thissell earnestly twanged at the *ganga*. "By no means; they all seem adequate. I am in great haste and will gladly accept any of the group."

The hostler played a brittle cascading crescendo. "Ser Moon Moth," he sang, "the steeds are ill and dirty. I am flattered that you consider them adequate to your use. I cannot accept the merit you offer me. And"—here, switching instruments, he struck a cool tinkle from his *krodatch*†—"somehow I fail to recognize the boon companion and co-

---

* *Kiv*: five banks of resilient metal strips, fourteen to the bank, played by touching, twisting, twanging.
** *Stimic*: three flutelike tubes equipped with plungers. Thumb and forefinger squeeze a bag to force air across the mouthpieces; the second, third and fourth little fingers manipulate the slide. The *stimic* is an instrument well adapted to the sentiments of cool withdrawal, or even disapproval.
† *Krodatch*: a small square sound-box strung with resined gut. The musician scratches the strings with his fingernail, or strokes them with his fingertips, to produce a variety of quietly formal sounds. The *krodatch* is also used as an instrument of insult.

craftsman who accosts me so familiarly with his *ganga*."
The implication was clear. Thissell would receive no
mount. He turned, set off at a run for the landing field.
Behind him sounded a clatter of the hostler's *hymerkin*—
whether directed toward the hostler's slaves or toward himself Thissell did not pause to learn.

The previous Consular Representative of the Home
Planets on Sirene had been killed at Zundar. Masked as a
Tavern Bravo he had accosted a girl beribboned for the
Equinoctial Attitudes, a solecism for which he had been
instantly beheaded by a Red Demiurge, a Sun Sprite and a
Magic Hornet. Edwer Thissell, recently graduated from the
Institute, had been named his successor, and allowed three
days to prepare himself. Normally of a contemplative, even
cautious disposition, Thissell had regarded the appointment
as a challenge. He learned the Sirenese language by sub-
cerebral techniques, and found it uncomplicated. Then, in
the *Journal of Universal Anthropology,* he read:

> The population of the Titanic littoral is highly in-
> dividualistic, possibly in response to a bountiful environ-
> ment which puts no premium upon group activity. The
> language, reflecting this trait, expresses the individual's
> mood, his emotional attitude toward a given situation.
> Factual information is regarded as a secondary con-
> comitant. Moreover, the language is sung, characteris-
> tically to the accompaniment of a small instrument. As
> a result, there is great difficulty in ascertaining fact from
> a native of Fan, or the forbidden city Zundar. One will
> be regaled with elegant arias and demonstrations of
> astonishing virtuosity upon one or another of the nu-
> merous musical instruments. The visitor to this fasci-
> nating world, unless he cares to be treated with the most
> consummate contempt, must therefore learn to express
> himself after the approved local fashion.

Thissell made a note in his memorandum book: *Procure
small musical instrument, together with directions as to use.*
He read on.

There is everywhere and at all times a plenitude,

not to say superfluity, of food, and the climate is benign.
With a fund of racial energy and a great deal of leisure
time, the population occupies itself with intricacy. Intricacy in all things: intricate craftmanship, such as the
carved panels which adorn the houseboats; intricate
symbolism, as exemplified in the masks worn by everyone; the intricate half-musical language which admirably
expresses subtle moods and emotions; and above all the
fantastic intricacy of interpersonal relationships. Prestige, face, *mana*, repute, glory: the Sirenese word is
strakh. Every man has his characterstic *strakh*, which
determines whether, when he needs a houseboat, he will
be urged to avail himself of a floating palace, rich with
gems, alabaster lanterns, peacock faience and carved
wood, or grudgingly permitted an abandoned shack on
a raft. There is no medium of exchange on Sirene; the
single and sole currency is *strakh*. . . .

Thissell rubbed his chin and read further.

Masks are worn at all times, in accordance with the
philosophy that a man should not be compelled to use
a similitude foisted upon him by factors beyond his
control; that he should be at liberty to choose that
semblance most consonant with his *strakh*. In the civilized areas of Sirene—which is to say the Titanic littoral
—a man literally never shows his face; it is his basic
secret.

Gambling, by this token, is unknown on Sirene; it
would be catastrophic to Sirenese self-respect to gain
advantage by means other than the exercise of *strakh*.
The word "luck" has no counterpart in the Sirenese
language.

Thissell made another note: *Get mask. Museum? Drama
guild?*

He finished the article, hastened forth to complete his
preparations, and the next day embarked aboard the *Robert
Astroguard* for the first leg of the passage to Sirene.

The lighter settled upon the Sirenese spaceport, a topaz
disk isolated among the black, green and purple hills. The

lighter grounded and Edwer Thissell stepped forth. He was met by Esteban Rolver, the local agent for Spaceways. Rolver threw up his hands, stepped back. "Your mask," he cried huskily. "Where is your mask?"

Thissell held it up rather self-consciously. "I wasn't sure—"

"Put it on," said Rolver, turning away. He himself wore a fabrication of dull green scales, blue-lacquered wood. Black quills protruded at the cheeks, and under his chin hung a black-and-white-checked pompom, the total effect creating a sense of sardonic supple personality.

Thissell adjusted the mask to his face, undecided whether to make a joke about the situation or to maintain a reserve suitable to the dignity of his post.

"Are you masked?" Rolver inquired over his shoulder.

Thissell replied in the affirmative and Rolver turned. The mask hid the expression of his face, but his hand unconsciously flicked a set of keys strapped to his thigh. The instrument sounded a trill of shock and polite consternation. "You can't wear that mask!" sang Rolver. "In fact—how, where, did you get it?"

"It's copied from a mask owned by the Polypolis museum," Thissell declared stiffly. "I'm sure it's authentic."

Rolver nodded, his own mask seeming more sardonic than ever. "Its authentic enough. It's a variant of the type known as the Sea Dragon Conqueror, and is worn on ceremonial occasions by persons of enormous prestige: princes, heroes, master craftsmen, great musicians."

"I wasn't aware—"

Rolver made a gesture of languid understanding. "It's something you'll learn in due course. Notice my mask. Today I'm wearing a Tarn Bird. Persons of minimal prestige—such as you, I, any other out-worlder—wear this sort of thing."

"Odd," said Thissell, as they started across the field toward a low concrete blockhouse. "I assumed that a person wore whatever he liked."

"Certainly," said Rolver. "Wear any mask you like—if you can make it stick. This Tarn Bird for instance. I wear it to indicate that I presume nothing. I make no claims to wisdom, ferocity, versatility, musicianship, truculence, or any of a dozen other Sirenese virtues."

"For the sake of argument," said Thissell, "what would happen if I walked through the streets of Zundar in this mask?"

Rolver laughed, a muffled sound behind his mask. "If you walked along the docks of Zundar—there are no streets—in any mask, you'd be killed within the hour. That's what happened to Benko, your predecessor. He didn't know how to act. None of us out-worlders know how to act. In Fan we're tolerated—so long as we keep our place. But you couldn't even walk around Fan in that regalia you're sporting now. Somebody wearing a Fire Snake or a Thunder Goblin—masks, you understand—would step up to you. He'd play his *krodatch,* and if you failed to challenge his audacity with a passage on the *skaranyi*,* a devilish instrument, he'd play his *hymerkin*—the instrument we use with the slaves. That's the ultimate expression of contempt. Or he might ring his dueling-gong and attack you then and there."

"I had no idea that people here were quite so irascible," said Thissell in a subdued voice.

Rolver shrugged and swung open the massive steel door into his office. "Cerain acts may not be committed on the Concourse at Polypolis without incurring criticism."

"Yes, that's quite true," said Thissell. He looked around the office. "Why the security? The concrete, the steel?"

"Protection against the savages," said Rolver. "They come down from the mountains at night, steal what's available, kill anyone they find ashore." He went to a closet, brought forth a mask. "Here. Use this Moon Moth; it won't get you in trouble."

Thissell unenthusiastically inspected the mask. It was constructed of mouse-colored fur; there was a tuft of hair at each side of the mouth-hole, a pair of featherlike antennae at the forehead. White lace flaps dangled beside the temples and under the eyes hung a series of red folds, creating an effect at once lugubrious and comic.

Thissell asked, "Does this mask signify any degree of prestige?"

"Not a great deal."

"After all, I'm Consular Representative," said Thissell. "I represent the Home Planets, a hundred billion people—"

---

* *Skaranyi*: a miniature bagpipe, the sac squeezed between thumb and palm, the four fingers controlling the stops along four tubes.

"If the Home Planets want their representative to wear a Sea Dragon Conqueror mask, they'd better send out a Sea Dragon Conqueror type of man."

"I see," said Thissell in a subdued voice. "Well, if I must . . ."

Rolver politely averted his gaze while Thissell doffed the Sea Dragon Conqueror and slipped the more modest Moon Moth over his head. "I suppose I can find something just a bit more suitable in one of the shops," Thissell said. "I'm told a person simply goes in and takes what he needs, correct?"

Rolver surveyed Thissell critically. "That mask—temporarily, at least—is perfectly suitable. And it's rather important not to take anything from the shops until you know the *strakh* value of the article you want. The owner loses prestige if a person of low *strakh* makes free with his best work."

Thissell shook his head in exasperation. "Nothing of this was explained to me! I knew of the masks, of course, and the painstaking integrity of the craftsmen, but this insistence on prestige—*strakh*, whatever the word is. . . ."

"No matter," said Rolver. "After a year or two you'll begin to learn your way around. I suppose you speak the language?"

"Oh, indeed. Certainly."

"And what instruments do you play?"

"Well—I was given to understand that any small instrument was adequate, or that I could merely sing."

"Very inaccurate. Only slaves sing without accompaniment. I suggest that you learn the following instruments as quickly as possible: The *hymerkin* for your slaves. The *ganga* for conversation between intimates or one a trifle lower than yourself in *strakh*. The *kiv* for casual polite intercourse. The *zachinko* for more formal dealings. The *strapan* or the *krodatch* for your social inferiors—in your case, should you wish to insult someone. The *gomapard** or the double-*kamanthil*** *for* ceremonials." He considered a moment. "The *crebarin*, the water-lute and the *slobo* are highly use-

* *Gomapard*: one of the few electric instruments used on Sirene. An oscillator produces an oboelike tone which is modulated, choked, vibrated, raised and lowered in pitch by four keys.
** Double-*kamanthil*: an instrument similar to the *ganga*, except the tones are produced by twisting and inclining a disk of resined leather against one or more of the forty-six strings.

ful also—but perhaps you'd better learn the other instruments first. They should provide at least a rudimentary means of communication."

"Aren't you exaggerating?" suggested Thissell. "Or joking?"

Rolver laughed his saturnine laugh. "Not at all. First of all, you'll need a houseboat. And then you'll want slaves."

Rolver took Thissell from the landing field to the docks of Fan, a walk of an hour and a half along a pleasant path under enormous trees loaded with fruit, cereal pods, sacs of sugary sap.

"At the moment," said Rolver, "there are only four outworlders in Fan, counting yourself. I'll take you to Welibus, our Commercial Factor. I think he's got an old houseboat he might let you use."

Cornely Welibus had resided fifteen years in Fan, acquiring sufficient *strakh* to wear his South Wind mask with authority. This consisted of a blue disk inlaid with cabochons of lapis lazuli, surrounded by an auerole of shimmering snakeskin. Heartier and more cordial than Rolver, he not only provided Thissell with a houseboat, but also a score of various musical instruments and a pair of slaves.

Embarrassed by the largesse, Thissell stammered something about payment, but Welibus cut him off with an expansive gesture. "My dear fellow, this is Sirene. Such trifles cost nothing."

"But a houseboat—"

Welibus played a courtly little flourish on his *kiv*. "I'll be frank, Ser Thissell. The boat is old and a trifle shabby. I can't afford to use it; my status would suffer." A graceful melody accompanied his words. "Status as yet need not concern you. You require merely shelter, comfort and safety from the Night-men."

" 'Night-men'?"

"The cannibals who roam the shore after dark."

"Oh, yes. Ser Rolver mentioned them."

"Horrible things. We won't discuss them." A shuddering little trill issued from his *kiv*. "Now, as to slaves." He tapped the blue disk of his mask with a thoughtful forefinger. "Rex and Toby should serve you well." He raised his voice, played a swift clatter on the *hymerkin.* "*Avan esx trobu!*"

A female slave appeared wearing a dozen tight bands of pink cloth, and a dainty black mask sparkling with mother-of-pearl sequins.

"*Fascu etz Rex ae Toby.*"

Rex and Toby appeared, wearing loose masks of black cloth, russet jerkins. Welibus addressed them with a resonant clatter of *hymerkin,* enjoining them to the service of their new master, on pain of return to their native islands. They prostrated themselves, sang pledges of servitude to Thissell in soft husky voices. Thissell laughed nervously and essayed a sentence in the Sirenese language. "Go to the houseboat, clean it well, bring aboard food."

Toby and Rex stared blankly through the holes in their masks. Welibus repeated the orders with *hymerkin* accompaniment. The slaves bowed and departed.

Thissell surveyed the musical instruments with dismay. "I haven't the slightest idea how to go about learning these things."

Welibus turned to Rolver. "What about Kershaul? Could he be persuaded to give Ser Thissell some basic instruction?"

Rolver nodded judicially. "Kershaul might undertake the job."

Thissell asked, "Who is Kershaul?"

"The fourth of our little group of expatriates," replied Welibus; "an anthropologist. You've read *Zundar the Splendid? Rituals of Sirene? The Faceless Folk?* No? A pity. All excellent works. Kershaul is high in prestige and I believe visits Zundar from time to time. Wears a Cave Owl, sometimes a Star Wanderer, or even a Wise Arbiter."

"He's taken to an Equatorial Serpent," said Rolver. "The variant with the gilt tusks."

"Indeed!" marveled Welibus. "Well, I must say he's earned it. A fine fellow, good chap indeed." And he strummed his *zachinko* thoughtfully.

Three months passed. Under the tutelage of Mathew Kershaul, Thissell practiced the *hymerkin,* the *ganga,* the *strapan,* the *kiv,* the *gomapard,* and the *zachinko.* The double-*kamanthil,* the *krodatch,* the *slobo,* the water-lute and a number of others could wait, said Kershaul, until Thissell had mastered the six basic instruments. He lent Thissell recordings of noteworthy Sirenese conversing in various moods and to various accompaniments, so that Thissell might learn the melodic conventions currently in vogue, and perfect himself in the niceties of intonation, the various rhythms, cross-rhythms, compound rhythms, implied rhythms and supressed rhythms. Kershaul professed to find Sirenese music a fascinating study, and Thissell admitted that it was a subject not readily exhausted. The quarter-tone tuning of the instruments admitted the use of twenty-four tonalities, which multiplied by the five modes in general use, resulted in one hundred and twenty separate scales. Kershaul, however, advised that Thissell primarily concentrate on learning each instrument in its fundamental tonality, using only two of the modes.

With no immediate business at Fan except the weekly visits to Mathew Kershaul, Thissell took his houseboat eight miles south and moored it in the lee of a rocky promontory. Here, if it had not been for the incessant practicing, Thissell lived an idyllic life. The sea was calm and crystal-clear; the beach, ringed by the gray, green and purple foliage of the forest, lay close at hand if he wanted to stretch his legs.

Toby and Rex occupied a pair of cubicles forward, Thissell had the after-cabins to himself. From time to time he toyed with the idea of a third slave, possibly a young female, to contribute an element of charm and gaiety to the ménage, but Kershaul advised against the step, fearing that the intensity of Thissell's concentration might somehow be diminished. Thissell acquiesced and devoted himself to the study of the six instruments.

The days passed quickly. Thissell never became bored with the pageantry of dawn and sunset; the white clouds and blue sea of noon; the night sky blazing with the twenty-nine stars of Cluster SI 1-715. The weekly trip to Fan broke the tedium: Toby and Rex foraged for food; Thissell visited the luxurious houseboat of Mathew Kershaul for instruction and advice. Then, three months after Thissell's arrival, came the message completely disorganizing the routine: Haxo Angmark, assassin, agent provocateur, ruthless and crafty criminal, had come to Sirene. *Effective detention and incarceration of this man!* read the orders. *Attention! Haxo Angmark superlatively dangerous. Kill without hesitation!*

Thissell was not in the best of condition. He trotted fifty yards until his breath came in gasps, then walked: through low hills crowned with white bamboo and black tree-ferns; across meadows yellow with grass-nuts; through orchards and wild vineyards. Twenty minutes passed, twenty-five minutes passed—twenty-five minutes!; with a heavy sensation in his stomach Thissell knew that he was too late. Haxo Angmark had landed, and might be traversing this very road toward Fan. But along the way Thissell met only four persons: a boy-child in a mock-fierce Alk Islander mask; two young women wearing the Red Bird and the Green Bird; a man masked as a Forest Goblin. Coming upon the man, Thissell stopped short. Could this be Angmark?

Thissell essayed a strategem. He went boldly to the man, stared into the hideous mask. "Angmark," he called in the language of the Home Planets, "you are under arrest!"

The Forest Goblin stared uncomprehendingly, then started forward along the track.

Thissell put himself in the way. He reached for his *ganga*, then recalling the hostler's reaction, instead struck a chord on the *zachinko*. "You travel the road from the spaceport," he sang. "What have you seen there?"

The Forest Goblin grasped his hand-bugle, an instrument used to deride opponents on the field of battle, to summon animals or occasionally to evince a rough and ready truculence. "Where I travel and what I see are the concern solely of myself. Stand back or I walk upon your face." He marched forward, and had not Thissell leaped aside the Forest Goblin might well have made good his threat.

Thissell stood gazing after the retreating back. Angmark? Not likely, with so sure a touch on the hand-bugle. Thissell hesitated, then turned and continued on his way.

Arriving at the spaceport, he went directly to the office. The heavy door stood ajar; as Thissell approached, a man appeared in the doorway. He wore a mask of dull green scales, mica plates, blue-lacquered wood and black quills— the Tarn Bird.

"Ser Rolver," Thissell called out anxiously, "who came down from the *Carina Cruzeiro?*"

Rolver studied Thissell a long moment. "Why do you ask?"

"Why do I ask?" demanded Thissell. "You must have seen the spacegram I received from Castel Cromartin!"

"Oh, yes," said Rolver. "Of course. Naturally."

"It was delivered only half an hour ago," said Thissell bitterly. "I rushed out as fast as I could. Where is Angmark?"

"In Fan, I assume," said Rolver.

Thissell cursed softly. "Why didn't you hold him up, delay him in some way?"

Rolver shrugged. "I had neither authority, inclination nor the capability to stop him."

Thissell fought back his annoyance. In a voice of studied calm he said, "On the way I passed a man in rather a ghastly mask—saucer eyes, red wattles."

"A Forest Goblin," said Rolver. "Angmark brought the mask with him."

"But he played the hand-bugle," Thissell protested. "How could Angmark—"

"He's well acquainted with Sirene; he spent five years here in Fan."

Thissell grunted in annoyance. "Cromartin made no mention of this."

"It's common knowledge," said Rolver with a shrug. "He was Commercial Representative before Welibus took over."

"Were he and Welibus acquainted?"

Rolver laughed shortly. "Naturally. But don't suspect poor Welibus of anything more venal than juggling his accounts; I assure you he's no consort of assassins."

"Speaking of assassins," said Thissell, "do you have a weapon I might borrow?"

Rolver inspected him in wonder. "You came out here to take Angmark bare-handed?"

"I had no choice," said Thissell. "When Cromartin gives orders he expects results. In any event you were here with your slaves."

"Don't count on me for help," Rolver said testily. "I wear the Tarn Bird and make no pretensions of valor. But I can lend you a power pistol. I haven't used it recently; I won't guarantee its charge."

Rolver went into the office and a moment later returned with the gun. "What will you do now?"

Thissell shook his head wearily. "I'll try to find Angmark in Fan. Or might he head for Zundar?"

Rolver considered. "Angmark might be able to survive in Zundar. But he'd want to brush up on his musicianship. I imagine he'll stay in Fan a few days."

"But how can I find him? Where should I look?"

"That I can't say," replied Rolver. "You might be safer not finding him. Angmark is a dangerous man."

Thissell returned to Fan the way he had come.

Where the path swung down from the hills into the esplanade a thick-walled *pisé de terre* building had been constructed. The door was carved from a solid black plank; the windows were guarded by enfoliated bands of iron. This was the office of Cornely Welibus, Commercial Factor, Importer and Exporter. Thissell found Welibus sitting at his ease on the tiled veranda, wearing a modest adaptation of the Waldemar mask. He seemed lost in thought, and might or might not have recognized Thissell's Moon Moth; in any event he gave no signal of greeting.

Thissell approached the porch. "Good morning, Ser Welibus."

Welibus nodded abstractedly and said in a flat voice, plucking at his *krodatch,* "Good morning."

Thissell was rather taken aback. This was hardly the instrument to use toward a friend and fellow out-worlder, even if he did wear the Moon Moth.

Thissell said coldly, "May I ask how long you have been sitting here?"

Welibus considered half a minute, and now when he spoke he accompanied himself on the more cordial *crebarin.* But the recollection of the *krodatch* chord still rankled in Thissell's mind.

"I've been here fifteen or twenty minutes. Why do you ask?"

"I wonder if you noticed a Forest Goblin pass?"

Welibus nodded. "He went on down the esplanade—turned into the first mask shop, I believe."

Thissell hissed between his teeth. This would naturally be Angmark's first move. "I'll never find him once he changes masks," he muttered.

"Who is this Forest Goblin?" asked Welibus, with no more than casual interest.

Thissell could see no reason to conceal the name. "A notorious criminal: Haxo Angmark."

"Haxo Angmark!" croaked Welibus, leaning back in his chair. "You're sure he's here?"

"Reasonably sure.'

Welibus rubbed his shaking hands together. "This is bad news—bad news indeed! Hes an unscrupulous scoundrel."

"You knew him well?"

"As well as anyone." Welibus was now accompanying himself with the *kiv*. "He held the post I now occupy. I came out as an inspector and found that he was embezzling four thousand UMI's a month. I'm sure he feels no great gratitude toward me." Welibus glanced nervously up the esplanade. "I hope you catch him."

"I'm doing my best. He went into the mask shop, you say?"

"I'm sure of it."

Thissell turned away. As he went down the path he heard the black plank door thud shut behind him.

He walked down the esplanade to the mask-maker's shop, paused outside as if admiring the display: a hundred miniature masks, carved from rare woods and minerals, dressed with emerald flakes, spider-web silk, wasp wings, petrified fish scales and the like. The shop was empty except for the mask-maker, a gnarled knotty man in a yellow robe, wearing a deceptively simple Universal Expert mask, fabricated from over two thousand bits of articulated wood.

Thissell considered what he would say, how he would accompany himself, then entererd. The mask-maker, noting the Moon Moth and Thissell's diffident manner, continued with his work.

Thissell, selecting the easiest of his instruments, stroked his *strapan*—possibly not the most felicitous choice, for it conveyed a certain degree of condescension. Thissell tried to counteract his flavor by singing in warm, almost effusive, tones, shaking the *strapan* whimsically when he struck a wrong note: "A stranger is an interesting person to deal with; his habits are unfamiliar, he excites curiosity. Not twenty minutes ago a stranger entered this fascinating shop, to exchange his drab Forest Goblin for one of the remarkable and adventurous creations assembled on the premises."

The mask-maker turned Thissell a side-glance, and without words played a progression of chords on an instrument Thissell had never seen before: a flexible sac gripped in the palm with three short tubes leading between the fingers. When the tubes were squeezed almost shut and air forced through the slit, an oboelike tone ensued. To Thissell's developing ear the instrument seemed difficult, the mask-maker expert, and the music conveyed a profound sense of disinterest.

Thissell tried again, laboriously manipulating the *strapan*. He sang, "To an out-worlder on a foreign planet, the voice of one from his home is like water to a wilting plant. A person who could unite two such persons might find satisfaction in such an act of mercy."

The mask-maker casually fingered his own *strapan*, and drew forth a set of rippling scales, his fingers moving faster than the eyes could follow. He sank in the formal style: "An artist values his moments of concentration; he does not care to spend time exchanging banalities with persons of at best average prestige." Thissell attempted to insert a counter melody, but the mask-maker struck a new set of complex chords whose portent evaded Thissell's understanding, and continued: "Into the shop comes a person who evidently has picked up for the first time an instrument of unparalleled complication, for the execution of his music is open to criticism. He sings of homesickness and longing for the sight of others like himself. He dissembles his enormous *strakh* behind a Moon Moth, for he plays the *strapan* to a Master Craftsman, and sings in a voice of contemptuous raillery. The refined and creative artist ignores the provocation. He plays a polite instrument, remains noncommittal, and trusts that the stranger will tire of his sport and depart."

Thissell took up his *kiv*. "The noble mask-maker completely misunderstands me—"

He was interrupted by staccato rasping of the mask-maker's *strapan*. "The stranger now sees fit to ridicule the artist's comprehension."

Thissell scratched furiously at his *strapan*: "To protect myself from the heat, I wander into a small and unpretentious mask shop. The artisan, though still distracted by the novelty of his tools, gives promise of development. He works zealously to perfect his skill, so much so that he refuses to converse with strangers, no matter what their need."

The mask maker carefully laid down his carving tool. He rose to his feet, went behind a screen and shortly returned wearing a mask of gold and iron, with simulated flames licking up from the scalp. In one hand he carried a *skaranyi,* in the other a scimitar. He struck off a brilliant series of wild tones, and sang: "Even the most accomplished artist can augment his *strakh* by killing sea-monsters, Night-men and importunate idlers. Such an occasion is at hand. The artist delays his attack exactly ten seconds, because the offender wears a Moon Moth." He twirled his scimitar, spun it in the air.

Thissell desperately pounded the *strapan.* "Did a Forest Goblin enter the shop? Did he depart with a new mask?"

"Five seconds have lapsed," sang the mask-maker in steady ominous rhythm.

Thissell departed in frustrated rage. He crossed the square, stood looking up and down the esplanade. Hundreds of men and women sauntered along the docks, or stood on the decks of their houseboats, each wearing a mask chosen to express his mood, prestige and special attributes, and everywhere sounded the twitter of musical instruments.

Thissell stood at a loss. The Forest Goblin had disappeared. Haxo Angmark walked at liberty in Fan, and Thissell had failed the urgent instructions of Castel Cromartin.

Behind him sounded the casual notes of a *kiv.* "Ser Moon Moth Thissell, you stand engrossed in thought."

Thissell turned, to find beside him a Cave Owl, in a somber cloak of black and gray. Thissell recognized the mask, which symbolized erudition and patient exploration of abstract ideas; Mathew Kershaul had worn it on the occasion of their meeting a week before.

"Good morning, Ser Kershaul," muttered Thissell.

"And how are the studies coming? Have you mastered the C-Sharp Plus scale on the *gomapard?* As I recall, you were finding those inverse intervals puzzling."

"I've worked on them," said Thissell in a gloomy voice. "However, since I'll probably be recalled to Polypolis, it may be all time wasted."

"Eh? What's this?"

Thissell explained the situation in regard to Haxo Angmark. Kershaul nodded gravely. "I recall Angmark. Not a gracious personality, but an excellent musician, with quick fingers and a real talent for new instruments." Thoughtfully he twisted the goatee of his Cave Owl mask. "What are your plans?"

"They're nonexistent," said Thissell, playing a doleful phrase on the *kiv*. "I haven't any idea what masks he'll be wearing and if I don't know what he looks like, how can I find him?"

Kershaul tugged at his goatee. "In the old days he favored the Exo Cambian Cycle, and I believe he used an entire set of Nether Denizens. Now of course his tastes may have changed."

"Exactly," Thissell complained. "He might be twenty feet away and I'd never know it." He glanced bitterly across the esplanade toward the mask-maker's shop. "No one will tell me anything; I doubt if they care that a murderer is walking their docks."

"Quite correct," Kershaul agreed. "Sirenese standards are different from ours."

"They have no sense of responsibility," declared Thissell. "I doubt if they'd throw a rope to a drowning man."

"It's true that they dislike interference," Kershaul agreed. "They emphasize individual responsibility and self-sufficiency."

"Interesting," said Thissell, "but I'm still in the dark about Angmark."

Kershaul surveyed him gravely. "And should you locate Angmark, what will you do then?"

"I'll carry out the orders of my superior," said Thissell doggedly.

"Angmark is a dangerous man," mused Kershaul. "He's got a number of advantages over you."

"I can't take that into account. It's my duty to send him back to Polypolis. He's probably safe, since I haven't the remotest idea how to find him."

Kershaul reflected. "An out-worlder can't hide behind a mask, not from the Sirenes, at least. There are four of us here at Fan—Rolver, Welibus, you and me. If another out-worlder tries to set up housekeeping the news will get around in short order."

"What if he heads for Zundar?"

Kershaul shrugged. "I doubt if he'd dare. On the other

hand—" Kershaul paused, then noting Thissell's sudden inattention, turned to follow Thissell's gaze.

A man in a Forest Goblin mask came swaggering toward them along the esplanade. Kershaul laid a restraining hand on Thissell's arm, but Thissell stepped out into the path of the Forest Goblin, his borrowed gun ready. "Haxo Angmark," he cried, "don't make a move, or I'll kill you. You're under arrest."

"Are you sure this is Angmark?" asked Kershaul in a worried voice.

"I'll find out," said Thissell. "Angmark, turn around, hold up your hands."

The Forest Goblin stood rigid with surprise and puzzlement. He reached to his *zachinko,* played an interrogatory arpeggio, and sang, "Why do you molest me, Moon Moth?"

Kershaul stepped forward and played a placatory phrase on his *slobo.* "I fear that a case of confused identity exists, Ser Forest Goblin. Ser Moon Moth seeks an out-worlder in a Forest Goblin mask."

The Forest Goblin's music became irritated, and he suddenly switched to his *stimic.* "He asserts that I am an out-worlder? Let him prove his case, or he has my retaliation to face."

Kershaul glanced in embarrassment around the crowd which had gathered and once more struck up an ingratiating melody. "I am sure that Ser Moon Moth—"

The Forest Goblin interrupted with a fanfare of *skaranyi* tones. "Let him demonstrate his case or prepare for the flow of blood."

Thissell said, "Very well, I'll prove my case." He stepped forward, grasped the Forest Goblin's mask. "Let's see your face, that'll demonstrate your identity!"

The Forest Goblin sprang back in amazement. The crowd gasped, then set up an ominous strumming and toning of various instruments.

The Forest Goblin reached to the nape of his neck, jerked the cord to his duel-gong, and with his other hand snatched forth his scimitar.

Kershaul stepped forward, playing the *slobo* with great agitation. Thissell, now abashed, moved aside, conscious of the ugly sound of the crowd.

Kershaul sang explanations and apologies, the Forest

Goblin answered; Kershaul spoke over his shoulder to Thissell: "Run for it, or you'll be killed! Hurry!"

Thissell hesitated; the Forest Goblin put up his hand to thrust Kershaul aside. "Run!" screamed Kershaul. "To Welibus' office, lock yourself in!"

Thissell took to his heels. The Forest Goblin pursued him a few yards, then stamped his feet, sent after him a set of raucous and derisive blasts of the hand-bugle, while the crowd produced a contemptuous counterpoint of clacking *hymerkins*.

There was no further pursuit. Instead of taking refuge in the Import-Export office, Thissell turned aside and after cautious reconnaissance proceeded to the dock where his houseboat was moored.

The hour was not far short of dusk when he finally returned aboard. Toby and Rex squatted on the forward deck, surrounded by the provisions they had brought back: reed baskets of fruit and cereal, blue-glass jugs containing wine, oil and pungent sap, three young pigs in a wicker pen. They were cracking nuts between their teeth, spitting the shells over the side. They looked up at Thissell, and it seemed that they rose to their feet with a new casualness. Toby muttered something under his breath; Rex smothered a chuckle.

Thissell clacked his *hymerkin* angrily. He sang, "Take the boat offshore; tonight we remain at Fan."

In the privacy of his cabin he removed the Moon Moth, stared into a mirror at his almost unfamiliar features. He picked up the Moon Moth, examined the detested lineaments: the furry gray skin, the blue spines, the ridiculous lace flaps. Hardly a dignified presence for the Consular Representative of the Home Planets. If, in fact, he still held the position when Cromartin learned of Angmark's winning free!

Thissell flung himself into a chair, stared moodily into space. Today he'd suffered a series of setbacks, but he wasn't defeated yet; not by any means. Tomorrow he'd visit Mathew Kershaul; they'd discuss how best to locate Angmark. As Kershaul had pointed out, another out-world establishment could not be camouflaged; Haxo Angmark's identity would soon become evident. Also, tomorrow he must procure another mask. Nothing extreme or vainglorious, but a mask which expressed a modicum of dignity and self-respect.

At this moment one of the slaves tapped on the door panel, and Thissell hastily pulled the hated Moon Moth back over his head.

Early next morning, before the dawn light had left the sky, the slaves sculled the houseboat back to that section of the dock set aside for the use of out-worlders. Neither Rolver nor Welibus nor Kershaul had yet arrived and Thissell waited impatiently. An hour passed, and Welibus brought his boat to the dock. Not wishing to speak to Welibus, Thissell remained inside his cabin.

A few moments later Rolver's boat likewise pulled in alongside the dock. Through the window Thissell saw Rolver, wearing his usual Tarn Bird, climb to the dock. Here he was met by a man in a yellow-tufted Sand Tiger mask, who played a formal accompaniment on his *gomapard* to whatever message he brought Rolver.

Rolver seemed surprised and disturbed. After a moment's thought he manipulated his own *gomapard,* and as he sang, he indicated Thissell's houseboat. Then, bowing, he went on his way.

The man in the Sand Tiger mask climbed with rather heavy dignity to the float and rapped on the bulwark of Thissell's houseboat.

Thissell presented himself. Sirenese etiquette did not demand that he invite a casual visitor aboard, so he merely struck an interrogation on his *zachinko.*

The Sand Tiger played his *gomapard* and sang, "Dawn over the bay of Fan is customarily a splendid occásion; the sky is white with yellow and green colors; when Mireille rises, the mists burn and writhe like flames. He who sings derives a greater enjoyment from the hour when the floating corpse of an out-worlder does not appear to mar the serenity of the view."

Thissell's *zachinko* gave off a startled interrogation almost of its own accord; the Sand Tiger bowed with dignity. "The singer acknowledges no peer in steadfastness of disposition; however, he does not care to be plagued by the antics of a dissatisfied ghost. He therefore has ordered his slaves to attach a thong to the ankle of the corpse, and while we have conversed they have linked the corpse to the stern of your houseboat. You will wish to administer whatever rites are prescribed in the out-world. He who sings wishes you a good morning and now departs."

Thissell rushed to the stern of his houseboat. There, near-naked and maskless, floated the body of a mature man, supported by air trapped in his pantaloons.

Thissell studied the dead face, which seemed character-less and vapid—perhaps in direct consequence of the mask-wearing habit. The body appeared of medium stature and weight, and Thissell estimated the age as between forty-five and fifty. The hair was nondescript brown, the features bloated by the water. There was nothing to indicate how the man had died.

This must be Haxo Angmark, thought Thissell. Who else could it be? Mathew Kershaul? Why not? Thissell asked himself uneasily. Rolver and Welibus had already disem-barked and gone about their business. He searched across the bay to locate Kershaul's houseboat, and discovered it already tying up to the dock. Even as he watched, Kershaul jumped ashore, wearing his Cave Owl mask.

He seemed in an abstracted mood, for he passed Thissell's houseboat without lifting his eyes from the dock.

Thissell turned back to the corpse. Angmark, then, beyond a doubt. Had not three men disembarked from the house-boats of Rolver, Welibus and Kershaul, wearing masks characteristic of these men? Obviously, the corpse of Ang-mark. . . . The easy solution refused to sit quiet in Thissell's mind. Kershaul had pointed out that another out-worlder would be quickly identified. How else could Angmark main-tain himself unless he . . . Thissell brushed the thought aside. The corpse was obviously Angmark.

And yet . . .

Thissell summoned his slaves, gave orders that a suitable container be brought to the dock, that the corpse be trans-ferred therein, and conveyed to a suitable place of repose. The slaves showed no enthusiasm for the task and Thissell was compelled to thunder forcefully, if not skillfully, on the *hymerkin* to emphasize his orders.

He walked along the dock, turned up the esplanade, passed the office of Cornely Welibus and set out along the pleasant little lane to the landing field.

When he arrived, he found that Rolver had not yet made

an appearance. An over-slave, given status by a yellow rosette on his black cloth mask, asked how he might be of service. Thissell stated that he wished to dispatch a message to Polypolis.

There was no difficulty here, declared the slave. If Thissell would set forth his message in clear block-print it would be dispatched immediately.

Thissell wrote:

Out-worlder found dead, possibly Angmark. Age 48, medium physique, brown hair. Other means of identification lacking. Await acknowledgment and/or instructions.

He addressed the message to Castel Cromartin at Polypolis and handed it to the over-slave. A moment later he heard the characteristic sputter of trans-space discharge.

An hour passed. Rolver made no appearance. Thissell paced restlessly back and forth in front of the office. There was no telling how long he would have to wait: trans-space transmission time varied unpredictably. Sometimes the message snapped through in microseconds; sometimes it wandered through unknowable regions for hours; and there were several authenticated examples of messages being received before they had been transmitted.

Another half hour passed, and Rolver finally arrived, wearing his customary Tarn Bird. Coincidentally Thissell heard the hiss of the incoming message.

Rolver seemed surprised to see Thissell. "What brings you out so early?"

Thissell explained. "It concerns the body which you referred to me this morning. I'm communicating with my superiors about it."

Rolver raised his head and listened to the sound of the incoming message. "You seem to be getting an answer. I'd better attend to it."

"Why bother?" asked Thissell. "Your slave seems efficient."

"It's my job," declared Rolver. "I'm responsible for the accurate transmission and receipt of all spacegrams."

"I'll come with you," said Thissell. "I've always wanted to watch the operation of the equipment."

"I'm afraid that's irregular," said Rolver. He went to the door which led into the inner compartment. "I'll have your message in a moment."

Thissell protested, but Rolver ignored him and went into the inner office.

Five minutes later he reappeared, carrying a small yellow envelope. "Not too good news," he announced with unconvincing commiseration.

Thissell glumly opened the envelope. The message read:

Body not Angmark. Angmark has black hair. Why did you not meet landing? Serious infraction, highly dissatisfied. Return to Polypolis next opportunity.
Castel Cromartin

Thissell put the message in his pocket. "Incidentally, may I inquire the color of your hair?"

Rolver played a surprised little trill on his *kiv*. "I'm quite blond. Why do you ask?"

"Mere curiosity."

Rolver played another run on the *kiv*. "Now I understand. My dear fellow, what a suspicious nature you have! Look!" He turned and parted the folds of his mask at the nape of his neck. Thissell saw that Rolver was indeed blond.

"Are you reassured?" asked Rolver jocularly.

"Oh, indeed," said Thissell. "Incidentally, have you another mask you could lend me? I'm sick of this Moon Moth."

"I'm afraid not," said Rolver. "But you need merely go into a mask-maker's shop and make a selection."

"Yes, of course," said Thissell. He took his leave of Rolver and returned along the trail to Fan. Passing Welibus' office he hesitated, then turned in. Today Welibus wore a dazzling confection of green glass prisms and silver beads, a mask Thissell had never seen before.

Welibus greeted him cautiously to the accompaniment of a *kiv*. "Good morning, Ser Moon Moth."

"I won't take too much of your time," said Thissell, "but I have a rather personal question to put to you. What color is your hair?"

Welibus hesitated a fraction of a second, then turned his back, lifted the flap of his mask. Thissell saw heavy black ringlets. "Does that answer your question?" inquired Welibus.

"Completely," said Thissell. He crossed the esplanade, went out on the dock to Kershaul's houseboat. Kershaul greeted him without enthusiasm, and invited him aboard with a resigned wave of the hand.

"A question I'd like to ask," said Thissell; "what color is your hair?"

Kershaul laughed woefully. "What little remains is black. Why do you ask?"

"Curiosity."

"Come, come," said Kershaul with an unaccustomed bluffness. "There's more to it than that."

Thissell, feeling the need of counsel, admitted as much. "Here's the situation. A dead out-worlder was found in the harbor this morning. His hair was brown. I'm not entirely certain, but the chances are—let me see, yes—two out of three that Angmark's hair is black."

Kershaul pulled at the Cave Owl's goatee. "How do you arrive at that probability?"

"The information came to me through Rolver's hands. He has blond hair. If Angmark has assumed Rolver's identity, he would naturally alter the information which came to me this morning. Both you and Welibus admit to black hair."

"Hm," said Kershaul. "Let me see if I follow your line of reasoning. You feel that Haxo Angmark has killed either Rolver, Welibus or myself and assumed the dead man's identity. Right?"

Thissell looked at him in surprise. "You yourself emphasized that Angmark could not set up another out-world establishment without revealing himself! Don't you remember?"

"Oh, certainly. To continue. Rolver delivered a message to you stating that Angmark was dark, and announced himself to be blond."

"Yes. Can you verify this? I mean for the old Rolver?"

"No," said Kershaul sadly. "I've seen neither Rolver nor Welibus without their masks."

"If Rolver is not Angmark," Thissell mused, "if Angmark indeed has black hair, then both you and Welibus come under suspicion."

"Very interesting," said Kershaul. He examined Thissell

warily. "For that matter, you yourself might be Angmark. What color is your hair?"

"Brown," said Thissell curtly. He lifted the gray fur of the Moon Moth mask at the back of his head.

"But you might be deceiving me as to the text of the message," Kershaul put forward.

"I'm not," said Thissell wearily. "You can check with Rolver if you care to."

Kershaul shook his head. "Unnecessary. I believe you. But another matter: what of voice? You've heard all of us before and after Angmark arrived. Isn't there some indication there?"

"No. I'm so alert for any evidence of change that you all sound rather different. And the masks muffle your voices."

Kershaul tugged the goatee. "I don't see any immediate solution to the problem." He chuckled. "In any event, need there be? Before Angmark's advent, there were Rolver, Welibus, Kershaul and Thissell. Now—for all practical purposes—there are still Rolver, Welibus, Kerhsaul and Thissell. Who is to say that the new member may not be an improvement upon the old?"

"An interesting thought," agreed Thissell, "but it so happens that I have a personal interest in identifying Angmark. My career is at stake."

"I see," murmured Kershaul. "The situation then becomes an issue between yourself and Angmark."

"You won't help me?"

"Not actively. I've become pervaded with Sirenese individualism. I think you'll find that Rolver and Welibus will respond similarly." He sighed. "All of us have been here too long."

Thissell stood deep in thought. Kershaul waited patiently a moment, then said, "Do you have any further questions?"

"No," said Thissell. "I have merely a favor to ask you."

"I'll oblige if I possibly can," Kershaul replied courteously.

"Give me, or lend me, one of your slaves, for a week or two."

Kershaul played an exclamation of amusement on the *ganga*. "I hardly like to part with my slaves; they know me and my ways—"

"As soon as I catch Angmark you'll have him back."

"Very well," said Kershaul. He rattled a summons on his

hymerkin, and a slave appeared. "Anthony," sang Kershaul, "you are to go with Ser Thissell and serve him for a short period."

The slave bowed, without pleasure.

Thissell took Anthony to his houseboat, and questioned him at length, noting certain of the responses upon a chart. He then enjoined Anthony to say nothing of what had passed, and consigned him to the care of Toby and Rex. He gave further instructions to move the houseboat away from the dock and allow no one aboard until his return.

He set forth once more along the way to the landing field, and found Rolver at a lunch of spiced fish, shredded bark of the salad tree and a bowl of native currants. Rolver clapped an order on the *hymerkin,* and a slave set a place for Thissell. "And how are the investigations proceeding?"

"I'd hardly like to claim any progress," said Thissell. "I assume that I can count on your help?"

Rolver laughed briefly. "You have my good wishes."

"More concretely," said Thissell, "I'd like to borrow a slave from you. Temporarily."

Rolver paused in his eating. "Whatever for?"

"I'd rather not explain," said Thissell. "But you can be sure that I make no idle request."

Without graciousness Rolver summoned a slave and consigned him to Thissell's service.

On the way back to his houseboat, Thissell stopped at Welibus' office.

Welibus looked up from his work. "Good afternoon, Ser Thissell."

Thissell came directly to the point. "Ser Welibus, will you lend me a slave for a few days?"

Welibus hesitated, then shrugged. "Why not?" He clacked his *hymerkin;* a slave appeared. "Is he satisfactory? Or would you prefer a young female?" He chuckled rather offensively, to Thissell's way of thinking.

"He'll do very well. I'll return him in a few days."

"No hurry." Welibus made an easy gesture and returned to his work.

Thissell continued to his houseboat, where he separately interviewed each of his two new slaves and made notes upon his chart.

Dusk came soft over the Titanic Ocean. Toby and Rex

sculled the houseboat away from the dock, out across the silken waters. Thissell sat on the deck listening to the sound of soft voices, the flutter and tinkle of musical instruments. Lights from the floating houseboats glowed yellow and wan watermelon-red. The shore was dark; the Night-men would presently come slinking to paw through refuse and stare jealously across the water.

In nine days the *Buenaventura* came past Sirene on its regular schedule; Thissell had his orders to return to Polypolis. In nine days, could he locate Haxo Angmark?

Nine days weren't too many, Thissell decided, but they might possibly be enough.

Two days passed, and three and four and five. Every day Thissell went ashore and at least once a day visited Rolver, Welibus and Kershaul.

Each reacted differently to his presence. Rolver was sardonic and irritable; Welibus formal and at least superficially affable; Kershaul mild and suave, but ostentatiously impersonal and detached in his conversation.

Thissell remained equally bland to Rolver's dour jibes, Welibus' jocundity, Kershaul's withdrawal. And every day, returning to his houseboat he made marks on his chart.

The sixth, the seventh, the eighth day came and passed. Rolver, with rather brutal directness, inquired if Thissell wished to arrange for passage on the *Buenaventura*. Thissell considered, and said, "Yes, you had better reserve passage for one."

"Back to the world of faces." Rolver shuddered. "Faces! Everywhere pallid, fish-eyed faces. Mouths like pulp, noses knotted and punctured; flat, flabby faces. I don't think I could stand it after living here. Luckily you haven't become a real Sirenese."

"But I won't be going back," said Thissell.

"I thought you wanted me to reserve passage."

"I do. For Haxo Angmark. He'll be returning to Polypolis in the brig."

"Well, well," said Rolver. "So you've picked him out."

"Of course," said Thissell. "Haven't you?"

Rolver shrugged. "He's either Welibus or Kershaul, that's as close as I can make it. So long as he wears his mask and calls himself either Welibus or Kershaul, it means nothing to me."

"It means a great deal to me," said Thissell. "What time tomorrow does the lighter go up?"

"Eleven twenty-two sharp. If Haxo Angmark's leaving, tell him to be on time."

"He'll be here," said Thissell.

He made his usual call upon Welibus and Kershaul, then returning to his houseboat, put three final marks on his chart.

The evidence was here, plain and convincing. Not absolutely incontrovertible evidence, but enough to warrant a definite move. He checked over his gun. Tomorrow, the day of decision. He could afford no errors.

The day dawned bright white, the sky like the inside of an oyster shell; Mireille rose through iridescent mists. Toby and Rex sculled the houseboat to the dock. The remaining three out-world houseboats floated somnolently on the slow swells.

One boat Thissell watched in particular, that whose owner Haxo Angmark had killed and dropped into the harbor. This boat presently moved toward the shore, and Haxo Angmark himself stood on the front deck, wearing a mask Thissell had never seen before: a construction of scarlet feathers, black glass and spiked green hair.

Thissell was forced to admire his poise. A clever scheme, cleverly planned and executed—but marred by an insurmountable difficulty.

Angmark returned within. The houseboat reached the dock. Slaves flung out mooring lines, lowered the gangplank. Thissell, his gun ready in the pocket flap of his robes, walked down the dock, went aboard. He pushed open the door to the saloon. The man at the table raised his red, black and green mask in surprise.

Thissell said, "Angmark, please don't argue or make any —"

Something hard and heavy tackled him from behind; he was flung to the floor, his gun wrested expertly away.

Behind him the *hymerkin* clattered; a voice sang, "Bind the fool's arms."

The man sitting at the table rose to his feet, removed the red, black and green mask to reveal the black cloth of a slave. Thissell twisted his head. Over him stood Haxo Angmark, wearing a mask Thissell recognized as a Dragon Tamer, fabricated from black metal, with a knife-blade nose, socketed eyelids and three crests running back over the scalp.

The mask's expression was unreadable, but Angmark's voice was triumphant. "I trapped you very easily."

"So you did," said Thissell. The slave finished knotting his wrists together. A clatter of Angmark's *hymerkin* sent him away. "Get to your feet," said Angmark. "Sit in that chair."

"What are we waiting for?" inquired Thissell.

"Two of our fellows still remain out on the water. We won't need them for what I have in mind."

"Which is?"

"You'll learn in due course," said Angmark. "We have an hour or so on our hands."

Thissell tested his bonds. They were undoubtedly secure. Angmark seated himself. "How did you fix on me? I admit to being curious. . . . Come, come," he chided as Thissell sat silently. "Can't you recognize that I have defeated you? Don't make affairs unpleasant for yourself."

Thissell shrugged. "I operated on a basic principle. A man can mask his face, but he can't mask his personality."

"Aha," said Angmark. "Interesting. Proceed."

"I borrowed a slave from you and the other two outworlders, and I questioned them carefully. What masks had their masters worn during the month before your arrival? I prepared a chart and plotted their responses. Rolver wore the Tarn Bird about eighty percent of the time, the remaining twenty percent divided between the Sophist Abstraction and the Black Intricate. Welibus had a taste for the heroes of Kan Dachan Cycle. He wore the Chalekun, the Prince Intrepid, the Seavain most of the time: six days out of eight. The other two days he wore his South Wind or his Gay Companion. Kershaul, more conservative, preferred the Cave Owl, the Star Wanderer, and two or three other masks he wore at odd intervals.

"As I say, I acquired this information from possibly its most accurate source, the slaves. My next step was to keep watch upon the three of you. Every day I noted what masks you wore and compared it with my chart. Rolver wore his Tarn Bird six times, his Black Intricate twice. Kershaul wore his Cave Owl five times, his Star Wanderer once, his Quincunx once and his Ideal of Perfection once. Welibus wore the Emerald Mountain twice, the Triple Phoenix three times, the Prince Intrepid once and the Shark God twice."

Angmark nodded thoughtfully. "I see my error. I selected from Welibus' masks, but to my own taste—and as you point out, I revealed myself. But only to you." He rose and went to the window. "Kershaul and Rolver are now coming ashore; they'll soon be past and about their business—though I doubt if they'd interfere in any case; they've both become good Sirenese."

Thissell waited in silence. Ten minutes passed. Then Angmark reached to a shelf and picked up a knife. He looked at Thissell. "Stand up."

Thissell slowly rose to his feet. Angmark approached from the side, reached out, lifted the Moon Moth from Thissell's head. Thissell gasped and made a vain attempt to seize it. Too late; his face was bare and naked.

Angmark turned away, removed his own mask, donned the Moon Moth. He struck a call on his *hymerkin*. Two slaves entered, stopped in shock at the sight of Thissell.

Angmark played a brisk tattoo, sang, "Carry this man up to the dock."

"Angmark!" cried Thissell. "I'm maskless!"

The slaves seized him and in spite of Thissell's desperate struggles, conveyed him out on the dock, along the float and up on the dock.

Angmark fixed a rope around Thissell's neck. He said, "You are now Haxo Angmark, and I am Edwer Thissell. Welibus is dead, you shall soon be dead. I can handle your job without difficulty. I'll play musical instruments like a Night-man and sing like a crow. I'll wear the Moon Moth till it rots and then I'll get another. The report will go to Polypolis, Haxo Angmark is dead. Everything will be serene."

Thissell barely heard. "You can't do this," he whispered. "My mask, my face . . ." A large woman in a blue and pink flower mask walked down the dock. She saw Thissell and emitted a piercing shriek, flung herself prone on the dock.

"Come along," said Angmark brightly. He tugged at the rope, and so pulled Thissell down the dock. A man in a Pirate Captain mask coming up from his houseboat stood rigid in amazement.

Angmark played the *zachinko* and sang, "Behold the notorious criminal Haxo Angmark. Through all the outerworlds his name is reviled; now he is captured and led in shame to his death. Behold Haxo Angmark!"

They turned into the esplanade. A child screamed in fright; a man called hoarsely. Thissell stumbled; tears tumbled from his eyes; he could see only disorganized shapes and colors. Angmark's voice belled out richly: "Everyone behold, the criminal of the out-worlds, Haxo Angmark! Approach and observe his execution!"

Thissell feebly cried out, "I'm not Angmark; I'm Edwer Thissell; he's Angmark." But no one listened to him; there were only cries of dismay, shock, disgust at the sight of his face. He called to Angmark, "Give me my mask, a slavecloth. . . ."

Angmark sang jubilantly, "In shame he lived, in maskless shame he dies."

A Forest Goblin stood before Angmark. "Moon Moth, we meet once more."

Angmark sang, "Stand aside, friend Goblin; I must execute this criminal. In shame he lived, in shame he dies!"

A crowd had formed around the group; masks stared in morbid titillation at Thissell.

The Forest Goblin jerked the rope from Angmark's hand, threw it to the ground. The crowd roared. Voices cried, "No duel, no duel! Execute the monster!"

A cloth was thrown over Thissell's head. Thissell awaited the thrust of a blade. But instead his bonds were cut. Hastily he adjusted the cloth, hiding his face, peering between the folds.

Four men clutched Haxo Angmark. The Forest Goblin confronted him, playing the *skaranyi*. "A week ago you reached to divest me of my mask; you have now achieved your perverse aim!"

"But he is a criminal," cried Angmark. "He is notorious, infamous!"

"What are his misdeeds?" sang the Forest Goblin.

"He has murdered, betrayed; he has wrecked ships; he has tortured, blackmailed, robbed, sold children into slavery; he has—"

The Forest Goblin stopped him. "Your religious differences are of no importance. We can vouch however for your present crimes!"

The hostler stepped forward. He sang fiercely, "This insolent Moon Moth nine days ago sought to preempt my choicest mount!"

Another man pushed close. He wore a Universal Expert, and sang, "I am a Master Mask-maker; I recognize this Moon Moth out-worlder! Only recently he entered my shop and derided my skill. He deserves death!"

"Death to the out-world monster!" cried the crowd. A wave of men surged forward. Steel blades rose and fell, the deed was done.

Thissell watched, unable to move. The Forest Goblin approached, and playing the *stimic* sang sternly, "For you we have pity, but also contempt. A true man would never suffer such indignities!"

Thissell took a deep breath. He reached to his belt and found his *zachinko*. He sang, "My friend, you malign me! Can you not appreciate true courage? Would you prefer to die in combat or walk maskless along the esplanade?"

The Forest Goblin sang, "There is only one answer. First I would die in combat; I could not bear such shame."

Thissell sang, "I had such a choice. I could fight with my hands tied, and so die—or I could suffer shame, and through this shame conquer my enemy. You admit that you lack sufficient *strakh* to achieve this deed. I have proved myself a hero of bravery! I ask, who here has courage to do what I have done?"

"Courage?" demanded the Forest Goblin. "I fear nothing, up to and beyond death at the hands of the Night-men!"

"Then answer."

The Forest Goblin stood back. He played his double-*kamanthil*. "Bravery indeed, if such were your motives."

The hostler struck a series of subdued *gomapard* chords and sang, "Not a man among us would dare what this maskless man has done."

The crowd muttered approval.

The mask-maker approached Thissell, obsequiously stroking his double-*kamanthil*. "Pray Lord Hero, step into my nearby shop, exchange this vile rag for a mask befitting your quality."

Another mask-maker sang, "Before you choose, Lord Hero, examine my magnificent creations!"

A man in a Bright Sky Bird mask approached Thissell reverently.

"I have only just completed a sumptuous houseboat; seventeen years of toil have gone into its fabrication. Grant me the good fortune of accepting and using this splendid craft; aboard waiting to serve you are alert slaves and pleasant maidens; there is ample wine in storage and soft silken carpets on the decks."

"Thank you," said Thissell, striking the *zachinko* with vigor and confidence. "I accept with pleasure. But first a mask."

The mask-maker struck an interrogative trill on the *gomapard*. "Would the Lord Hero consider a Sea Dragon Conqueror beneath his dignity?"

"By no means," said Thissell. "I consider it suitable and satisfactory. We shall go now to examine it."

"**R**UMFUDDLE" WAS originally commissioned by Robert Silverberg for a collection of three stories founded upon the same theme but produced by different writers. Opinions seem to vary as to the complete success of such an approach. From one perspective the idea is provocative and appealing; the theme is explored in many aspects. Another viewpoint suspects that the stories tend to vitiate each other.

What, then, is Robert Silverberg? An impractical theoretician? A dreamer in an ivory tower? To the contrary, he is a pragmatist of no mean distinction; he has performed a deed of altruism by giving substance to an amusing caprice which otherwise might have dissolved into a few rhetorical glimmers. The writers are complacent; so far as I know, all were paid and none seem to be agonized by misgivings.

VI

RUMFUDDLE

1

From *Memoirs and Reflections*, by Alan Robertson:

Often I hear myself declared humanity's preeminent benefactor, though the jocular occasionally raise a claim in favor of the original Serpent. After all circumspection, I really cannot dispute the judgment. My place in history is secure; my name will persist as if it were printed indélibly across the sky. All of which I find absurd but understandable. For I have given wealth beyond calculation. I have expunged deprivation, famine, overpopulation, territorial constriction: all the first-order causes of contention have vanished. My gifts go freely and carry with them my personal joy, but as a reasonable man (and for lack of other restrictive agency), I feel that I cannot relinquish all control, for when has the human animal ever been celebrated for abnegation and self-discipline?

We now enter an era of plenty and a time of new concerns. The old evils are gone; we must resolutely prohibit a flamboyant and perhaps unnatural set of new vices.

The three girls gulped down breakfast, assembled their homework and departed noisily for school.

Elizabeth poured coffee for herself and Gilbert. He thought she seemed pensive and moody. Presently she said, "It's so beautiful here. . . . We're very lucky, Gilbert."

"I never forget it."

Elizabeth sipped her coffee and mused a moment, following some vagrant train of thought. She said, "I never liked growing up. I always felt strange—different from the other girls. I really don't know why."

"It's no mystery. Everyone for a fact is different."

"Perhaps . . . but Uncle Peter and Aunt Emma always acted as if I were more different than usual. I remember a hundred little signals. And yet I was such an ordinary little girl. . . . Do you remember when you were little?"

"Not very well." Duray looked out the window he himself had glazed, across green slopes and down to the placid water his daughters had named the Silver River. The Sounding Sea was thirty miles south; directly behind the house stood the first trees of the Robber Woods.

Duray considered his past. "Bob owned a ranch in Arizona during the 1870's: one of his fads. The Apaches killed my father and mother. Bob took me to the ranch, and then when I was three he brought me to Alan's house in San Francisco and that's where I was brought up."

Elizabeth sighed. "Alan must have been wonderful. Uncle Peter was so grim. Aunt Emma never told me anything. Literally, not anything! They never cared the slightest bit for me, one way or the other. . . . I wonder why Bob brought the subject up—about the Indians and your mother and father being scalped and all. . . . He's such a strange man."

"Was Bob here?"

"He looked in a few minutes yesterday to remind us of his 'Rumfuddle.' I told him I didn't want to leave the girls. He said to bring them along."

"Hah!"

"I told him I didn't want to go to his damn Rumfuddle with or without the girls. In the first place, I don't want to see Uncle Peter, who's sure to be there. . . ."

2

From *Memoirs and Reflections:*

I insisted then and I insist now that our dear old Mother Earth, so soiled and toil-worn, never be neglected. Since I pay the piper (in a manner of speaking)

I call the tune, and to my secret amusement I am
heeded most briskly the world around, in the manner
of bellboys jumping to the command of an irascible
old gentleman who is known to be a good tipper. No
one dares to defy me. My whims become actualities;
my plans progress.

Paris, Vienna, San Francisco, St. Petersburg, Venice,
London, Dublin surely will persist, gradually to become
idealized essences of their former selves, as wine in due
course becomes the soul of the grape. What of the old
vitality? The shouts and curses, the neighborhood quarrels, the raucous music, the vulgarity? Gone, all gone!
(But easy of reference at any of the cognates.) Old
Earth is to be a gentle, kindly world, rich in treasures
and artifacts, a world of old places: old inns, old roads,
old forests, old palaces, where folk come to wander and
dream, to experience the best of the past without suffering the worst.

Material abundance can now be taken for granted:
our resources are infinite. Metal, timber, soil, rock,
water, air: free for anyone's taking. A single commodity
remains in finite supply: human toil.

Gilbert Duray, the informally adopted grandson of Alan
Robertson, worked on the Urban Removal Program. Six
hours a day, four days a week, he guided a trashing-machine
across deserted Cupertino, destroying tract houses, service
stations and supermarkets. Knobs and toggles controlled
a stool hammer at the end of a hundred-foot boom; with a
twitch of the finger Duray toppled power poles, exploded
picture windows, smashed siding and stucco, pulverized
concrete, first to the left, then to the right. A disposal rig
crawled fifty feet behind. The detritus was clawed upon a
conveyor belt, carried to a twenty-foot orifice and dumped
with a rush and a rumble into Apathetic Ocean. Alumimum
siding, asphalt shingles, corrugated fiber-glass, TV's and
barbeques, Swedish Modern furniture, Book-of-the-Month
selections, concrete patio tiles, finally the sidewalk and street
itself: all to the bottom of Apathetic Ocean. Only the trees
remained: a strange eclectic forest stretching as far as the

eye could reach: liquidambar and Scotch pine; Chinese pistachio, Atlas cedar and ginkgo; white birch and Norway maples.

At one o'clock Howard Wirtz emerged from the caboose, as they called the small locker room at the rear of the machine. Wirtz had homesteaded a Miocene world; Duray, with a wife and three children, had preferred the milder environment of a contemporary semi-cognate: the popular Type A world on which man had never evolved.

Duray gave Wirtz the work schedule. "More or less like yesterday; straight out Persimmon to Walden, then right a block and back."

Wirtz, a dour and laconic man, acknowledged the information with a jerk of the head. On his Miocene world he lived alone, in a houseboat on a mountain lake. He harvested wild rice, mushrooms and berries; he shot geese, ground fowl, deer, young bison, and had once informed Duray that after his five-year work-time he might just retire to his lake and never appear on Earth again, except maybe to buy clothes and ammunition. "Nothing here I want, nothing at all."

Duray gave a derisive snort. "And what will you do with all your time?"

"Hunt, fish, eat and sleep, maybe sit on the front deck once in a while and look out across the lake."

"Nothing else?"

"I just might learn to fiddle. Nearest neighbor is fifteen million years away."

"You can't be too careful, I suppose."

Duray descended to the ground and looked over his day's work: a quarter-mile swath of desolation. Duray, who allowed his subconscious few extravagances, nevertheless felt a twinge for the old times, which, for all their disadvantages, at least had been lively. Voices, bicycle bells, the barking of dogs, the slam of doors, still echoed along Persimmon Avenue. The former inhabitants presumably preferred their new homes. The self-sufficient had taken private worlds, the more gregarious lived in communities on worlds of every description: as early as the Carboniferous, as current as the Type A. A few had even returned to the now uncrowded cities. An exciting era to live in: a time of flux. Duray, thirty-four years old, remembered no other way of life; the old existence, as exemplified by Persimmon Avenue, seemed antique, cramped, constricted.

He had a word with the operator of the trashing-machine; returning to the caboose he paused to look through the orifice across the Apathetic Ocean. A squall hung black above the southern horizon, toward which a trail of broken lumber drifted, to wash ultimately up on some unknown pre-Cambrian shore. There never would be an inspector sailing forth to protest; the world knew no life other than mollusks and algae, and all the trash of Earth would never fill its submarine gorges. Duray tossed a rock through the gap and watched the alien water splash up and subside. Then he turned away and entered the caboose.

Along the back wall were four doors. The second from the left was marked *G. Duray.* He unlocked the door, pulled it open and stopped short, staring in astonishment at the blank back wall. He lifted the transparent plastic flap which functioned as an air-seal and brought out the collapsed metal ring which had been the flange surrounding his passway. The inner surface was bare metal; looking through he saw only the interior of the caboose.

A long minute passed. Duray stood staring at the useless ribbon as if hypnotized, trying to grasp the implications of the situation. To his knowledge no passway had ever failed, unless it had been purposefully closed. Who would play him such a spiteful, idiotic trick? Certainly not his wife Elizabeth. She detested practical jokes, and, if anything, like Duray himself, was perhaps a trifle too intense and literal minded. He jumped down from the caboose and strode off across Cupertino forest: a sturdy, heavy-shouldered man of about average stature. His features were rough and uncompromising; his brown hair was cut crisply short; his eyes glowed golden-brown and exerted an arresting force. Straight heavy eyebrows crossed his long thin nose like the bar of a *T*; his mouth, compressed against some strong inner urgency, formed a lower horizontal bar. All in all, not a man to be trifled with, or so it would seem.

He trudged through the haunted Cupertino forest, preoccupied by the strange and inconvenient event which had befallen him. What had happened to the passway? Unless Elizabeth had invited friends out to Home, as they called their world, she was alone, with the three girls at school. . . .

Duray came out upon Stevens Creek Road. A farmer's pick-up truck halted at his signal and took him into San Jose, now little more than a country town.

At the transit center he dropped a coin in the turnstile and entered the lobby. Four portals, designated *Local, California, North America, World,* opened in the walls, each portal leading to a hub on Utilis *.

Duray passed into the "California" hub, found the "Oakland" portal, returned to the Oakland Transit Center on Earth, passed back through the "Local" portal to the "Oakland" hub on Utilis, returned to Earth through the "Montclair West" portal to a depot only a quarter-mile from Thornhill School**, to which Duray walked.

In the office Duray identified himself to the clerk and requested the presence of his daughter Dolly.

The clerk sent forth a messenger who, after an interval, returned alone. "Dolly Duray isn't at school."

Duray was surprised; Dolly had been in good health and had set off to school as usual. He said, "Either Joan or Ellen will do as well."

The messenger again went forth and again returned. "Neither one is in their classrooms, Mr. Duray. All three of your children are absent."

"I can't understand it," said Duray, now fretful. "All three set off to school this morning."

"Let me ask Miss Haig. I've just come on duty." The clerk spoke into a telephone, listened, then turned back to Duray. "The girls went home at ten o'clock. Mrs. Duray called for them and took them back through the passway."

"Did she give any reason whatever?"

---

* Utilis: a world cognate to Palaeocene Earth, where, by Alan Robertson's decree, all the industries, institutions, warehouses, tanks, dumps and commercial offices of old Earth were now located. The name 'Utilis', so it had been remarked, accurately captured the flavor of Alan Robertson's pedantic, quaint and idealistic personality.

** Alan Robertson had proposed another specialized world, to be known as "Tutelar," where the children of all the settled worlds should receive their education in a vast array of pedagogical facilities. To his hurt surprise, he encountered a storm of wrathful opposition from parents. His scheme was termed mechanistic, vast, dehumanizing, repulsive. What better world for schooling than old Earth itself? Here was the source of all tradition; let Earth become "Tutelar"! So insisted the parents and Alan Robertson had no choice but to agree.

"Miss Haig says no; Mrs. Duray just told her she needed the girls at home."

Duray stifled a sigh of baffled irritation. "Could you take me to their locker? I'll use their passway to get home."

"That's contrary to school regulations, Mr. Duray. You'll understand, I'm sure."

"I can identify myself quite definitely," said Duray. "Mr. Carr knows me well. As a matter of fact, my passway collapsed and I came here to get home."

"Why don't you speak to Mr. Carr?"

"I'd like to do so."

Duray was conducted into the principal's office where he explained his predicament. Mr. Carr expressed sympathy and made no difficulty about taking Duray to the children's passway.

They went to a hall at the back of the school and found the locker numbered "382." "Here we are," said Carr. "I'm afraid that you'll find it a tight fit." He unlocked the metal door with his master key and threw it open. Duray looked inside and saw only the black metal at the back of the locker. The passway, like his own, had been closed.

Duray drew back and for a moment could find no words.

Carr spoke in a voice of polite amazement. "How very perplexing! I don't believe I've ever seen anything like it before! Surely the girls wouldn't play such a silly prank?"

"They know better than to touch the passway," Duray said gruffly. "Are you sure that this is the right locker?"

Carr indicated the card on the outside of the locker, where three names had been typed: *Dorothy Duray, Joan Duray, Ellen Duray.* "No mistake," said Carr, "and I'm afraid that I can't help you any further. Are you in common residency?"

"It's our private homestead."

Carr nodded with lips judiciously pursed, to suggest that such insistence upon privacy seemed eccentric. He gave a deprecatory little chuckle. "I suppose if you isolate yourself to such an extent, you more or less must expect a series of emergencies."

"To the contrary," Duray said crisply. "Our life is uneventful, because there's no one to bother us. We love the wild animals, the quiet, the fresh air. We wouldn't have it any differently."

Carr smiled a dry smile. "Mr. Robertson has certainly altered the lives of us all. I understand that he is your grandfather?"

"I was raised in his household. I'm his nephew's foster son. The blood relationship isn't all that close."

3

From *Memoirs and Reflections:*

I early became interested in magnetic fluxes and their control. After taking my degree I worked exclusively in this field, studying all varieties of magnetic envelopes and developing controls over their formation. For many years my horizons were thus limited, and I lived a placid existence.

Two contemporary developments forced me down from my "ivory castle." First: the fearful overcrowding of the planet and the prospect of worse to come. Cancer already was an affliction of the past; heart diseases were under control; I feared that in another ten years immortality might be a practical reality for many of us, with a consequent augmentation of population pressure.

Second: the theoretical work done upon "black holes" and "white holes" suggested that matter compacted in a "black hole" broke through a barrier to spew forth from a "white hole" into another universe. I calculated pressures and considered the self-focusing magnetic sheaths, cones and whorls with which I was experimenting. Through their innate properties, these entities constricted themselves to apices of a cross-section indistinguishable from a geometric point. What if two or more cones (I asked myself) could be arranged in contraposition to produce an equilibrium? In this condition charged particles must be accelerated to near light speed and at the mutual focus constricted and impinged together. The pressures thus created, though of small scale, would be far in excess of those characteristic of the "black holes": to unknown effect.

I can now report that the mathematics of the multiple focus are a most improbable thicket, and the useful service I enforced upon what I must call a set of absurd contradictions is one of my secrets. I know that thousands of scientists, at home and abroad, are attempting to duplicate my work; they are welcome to the effort. None will succeed. Why do I speak so positively? This is my other secret.

Duray marched back to the Montclair West depot in a state of angry puzzlement. There had been four passways to Home, of which two were closed. The third was located in his San Francisco locker: the "front door," so to speak. The last and the original orifice was cased, filed and indexed in Alan Robertson's vault.

Duray tried to deal with the problem in rational terms. The girls would never tamper with the passways. As for Elizabeth, no more than the girls would she consider such an act. At least Duray could imagine no reason which would so urge or impel her. Elizabeth, like himself a foster child, was a beautiful passionate woman, tall, dark-haired, with lustrous dark eyes and a wide mouth which tended to curve in an endearingly crooked grin. She was also responsible, loyal, careful, industrious; she loved her family and Riverview Manor. The theory of erotic intrigue seemed to Duray as incredible as the fact of the closed passways. Though, for a fact, Elizabeth was prone to wayward and incomprehensible moods. Suppose Elizabeth had received a visitor, who for some sane or insane purpose had forced her to close the passway? . . . Duray shook his head in frustration, like a harassed bull. The matter no doubt had some simple cause. Or on the other hand, Duray reflected, the cause might be complex and intricate. The thought by some obscure connection brought before him the image of his nominal foster father, Alan Robertson's nephew, Bob Robertson. Duray gave his head a nod of gloomy asseveration, as if to confirm a fact he long ago should have suspected. He went to the phone booth and called Bob Robertson's apartment in San Francisco. The screen glowed white and an instant later displayed Bob Robertson's alert, clean and handsome face. "Good afternoon, Gil. Glad you called; I've been anxious to get in touch with you."

Duray became warier than ever. "How so?"

"Nothing serious, or so I hope. I dropped by your locker to leave off some books that I promised Elizabeth, and I noticed through the glass that your passway is closed. Collapsed. Useless."

"Strange," said Duray. "Very strange indeed. I can't understand it. Can you?"

"No . . . not really."

Duray thought to detect a subtlety of intonation. His eyes narrowed in concentration. "The passway at my rig was closed. The passway at the girls' school was closed. Now you tell me that the downtown passway is closed."

Bob Robertson grinned. "That's a pretty broad hint, I would say. Did you and Elizabeth have a row?"

"No."

Bob Robertson rubbed his long aristocratic chin. "A mystery. There's probably some very ordinary explanation."

"Or some very extraordinary explanation."

"True. Nowadays a person can't rule out anything. By the way, tomorrow night is the Rumfuddle, and I expect both you and Elizabeth to be on hand."

"As I recall," said Duray, "I've already declined the invitation." The "Rumfuddlers" were a group of Bob's cronies. Duray suspected that their activities were not altogether wholesome. "Excuse me; I've got to find an open passway or Elizabeth and the kids are marooned."

"Try Alan," said Bob. "He'll have the original in his vault."

Duray gave a curt nod. "I don't like to bother him, but that's my last hope."

"Let me know what happens," said Bob Robertson. "And if you're at loose ends, don't forget the Rumfuddle tomorrow night. I mentioned the matter to Elizabeth and she said she'd be sure to attend."

"Indeed. And when did you consult Elizabeth?"

"A day or so ago. Don't look so damnably gothic, my boy."

"I'm wondering if there's a connection between your invitation and the closed passways. I happen to know that Elizabeth doesn't care for your parties."

Bob Robertson laughed with easy good grace. "Reflect a moment. Two events occur. I invite you and wife Elizabeth to the Rumfuddle. This is event one. Your passways close up, which is event two. By a feat of structured absurdity you equate the two and blame me. Now, is that fair?"

"You call it 'structured absurdity,'" said Duray. "I call it instinct."

Bob Robertson laughed again. "You'll have to do better than that. Consult Alan and if for some reason he can't help you, come to the Rumfuddle. We'll rack our brains and either solve your problem, or come up with new and better ones." He gave a cheery nod and before Duray could roar an angry expostulation the screen faded.

Duray stood glowering at the screen, convinced that Bob Robertson knew much more about the closed passways than he admitted. Duray went to sit on a bench. . . . If Elizabeth had closed him away from Home, her reasons must have been compelling indeed. But, unless she intended to isolate herself permanently from Earth, she would leave at least one passway ajar, and this must be the master orifice in Alan Robertson's vault.

Duray rose to his feet, somewhat heavily, and stood a moment, head bent and shoulders hunched. He gave a surly grunt and returned to the phone booth, where he called a number known to not more than a dozen persons.

The screen glowed white, while the person at the other end of the line scrutinized his face. . . . The screen cleared, revealing a round pale face from which pale blue eyes stared forth with a passionless intensity. "Hello, Ernest," said Duray. "Is Alan busy at the moment?"

"I don't think he's doing anything particular—except resting."

Ernest gave the last two words a meaningful emphasis.

"I've got some problems," said Duray. "What's the best way to get in touch with him?"

"You'd better come up here. The code is changed. It's *MHF* now."

"I'll be there in a few minutes."

Back in the "California" hub on Utilis, Duray went into a side chamber lined with private lockers, numbered and variously marked with symbols, names, colored flags, or not marked at all. Duray went to Locker 122, and ignoring the keyhole, set the code lock to the letters *MHF*. The door opened; Duray stepped into the locker and through the passway to the High Sierra headquarters of Alan Robertson.

4

From *Memoirs and Reflections:*

If one Basic Axiom controls the cosmos, it must be this:

In a situation of infinity, every possible condition occurs, not once, but an infinite number of times.

There is no mathematical nor logical limit to the number of dimensions. Our perceptions assure us of three only, but many indications suggest otherwise: parapsychic occurrences of a hundred varieties, the "white holes," the seemingly finite state of our own universe, which, by corollary, asserts the existence of others.

Hence, when I stepped behind the lead slab and first touched the button I felt confident of success; failure would have surprised me!

But (and here lay my misgivings) what sort of success might I achieve?

Suppose I opened a hole into the interplanetary vacuum?

The chances of this were very good indeed; I surrounded the machine in a strong membrane, to prevent the air of Earth from rushing off into the void.

Suppose I discovered a condition totally beyond imagination?

My imagination yielded no safeguards.

I proceeded to press the button.

Duray stepped out into a grotto under damp granite walls. Sunlight poured into the opening from a dark blue sky. This was Alan Robertson's link to the outside world; like many other persons, he disliked a passway opening directly into his home. A path led fifty yards across bare granite mountainside to the lodge. To the west spread a great vista of diminishing ridges, valleys and hazy blue air; to the east rose a pair of granite crags with snow caught in the saddle between. Alan Robertson's lodge was built just below the timberline, beside a small lake fringed with tall dark firs. The lodge was built of rounded granite stones, with a wooden porch across the front; at each end rose a massive chimney. Duray had visited the lodge on many occasions; as a boy he had scaled both of the crags behind the house, to look wondering off across the stillness, which on old Earth had a poignant breathing quality different from the uninhabited solitudes of worlds such as Home.

Ernest came to the door: a middle-aged man with an ingenuous face, small white hands and soft, damp mouse-colored hair. Ernest disliked the lodge, the wilderness and solitude in general; he nevertheless would have suffered tortures before relinquishing his post as subaltern to Alan Robertson. Ernest and Duray were almost antipodal in outlook; Ernest thought Duray brusque, indelicate, a trifle coarse and probably not disinclined to violence as an argu-mentative adjunct. Duray considered Ernest, when he thought of him at all, as the kind of man who takes two bites out of a cherry. Ernest had never married; he showed no interest in women, and Duray, as a boy, had often fretted at Ernest's overcautious restrictions.

In particular Ernest resented Duray's free and easy access to Alan Robertson. The power to restrict or admit those countless persons who demanded Alan Robertson's attention was Ernest's most cherished perquisite, and Duray denied him the use of it by simply ignoring Ernest and all his regu-lations. Ernest had never complained to Alan Robertson for fear of discovering that Duray's influence exceeded his own. A wary truce existed between the two, each conceding the other his privileges.

Ernest performed a polite greeting and admitted Duray into the lodge. Duray looked around the interior, which had not changed during his lifetime: varnished plank floors with red, black and white Navaho rugs, massive pine furniture with leather cushions, a few shelves of books, a half dozen pewter mugs on the mantel over the big fireplace: a room almost ostentatiously bare of souvenirs and mementos. Duray turned back to Ernest: "Whereabouts is Alan?"

"On his boat."

"With guests?"

"No," said Ernest, with a faint sniff of disapproval. "He's alone, quite alone."

"How long has he been gone?"

"He just went through an hour ago. I doubt if he's left the dock yet. What is your problem, if I may ask?"

"The passways to my world are closed. All three. There's only one left, in the vault."

Ernest arched his flexible eyebrows. "Who closed them?"

"I don't know. Elizabeth and the girls are alone, so far as I know."

"Extraordinary," said Ernest, in a flat metallic voice. "Well, then, come along." He led the way down a hall to a back room. With his hand on the knob Ernest paused and looked back over his shoulder. "Did you mention the matter to anyone? Robert, for instance?"

"Yes," said Duray curtly, "I did. Why do you ask?"

Ernest hesitated a fraction of a second. "No particular reason. Robert occasionally has a somewhat misplaced sense of humor, he and his Rumfuddlers." He spoke the word with a hiss of distaste.

Duray said nothing of his own suspicions. Ernest opened the door; they entered a large room illuminated by a sky-light. The only furnishing was a rug on the varnished floor. Into each wall opened four doors. Ernest went to one of these doors, pulled it open and made a resigned gesture. "You'll probably find Alan at the dock."

Duray looked into the interior of a rude hut with palm-frond walls, resting on a platform of poles. Through the doorway he saw a path leading under sunlit green foliage toward a strip of white beach. Surf sparkled below a layer of dark blue ocean and a glimpse of the sky. Duray hesitated, rendered wary by the events of the morning. Anyone and everyone was suspect, even Ernest, who now gave a quiet sniff of contemptuous amusement. Through the foliage Duray glimpsed a spread of sail; he stepped through the passway.

5

From *Memoirs and Reflections:*

Man is a creature whose evolutionary environment has been the open air. His nerves, muscles and senses have developed across three million years in intimate contiguity with natural earth, crude stone, live wood, wind and rain. Now this creature is suddenly—on the geologic scale, instantaneously—shifted to an unnatural environment of metal and glass, plastic and plywood, to which his psychic substrata lack all compatibility.

The wonder is not that we have so much mental instability but so little. Add to this the weird noises, electrical pleasures, bizarre colors, synthetic foods, abstract entertainments! We should congratulate ourselves on our durability.

I bring this matter up because, with my little device, so simple, so easy, so flexible, I have vastly augmented the load upon our poor primeval brains, and for a fact many persons find the instant transition from one locale to another unsettling, and even actively unpleasant.

Duray stood on the porch of the cabin, under a vivid green canopy of sunlit foliage. The air was soft and warm and smelled of moist vegetation. Duray stood listening. The mutter of the surf came to his ears and from a far distance a single bird-call.

Duray stepped down to the ground and followed the path under tall palm trees to a river bank. A few yards downstream, beside a rough pier of poles and planks, floated a white and blue trimaran ketch, sails hoisted and distended to a gentle breeze. On the deck stood Alan Robertson, on the poinst of casting off the mooring lines. Duray hailed him; Alan Robertson turned in surprise and vexation, which vanished when he recognized Duray.

"Hello, Gil; glad you're here! For a moment I thought it might be someone to bother me. Jump aboard; you're just in time for a sail."

Duray somberly joined Alan Robertson on the boat. "I'm afraid I am here to bother you."

"Oh?" Alan Robertson raised his eyebrows in instant solicitude. He was a man of no great height, thin, nervously active. Wisps of rumpled white hair fell over his forehead; mild blue eyes inspected Duray with concern, all thought of sailing forgotten. "What in the world has happened?"

"I wish I knew. If it were something I could handle myself I wouldn't bother you."

"Don't worry about me; there's all the time in the world for sailing. Now tell me what's happened."

"I can't get through to Home. All the passways are closed off: why and how I have no idea. Elizabeth and the girls are out there alone; at least I think they're out there."

Alan Robertson rubbed his chin. "What an odd business!

I can certainly understand your agitation. . . . You think Elizabeth closed the passways?"

"It's unreasonable—but there's no one else."

Alan Robertson turned Duray a shrewd, kindly glance. "No little family upsets? Nothing to cause her despair and anguish?"

"Absolutely nothing. I've tried to reason things out, but I draw a blank. I thought that maybe someone—a man— had gone through to visit her and decided to take over— but if this were the case, why did she come to the school for the girls? That possibility is out. A secret love affair? Possible but so damned unlikely. Since she wants to keep me off the planet, her only motive could be to protect me, or herself, or the girls from danger of some sort. Again this means that another person is concerned in the matter. Who? How? Why? I spoke to Bob. He claims to know nothing about the situation, but he wants me to come to his damned Rum-fuddle and he hints very strongly that Elizabeth will be on hand. I can't prove a thing against Bob, but I suspect him. He's always had a taste for odd jokes."

Alan Robertson gave a lugubrious nod. "I won't deny that." He sat down in the cockpit and stared off across the water. "Bob has a complicated sense of humor, but he'd hardly close you away from your world. . . . I hardly think that your family is in actual danger, but of course we can't take chances. The possibility exists that Bob is not respon-sible, that something uglier is afoot." He jumped to his feet. "Our obvious first step is to use the master orifice in the vault." He looked a shade regretfully toward the ocean. "My little sail can wait. . . . A lovely world this: not fully cog-nate with Earth—a cousin, so to speak. The fauna and flora are roughly contemporary except for man. The homonids have never developed."

The two men returned up the path, Alan Robertson chat-ting lightheartedly: "—thousands and thousands of worlds I've visited, and looked into even more, but do you know I've never hit upon a good system of classification? There are exact cognates—of course we're never sure exactly *how* exact they are. These cases are relatively simple, but then the problems begin. . . . Bah! I don't think about such things anymore. I know that when I keep all the nomi nates at zero the cognates appear. Overintellectualizing is the bane of this, and every other era. Show me a man who deals only with abstraction and I'll show you the dead futile end of evolution. . . ." Alan Robertson chuckled. "If I could control the machine tightly enough to produce real cognates, our troubles would be over. . . . Much confusion of course. I might step through into the cognate world immediately as a true cognate Alan Robertson steps through into our world, with net effect of zero. An amazing business, really; I never tire of it. . . ."

They returned to the transit room of the mountain lodge. Ernest appeared almost instantly. Duray suspected he had been watching through the passway.

Alan Robertson said briskly, "We'll be busy for an hour or two, Ernest. Gilbert is having difficulties and we've got to set things straight."

Ernest nodded somewhat grudgingly, or so it seemed to Duray. "The progress report on the Ohio Plan has arrived. Nothing particularly urgent."

"Thank you, Ernest, I'll see to it later. Come along, Gilbert; let's get to the bottom of this affair." They went to Door No. 1, and passed through to the Utilis hub. Alan Robertson led the way to a small green door with a three-dial coded lock, which he opened with a flourish. "Very well; in we go." He carefully locked the door behind them and they walked the length of a short hall. "A shame that I must be so cautious," said Alan Robertson. "You'd be astonished at the outrageous requests otherwise sensible people make of me. I sometimes become exasperated. . . . Well, it's understandable, I suppose."

At the end of the hall Alan Robertson worked the locking dials of a red door. "This way, Gilbert; you've been through before." They stepped through a passway into a hall, which opened into a circular concrete chamber fifty feet in diameter, located, so Duray knew, deep under the Mad Dog Mountains of the Mojave Desert. Eight halls extended away into the rock; each hall communicated with twelve aisles. The center of the chamber was occupied by a circular desk twenty feet in diameter: here six clerks in white smocks worked at computers and collating machines. In accordance with their instructions they gave Alan Robertson neither recognition nor greeting.

Alan Robertson went up to the desk, at which signal the chief clerk, a solemn young man bald as an egg, came forward. "Good afternoon, sir."

"Good afternoon, Harry. Find me the index for 'Gilbert Duray,' on my personal list."

The clerk bowed smartly. He went to an instrument and ran his fingers over a bank of keys; the instrument ejected a card which Harry handed to Alan Robertson. "There you are, sir."

Alan Robertson showed the card to Duray, who saw the code: 4:8:10/6:13:29.

"That's your world," said Alan Robertson. "We'll soon learn how the land lies. This way, to Radiant Four." He led the way down the hall, turned into the aisle numbered 8, and proceeded to Stack 10. "Shelf six," said Alan Robertson. He checked the card. "Drawer thirteen. Here we are." He drew forth the drawer, ran his fingers along the tabs. "Item twenty-nine. This should be Home." He brought forth a metal frame four inches square, and held it up to his eyes. He frowned in disbelief. "We don't have anything here either." He turned to Duray a glance of dismay. "This is a serious situation!"

"It's no more than I expected," said Duray tonelessly.

"All this demands some careful thought." Alan Robertson clicked his tongue in vexation. "Tsk, tsk, tsk. . . ." He examined the identification plaque at the top of the frame. "Four: eight: ten/six: thirteen: twenty-nine," he read. "There seems to be no question of error." He squinted carefully at the numbers, hesitated, then slowly replaced the frame. On second thought he took the frame forth once more. "Come along, Gilbert," said Alan Robertson. "We'll have a cup of coffee and think this matter out."

The two returned to the central chamber, where Alan Robertson gave the empty frame into the custody of Harry the clerk. "Check the records, if you please," said Alan Robertson. "I want to know how many passways were pinched off the master."

Harry manipulated the buttons of his computer. "Three only, Mr. Robertson."

"Three passways and the master—four in all?"

"That's right, sir."

"Thank you, Harry."

6

From *Memoirs and Reflections:*

I recognized the possibility of many cruel abuses, but the good so outweighed the bad that I thrust aside all thought of secrecy and exclusivity. I consider myself not Alan Robertson, but, like Prometheus, an archetype of Man, and my discovery must serve all men.

But caution, caution, caution!

I sorted out my ideas. I myself coveted the amplitude of a private, personal, world; such a yearning was not ignoble, I decided. Why should not everyone have the same if he so desired, since the supply was limitless? Think of it! The wealth and beauty of an entire world: mountains and plains, forests and flowers, ocean cliffs and crashing seas, winds and clouds—all beyond value, yet worth no more than a few seconds of effort and a few watts of energy.

I became troubled by a new idea. Would everyone desert old Earth and leave it a vile junk-heap? I found the concept intolerable. . . . I exchange access to a world for three to six years of remedial toil, depending upon occupancy.

A lounge overlooked the central chamber. Alan Robertson gestured Duray to a seat and drew two mugs of coffee from a dispenser. Settling in a chair, he turned his eyes up to the ceiling. "We must collect our thoughts. The circumstances are somewhat unusual; still, I have lived with unusual circumstances for almost fifty years.

"So then: the situation. We have verified that there are only four passways to Home. These four passways are closed, though we must accept Bob's word in regard to your downtown locker. If this is truly the case, if Elizabeth and the girls are still on Home, you will never see them again."

"Bob is mixed up in this business. I could swear to nothing but—"

Alan Robertson held up his hand. "I will talk to Bob; this is the obvious first step." He rose to his feet and went to the telephone in the corner of the lounge. Duray joined him. Alan spoke into the screen. "Get me Robert Robertson's apartment in San Francisco."

The screen glowed white. Bob's voice came from the speaker. "Sorry; I'm not at home. I have gone out to my world Fancy, and I cannot be reached. Call back in a week, unless your business is urgent, in which case call back in a month."

"Mmph," said Alan Robertson, returning to his seat. "Bob is sometimes a trifle too flippant. A man with an under-extended intellect. . . ." He drummed his fingers on the arm of his chair. "Tomorrow night is his party? What does he call it? A Rumfuddle?"

"Some such nonsense. Why does he want me? I'm a dull dog; I'd rather be home building a fence."

"Perhaps you had better plan to attend the party."

"That means, submit to his extortion."

"Do you want to see your wife and family again?"

"Naturally. But whatever he has in mind won't be for my benefit, or Elizabeth's."

"You're probably right there. I've heard one or two unsavory tales regarding the Rumfuddlers. . . . The fact remains that the passways are closed. All four of them."

Duray's voice became harsh. "Can't you open a new orifice for us?"

Alan Robertson gave his head a sad shake. "I can tune the machine very finely. I can code accurately for the 'Home' class of worlds, and as closely as necessary approximate a particular world-state. But at each setting, no matter how fine the tuning, we encounter an infinite number of worlds. In practice, inaccuracies in the machine, backlash, the gross size of electrons, the very difference between one electron and another, make it difficult to tune with absolute precision. So even if we tuned exactly to the 'Home' class, the probability of opening into your particular Home is one in an infinite number: in short, negligible."

Duray stared off across the chamber. "Is it possible that a space once entered might tend to open more easily a second time?"

Alan Robertson smiled. "As to that, I can't say. I suspect not, but I really know so little. I see no reason why it should be so."

"If we can open into a world precisely cognate, I can at least learn why the passways are closed."

Alan Robertson sat up in his chair. "Here is a valid point. Perhaps we can accomplish something in this regard." He glanced humorously sidewise at Duray. "On the other hand —consider this situation. We create access into a 'Home' almost exactly cognate to your own—so nearly identical that the difference is not readily apparent. You find there an Elizabeth, a Dolly, a Joan and an Ellen indistinguishable from your own, and a Gilbert marooned on Earth. You might even convince yourself that this is your very own Home."

"I'd know the difference," said Duray shortly, but Alan Robertson seemed not to hear.

"Think of it! An infinite number of Homes isolated from Earth, an infinite number of Elizabeths, Dollys, Joans and Ellens marooned; an infinite number of Gilbert Durays trying to regain access. . . . The sum effect might be a wholesale reshuffling of families with everyone more or less good-natured about the situation. I wonder if this could be Bob's idea of a joke to share with his Rumfuddlers."

Duray looked sharply at Alan Robertson, wondering whether the man were serious. "It doesn't sound funny, and I wouldn't be very good-natured."

"Of course not," Alan Robertson said hastily. "An idle thought—in rather poor taste, I'm afraid."

"In any event, Bob hinted that Elizabeth would be at his damned Rumfuddle. If that's the case she must have closed the passways from this side."

"A possibility," Alan Robertson conceded, "but unreasonable. Why should she seal you away from Home?"

"I don't know, but I'd like to find out."

Alan Robertson slapped his hands down upon his thin shanks and jumped to his feet, only to pause once more. "You're sure you want to look into these cognates? You might see things you wouldn't like."

"So long as I know the truth, I don't care whether I like it or not."

"So be it."

The machine occupied a room behind the balcony. Alan Robertson surveyed the device with pride and affection.

"This is the fourth model, and probably optimum; at least I don't see any place for significant improvements. I use a hundred and sixty-seven rods converging upon the center of the reactor sphere. Each rod produces a quotum of energy, and is susceptible to several types of adjustment, to cope with the very large number of possible states. The number of particles to pack the universe full is on the order of   ; the possible permutations of these particles would number   The universe of course is built of many different particles, which makes the final number of possible, or let us say thinkable, states, a number like   where 'x' is the number of particles under consideration. A large, unmanageable number, which we need not consider because the conditions we deal with—the possible variations of planet Earth—are far fewer."

"Still a very large number," said Duray.

"Indeed, yes. But again the sheer unmanageable bulk is cut away by a self-normalizing property of the machine. In what I call 'floating neutral' the machine reaches the closest cycles, which is to say, that infinite class of perfect cognates. In practice, because of infinitesimal inaccuracies, 'floating neutral' reaches cognates more or less imperfect, perhaps by no more than the shape of a single grain of sand. Still, 'floating neutral' provides a natural base, and by adjusting the controls we reach cycles at an ever greater departure from Base. In practice I search out a good cycle, and strike a large number of passways, as many as a hundred thousand. So now to our business." He went to a console at the side. "Your code number, what was it now?"

Duray brought forth the card and read the numbers: "Four: eight: ten/six: thirteen: twenty-nine."

"Very good. I give the code to the computer, which searches the files and automatically adjusts the machine. Now then, step over here; the process releases dangerous radiation."

The two stood behind lead slabs. Alan Robertson touched a button; watching through a periscope Duray saw a spark of purple light, and heard a small groaning, rasping sound seeming to come from the air itself.

Alan Robertson stepped forth and walked to the machine. In the delivery tray rested an extensible ring. He picked up the ring, looked through the hole. "This seems to be right." He handed the ring to Duray. "Do you see anything you recognize?"

Duray put the ring to his eye. "That's Home."

"Very good. Do you want me to come with you?"

Duray considered. "The time is Now?"

"Yes. This is a time-neutral setting."

"I think I'll go alone."

Alan Robertson nodded. "Whatever you like. Return as soon as you can, so I'll know you're safe."

Duray frowned at him sidewise. "Why shouldn't I be safe? No one is there but my family."

"Not *your* family. The family of a cognate Gilbert Duray. The family may not be absolutely identical. The cognate Duray may not be identical. You can't be sure exactly what you will find—so be careful."

7

From *Memoirs and Reflections:*

When I think of my machine and my little forays in and out of infinity, an idea keeps recurring to me which is so rather terrible that I close it out of my mind, and I will not even mention it here.

Duray stepped out upon the soil of Home, and stood appraising the familiar landscape. A vast meadow drenched in sunlight rolled down to wide Silver River. Above the opposite shore rose a line of low bluffs, with copses of trees in the hollows. To the left, landscape seemed to extend indefinitely and at last become indistinct in the blue haze of distance. To the right, the Robber Woods ended a quarter-mile from where Duray stood. On a flat beside the forest, on the bank of a small stream, stood a house of stone and timber: a sight which seemed to Duray the most beautiful he had ever seen. Polished glass windows sparkled in the sunlight; banks of geraniums glowed green and red. From the chimney rose a wisp of smoke.

The air smelled cool and sweet, but seemed—so Duray imagined—to carry a strange tang, different—so he imagined —from the meadow-scent of his own Home. Duray started forward, then halted. The world was his own, yet not his own. If he had not been conscious of the fact, would he have recognized the strangeness? Nearby rose an outcrop of weathered gray field-rock: a rounded mossy pad on which he had sat only two days before, contemplating the building of a dock. He walked over and looked down at the stone. Here he had sat, here were the impressions of his heels in the soil; here was the pattern of moss from which he had absently scratched a fragment. Duray bent close. The moss was whole. The man who had sat here, the cognate Duray, had not scratched at the moss. So then: the world was perceptibly different from his own.

Duray was relieved and yet vaguely disturbed. If the world had been the exact simulacrum of his own, he might have been subjected to unmanageable emotions—which still might be the case. He walked toward the house, along the path which led down to the river. He stepped up to the porch. On a deck chair was a book: *Down There, A Study in Satanism*, by J. K. Huysmans. Elizabeth's tastes were eclectic. Duray had not previously seen the book; was it perhaps that Bob Robertson had put through the parcel delivery?

Duray went into the house. Elizabeth stood across the room. She had evidently watched him coming up the path. She said nothing; her face showed no expression.

Duray halted, somewhat at a loss as to how to address this woman. "Good afternoon," he said at last.

Elizabeth allowed a wisp of a smile to show. "Hello, Gilbert."

At least, thought Duray, on cognate worlds the same language was spoken. He studied Elizabeth. Lacking prior knowledge, would he have perceived her to be someone different from his own Elizabeth? Both were beautiful women: tall and slender, with curling black shoulder-length hair, worn without artifice. Their skins were pale with a dusky undertone; their mouths were wide, passionate, stubborn. Duray knew his Elizabeth to be a woman of inexplicable moods, and this Elizabeth was doubtless no different —yet somehow a difference existed, which Duray could not define, deriving perhaps from the strangeness of her atoms, the stuff of a different universe. He wondered if she sensed the same difference in him.

He asked, "Did you close off the passways?"

Elizabeth nodded, without change of expression.

"Why?"

"I thought it the best thing to do," said Elizabeth in a soft voice.

"That's no answer."

"I suppose not. How did you get here?"

"Alan made an opening."

Elizabeth raised her eyebrows. "I thought that was impossible."

"True. This is a different world to my own. Another Gilbert Duray built this house. I'm not your husband."

Elizabeth's mouth drooped in astonishment. She swayed back a step and put her hand up to her neck: a mannerism Duray could not recall in his own Elizabeth. The sense of strangeness came ever more strongly upon him. He felt an intruder. Elizabeth was watching him with a wide-eyed fascination. She said in a hurried mutter: "I wish you'd leave; go back to your own world; do!"

"If you've closed off all the passways, you'll be isolated," growled Duray. "Marooned, probably forever."

"Whatever I do," said Elizabeth, "it's not your affair."

"It is my affair, if only for the sake of the girls. I won't allow them to live and die alone out here."

"The girls aren't here," said Elizabeth in a flat voice. "They are where neither you nor any other Gilbert Duray will find them. So now go back to your own world, and leave me in whatever peace my soul allows me."

Duray stood glowering at the fiercely beautiful woman. He had never heard his own Elizabeth speak so wildly. He wondered if on his own world another Gilbert Duray similarly confronted his own Elizabeth, and as he analyzed his feelings toward this woman before him he felt a throb of annoyance. A curious situation. He said in a quiet voice, "Very well. You, and my own Elizabeth, have decided to isolate yourselves. I can't imagine your reasons."

Elizabeth gave a wild laugh. "They're real enough."

"They may be real now, but ten years from now, or forty years from now, they may seem unreal. I can't give you access to your own Earth, but if you wish, you can use the passway to the Earth from which I've just come, and you need never see me again."

Elizabeth turned away and went to look out over the valley. Duray spoke to her back. "We've never had secrets

between us, you and I—or I mean, Elizabeth and I. Why
now? Are you in love with some other man?"

Elizabeth gave a snort of sardonic amusement. "Certainly
not. . . . I'm disgusted with the entire human race."

"Which presumably includes me."

"It does indeed, and myself as well."

"And you won't tell me why?"

Elizabeth, still looking out the window, wordlessly shook
her head.

"Very well," said Duray in a cold voice. "Will you tell me
where you've sent the girls? They're mine as much as yours,
remember."

"These particular girls aren't yours at all."

"That may be, but the effect is the same."

Elizabeth said tonelessly: "If you want to find your own
particular girls, you'd better find your own particular Elizabeth and ask her. I can only speak for myself. . . . To tell
you the truth, I don't like being part of a composite person,
and I don't intend to act like one. I'm just me. You're you,
a stranger, whom I've never seen before in my life. So I
wish you'd leave."

Duray strode from the house, out into the sunlight. He
looked once around the wide landscape, then gave his head
a surly shake and marched off along the path.

8

From *Memoirs and Reflections:*

The past is exposed for our scrutiny; we can wander
the epochs like lords through a garden, serene in our
purview. We argue with the noble sages, refuting their
laborious concepts, should we be so unkind. Remember
(at least) two things. First: the more distant from Now,
the less precise our conjunctures, the less our ability to
strike to any given instant. We can break in upon yesterday at a stipulated second; during the Eocene plus
or minus ten years is the limit of our accuracy; as for
the Cretaceous or earlier, an impingement within three
hundred years of a given date can be considered satisfactory. Second: the past we broach is never our own
past, but at best the past of a cognate world, so that
any illumination cast upon historical problems is ques-

tionable and perhaps deceptive. We cannot plumb the future; the process involves a negative flow of energy, which is inherently impractical. An instrument constructed of antimatter has been jocularly recommended, but would yield no benefit to us. The future, thankfully, remains forever shrouded.

"Aha, you're back!" exclaimed Alan Robertson. "What did you learn?"

Duray described the encounter with Elizabeth. "She makes no excuse for what she's done; she shows hostility which doesn't seem real, especially since I can't imagine a reason for it."

Alan Robertson had no comment to make.

"The woman isn't my wife, but their motivations must be the same. I can't think of one sensible explanation for conduct so strange, let alone two."

"Elizabeth seemed normal this morning?" asked Alan Robertson.

"I noticed nothing unusual."

Alan Robertson went to the control panel of his machine. He looked over his shoulder at Duray. "What time do you leave for work?"

"About nine."

Alan Robertson set one dial, turned two others until a ball of green light balanced wavering precisely halfway along a glass tube. He signaled Duray behind the lead slab and touched the button. From the center of the machine came the impact of one hundred and sixty-seven colliding nodules of force, and the groan of rending dimensional fabric.

Alan Robertson brought forth the new passway. "The time is morning. You'll have to decide for yourself how to handle the situation. You can try to watch without being seen; you can say that you have paperwork to catch up on, that Elizabeth should ignore you and go about her normal routine, while you unobtrusively see what happens."

Duray frowned. "Presumably for each of these worlds there is a Gilbert Duray who finds himself in my fix. Suppose each tries to slip inconspicuously into someone else's world to learn what is happening. Suppose each Elizabeth catches him in the act and furiously accuses the man she believes to be her husband of spying on her—this in itself might be the source of Elizabeth's anger."

"Well, be as discreet as you can. Presumably you'll be several hours, so I'll go back to the boat and putter about. Locker Five in my private hub yonder; I'll leave the door open."

Once again Duray stood on the hillside above the river, with the rambling stone house, built by still another Gilbert Duray, two hundred yards along the slope. From the height of the sun, Duray judged local time to be about nine o'clock: somewhat earlier than necessary. From the chimney of the stone house rose a wisp of smoke; Elizabeth had built a fire in the kitchen fireplace. Duray stood reflecting. This morning in his own house Elizabeth had built no fire. She had been on the point of striking a match and then had decided that the morning was already warm. Duray waited ten minutes, to make sure that the local Gilbert Duray had departed, then set forth toward the house. He paused by the big flat stone to inspect the pattern of moss. The crevice seemed narrower than he remembered, and the moss was dry and discolored. Duray took a deep breath. The air, rich with the odor of grasses and herbs, again seemed to carry an odd, unfamiliar scent. Duray proceeded slowly to the house, uncertain whether, after all, he were engaged in a sensible course of action.

He approached the house. The front door was open. Elizabeth came to look out at him in surprise. "That was a quick day's work!"

Duray said lamely, "The rig is down for repairs. I thought I'd catch up on some paperwork. You go ahead with whatever you were doing."

Elizabeth looked at him curiously. "I wasn't doing anything in particular."

He followed Elizabeth into the house. She wore soft black slacks and an old gray jacket; Duray tried to remember what his own Elizabeth had worn, but the garments had been so familiar that he could summon no recollection.

Elizabeth poured coffee into a pair of stoneware mugs and Duray took a seat at the kitchen table, trying to decide how this Elizabeth differed from his own—if she did. This Elizabeth seemed more subdued and meditative; her mouth might have been a trifle softer. "Why are you looking at me so strangely?" she asked suddenly.

Duray laughed. "I was merely thinking what a beautiful girl you are."

Elizabeth came to sit in his lap and kissed him, and Duray's blood began to flow warm. He restrained himself; this was not his wife; he wanted no complications. And if he yielded to temptations of the moment, might not another Gilbert Duray visiting his own Elizabeth do the same . . . ? He scowled.

Elizabeth, finding no surge of ardor, went to sit in the chair opposite. For a moment she sipped her coffee in silence. Then she said, "Just as soon as you left Bob called through."

"Oh?" Duray was at once attentive. "What did he want?"

"That foolish party of his—the Rubble-menders or some such thing. He wants us to come."

"I've already told him 'no' three times."

"I told him 'no' again. His parties are always so peculiar. He said he wanted us to come for a very special reason, but he wouldn't tell me the reason. I told him thank you but no."

Duray looked around the room. "Did he leave any books?"

"No. Why should he leave me books?"

"I wish I knew."

"Gilbert," said Elizabeth, "you're acting rather oddly."

"Yes, I suppose I am." For a fact Duray's mind was whirling. Suppose now he went to the school passway, brought the girls home from school, then closed off all the passways, so that once again he had an Elizabeth and three daughters, more or less his own; then the conditions he had encountered would be satisfied. And another Gilbert Duray, now happily destroying the tract houses of Cupertino, would find himself bereft. . . . Duray recalled the hostile conduct of the previous Elizabeth. The passways in that particular world had certainly not been closed off by an intruding Duray. . . . A startling possibility came to his mind. Suppose a Duray had come to the house and succumbing to temptation had closed off all passways except that one communicating with his own world; suppose, then, that Elizabeth, discovering the impostor, had killed him. . . . The theory had a grim plausibility, and totally extinguished whatever inclination Duray might have had for making this world his home.

Elizabeth said, "Gilbert, why are you looking at me with that strange expression?"

Duray managed a feeble grin. "I guess I'm just in a bad mood this morning. Don't mind me. I'll go make out my report." He went into the wide cool living room, at once familiar and strange, and brought out the work records of the other Gilbert Duray. . . . He studied the handwriting: like his own, firm and decisive, but in some indefinable way different—perhaps a trifle more harsh and angular. The three Elizabeths were not identical, nor were the Gilbert Durays.

An hour passed. Elizabeth occupied herself in the kitchen; Duray pretended to write a report.

A bell sounded. "Somebody at the passway," said Elizabeth.

Duray said, "I'll take care of it."

He went to the passage room, stepped through the passway, looked through the peephole—into the large bland, suntanned face of Bob Robertson.

Duray opened the door. For a moment he and Bob Robertson confronted each other. Bob Robertson's eyes narrowed. "Why, hello, Gilbert. What are you doing at home?"

Duray pointed to the parcel Bob Robertson carried. "What do you have there?"

"Oh, these?" Bob Robertson looked down at the parcel as if he had forgotten it. "Just some books for Elizabeth."

Duray found it hard to control his voice. "You're up to some mischief, you and your Rumfuddlers. Listen, Bob: keep away from me and Elizabeth. Don't call here, and don't bring around any books. Is this definite enough?"

Bob raised his sun-bleached eyebrows. "Very definite, very explicit. But why the sudden rage? I'm just friendly old Uncle Bob."

"I don't care what you call yourself; stay away from us."

"Just as you like, of course. But do you mind explaining this sudden decree of banishment?"

"The reason is simple enough. We want to be left alone."

Bob made a gesture of mock despair. "All this over a simple invitation to a simple little party, which I'd really like you to come to."

"Don't expect us. We won't be there."

Bob's face suddenly went pink. "You're coming a very high horse over me, my lad, and it's a poor policy. You might just get hauled up with a jerk. Matters aren't all the way you think they are."

"I don't care a rap one way or another," said Duray. "Goodbye." He closed the locker door and backed through the passway. He returned to the living room. Elizabeth called from the kitchen. "Who was it, dear?"

"Bob Robertson, with some books."

"Books? Why books?"

"I didn't trouble to find out. I told him to stay away. After this, if he's at the passway, don't open it."

Elizabeth looked at him intently. "Gil—you're so strange today! There's something about you that almost scares me."

"Your imagination is working too hard."

"Why should Bob trouble to bring me books? What sort of books? Did you see?"

"Demonology. Black magic. That sort of thing."

"Mmf. Interesting—but not all *that* interesting. . . . I wonder if a world like ours, where no one has ever lived, would have things like goblins and ghosts?"

"I suspect not," said Duray. He looked toward the door. There was nothing more to be accomplished here and it was time to return to his own Earth. He wondered how to make a graceful departure. And what would occur when the Gilbert Duray now working his rig came home?

Duray said, "Elizabeth, sit down in this chair here."

Elizabeth slowly slid into the chair at the kitchen table and watched him with a puzzled gaze.

"This may come as a shock," he said. "I am Gilbert Duray, but not your personal Gilbert Duray. I'm his cognate."

Elizabeth's eyes widened to lustrous dark pools.

Duray said, "On my own world Bob Robertson caused me and my Elizabeth trouble. I came here to find out what he had done and why, and to stop him from doing it again."

Elizabeth asked, "What has he done?"

"I still don't know. He probably won't bother you again. You can tell your personal Gilbert Duray whatever you think best, or even complain to Alan."

"I'm bewildered by all this!"

"No more so than I." He went to the door. "I've got to leave now. Good-bye."

Elizabeth jumped to her feet and came impulsively forward. "Don't say good-bye. It has such a lonesome sound, coming from you. . . . It's like my own Gilbert saying good-bye."

"There's nothing else to do. Certainly I can't follow my inclinations and move in with you. What good are two Gilberts? Who'd get to sit at the head of the table?"

"We could have a round table," said Elizabeth. "Room for six or seven. I like my Gilberts."

"Your Gilberts like their Elizabeths." Duray sighed and said, "I'd better go now."

Elizabeth held out her hand. "Good-bye, cognate Gilbert."

9

From *Memoirs and Reflections:*

The Oriental world-view differs from our own—specifically my own—in many respects, and I was early confronted with a whole set of dilemmas. I reflected upon Asiatic apathy and its obverse, despotism; warlords and brain-laundries; indifference to disease, filth and suffering; sacred apes and irresponsible fecundity.

I also took note of my resolve to use my machine in the service of all men.

In the end I decided to make the "mistake" of many before me; I proceeded to impose my own ethical point of view upon the Oriental life-style.

Since this was precisely what was expected of me; since I would have been regarded as a fool and a mooncalf had I done otherwise; since the rewards of cooperation far exceeded the gratifications of obduracy and scorn: my programs are a wonderful success, at least to the moment of writing.

Duray walked along the river bank toward Alan Robertson's boat. A breeze sent twinkling cat's-paws across the water and bellied the sails which Alan Robertson had raised to air; the boat tugged at the mooring lines.

Alan Robertson, wearing white shorts and a white hat with a loose flapping brim, looked up from the eye he had been splicing at the end of a halyard. "Aha, Gil! you're back. Come aboard, and have a bottle of beer."

Duray seated himself in the shade of the sail and drank half the beer at a gulp. "I still don't know what's going on —except that one way or another Bob is responsible. He came while I was there. I told him to clear out. He didn't like it."

Alan Robertson heaved a melancholy sigh. "I realize that Bob has the capacity for mischief."

"I still can't understand how he persuaded Elizabeth to close the passways. He brought out some books, but what effect could they have?"

Alan Robertson was instantly interested. "What were the books?"

"Something about satanism, black magic; I couldn't tell you much else."

"Indeed, indeed!" muttered Alan Robertson. "Is Elizabeth interested in the subject?"

"I don't think so. She's afraid of such things."

"Rightly so. Well, well, that's disturbing." Alan Robertson cleared his throat and made a delicate gesture, as if beseeching Duray to geniality and tolerance. "Still, you mustn't be too irritated with Bob. He's prone to his little mischiefs, but—"

"'Little mischiefs'!" roared Duray. "Like locking me out of my home and marooning my wife and children? That's going beyond mischief!"

Alan Robertson smiled. "Here; have another beer; cool off a bit. Lot's reflect. First, the probabilities. I doubt if Bob has really marooned Elizabeth and the girls, or caused Elizabeth to do so."

"Then why are all the passways broken?"

"That's susceptible to explanation. He has access to the vaults; he might have substituted a blank for your master orifice. There's one possibility, at least."

Duray could hardly speak for rage. At last he cried out: "He has no right to do this!"

"Quite right, in the largest sense. I suspect that he only wants to induce you to his Rumfuddle."

"And I don't want to go, especially when he's trying to put pressure on me."

"You're a stubborn man, Gil. The easy way, of course,

would be to relax and look in on the occasion. You might even enjoy yourself."

Duray glared at Alan Robertson. "Are you suggesting that I attend the affair?"

"Well—no. I merely proposed a possible course of action."

Duray drank more beer and glowered out across the river. Alan Robertson said, "In a day or so, when this business is clarified, I think that we—all of us—should go off on a lazy cruise, out there among the islands. Nothing to worry us, no bothers, no upsets. The girls would love such a cruise."

Duray grunted. "I'd like to see them again before I plan any cruises. What goes on at these Rumfuddler events?"

"I've never attended. The members laugh and joke and eat and drink, and gossip about the worlds they've visited and show each other movies: that sort of thing. Why don't we look in on last year's party? I'd be interested myself."

Duray hesitated. "What do you have in mind?"

"We'll set the dials to a year-old cognate to Bob's world Fancy, and see precisely what goes on. What do you say?"

"I suppose it can't do any harm," said Duray grudgingly.

Alan Robertson rose to his feet. "Help me get these sails in."

10

From *Memoirs and Reflections:*

The problems which long have harassed historians have now been resolved. Who were the Cro-Magnons; where did they evolve? Who were the Etruscans? Where were the legendary cities of the proto-Sumerians before they migrated to Mesopotamia? Why the identity between the ideographs of Easter Island and Mohenjo-Daro? All these fascinating questions have now been settled and reveal to us the full scope of our early history. We have preserved the library at old Alexandria from the Mohammedans and the Inca codices from the Christians. The Guanches of the Canaries, the Ainu of Hokkaido, the Mandans of Missouri, the blond Kaffirs of Bhutan: all are now known to us. We can chart the development of every language syllable by syllable, from earliest formulation to the present. We have identified the Hellenic heroes, and I myself have searched the haunted forests of the ancient North and, in their own stone keeps, met face to face those mighty men who generated the Norse myths.

Standing before his machine, Alan Robertson spoke in a voice of humorous self-deprecation. "I'm not as trusting and forthright as I would like to be; in fact I sometimes feel shame for my petty subterfuges; and now I speak in reference to Bob. We all have our small faults, and Bob certainly does not lack his share. His imagination is perhaps his greatest curse: he is easily bored, and sometimes tends to overreach himself. So while I deny him nothing, I also make sure that I am in a position to counsel or even remonstrate, if need be. Whenever I open a passway to one of his formulas, I unobtrusively strike a duplicate which I keep in my private file. We will find no difficulty in visiting a cognate to Fancy."

Duray and Alan Robertson stood in the dusk, at the end of a pale white beach. Behind them rose a low basalt cliff. To their right the ocean reflected the afterglow and a glitter from the waning moon; to the left palms stood black against the sky. A hundred yards along the beach dozens of fairy lamps had been strung between the trees to illuminate a long table laden with fruit, confections, punch in crystal bowls. Around the table stood several dozen men and women in animated conversation; music and the sounds of gaiety came down the beach to Duray and Alan Robertson.

"We're in good time," said Alan Robertson. He reflected a moment. "No doubt we'd be quite welcome; still, it's probably best to remain inconspicuous. We'll just stroll unobtrusively down the beach, in the shadow of the trees. Be careful not to stumble or fall, and no matter what you see or hear, do nothing! Discretion is essential; we want no awkward confrontations."

Keeping to the shade of the foliage, the two approached the merry group. Fifty yards distant, Alan Robertson held up his hand to signal a halt. "This is as close as we need approach; most of the people you know, or more accurately, their cognates. For instance, there is Royal Hart, and there is James Parham and Elizabeth's aunt, Emma Bathurst, and her uncle Peter, and Maude Granger, and no end of other folk."

"They all seem very gay."

"Yes; this is an important occasion for them. You and I are surly outsiders who can't understand the fun."

"Is this all they do, eat and drink and talk?"

"I think not," said Alan Robertson. "Notice yonder; Bob seems to be preparing a projection screen. Too bad that we can't move just a bit closer." Alan Robertson peered through the shadows. "But we'd better take no chances; if we were discovered everyone would be embarrassed."

They watched in silence. Presently Bob Robertson went to the projection equipment and touched a button. The screen became alive with vibrating rings of red and blue. Conversations halted; the group turned toward the screen. Bob Robertson spoke, but his words were inaudible to the two who watched from the darkness. Bob Robertson gestured to the screen, where now appeared the view of a small country town, as if seen from an airplane. Surrounding was flat farm country, a land of wide horizons; Duray assumed the location to be somewhere in the Middle West. The picture changed, to show the local high school, with students sitting on the steps. The scene shifted to the football field, on the day of a game: a very important game to judge from the conduct of the spectators. The local team was introduced; one by one the boys ran out on the field to stand blinking into the autumn sunlight; then they ran off to the pre-game huddle.

The game began; Bob Robertson stood by the screen in the capacity of an expert commentator, pointing to one or another of the players, analyzing the play. The game proceeded, to the manifest pleasure of the Rumfuddlers. At half time the bands marched and countermarched, then play resumed. Duray became bored and made fretful comments to Alan Robertson, who only said: "Yes, yes; probably so," and "My word, the agility of that halfback!" and "Have you noticed the precision of the line play? Very good indeed!" At last the final quarter ended; the victorious team stood under a sign reading:

THE SHOWALTER TORNADOES
CHAMPION OF TEXAS
1951

The players came forward to accept trophies; there was a last picture of the team as a whole, standing proud and victorious; then the screen burst out into a red and gold starburst and went blank. The Rumfuddlers rose to their feet and congratulated Bob Robertson, who laughed modestly, and went to the table for a goblet of punch.

Duray said disgustedly, "Is this one of Bob's famous parties? Why does he make such a tremendous occasion of the affair? I expected some sort of debauch."

Alan Robertson said, "Yes, from our standpoint at least the proceedings seem somewhat uninteresting. Well, if your curiosity is satisfied, shall we return?"

"Whenever you like."

Once again in the lounge under the Mad Dog Mountains, Alan Robertson said: "So now and at last we've seen one of Bob's famous Rumfuddles. Are you still determined not to attend the occasion of tomorrow night?"

Duray scowled. "If I have to go to reclaim my family, I'll do so. But I just might lose my temper before the evening is over."

"Bob has gone too far," Alan Robertson declared. "I agree with you there. As for what we saw tonight, I admit to a degree of puzzlement."

"Only a degree? Do you understand it at all?"

Alan Robertson shook his head with a somewhat cryptic smile. "Speculation is pointless. I suppose you'll spend the night with me at the lodge?"

"I might as well," grumbled Duray. "I don't have anywhere else to go."

Alan Robertson clapped him on the back. "Good lad! We'll put some steaks on the fire and turn our problems loose for the night."

11

From *Memoirs and Reflections:*

When I first put the Mark I machine into operation I suffered great fears. What did I know of the forces which I might release? . . . With all adjustments at dead neutral, I punched a passway into a cognate Earth. This was simple enough; in fact, almost anticlimactic. . . .

Little by little I learned to control my wonderful toy; our own world and all its past phases became familiar to me. What of other worlds? I am sure that in due course we will move instantaneously from world to world, from galaxy to galaxy, using a special space-traveling hub on Utilis. At the moment I am candidly afraid to punch through passways at blind random. What if I opened into the interior of a sun? Or into the center of a black hole? Or into an antimatter universe? I would certainly destroy myself and the machine and conceivably Earth itself.

Still, the potentialities are too entrancing to be ignored. With painstaking precautions and a dozen protective devices, I will attempt to find my way to new worlds, and for the first time interstellar travel will be a reality.

Alan Robertson and Duray sat in the bright morning sunlight beside the flinty blue lake. They had brought their breakfast out to the table and now sat drinking coffee. Alan Robertson made cheerful conversation for the two of them. "These last few years have been easier on me; I've relegated a great deal of responsibility. Ernest and Henry know my policies as well as I do, if not better; and they're never frivolous or inconsistent." Alan Robertson chuckled. "I've worked two miracles: first, my machine, and second, keeping the business as simple as it is. I refuse to keep regular hours; I won't make appointments; I don't keep records; I pay no taxes; I exert great political and social influence, but only informally; I simply refuse to be bothered with administrative detail, and consequently I find myself able to enjoy life."

"It's a wonder some religious fanatic hasn't assassinated you," Duray said sourly.

"No mystery there! I've given them all their private worlds, with my best regards, and they have no energy left for violence! And as you know, I walk with a very low silhouette. My friends hardly recognize me on the street." Alan Robertson waved his hand. "No doubt you're more concerned with your immediate quandary. Have you come to a decision regarding the Rumfuddle?"

"I don't have any choice," Duray muttered. "I'd prefer

to wring Bob's neck. If I could account for Elizabeth's conduct, I'd feel more comfortable. She's not even remotely interested in black magic. Why did Bob bring her books on Satanism?"

"Well—the subject is inherently fascinating," Alan Robertson suggested, without conviction. "The name 'Satan' derives from the Hebrew word for 'adversary'; it never applied to a real individual. Zeus of course was an Aryan chieftain of about 3500 B.C., while Woden lived somewhat later. He was actually 'Othinn,' a shaman of enormous personal force, who did things with his mind that I can't do with the machine. . . . But again I'm rambling."

Duray gave a silent shrug.

"Well, then, you'll be going to the Rumfuddle," said Alan Robertson, "by and large the best course, whatever the consequences."

"I believe that you know more than you're telling me."

Alan Robertson smiled and shook his head. "I've lived with too much uncertainty among my cognate and near-cognate worlds. Nothing is sure; surprises are everywhere. I think the best plan is to fulfill Bob's requirements. Then, if Elizabeth is indeed on hand, you can discuss the event with her."

"What of you? Will you be coming?"

"I am of two minds. Would you prefer that I came?"

"Yes," said Duray. "You have more control over Bob than I do."

"Don't exaggerate my influence! He is a strong man, for all his idleness. Confidentially, I'm delighted that he occupies himself with games rather than. . . ." Alan Robertson hesitated.

"Rather than what?"

"Than that his imagination should prompt him to less innocent games. Perhaps I have been overingenuous in this connection. He can only wait and see."

12

From *Memoirs and Reflections:*

If the Past is a house of many chambers, then the Present is the most recent coat of paint.

At four o'clock Duray and Alan Robertson left the lodge and passed through Utilis to the San Francisco depot. Duray had changed into a somber dark suit; Alan Robertson wore a more informal costume: blue jacket and pale gray trousers. They went to Bob Robertson's locker, to find a panel with the sign: *Not home! For the Rumfuddle go to Roger Waille's locker, RC3-96 and pass through to Ekshayan!*

The two went on to Locker RC3-96 where a sign read: *Rumfuddlers, pass! All others: away!*

Duray shrugged contemptuously and parting the curtain looked through the passway, into a rustic lobby of natural wood, painted in black, red, yellow, blue and white floral designs. An open door revealed an expanse of open land and water glistening in the afternoon sunlight. Duray and Alan Robertson passed through, crossed the foyer and looked out upon a vast slow river flowing from north to south. A rolling plain spread eastward away and over the horizon. The western bank of the river was indistinct in the afternoon glitter. A path led north to a tall house of eccentric architecture. A dozen domes and cupolas stood against the sky; gables and ridges created a hundred unexpected angles. The walls showed a fish-scale texture of hand-hewn shingles; spiral columns supported the second- and third-story entablatures, where wolves and bears carved in vigorous curves and masses, snarled, fought, howled and danced. On the side overlooking the river a pergola clothed with vines cast a dappled shade; here sat the Rumfuddlers.

Alan Robertson looked at the house, up and down the river, across the plain. "From the architecture, the vegetation, the height of the sun, the characteristic haze, I assume the river to be either the Don or the Volga, and yonder the steppes. From the absence of habitation, boats and artifacts, I would guess the time to be early historic—perhaps 2,000 or 3,000 B.C., a colorful era. The inhabitants of the steppes are nomads; Scyths to the east, Celts to the west, and to the north the homeland of the Germanic and Scandinavian tribes; and yonder the mansion of Roger Waille, ʳnd very interesting too, after the extravagant fashion of the Russian Baroque. And, my word! I believe I see an ox on the spit! We may even enjoy our little visit!"

"You do as you like," muttered Duray, "I'd just as soon eat at home."

Alan Robertson pursed his lips. "I understand your point of view, of course, but perhaps we should relax a bit. The scene is majestic, the house is delightfully picturesque; the roast beef is undoubtedly delicious; perhaps we should meet the situation on its own terms."

Duray could find no adequate reply, and kept his opinions to himself.

"Well, then," said Alan Robertson, "equability is the word. So now let's see what Bob and Roger have up their sleeves." He set off along the path to the house, with Duray sauntering morosely a step or two behind.

Under the pergola a man jumped to his feet and flourished his hand; Duray recognized the tall spare form of Bob Robertson. "Just in time," Bob called jocosely. "Not too early, not too late. We're glad you could make it!"

"Yes, we found we could accept your invitation after all," said Alan Robertson. "Let me see, do I know anyone here? Roger, hello! . . . And William . . . Ah! the lovely Dora Gorski! . . . Cypriano. . . ." He looked around the circle of faces, waving to his acquaintances.

Bob clapped Duray on the shoulder. "Really pleased you could come! What'll you drink? The locals distill a liquor out of fermented mare's milk, but I don't recommend it."

"I'm not here to drink," said Duray. "Where's Elizabeth?"

The corners of Bob's wide mouth twitched. "Come now, old man; let's not be grim. This is the Rumfuddle! A time for joy and self-renewal! Go dance about a bit! Cavort! Pour a bottle of champagne over your head! Sport with the girls!"

Duray looked into the blue eyes for a long second. He strained to keep his voice even. "Where is Elizabeth?"

"Somewhere about the place. A charming girl, your Elizabeth! We're delighted to have you both!"

Duray swung away. He walked to the dark and handsome Roger Waille. "Would you be good enough to take me to my wife?"

Waille raised his eyebrows as if puzzled by Duray's tone of voice. "She's in primping and gossiping. If necessary I suppose I could pull her away for a moment or two."

Duray began to feel ridiculous, as if he had not been locked away from his world, subjected to harassments and doubts, and made the butt of some obscure joke. "It's necessary," he said. "We're leaving."

"But you've just arrived!"

"I know."

Waille gave a shrug of amused perplexity, and turned away toward the house. Duray followed. They went through a tall narrow doorway into an entry hall paneled with a beautiful brown-gold wood, which Duray automatically identified as chestnut. Four high panes of tawny glass turned to the west filled the room with a smoky half-melancholy light. Oak settees, upholstered in leather, faced each other across a black, brown and gray rug. Taborets stood at each side of the settees, and each supported an ornate golden candelabrum in the form of conventionalized stag's-heads. Waille indicated these last. "Striking, aren't they? The Scythians made them for me. I paid them in iron knives. They think I'm a great magician; and for a fact, I am." He reached into the air and plucked forth an orange, which he tossed upon a settee. "Here's Elizabeth now, and the other maenads as well."

Into the chamber came Elizabeth, with three other young women whom Duray vaguely recalled having met before. At the sight of Duray, Elizabeth stopped short. She essayed a smile, and said in a light, strained voice, "Hello, Gil. You're here after all." She laughed nervously and, Duray felt, unnaturally. "Yes, of course you're here. I didn't think you'd come."

Duray glanced toward the other women, who stood with Waille watching half expectantly. Duray said, "I'd like to speak to you alone."

"Excuse us," said Waille. "We'll go on outside."

They departed. Elizabeth looked longingly after them, and fidgeted with the buttons of her jacket.

"Where are the children?" Duray demanded curtly.

"Upstairs, getting dressed." She looked down at her own costume, the festival raiment of a Transylvanian peasant girl: a green skirt embroidered with red and blue flowers, a white blouse, a black velvet vest, glossy black boots.

Duray felt his temper slipping; his voice was strained and fretful. "I don't understand anything of this. Why did you close the passways?"

Elizabeth attempted a flippant smile. "I was bored with routine."

"Oh? Why didn't you mention it to me yesterday morning? You didn't need to close the passways."

"Gilbert, please, Let's not discuss it."

Duray stood back, tongue-tied with astonishment. "Very well," he said at last. "We won't discuss it. You go up and get the girls. We're going home."

Elizabeth shook her head. In a neutral voice she said, "It's impossible. There's only one passway open. I don't have it."

"Who does? Bob?"

"I guess so; I'm not really sure."

"How did he get it? There were only four, and all four were closed."

"It's simple enough. He moved the downtown passway from our locker to another, and left a blank in its place."

"And who closed off the other three?"

"I did."

"Why?"

"Because Bob told me to. I don't want to talk about it; I'm sick to death of the whole business." And she half whispered: "I don't know what I'm going to do with myself."

"I know what I'm going to do," said Duray. He turned toward the door.

Elizabeth held up her hands and clenched her fists against her breast. "Don't make trouble—please! He'll close our last passway!"

"Is that why you're afraid of him? If so—don't be. Alan wouldn't allow it."

Elizabeth's face began to crumple. She pushed past Duray and walked quickly out upon the terrace. Duray followed, baffled and furious. He looked back and forth across the terrace. Bob was not to be seen. Elizabeth had gone to Alan Robertson; she spoke in a hushed urgent voice. Duray went to join them. Elizabeth became silent and turned away, avoiding Duray's gaze.

Alan Robertson spoke in a voice of easy geniality. "Isn't this a lovely spot? Look how the setting sun shines on the river!"

Roger Waille came by rolling a cart with ice, goblets and a dozen bottles. Now he said: "Of all the places on all the Earths this is my favorite. I call it 'Ekshayan,' which is the Scythian name for this district."

A woman asked, "Isn't it cold and bleak in the winter?"

"Frightful" said Waille. "The blizzards howl down from the north; then they stop and the land is absolutely still. The days are short and the sun comes up red as a poppy. The wolves slink out of the forests, and at dusk they circle the house. When a full moon shines, they howl like banshees, or maybe the banshees are howling! I sit beside the fireplace, entranced."

"It occurs to me," said Manfred Funk, "that each person, selecting a site for his home, reveals a great deal about himself. Even on old Earth, a man's home was ordinarily a symbolic simulacrum of the man himself; now, with every option available, a person's house is himself."

"This is very true," said Alan Robertson, "and certainly Roger need, not fear that he has revealed any discreditable aspects of himself by showing us his rather grotesque home on the lonely steppes of prehistoric Russia."

Roger Waille laughed. "The grotesque house isn't me; I merely felt that it fitted its setting. . . . Here, Duray, you're not drinking. That's chilled vodka; you can mix it or drink it straight in the time-tested manner."

"Nothing for me, thanks."

"Just as you like. Excuse me; I'm wanted elsewhere." Waille moved away, rolling the cart. Elizabeth leaned as if she wanted to follow him, then remained beside Alan Robertson, looking thoughtfully over the river.

Duray spoke to Alan Robertson as if she were not there. "Elizabeth refuses to leave. Bob has hypnotized her."

"That's not true," said Elizabeth softly.

"Somehow, one way or another, he's forced her to stay. She won't tell me why."

"I want the passway back," said Elizabeth. But her voice was muffled and uncertain.

Alan Robertson cleared his throat. "I hardly know what to say. It's a very awkward situation. None of us wants to create a disturbance—"

"There you're wrong," said Duray.

Alan Robertson ignored the remark. "I'll have a word with Bob after the party. In the meantime I don't see why we shouldn't enjoy the company of our friends, and that wonderful roast ox! Who is that turning the spit? I know him from somewhere."

Duray could hardly speak for outrage. "After what he's done to us?"

"He's gone too far, much too far," Alan Robertson agreed. "Still, he's a flamboyant feckless sort and I doubt if he understands the full inconvenience he's caused you."

"He understands well enough. He just doesn't care."

"Perhaps so," said Alan Robertson sadly. "I had always hoped—but that's neither here nor there. I still feel that we should act with restraint. It's much easier not to do than to undo."

Elizabeth abruptly crossed the terrace and went to the front door of the tall house, where her three daughters had appeared: Dolly, twelve; Joan, ten; Ellen, eight: all wearing green, white and black peasant frocks and glossy black boots. Duray thought they made a delightful picture. He followed Elizabeth across the terrace.

"It's Daddy," screamed Ellen, and threw herself in his arms. The other two, not to be outdone, did likewise.

"We thought you weren't coming to the party," cried Dolly. "I'm glad you did, though." "So'm I." "So'm I."

"I'm glad I came too, if only to see you in these pretty costumes. Let's go see Grandpa Alan." He took them across the terrace, and after a moment's hesitation, Elizabeth followed. Duray became aware that everyone had stopped talking to look at him and his family, with, so it seemed, an extraordinary, even avid, curiosity, as if in expectation of some entertaining extravagance of conduct. Duray began to burn with emotion. Once, long ago, while crossing a street in downtown San Francisco, he had been struck by an automobile, suffering a broken leg and a fractured clavicle. Almost as soon as he had been knocked down, pedestrians came pushing to stare down at him, and Duray, looking up in pain and shock, had seen only the ring of white faces and intent eyes, greedy as flies around a puddle of blood. In hysterical fury he had staggered to his feet, striking out into every face within reaching distance, man and woman alike. He hated them more than the man who had run him down: the ghouls who had come to enjoy his pain. Had he the miraculous power, he would have crushed them into a screaming bale of detestable flesh, hurled the bundle twenty miles out into the Pacific Ocean. . . . Some faint shadow of this emotion affected him now, but today he could provide them no unnatural pleasure. He turned a single glance of cool contempt around the group, then took his three eager-faced daughters to a bench at the back of the terrace. Elizabeth followed, moving like a mechanical object. She seated herself at the end of the bench and looked off across the river. Duray stared heavily back at the Rumfuddlers, compelling them to shift their gazes, to where the ox roasted over a great bed of coals. A young man in a white jacket turned the spit; another basted the meat with a long-handled brush. A pair of Orientals carried out a carving table; another brought a carving set; a fourth wheeled out a cart laden with salads, round crusty loaves, trays of cheese and herrings. A fifth man, dressed as a Transylvanian gypsy, came from the house with a violin. He went to the corner of the terrace and began to play melancholy music of the steppes.

Bob Robertson and Roger Waille inspected the ox, a magnificent sight indeed. Duray attempted a stony detachment, but his nose was under no such strictures; the odor of the roast meat, garlic and herbs tantalized him unmercifully. Bob Robertson returned to the terrace and held up his hands for attention; the fiddler put down his instrument. "Control your appetites; there'll still be a few minutes, during which we can discuss our next Rumfuddle. Our clever colleague Bernard Ulman recommends a hostelry in the Adirondacks: the Sapphire Lake Lodge. The hotel was built in 1902, to the highest standards of Edwardian comfort. The clientele is derived from the business community of New York. The cuisine is kosher; the management maintains an atmosphere of congenial gentility; the current date is 1930. Bernard has furnished photographs. Roger, if you please. . . ."

Waille drew back a curtain to reveal a screen. He manipulated the projection machine and the hotel was displayed on the screen: a rambling half-timbered structure overlooking several acres of park and a smooth lake.

"Thank you, Roger. I believe that we also have a photograph of the staff. . . ."

On the screen appeared a stiffly posed group of about thirty men and women, all smiling with various degrees of affability. The Rumfuddlers were amused; some among them tittered.

"Bernard gives a very favorable report as to the cuisine,

the amenities and the charm of the general area. Am I right, Bernard?"

"In every detail," declared Bernard Ulman. "The management is attentive and efficient; the clientele is well established."

"Very good," said Bob Robertson. "Unless someone has a more entertaining idea, we will hold our next Rumfuddle at the Sapphire Lake Lodge. And now I believe that the roast beef should be ready: done to a turn as the expression goes."

"Quite right," said Roger Waille. "Tom, as always, has done an excellent job at the spit."

The ox was lifted to the table. The carver set to work with a will. Duray went to speak to Alan Robertson, who blinked uneasily at his approach. Duray asked, "Do you understand the reason for these parties? Are you in on the joke?"

Alan Robertson spoke in a precise manner: "I certainly am not 'in on the joke,' as you put it." He hesitated, then said: "The Rumfuddlers will never again intrude upon your life or that of your family. I am sure of this. Bob became overexuberant; he exercised poor judgment, and I intend to have a quiet word with him. In fact, we have already exchanged certain opinions. At the moment your best interests will be served by detachment and unconcern."

Duray spoke with sinister politeness: "You feel, then, that I and my family should bear the brunt of Bob's jokes?"

"This is a harsh view of the situation, but my answer must be 'yes.' "

"I'm not so sure. My relationship with Elizabeth is no longer the same. Bob has done this to me."

"To quote an old apothegm: 'Least said, soonest mended.' "

Duray changed the subject. "When Waille showed the photograph of the hotel staff, I thought some of the faces were familiar. Before I could be quite sure the picture was gone."

Alan Robertson nodded unhappily. "Let's not develop the subject, Gilbert. Instead—"

"I'm into the situation too far," said Duray. "I want to know the truth."

"Very well, then," said Alan Robertson hollowly, "you're

instincts are accurate. The management of the Sapphire Lake Lodge, in cognate circumstances, has achieved an unsavory reputation. As you have guessed, they comprise the leadership of the National Socialist Party during 1938 or thereabouts. The manager of course is Hitler, the desk clerk is Goebbels, the headwaiter is Goering, the bellboys are Himmler and Hess, and so on down the line. They are of course not aware of the activities of their cognates on other worlds. The hotel's clientele is for the most part Jewish, which brings a macabre humor to the situation."

"Undeniably," said Duray. "What of that Rumfuddlers party that we looked in on?"

"You refer to the high-school football team? The 1951 Texas champions as I recall." Alan Robertson grinned. "And well they should be. Bob identified the players for me. Are you interested in the lineup?"

"Very much so."

Alan Robertson drew a sheet of paper from his pocket. "I believe—yes, this is it." He handed the sheet to Duray, who saw a schematic lineup:

LE	LT	LG	C	RG	RT	RE
Achilles	Charle-magne	Hercules	Goliath	Samson	Richard the Lion Hearted	Billy the Kid

Q
Machiavelli

LHB
Sir Galahad

RHB
Geronimo

FB
Cuchulain

Duray returned the paper. "You approve of this?"

"I had best put it like this," said Alan Robertson, a trifle uneasily. "One day, chatting with Bob, I remarked that much travail could be spared the human race if the most notorious evil-doers were early in their lives shifted to environments which afforded them constructive outlets for their energies. I speculated that having the competence to make such changes it was perhaps our duty to do so. Bob became interested in the concept and formed his group, the Rumfuddlers, to serve the function I had suggested. In all candor I

believe that Bob and his friends have been attracted more by
the possibility of entertainment than by altruism, but the
effect has been the same."

"The football players aren't evil-doers," said Duray. "Sir
Galahad, Charlemagne, Samson, Richard the Lion Hearted.
. . ."

"Exactly true," said Alan Robertson, "and I made this
point to Bob. He asserted that all were brawlers and bully-
boys, with the possible exception of Sir Galahad; that
Charlemagne, for example, had conquered much territory
to no particular achievement; that Achilles, a national hero
to the Greeks, was a cruel enemy to the Trojans; and so
forth. His justifications are somewhat specious perhaps. . . .
Still, these young men are better employed making touch-
downs than breaking heads."

After a pause Duray asked: "How are these matters
arranged?"

"I'm not entirely sure. I believe that by one means or
another, the desired babies are exchanged with others of
similar appearance. The child so obtained is reared in
appropriate circumstances."

"The jokes seem elaborate and rather tedious."

"Precisely!" Alan Robertson declared. "Can you think of
a better method to keep someone like Bob out of mischief?"

"Certainly," said Duray. "Fear of the consequences." He
scowled across the terrace. Bob had stopped to speak to
Elizabeth. She and the three girls rose to their feet.

Duray strode across the terrace. "What's going on?"

"Nothing of consequence," said Bob. "Elizabeth and the
girls are going to help serve the guests." He glanced toward
the serving table, then turned back to Duray. "Would you
help with the carving?"

Duray's arm moved of its own volition. His fist caught
Bob on the angle of the jaw, and sent him reeling back into
one of the white-coated Orientals, who carried a tray of
food. The two fell into an untidy heap. The Rumfuddlers
were shocked and amused, and watched with attention.

Bob rose to his feet gracefully enough and gave a hand to
the Oriental. Looking toward Duray he shook his head ruefully. Meeting his glance, Duray noted a pale blue glint; then
Bob once more became bland and debonair.

Elizabeth spoke in a low despairing voice: "Why couldn't

you have done as he asked? It would have all been so simple."

"Elizabeth may well be right," said Alan Robertson.

"Why should she be right?" demanded Duray. "We are his victims! You've allowed him a taste of mischief, and now you can't control him!"

"Not true!" declared Alan. "I intend to impose rigorous curbs upon the Rumfuddlers, and I will be obeyed."

"The damage is done, so far as I am concerned," said Duray bitterly. "Come along, Elizabeth, we're going home."

"We can't go home. Bob has the passway."

Alan Robertson drew a deep sigh, and came to a decision. He crossed to where Bob stood with a goblet of wine in one hand, massaging his jaw with the other. Alan Robertson spoke to Bob politely, but with authority. Bob was slow in making reply. Alan Robertson spoke again, sharply. Bob only shrugged. Alan Robertson waited a moment, then returned to Duray, Elizabeth and the three children.

"The passway is at his San Francisco apartment," said Alan Robertson in a measured voice. "He will give it back to you after the party. He doesn't choose to go for it now."

Bob once more commanded the attention of the Rumfuddlers. "By popular request we replay the record of our last but one Rumfuddle, contrived by one of our most distinguished, diligent and ingenious Rumfuddlers, Manfred Funk. The locale is the Red Barn, a roadhouse twelve miles west of Urbana, Illinois; the time is the late summer of 1926; the occasion is a Charleston dancing contest. The music is provided by the legendary Wolverines, and you will hear the fabulous cornet of Leon Bismarck Beiderbecke." Bob gave a wry smile, as if the music were not to his personal taste. "This was one of our most rewarding occasions, and here it is again."

The screen showed the interior of a dance hall, crowded with excited young men and women. At the back of the stage sat the Wolverines, wearing tuxedos; to the front stood the contestants: eight dapper young men and eight pretty girls in short skirts. An announcer stepped forward and spoke to the crowd through a megaphone: "Contestants are numbered one through eight! Please, no encouragement from the audience. The prize is this magnificent trophy and fifty dollars cash; the presentation will be made by last year's winner, Boozy Horman. Remember, on the first number we eliminate four contestants, on the second number two; and after the third number we select our winner. So then: Bix and the Wolverines, and 'Sensation Rag'!"

From the band came music, from the contestants agitated motion.

Duray asked, "Who are these people?"

Alan Robertson replied in an even voice: "The young men are locals and not important. But notice the girls: no doubt you find them attractive. You are not alone. They are Helen of Troy, Deirdre, Marie Antoinette, Cleopatra, Salome, Lady Godiva, Nefertiti and Mata Hari."

Duray gave a dour grunt. The music halted; judging applause from the audience, the announcer eliminated Marie Antoinette, Cleopatra, Deirdre, Mata Hari, and their respective partners. The Wolverines played "Fidgety Feet"; the four remaining contestants danced with verve and dedication; but Helen and Nefertiti were eliminated. The Wolverines played "Tiger Rag." Salome and Lady Godiva and their young men performed with amazing zeal. After carefully appraising the volume of applause, the announcer gave his judgment to Lady Godiva and her partner. Large on the screen appeared a close-up view of the two happy faces; in an excess of triumphant joy they hugged and kissed each other. The screen went dim; after the vivacity of the Red Barn the terrace above the Don seemed drab and insipid.

The Rumfuddlers shifted in their seats. Some uttered exclamations to assert their gaiety; others stared out across the vast empty face of the river.

Duray glanced toward Elizabeth; she was gone. Now he saw her circulating among the guests with three other young women, pouring wine from Scythian decanters.

"It makes a pretty picture, does it not?" said a calm voice. Duray turned to find Bob standing behind him; his mouth twisted in an easy half-smile but his eyes glinted pale blue.

Duray turned away. Alan Robertson said, "This is not at all a pleasant situation, Bob, and in fact completely lacks charm."

"Perhaps at future Rumfuddles, when my face feels better, the charm will emerge. . . . Excuse me; I see that I must enliven the meeting." He stepped forward. "We have a final pastiche: oddments and improvisations, vignettes and glimpses, each in its own way entertaining and instructive. Roger, start the mechanism, if you please."

Roger Waille hesitated and glanced sidelong toward Alan Robertson.

"The item number is sixty-two, Roger," said Bob in a calm voice. Roger Waille delayed another instant, then shrugged and went to the projection machine.

"The material is new," said Bob, "hence I will supply a commentary. First we have an episode in the life of Richard Wagner, the dogmatic and occasionally irascible composer. The year is 1843; the place is Dresden. Wagner sets forth on a summer night to attend a new opera, *Der Sanger Krieg*, by an unknown composer. He alights from his carriage before the hall; he enters; he seats himself in his loge. Notice the dignity of his posture; the authority of his gestures! The music begins: listen!" From the projector came the sound of music. "It is the overture," stated Bob. "But notice Wagner: why is he stupefied? Why is he overcome with wonder? He listens to the music as if he has never heard it before. And in fact he hasn't; he has only just yesterday set down a few preliminary notes for this particular opus, which he planned to call *Tannhauser;* today, magically, he hears it in its final form. Wagner will walk home slowly tonight, and perhaps in his abstraction he will kick the dog Schmutzi. . . . Now, to a different scene: St. Petersburg in the year 1880 and the stables in back of the Winter Palace. The ivory and gilt carriage rolls forth to convey the Czar and the Czarina to a reception at the British Embassy. Notice the drivers: stern, well-groomed, intent at their business. Marx's beard is well trimmed; Lenin's goatee is not so pronounced. A groom comes to watch the carriage roll away. He has a kindly twinkle in his eye, does Stalin." The screen went dim once more, then brightened to show a city street lined with automobile showrooms and used-car lots. "This is one of Shawn Henderson's projects. The four used-car lots are operated by men who in other circumstances were religious notables: prophets and so forth. That alert keen-featured man in front of 'Quality Motors,' for instance, is Mohammed. Shawn is conducting a careful survey, and at our next Rumfuddle he will report upon his dealings with these four famous figures."

Alan Robertson stepped forward, somewhat diffidently. He cleared his throat. "I don't like to play the part of spoilsport, but I'm afraid I have no choice. There will be no further Rumfuddles. Our original goals have been neglected and I note far too many episodes of purposeless frivolity and even cruelty. You may wonder at what seems a sudden decision, but I have been considering the matter for several days. The Rumfuddles have taken a turn in an unwholesome direction, and conceivably might become a grotesque new vice, which of course is far from our original ideal. I'm sure that every sensible person, after a few moments' reflection, will agree that now is the time to stop. Next week you may return to me all passways except those to worlds where you maintain residence."

The Rumfuddlers sat murmuring together. Some turned resentful glances toward Alan Robertson; others served themselves more bread and meat. Bob came over to join Alan and Duray. He spoke in an easy manner. "I must say that your admonitions arrive with all the delicacy of a lightning bolt. I can picture Jehovah smiting the fallen angels in a similar style."

Alan Robertson smiled. "Now then, Bob, you're talking nonsense. The situations aren't at all similar. Jehovah struck out in fury; I impose my restrictions in all goodwill, in order that we can once again turn our energies to constructive ends."

Bob threw back his head and laughed. "But the Rumfuddlers have lost the habit of work. We want only to amuse ourselves, and after all, what is so noxious in our activities?"

"The trend is menacing, Bob." Alan Robertson's voice was reasonable. "Unpleasant elements are creeping into your fun, so stealthily that you yourself are unaware of them. For instance, why torment poor Wagner? Surely there was gratuitous cruelty, and only to provide you a few instants of amusement. And, since the subject is in the air, I heartily deplore your treatment of Gilbert and Elizabeth. You have brought them both an extraordinary inconvenience, and in Elizabeth's case, actual suffering. Gilbert got something of his own back, and the balance is about even."

"Gilbert is far too impulsive," said Bob. "Self-willed and egocentric, as he always has been."

Alan held up his hand. "There is no need to go further into the subject, Bob. I suggest that you say no more."

"Just as you like, though the matter, considered as practical rehabilitation, isn't irrelevant. We can amply justify the work of the Rumfuddlers."

Duray asked quietly, "Just how do you mean, Bob?"

Alan Robertson made a peremptory sound, but Duray said, "Let him say what he likes, and make an end to it. He plans to do so anyway."

There was a moment of silence. Bob looked across the terrace to where the three Orientals were transferring the remains of the beef to a service cart.

"Well?" Alan Robertson asked softly. "Have you made your choice?"

Bob held out his hands in ostensible bewilderment. "I don't understand you! I want only to vindicate myself and the Rumfuddlers. I think we have done splendidly. Today we have allowed Torquemada to roast a dead ox instead of a living heretic; the Marquis de Sade has fulfilled his obscure urges by caressing seared flesh with a basting brush, and did you notice the zest with which Ivan the Terrible hacked up the carcass? Nero, who has real talent, played his violin; Attila, Genghis Khan, and Mao Tse Tung efficiently served the guests. Wine was poured by Messalina, Lucrezia Borgia, Delilah, and Gilbert's charming wife Elizabeth. Only Gilbert failed to demonstrate his rehabilitation, but at least he provided us a touching and memorable picture: Gilles de Rais, Elizabeth Báthory and their three virgin daughters. It was sufficient. In every case we have shown that rehabilitation is not an empty word."

"Not in every case," said Alan Robertson, "specifically that of your own."

Bob looked at him askance. "I don't follow you."

"No less than Gilbert are you ignorant of your background. I will now reveal the circumstances so that you may understand something of yourself and try to curb the tendencies which have made your cognate an exemplar of cruelty, stealth and treachery."

Bob laughed: a brittle sound like cracking ice. "I admit to a horrified interest."

"I took you from a forest a thousand miles north of this very spot, while I traced the phylogeny of the Norse gods.

Your name was Loki. For reasons which are not now important I brought you back to San Francisco and there you grew to maturity."

"So I am Loki."

"No. You are Bob Robertson, just as this is Gilbert Duray, and here is his wife Elizabeth. Loki, Gilles de Rais, Elizabeth Báthory: these are names applied to human material which has not functioned quite as well. Gilles de Rais, judging from all evidence, suffered from a brain tumor; he fell into his peculiar vices after a long and honorable career. The case of Princess Elizabeth Báthory is less clear, but one might suspect syphilis and consequent cerebral lesions."

"And what of poor Loki?" inquired Bob with exaggerated pathos.

"Loki seemed to suffer from nothing except a case of old-fashioned meanness."

Bob seemed concerned. "So that these qualities apply to me?"

"You are not necessarily identical to your cognate. Still, I advise you to take careful stock of yourself, and, so far as I am concerned, you had best regard yourself as on probation."

"Just as you say." Bob looked over Alan Robertson's shoulder. "Excuse me; you've spoiled the party and everybody is leaving. I want a word with Roger."

Duray moved to stand in his way, but Bob shouldered him aside and strode across the terrace, with Duray glowering at his back.

Elizabeth said in a mournful voice, "I hope we're at the end of all this."

Duray growled, "You should never have listened to him."

"I didn't listen; I read about it in one of Bob's books; I saw your picture; I couldn't—"

Alan Robertson intervened. "Don't harass poor Elizabeth; I consider her both sensible and brave; she did the best she could."

Bob returned. "Everything taken care of," he said cheerfully. "All except one or two details."

"The first of these is the return of the passway. Gilbert and Elizabeth, not to mention Dolly, Joan and Ellen, are anxious to return home."

"They can stay here with you," said Bob. "That's probably the best solution."

"I don't plan to stay here," said Alan Robertson in mild wonder. "We are leaving at once."

"You must change your plans," said Bob. "I have finally become bored with your reproaches. Roger doesn't particularly care to leave his home, but he agrees that now is the time to make a final disposal of the matter."

Alan Robertson frowned in displeasure. "The joke is in very poor taste, Bob."

Roger Waille came from the house, his face somewhat glum. "They're all closed. Only the main gate is open."

Alan Robertson said to Gilbert: "I think that we will leave Bob and Roger to their Rumfuddle fantasies. When he returns to his senses we'll get your passway. Come along then, Elizabeth! Girls!"

"Alan," said Bob gently. "You're staying here. Forever. I'm taking over the machine."

Alan Robertson asked mildly: "How do you propose to restrain me? By force?"

"You can stay here alive or dead; take your choice."

"You have weapons, then?"

"I certainly do." Bob displayed a pistol. "There are also the servants. None have brain tumors or syphilis, they're all just plain bad."

Roger said in an awkward voice, "Let's go and get it over."

Alan Robertson's voice took on a harsh edge. "You seriously plan to maroon us here, without food?"

"Consider yourself marooned."

"I'm afraid that I must punish you, Bob, and Roger as well."

Bob laughed gaily. "You yourself are suffering from brain disease—megalomania. You haven't the power to punish anyone."

"I still control the machine, Bob."

"The machine isn't here. So now—"

Alan Robertson turned and looked around the landscape, with a frowning air of expectation. "Let me see: I'd probably come down from the main gate; Gilbert and a group from behind the house. Yes; here we are."

Down the path from the main portal, walking jauntily,

came two Alan Robertsons with six men armed with rifles and gas grenades. Simultaneously from behind the house appeared two Gilbert Durays and six more men, similarly armed.

Bob stared in wonder. "Who are these people?"

"Cognates," said Alan, smiling. "I told you I controlled the machine, and so do all my cognates. As soon as Gilbert and I return to our Earth, we must similarly set forth and in our turn do our part on other worlds cognate to this. . . . Roger, be good enough to summon your servants. We will take them back to Earth. You and Bob must remain here."

Waille gasped in distress. "Forever?"

"You deserve nothing better," said Alan Robertson. "Bob perhaps deserves worse." He turned to the cognate Alan Robertsons. "What of Gilbert's passway?"

Both replied, "It's in Bob's San Francisco apartment, in a box on the mantelpiece."

"Very good," said Alan Robertson. "We will now depart. Good-bye, Bob. Good-bye, Roger. I am sorry that our association ended on this rather unpleasant basis."

"Wait!" cried Roger. "Take me back with you!"

"Good-bye," said Alan Robertson. "Come along, then, Elizabeth. Girls! Run on ahead!"

13

Elizabeth and the children had returned to Home; Alan Robertson and Duray sat in the lounge above the machine. "Our first step," said Alan Robertson, "is to dissolve our obligation. There are of course an infinite number of Rumfuddles at Ekshayans and an infinite number of Alans and Gilberts. If we visited a single Rumfuddle, we would, by the laws of probability, miss a certain number of the emergency situations. The total number of permutations, assuming that an infinite number of Alans and Gilberts makes a random choice among an infinite number of Ekshayans, is infinity raised to the infinite power. What percentage of this number yields blanks for any given Ekshayan, I haven't calculated. If we visited Ekshayans until we had by our own efforts rescued at least one Gilbert and Alan set, we might be forced to scour fifty or a hundred worlds, or more. Or we might achieve our rescue on the first visit. The wisest course, I believe, is for you and I to visit, say, twenty Ekshayans. If each of the Alan and Gilbert sets does the same, then the chances for any particular Alan and Gilbert to be abandoned are one in twenty times nineteen times eighteen times seventeen, et cetera. Even then I think I will arrange that an operator check another five or ten thousand worlds to gather up that one lone chance. . . ."